THE CARTHAGINIAN ROSE

THE
CARTHAGINIAN
ROSE

by ILKA CHASE

WITH DRAWINGS BY MIRCEA VASILIU

DOUBLEDAY & COMPANY, INC., GARDEN CITY, NEW YORK

1961

To those we met around the world who, woven inextricably into the fabric of our lives, have enriched and colored it—this book is dedicated with gratitude.

CONTENTS

CHAPTER ONE

France * Spain * England

How shall I know, unless I go
To Cairo and Cathay,
Whether or not this blessed spot
Is blest in every way?

Now it may be, the flower for me
Is this beneath my nose;
How shall I tell, unless I smell
The Carthaginian rose?

So SANG Edna St. Vincent Millay, and so echo I. The distant bloom is fair, the world is round and fat and fine. Who would miss it? In this book, covering a decade of travel ranging through the British Isles and the isles of Greece, through France, Spain, and Italy, Bangkok and Bali, Hong Kong and Japan, it is my hope to share with the reader some of the fun and excitement, not to mention the lunacy, that were our lot, my husband's and mine, as we journeyed about the globe.

To me travel is a triple delight: anticipation, performance, and recollection. The purest of these probably is anticipation, heightened and spurred by travel literature. Others may cling to the master stylists, but for unadulterated reading bliss give me travel folders; their provocation quotient is unbeatable. What other pages cause the heart to beat so fast, hopes to soar so high? What else makes the familiar routine more stagnant?

I love my native land, but after a lifetime in New York, a hiatus in Hollywood, and years spent crisscrossing the forty-eight continental states, I spark more to travel in Europe and the Orient. I am looking forward to Africa. I can't help it. I get a bigger thrill standing in an airport, hearing them announce departures for Vienna and Istanbul,

Algiers and Bangkok, than when I hear them exhorting passengers to board for Kansas City and Pittsburgh. It's not that I'm unwilling to concede happiness in the central plains and the Alleghenies, and possibly after East, West home *is* best, but how can we know that unless we've been East and West and proven it to our satisfaction? "What should they know of England who only England know?" is true of every homeland. In order to appreciate what we have let us sniff the Carthaginian rose.

Actually, for the travel addict—and the yearning to travel is as much an addiction as a yearning for drugs—"best" doesn't enter into it. Travel may be uncomfortable; it may be downright painful or dangerous, tedious or fatiguing; one may encounter climates that depress, freeze, or suffocate, foods that sicken, and bugs that bite, and the hotel doesn't exist that shelters one as felicitously as one's own home, but the traveler born is stimulated rather than deterred by hardship and the unexpected, and it is rare indeed that he regrets a journey into the unknown or a return visit to the foreign but familiar and beloved.

My husband, I think, in the beginning had not the same curiosity about the far places of the earth that has animated me since childhood, but I infected him, and we are now a pair—travelers dedicated if not constant. Our first trip abroad together took place in 1949 and hinged on a matter of thirteen dollars.

We were planning to go to Guatemala. Our friend Lee Barker had recently returned and was eloquent about the beauty of the Mayan ruins. "Superb," he said, "not to be missed," he said. Norton and I were discussing the trip one morning as I sat sipping my tea while he dressed. I had been in communication with the American Express and was detailing to him as tactfully as possible what the trip was going to cost. "That," he said, "seems like a lot of money."

"Well, yes, but think of the Mayan ruins."

"I'm thinking of them," he said. "It seems like a lot of money." There was a pause while he knotted his tie and I drank my tea.

"How much does it cost to fly to Paris?" he asked.

"Are you kidding? We couldn't possibly afford Paris."

"Let's see." I dialed Pan American. For thirteen dollars more we could fly to Paris, so we did. We were gone only two or three weeks, but it was a memorable adventure and we learned how to make French-fried potatoes. *Les frites* as done in France have always struck me as being one of the world's great dishes, and they bear no more relation to the average American French fries than a watered-down adaptation of a Paris model on sale in Stern's bears to the original Balenciaga.

The lesson took place at La Providence, an inn near the cathedral of Chartres which we had gone to visit. It was the second one of the lunch hour. The first was in the nature of a review, as it was my first trip back to France since the war and I had forgotten how agile they are with wine. When the French sit down at table, they look at the menu, decide what they will eat, and then call the sommelier. The wine they order is brought immediately, and they drink a little while waiting for the meal. This is pleasant. Here at home when we do have it it is the last item served. Indeed I know houses where they are so hellbent on getting everything onto your plate, including rolls, relishes, and jellies—these last two dubious accessories to meat at best—that the benison arrives just as you're polishing off the last mouthful. Sometimes they even pass seconds before the bottle! Wine should be an accompaniment, hostess dear, not an aftermath. And in the event that the service is not adequate, and in these days it rarely is, do not hesitate to set the bottle on the table. The richest and most pampered guest will not disdain to serve himself a delicious vintage.

Europeans lack many things that Americans cherish; hot dogs, chewing gum, good telephone service, but the service of wine is not among them.

That day in Chartres our bottle was quickly brought and we sampled it while awaiting our succulent *frites*. Thinking ahead to country weekends in the winter when, not tempted by garden or beach, the doctor has been known to spend all Saturday and Sunday happily presiding over a hot stove, we asked the proprietor if he would give us his secret. He was a saint and did. I shall be a saint and pass it on to you.

Allowing, obviously, for good potatoes, cut them into the usual strips and soak them for a while in ice water. To do the job well you must have a proper deep-frying iron saucepan with a basket. The great secret is the fat. Eschew prepared commercial shortening, use instead the suet from beef kidneys. You'll need a lot of it and you must render and strain it beforehand, but once this is done it will keep in a cool place indefinitely. Dry the potatoes and plunge them into the fat. In the course of the cooking, to make the potatoes truly delicious, the basket should be lifted three times from the bubbling fat and hung to dry for a couple of minutes on the little arm protruding up from the pot for that purpose. When the last of the fat has dripped off, put them in a hot dish, salt lightly, and serve. You might as well start on the second batch immediately, as the most rigid dieter will succumb to the hot, delicate crispiness outside and the light, soft mealy center.

Recipe collecting is one of the true joys of traveling. For some people, indeed, it is a primary urge. Gourmet tours, through France especially, are a respected form of self-indulgence with dedicated adherents. Norton and I hope to adhere ourselves in the near future, but certain crass considerations of practicality restrain us from unlimited wandering. After a trip we need time to recuperate. We also need time to accumulate more money, not only for another journey, but for the humdrum realities of home—familiar items such as taxes and rent, food, clothing, and service.

In order to obtain this wherewithal we must stick to our jobs. My husband is a knowledgeable, conscientious doctor; his life therefore is not easy. My own career is erratic, but fortunately for me one segment or another, as on a many-faceted revolving sphere, seems to catch the light of employment most of the time, so that with writing and acting, lecturing, television appearances, and fashion-show commentaries I am kept busy and modestly solvent.

It was July 1951, to be exact, two years after our first trip together, that the money bush bloomed again and we happily departed from the place there's no place like. We took off by air, and I learned afresh the lesson that every traveler must brace himself for and accept with philosophy. I'll call it Traveler's Tip No. 1: *There Will Be Delays.* One can suffer sad disillusion in traveling by failing to appreciate the basic meaning of the word itself. The stem is the same as "travail," meaning toil or trouble of a painful or oppressive nature. It is also like the French verb *travailler,* "to work." In the delay I mention there was not much work involved, but its nature was indeed oppressive. Norton and his son, Peter, at that time thirteen, had left on an earlier plane and were meeting me in Paris. Our rendezvous was the Orly airport.

My own departure time came, and we took off from Idlewild on the nose at 7 P.M. in one of those good old deep-bellied Strato-Clippers. We dined de luxe, and after dinner a gaggle of youngsters, boys in their teens, erupted into the aisle. Guided by a couple of older men, they were en route to an African safari sent by the Columbus, Ohio, *Dispatch*; a bonus for having been good salesmen. They asked me if I would have some pictures taken with them, so we wound down the tiny staircase to the lounge and flashlights were popping, laughter exploding, ice, in the glasses of the older passengers, tinkling cozily, and we were due in Goose Bay at any minute. Suddenly over the intercom came the voice of the captain saying, in effect, that he couldn't regret it more, folks, but guess what? We were heading back to Idlewild. It is really quite trying to have one's plans changed in mid-air, but I suppose if ever Better Be Sure Than Sorry applies, it is at twenty thousand feet. Back we went, the pilot assuring us that there was nothing the matter with the engines but that a fuel gauge had blown and they didn't want to head out over the ocean without it. I should think the great overseas lines would keep a little cache of spare parts at way stations along the route, but apparently that's not the way it's done.

We landed at 2 A.M. the morning of the Fourth of July, and hot and muggy it was. The gadget they needed took no time at all to install, but the powers then decided that as that crew had already been flying several hours they'd best get a new one. These had to be routed out of bed, so, rather than keep us in the hot and hideous shacks that were the original Idlewild terminal, the management transported us to Forest Hills to a White Tower and blew us all to hamburgers. To one who had been anticipating the garden of the Paris Ritz at about that hour, it was quite anticlimactic. Finally we were loaded back into the busses and delivered again to the airport. We filed into the plane, the doors were closed, the heat was stifling, and there we sat. Goose Bay, it seemed, had gone off the air. It was unthinkable to leave before it was back on, but when that would be there was no inkling. We waited, we fidgeted, we yawned, we softly swore, then, suddenly God came back from wherever he had been, Goose Bay spoke, and we took off. Nor was that the end of our blessings. At 7 A.M. we landed at Cape Breton. I have heard pampered types who have landed at Gander complain that it is dull. "Dear, there's nothing to *do*," they say. I have not been there, but I can tell these whimperers that Gander is opening night at the Met compared to Sydney, Cape Breton, which is an element—earth; that's all you can say for it. We were aired, fed after a fashion, and finally took off for Paris, where we arrived at 11:30 P.M. Paris time.

The doctor at the Orly airport was not in a good mood. The cables we had been promised would be sent to those awaiting us had not been delivered, and the only news he had been able to get was that the plane had turned back just short of Goose Bay. A thick silence covered its subsequent fate. However, and that's one of the good parts of travel, the trouble was behind us; the fun began.

Peter, who had been in Paris for ten hours, was a mine of information about the city and highly vocal on the subject. It took considerable restraint on my part not to blast the little chap with a few items of my own gleaned over the years when I went to school in Paris and during the many visits I had paid to the city since, but as he was crazy about it, we effected a happy truce.

Since we were planning to motor through France into Spain, we had arranged to hire a car, and young Monsieur Jacob was at Orly with our appetizing Ford Vedette. He drove us into Paris at the usual French tempo, eighty on the curves, trailed by another car, driven by his godfather. We had been introduced to him at the airport, and somehow the idea had charmed us. Where but in France does a grown man say to you, "I want you to meet my godfather"?

My last meal having been far away on the other side of the Atlantic, we stopped en route to the hotel at the Coupole, along with the Dôme and Select, a famous hangout for art students. It is not picturesque, being large and brightly lighted with a considerable display of brass, but I had a fine sandwich of French bread washed down with foaming beer. It was after midnight in the middle of the week, but the sidewalk tables were filled with Parisians, eating, drinking, talking, and enjoying themselves.

We came at last to our hotel, the Vendôme, situated directly off one of the beautiful urban centers of the world. To me the Place Vendôme, with its exquisite façade is the epitome of sophisticated beauty, just as the Piazza Navona in Rome is the focal point of urban romanticism.

The Vendôme is a small hotel, not swank, like its famous neighbor, the Ritz, or glossy like the George Cinq or the Plaza Athenée, but homey and admirably run by its owner, Monsieur Baguet. We had never stopped there before, but in my recently published novel, New York 22, one of the characters lived there during her sojourn in Paris, and I had described the hotel in considerable detail. Understandably enough, this puzzled our host, to whom I gave a copy of the book, since a good deal of the description was pure fantasy, although when I actually saw the place I found to my pleasure that I had been correct about the atmosphere if not the architecture. The Vendôme is rather crowded and jumbled; I had tended more to sweeping corridors.

The Vendôme does not have a dining room, but it has what is more important—a kitchen—and if a weary tourist decides that he will forgo Montmartre and spend a quiet evening in his own quarters, he will be served a delicious meal.

We spent our first night in a little suite at the corner of the Place Vendôme and the Rue St. Honoré, but the next day changed to rooms on the court. Less grand but quieter. Like most right-thinking Americans, I too consider Paris my second home, but the noises are sharp and individualistic, piercing the eardrum rather than blending into a low amorphous roar as in New York. My idea of hell is not so much heat as noise, and a combination of the two can shatter me.

Once caught up on our sleep, however, we set about our sight-seeing, and here, if I may, I should like to offer Traveler's Tip No. 2. It will be ignored, but I offer it anyhow: Rest before sight-seeing. Flying is fatiguing, and one needs time to recuperate. I suppose eventually we'll be getting to Europe in a couple of hours, to the Orient in five or six. They are still a long way from home. The machines can go that fast, but the human physique can't. Time is different, food and water unaccustomed, the pace of life one to which we must become acclimated, and if arriving in a country for the first time, the emotional tension is usually high.

Rest, therefore, is advisable, unless, of course, one is so taut with excitement and curiosity that trying to take a nap is tantamount to exploding. In that case, go out. *Sortez. Herausgehen.* We're a long time dead.

I think that most parents enjoy seeing foreign lands through the eyes of the young, but they are also aware of the cost of transporting the young. Enjoyment of the trip, God knows, is the intent, but a little culture should be absorbed too. To this end our first Sight was Notre Dame. I remembered how as a schoolgirl I had climbed into the towers for a close view of the gargoyles, but, my recollection being reasonably vivid, I told Pete that he could clamber if he liked but it would have to be on his own.

The French, I have always thought, have a unique gift for combining stockiness with grandeur. Notre Dame is not a soaring monument; neither is the other great Parisian landmark that followed it by six hundred years, the Arc de Triomphe. They are both compact rather than aspiring, but in both the proportion is superb.

It is only in recent years, however, that I have learned that compactness in the case of the church was not the original intention of the architect. Originally Notre Dame was to have had spires like those of other cathedrals. For reasons I do not know—financial, possibly, or political—the twin towers were never completed. The famous squared-off silhouette now seems completely right and will probably never be changed.

Like many men my husband is not a dedicated sight-seer when it comes to cathedrals, but he is dogged. If I say, "Darling, we really should," he will almost always come along with good grace, but sometimes he gets contrary.

When we visited Chartres, the time we learned about the *frites*, I told him that during the war every piece of the famous stained-glass windows had been numbered and removed to keep them from being destroyed by bombs. "I don't believe it," he said flatly. Movable iron scaffoldings and tremendously high ladders with platforms stood about. "Those," I said, "are there because they're still putting the glass back. You must believe it." "I don't," he said. Just then a priest came by. I asked him in French, "Father, is it not true that the windows were removed during the war?" "Yes," he said, "they were." "Yes," I said to the doctor, "they were. He says so." The doctor said, "Oh." Actually, one can't blame people for doubting. The labor involved is Herculean, yet throughout the cathedrals and museums of Europe the giant task has been performed not once but many times to save the art of man from man's barbarity.

On our current Paris visit Peter's cultural work was going forward. The Louvre, Napoleon's Tomb, and the jewel box Sainte Chapelle; we also went to Versailles. How I wish that Stanley Loomis' brilliant biography of Madame Du Barry had been published at that time. It re-creates in fascinating and colorful detail the life of the vast palace in its great era. When we were there, however, it was probably not even a gleam in its author's eye, so we made do with guidebooks.

One of the happy things about Europe is the way culture and good food seem inextricably blended. Notre Dame was leavened by a sustaining snack at La Bouteille d'Or, a small bistro on the *quai* opposite the cathedral, offering at noontime such dainties as a wide variety of hors d'oeuvres, fresh prawns, kidneys with a delectable sauce, salad, cheese, fruit, and coffee. Wine, naturally. Sometimes I feel that even the hamburger with the college education is not at the head of the class. If ever you must shepherd a reluctant husband or child to Versailles, seduce him with Le Coq Hardi, that superb restaurant at Bougival, which was on our way.

This robust rooster is notable, not only for food, as though that weren't enough, but for the charm of its décor as well. From the road it is nothing special, a perfectly plain façade, then you enter. The dining room is inviting, provincial in style, with a fine open fireplace, and cozy in the winter, but for the full impact go there in the summertime. The garden is a widely terraced hillside, each level set with tables and

bright parasols and bordered by enormous pots of pink and blue hydrangeas. The eye is carried up and up through splashing color into the
sunlight and the effect is indescribably gay. The food, however, is not
cheap, and we were pained in more ways than one when our young
man returned his costly luncheon some fifteen minutes after he had
swallowed it.

That particular timing was unfortunate, but afterward he pulled
himself together and in Spain thrived on some esoteric concoction
known as Zimba Cola, while his father and I, far far from happy, toyed
with a little ginger ale and bicarb.

We felt no pain, however, at a gala evening in Paris spent with Ken
McCormick and Frank Price of Doubleday. We dined and danced at
the Pré Catalan in the Bois. Dorothy Stickney and Howard Lindsay
were with us, and also that lady warrior and reporter, Marguerite Hig-
gins. General Hall, Marguerite Steen, and Eve Curie completed the
party. It was nice having Mademoiselle Curie. She created a French
aura and made us feel that we were not completely expatriot Americans who must cling together, never getting to know the natives.

It is curious the schism that still exists between the American colony
and the Parisians. Americans who have been there a long time do have
some French friends, of course, but for the most part the setup would
delight a Southern heart, everything equal but, thank God, separate.

That pleasant evening concluded our Paris stanza. The time had
come to see something of France itself as we motored south into Spain.

We left Paris of a Sunday morning, delayed by a lengthy conference
between the doctor and the hotel porter as how best to stow the luggage.
Norton settled matters to his satisfaction by cunningly concealing everything we'd need that night under the stuff we wouldn't want till
we hit Granada. I don't know why he did that; normally he's an extremely good planner. Moment of aberration, I guess.

Finally we set off. I was determined on Fontainebleau en route, but
some things just aren't meant for some people, and the château was one
of them. I have affection for it, as one of my school summers was
passed with a French family in a little house on the edge of the forest,
but when I had tried to sell it to the doctor a couple of years before,
I had had scant success. That time we were on our way back to Paris
from some little side trip, and he was anxious to get there. He stared
at the carp in the pond with an eye as fishy as their own and said he
doubted that they were as old as I maintained and that, anyway, he had
expected them to be bigger. The double staircase of the château, re-

nowned throughout the architectural world, interested him not one whit, and he had refused point blank to enter the building. I hoped to do better this time, but destiny was against me. As we neared the town, I dangled the château like a carrot before the noses of my loved ones, but found that a real carrot was more to their mood. They were hungry, and sight-seeing before lunch was out. I sprang blithely into the breach. A hotel I remembered from my school days, that's where we would go. True, it wasn't mentioned in the *Guide Michelin*, which only went to prove that they weren't as omniscient as poor gullible tourists were taught to believe. Could I, an old Francophile, show them a thing or two! As it turned out, I could not. The Michelin people were privy to a little secret that had escaped me. The place was out of business.

We had to eat somewhere, so in a grim little silence Norton manned the wheel and we started back in the direction of Paris. Six kilometers later we came to the turning for the village of Barbizon. As we drove through the forest, I dwelled, rather eloquently I thought, on the Barbizon school of painting. Millet, Corot, Dupré, *les gars*.

I also pointed out happy French families who had driven from Paris to picnic under the great trees in surroundings so spacious that each group could be quite private and by themselves, complete with food hamper, wine bottles, often a card table set up for greater comfort, camp chairs, and the family cat or dog. My little vignettes of *la vie en plein air* were received in stony silence. At last it dawned on me. My own poor beasts were now starving. The sight of others happily munching only added to the pangs that were consuming them.

Once arrived in Barbizon, settled at a table under the grape arbor at the restaurant of La Clef d'Or, an entirely different spirit animated our little band. After luncheon I said to myself, fed and cosseted, there will be no further resistance to the château, but once more I was defeated by that stern masculine sense of logic that always asserts itself on motor trips. It is more important to leave a place on time and to get to a place on time than it is to see the place. "We will do as you like, dear," the man said, "but I would point out that we are barely out of Paris, we have got to make Tours by evening, and we still have two hundred kilometers to go." Fontainebleau got the broom.

I saw it go with regret but not anguish. After all, we would be motoring through the Loire, the heart of the châteaux country, some of them we were bound to see. Besides, it is impossible to drive through the French countryside with a heavy heart. It's so lovely and fertile, it's a joy to behold even if one has no destination at all. The poplar-lined roads are excellent, and once we stopped the car and got out for the sheer pleasure of sitting at the edge of a wheat field laced with crimson poppies. Perhaps it is the poppies and the occasional cornflowers that flavor the flour and give French bread its delicious taste.

Late in the afternoon we came to Chambord. Having been gypped out of Fontainebleau, I was firm about this one. There it sat, a stupendous exquisite wedding cake with its great round towers and a forest of cupolas, dormers, and spirelike chimneys crowding the roof. Within is the fantastic spiraling double staircase so designed that anyone walking up would never pass anyone walking down. Not very sociable but a boon in case of bores.

Chambord was begun in 1526 by Francis I. Various kings used it as a hunting lodge and in it Molière wrote a couple of plays, though domestically speaking it must have been madly uncomfortable. In 1944 the Germans threatened to burn the château on the pretext that they were being shot at from the terraces, but the village priest dissuaded them and by so doing saved not only one of the world's architectural treasures but also the pictures placed there by French museums for safekeeping.

It was at Chambord that my husband gave me reason to brood, the result of which I shall call Traveler's Tip No. 3: If you're not feeling well when abroad, for heaven's sake, *say* so. I was thinking the poor man boorish and insensitive when he failed to react to the inspired masonry. I twitted him about it and only then discovered that for the last couple of hours he had been in misery. He had some bug—minor, thank heaven—but it made him wretched. Speak up, friends, when indisposed! Don't let your companions worry to death, fearful that this superlative, long-anticipated great adventure is a frightful frost. Colic everyone sympathizes with and forgives, and when touring there are enough hurdles little and big to be overcome—there's enough colic, too—without superimposing avoidable misunderstandings.

Poor Pete suffered several small discomforts of his own. We did our best to comfort him, but he was thirteen and filled with dignity, and it did not sit well when the woman who sold admittance tickets to the château regarded him as a child and let him go in free. It was also galling that the hotels never asked for his passport, only for his father's and mine.

All things considered, I could only feel Chambord a Pyrrhic victory, especially when a storm came up just as we were leaving and we had to drive through blinding rain to Blois, where we dined and where we did

Vasiliu

not visit the château. That night late we arrived at Tours. The doctor, as so frequently happens, had been right. To arrive at even a remotely Christian hour, we had needed to get out of Fontainebleau when we did.

Tours is a fair-sized town, so with Paris taxi horns still a cacophonous echo in our ears we asked for two quiet rooms on the court. The court was charming, a spacious graveled garden abloom with geraniums.

Hurray, we thought, the deep sleep of the just. Then we heard it, the town clock. The clock of Tours slumbered not and neither did the hotel guests. It rang the hour and it rang the half hour and its tone was not sonorous. It was in fact a clanging, loud-tongued shrew, a blot upon her native city, for in Tours they supposedly speak the most pure French of France. There is also the matter of French bedding. That may be one reason the French are so keen on *l'amour*. It distracts them from full awareness of their pillows and bolsters. The bolsters are extraordinary. Round and lumpy, they look like dead relatives stuffed into shrouds. Nor is that all. At night they become substructures for still more upholstery, great square pillows extending down under the shoulder blades so that it is impossible for the spine to have any contact with the mattress. Chin and chest are so out of alignment that one wakes in the morning with an ineradicable crick in the neck. Personally, I do not suffer too much, I use a baby pillow, but if one is not self-supplied, the results can be lamentable.

The feature of the hotel that filled us with curiosity and speculation was the bathroom. We had one to ourselves, and it was quite large,

but a big double window was cut into it opening directly into the bedroom. When sitting in the tub you could lean over the sill and have a chat with your roommate. That part was not without its advantages, but further privacy, sometimes desirable, was more difficult to achieve. One could close the double windows and the lower halves were curtained, but the fabric was transparent, and all in all it was more satisfactory to ask one's fellow occupant to leave the room, permitting solitude at given intervals.

The next day, even after our bell-ridden night, health and spirits were restored, the prospect of sight-seeing was inviting and we set out for Azay-le-Rideau. It is a very beautiful château, sometimes referred to as the Pearl of the Loire Valley, and was built early in the sixteenth century by a financier named Berthelot. Monsieur Berthelot in some way ran afoul of the king and fled the country, whereupon Francis I promptly clamped down on the property. The château is on a little island completely surrounded by a moat that is still filled with water. Most of the moats of Europe have long since been drained and are carpeted with grass, but Azay is reflected in a glimmering mirror. It's interesting, too, because there's quite a lot of furniture in it, and you get a feeling of what life must have been like in the old days.

In this sense of continuity, I think, lies much of the appeal of Europe. They built for keeps, anticipating future generations. Ours is the economy of waste. Tear it down, throw it out, burn it up. Makes more work for more people. I suppose it does, but it's a false philosophy just the same. The world's resources are not unlimited, nor beautiful objects commonplace.

Tradition means little to us here at home. Had we ever had a tower such as they have in London, it would long ago have been destroyed to make way for a parking lot.

From Azay we pushed on, stopping eventually at Loudun, a village of about six thousand people, dry and unattractive. We stopped only because we had not lunched. It was now past two and we were hungry.

The one café in the village was unprepossessing, but we had no choice. We went inside, and although the bar was empty, we discovered the owner and his wife and little boy having their own luncheon behind a striped canvas curtain. We apologized for intruding and asked if it would be possible to get something to eat even though it was late.

The woman said that it was never too late to do well and would we give ourselves the pain of sitting down. We sat. Shortly afterward she served us. The hors d'oeuvres consisted of delicious little artichokes, succulent tomatoes, eggs with homemade mayonnaise, sardines, slices of spicy sausage, olives, and radishes. This was followed by a tureen of fresh mussels with *sauce marinière* that left us speechless we were so busy mopping it up with excellent bread. After that we had cold roast chicken and salad, goat's-milk cheese, and fresh peaches. To wash it down, an excellent local wine and at the end strong black coffee. For the three of us the bill came to a little over six dollars including the tip.

In America it is not impossible to get a luncheon for three for six dollars but it would not be that luncheon. You would be lucky to get it in New York, Chicago, New Orleans or San Francisco regardless of what you paid, and in towns of six thousand it simply wouldn't exist.

I remember once when I was on a lecture tour, I spoke in Fond du Lac, Wisconsin. I was driven by the ladies who were looking after me to a Victorian house at the edge of town that had been turned into a restaurant and was decorated with taste and gaiety. We were served a luncheon of fricassee of veal, a real *blanquette de veau*, and an authentic tossed green salad. When I exclaimed over this delightful surprise, I was told that the owner of the house was a young French war bride who had married an American soldier and come back to Wisconsin to live with him. Wisconsin was lucky.

Our second night out of Paris we arrived at the Hotel Domino in Périgueux. Périgueux is famous for the cathedral of St. Front, its great domes giving it a curiously mosque-like appearance, and it's also the home of the truffle and *pâté de foie gras*.

We dined in an upstairs restaurant called La Montaigne, and from it saw a curious sight. Across the street on the corner was a house in which considerable alteration was going on. On two sides the walls were out, so you could look into it as if it were a doll's house. From the center of the ceiling in an upstairs room hung, in true French fashion, one naked electric light bulb with a table and chair under it. Ranged against the walls that were still standing were a few other tables and chairs. Presently a man came in, sat down at the center table, and proceeded to write. We speculated as to what he was doing there and decided he must be the architect going over the plans or possibly the owner going over the bills. In a few minutes, however, two or three other men came in. They were shortly joined by more until finally there was a small crowd standing about chatting, seating themselves at the tables, playing cards. A soiree was obviously in full swing. Unable to contain our curiosity, we asked the waiter what on earth went on. "Oh," he said, "downstairs is the café and upstairs is a club. As you see, the place is being renovated, but the members like it so much they come for their evening meetings anyway, even though there are no walls." *Vive l'esprit* that rises above life's petty inconveniences.

Our nocturnal disturbances at Périgueux were other than the taxi horns of Paris and the clanging clock of Tours, but they were with us. We got back from the restaurant and went to bed, only to find that in the garden our windows overlooked a festive dinner party was going on; twelve Germans all talking at the tops of their lungs, and they didn't break up until after 2 A.M. Sleepy, with nerves frayed by fatigue, more than once I was within a hairsbreadth of leaping from my bed to the window and screaming down at them, "Buchenwald, Dachau, monsters." In the morning I was glad my shattered self-control had held, for when I complained about them at the desk, the lady manager agreed they were noisy, but added, "They're Belgian, you know. What you thought was the German language was Flemish, but it's true that they talk very loud." I was still disgruntled, but took some consolation from the fact that the Belgians, at least, had suffered from the war, not inflicted it.

There was a very nice English girl behind the desk, and when I asked her how she happened to be working there, she said that she was married to a Frenchman, a native of Périgueux. During the war he was very young and the Germans sent him into Germany to do forced labor in a concentration camp. He escaped, aided, it must be said, by a German, returned to France, was deported into Spain, escaped from there to England, where he joined the R.A.F. and met and married our English girl. He sounded a man of parts.

From Périgueux we pushed on to Toulouse, the lush countryside changing to the more mountainous terrain of the Dordogne and the Garonne, but still very thoroughly cultivated. Toulouse is a thriving provincial city without charm but with good restaurants and a hairdressing establishment where, if one is brave, one may get a shampoo. Courage is required because at the time we were there—they may have modernized it by now—they used a geyser that would have been appropriate in an anteroom to hell—roaring flames, bubbling water, and tubes sticking out like octopus tentacles.

When the acolyte who tended this monster was finished with me, my hair was clean, but I was first cousin to a Fiji Islander, sprouting a frizzy, bushlike mop. As we walked along the street together, I noticed that Norton and Peter kept their distance, gazing with unaccustomed

concentration into shopwindows when other pedestrians went by staring at me with ill-concealed amusement.

The unexpected experience in Toulouse was the exhibition of modern tapestries we had the good luck to happen upon. After the ancient
beige-and-maroon hangings eternally churning with horses' haunches,
riotous with gods in armor and kings in plumed hats and brocaded coats
leading charging armies into battle, the brilliant abstractions, gay birds
and flowers, stars and shells of the moderns were a refreshing change.
The cartoons were drawn by contemporary French artists, but the weaving was done in the old workshops of Gobelin and Aubusson. I never
think of Aubusson without thinking of the exquisite rug at Mount
Vernon given to Washington by the Marquis de Lafayette.

The day we left Toulouse we lunched at Carcassonne. The island of
Rhodes, which we have since seen, is, I believe, supposed to be the most
complete example of medieval architecture extant, but it hasn't the romantic, fairy-tale quality of Carcassonne. The fortress city on the hillside dates from the pre-Roman era, but what one sees today is the
restored moats and towers and crenelated battlements of the thirteenth century, and they are pure Grimm. One may wander about and
see where the defenders poured molten lead on any enemy intrepid
enough to attack, and peer through the narrow slits through which the
arrows whizzed.

It is a spot to delight the hearts of small boys and tourists, and there
is a restaurant in the regular part of town, as distinguished from the
citadel, that is top flight, the Auter. Some pretty awful tapestries hang
on the wall, but what they set upon the table is fine art. For this treat
we were indebted to a young Dane who was having language troubles
and we were able to help him out, and he knew about the restaurant.
He was on a walking tour all by himself. He had been through Spain
and was now hiking northward back to Denmark.

Fortified by our luncheon, we rolled on to Perpignan, one of the
starred destinations of our trip, for the Casals music festival was in
progress. The concerts were usually held at Prades, on the Spanish border, but, due to political complications in which Casals was involved,
had been moved and were given in the palace of the kings of Marjorca,
who once ruled the small state of Perpignan. The courtyard of the
palace is open to the sky but the acoustics are perfect.

As much cannot be said for the plumbing. At one point in the concert I had to excuse myself. I wandered around and finally found myself outside the palace walls. A small soft-drink stand where the daring

could purchase alarming orange syrups was set up nearby, and I asked
the attendant where I might find a lavatory. She looked surprised and
said that as far as she knew there wasn't one. I looked surprised and,
I should fancy, alarmed. "But what is one to do?" I demanded. She
shrugged, then waved me airily behind the stand. "Madame, there are
always the fields." So there were, and I thanked heaven I had left in
the middle of a masterpiece rather than at intermission. At least I was
alone.

Why it does not occur to the French, normally realists in these matters, that with thousands of people converging on one spot a lavatory
system would see enough use to make it practical is mysterious. It
doesn't occur to them to install one at the château of Chambord, either,
and that is an old-established tourist mecca.

The night we were at the palace we sat on the uncomfortable
wooden chairs drinking in the beautiful sounds and assuaging our disappointment over the fact that Casals himself was not playing. He did,
however, conduct. Jennie Tourel sang, and Horshovsky, the pianist,
played superbly, notes of cascading crystal. It was a romantic occasion,
but the night was cool and windy, and the orchestra had its troubles
as the scores blew from the stands and there was desperate diving and
snatching to retrieve them before the down beat. Casals conducted
with his overcoat on, a muffler around his neck, and his hat upon his
head. He could have worn tails or a bathing suit; it wouldn't have mattered. He conducted like an angel.

Some time later I met Jennie Tourel at a party given by mutual
friends, the Gerald Warburgs, after she had sung at a Philharmonic
concert in New York conducted by Leonard Bernstein. She remembered the Perpignan evening well and how the wind had blown her
skirts and how Casals' scarf had whipped out like a banner.

We had hoped to stay in Perpignan, but because of the festival had
been unable to get accommodations. We had had recommended to us
the little village of Collioure, about twenty-seven kilometers nearer the
Spanish frontier.

We were supposed to stop at the Hôtel de la Frégate and indeed
had had our reservations for weeks before we left New York, all specifically stated in one of those books of tickets supplied to its clients
by the American Express Company.

We whipped out our book, explained who we were, and waited ex-
pectantly to be shown to our rooms. The manager looked distraught,

and it soon became clear that, tickets or not, might of American Express Co. or no, there was no room at the inn.

The manager was desolated, but the workmen—the hotel was still in the building—had let him down. He was desolated, he was also exasperated. Who could have foreseen anything like this influx of visitors? How could the town be expected to accommodate them? How did so many people know about Casals anyway? It was not reasonable! We would, however, be taken care of. He had got us rooms in a private house just across the road from the hotel belonging to a charming old lady who had, he assured us, a very great fortune. That sounded pretty good. The house would doubtless be delightful, and maybe, being so rich, she wouldn't want to be paid.

When we saw the house, we decided that she might have the money, but if so it was stashed away in her sock, as obviously little of it had been spent on gracious living. The bathroom arrangements were pixy and the beds pure fantasy. Pete's slanted so sharply from head to foot that he seemed to be leaning against one of those propped-up reclining boards they give you in Hollywood studios when your dress is tight or fragile and the wardrobe department doesn't want you to sit down in it. One entered the old lady's property through a door in the garden wall. The wall was covered with honeysuckle and that was lovely, but the fragrance found itself in sharp competition with the adjacent fish market. Peter invented a perfume called Peume. You smelled the fish, you started to say Phew, then you caught the honeysuckle and changed it to Hmmm.

We slept, in a manner of speaking, at the house and took our meals at the Frégate. The dining room was French provincial, and guests rolled their napkins into napkin rings from meal to meal and kept their own bottles of wine boardinghouse fashion.

The couple who ran the inn were pleasant, though harassed, and told us that their business had been made possible by the Marshall Plan. They'd been able to get in the foundation and the first two floors when the Plan money ran out. They had, however, gone ahead renting rooms, to us among others, in two nonexistent upper stories, hoping against hope that they could refinance and get the building completed in time for the tourist surge. This optimistic scheme had backfired as far as the present season was concerned, but they assured us that everything had now been straightened out and we must come back next year, when we should have what we gathered would be a princely suite.

So far we haven't been able to accept the invitation, but I should like someday to return. Collioure is a picturesque fishing village, its small harbor protected by a breakwater and an ancient round stone tower remarkably phallic in silhouette.

The long rust-colored nets bordered with cork floats are spread out to dry on the silvery jetty against the sparkling blue of the Mediterranean. The old gray stone houses, with their velvety terra-cotta-tiled roofs, climb the green and violet hills, and even the clothes the people wear are an integral part of the color scheme: the black dresses and shawls of the women, the deep blue blouses of the men, a white apron or a white head, striking a sharp contrasting note in the deep rich coloring of the backdrop. In one of the winding cobbled streets we saw a white and tortoise-shell cat, his tail tied with three red ribbons, and we saw a tiny bent old woman all in black, under her arm a huge bundle of fagots we assumed she would use for firewood.

Wood is precious in France, and the French find in our disregard of it something a little shocking. Norton and I once had a cook, Ketty, whom we had engaged in Paris. When we were at the place on Long Island, she would walk along the beach and come back to the house laden with a great harvest of driftwood that was often lovely in shape and burned beautifully, but it also shed sand all over the house, and this annoyed the doctor. He bore up under the driftwood, however, because there were often solid, businesslike pieces in Ketty's haul, but he rebelled when she started bringing in dried branches that had blown from the trees. He would sternly order her to exile the clutter, and she would mutter darkly, predicting ominous consequences from such waste.

Being from Luxembourg, she spoke German as well as French, and it was quite educational to take her out in the rowboat around sunset, when she might express her pleasure with something like "Ah, *das ist zer beau the sun qui couche.*"

We were not in Collioure long, but we slipped easily into the village life and would watch our landlady cross the road to gossip with her neighbor. The two women would sit knitting and chatting on the balcony, and Wolf, the landlady's big dog, would go out through the door in the garden wall, cross the road, go upstairs to the neighbor's house, and presently appear on the balcony and sit down beside them.

We wandered about and bought *espadrilles*, the canvas, rope-soled shoes, and we watched the old women sitting on the ground mending the fishing nets.

At night the sardine fleet went out with fat lanterns bobbing on the bows and came back just before dawn with the catch. In the daytime the red and blue and green boats were drawn up and beached on the edge of the little cove, and we strolled around them and bathed and lay on the warm sand.

Old men in faded blue jackets and trousers and the inevitable Basque beret sat like ancient blue jays along the stone wall or played a game like bowls under the trees of the village square. They had card games, too, like the old men in Paris in the Luxembourg Gardens who play endless hands of cards and dominoes.

It seems to me that the old people of Europe are less lonely than many of the elderly men and women of America. The sidewalk café, the village square, the parks are clubs where all are welcome. Europeans consider it natural and proper that the inhabitants of the village or the neighborhood should gather to pass the time companionably. Here at home we're fond of referring to all outdoors. As big as all outdoors, we say, but in all that vastness there are few corners either in town or country geared to the enjoyment and the quiet pleasures of the old.

We left Collioure reluctantly, but Spain lay ahead and we felt that we had best stick to our schedule.

I know there are two violently opposed schools of thought on the virtues and disadvantages of a tour that, if not guided, is at any rate mapped out with dates of arrival and departure to be rigidly adhered to. "Not for us," cry the freewheeling gypsies. "Get to a place, if you love it, stay, if you hate it, push on. Why be confined by a travel agency?" I sympathize with this spirit completely, and if one is traveling out of season, I think it's well worth taking a gamble on finding bed and board unannounced and unexpected. I do not recommend it when a million or so other Americans are also wandering the well-worn paths of Europe and, in ever-increasing numbers, Asia during the summer months.

We have seen that even a confirmed reservation is not necessarily a guarantee of accommodation, but it's a better-than-fifty-fifty chance, and the management at least feels guilty to the extent of making an effort to palm you off elsewhere. Totally unannounced, you run the risk of excessive bohemianism—sleeping under the stars or propped up in the lobby of some dubious hostelry. Furthermore, a schedule is not always that confined. On the spot you sometimes can make changes if willing to put up with a certain amount of inconvenience or delay.

We left Collioure on the morning of Friday, the thirteenth, riding with us. It was a glorious day, and we drove over the winding mountain roads under a blazing blue sky, the sparkling Mediterranean on our left. We got across the border with a minimum of red tape, traversed a few hundred yards of a sort of no man's land, and arrived at the Spanish frontier. There we presented our passports, signed for the number of pesetas we had with us, and brought out the papers for the car, a more impressive sheaf than anything we had relating to ourselves. Those they studied with great care, scrutinizing the car and looking us up and down as though it was obvious that we had stolen it. Finally with a shrug they passed us through. Spain at last!

The doctor expanded. "Can't see why people make such a fuss about customs," he observed. "Nothing to them. They balked at the car a little, but that's natural. Otherwise they couldn't have been nicer."

Within I heard a still, small voice. "I have a suspicion, darling," I said, "that we haven't seen the end of the Spanish Customs yet. That was just the frontier. Probably in this village we're coming to . . ." I spoke with the tongue of prophets. As we approached the village, the chaps in the green uniforms with the black patent-leather bicorn hats and the rifles slung over their shoulders stopped us in front of a square white house, and it didn't take extrasensory perception or a knowledge of Spanish to divine where we were: la aduana, la douane, customs. We went inside, and it was interesting to be in a Spanish house even though it was a municipal one. The first thing that struck us was the extreme cleanliness of everything; the whitewashed walls and the tiled floors were immaculate. The next thing—and although he may have been clean he was certainly not clean cut, being in fact a jowly type—was Franco in a large gilt frame. We were to see him in every hotel and bank throughout Spain. Dictators, due, I fancy, to insecurity, find it necessary to impinge their images on the public conscience a thousand times over, preferably in locations where the traffic is heavy.

The chap on duty, a bantamweight in spruce uniform looking rather like a diminutive member of the U. S. Navy in summer whites, asked politely to see our luggage. We hauled everything out and were asked to open a couple of pieces, which he and an assistant rummaged through perfunctorily. They actually disturbed very little beyond my emotions. I hate seeing my clothes pawed over by public officials.

Finally we were allowed to close the bags. Hieroglyphics were scrawled upon them in chalk, and we thought that we were in the clear, when our chum, Little White Wing, indicated courteously that he would like us to open a dispatch case we thought had gone unnoticed. We were not deliberately trying to smuggle it. It is just that after many

years of crossing many borders I have found it timesaving to draw
as little attention as possible to as few pieces as possible. This, shall
we say, might be Traveler's Tip No. 4. Of course, once a particular piece
is pin-pointed, the prudent voyager opens it with good grace, nay, with
eager co-operation and an engaging smile. Unfortunately the particular
piece pounced upon was Pandora's box. It contained—and the tongue
trips over the dirty word—film. It contained masses and masses and
masses of the stuff, plus light meters and lenses. The doctor is not a man
to stint in the photographic department. Traveler's Tip No. 5: When
estimating the cost of a journey do not forget to include film and
charges for developing same. It can be quite an item.

Logically there was no reason for customs-official censure, since the
three of us were so garlanded with cameras we looked like caricature
American tourists, and they had not taken us to task because of it.
What did they think we put in them? I suppose it must have been the
number of little yellow boxes, sixty-five or seventy, as I recall. Obviously
we were either international spies or were going to set up shop, taking
bread from the mouths of the Spanish representatives of Kodak. Sensing a mood of antipathy not conducive to international good will, we
started laughing gaily and dispensing charm like popcorn, my husband
explaining that Spain was so *hermosa* that *mucha fotografía* was inevitable. "*No es verdad?*" I said hopefully, my one Spanish phrase to date.

Little White Wing looked at us coldly and went away, he said to telephone, but we heard him in another room shouting so loudly we were
convinced he was simply hollering to Franco in Madrid without benefit of wires.

He came back after a while and via much pantomime and flooding
Spanish gave us to understand that we might pass but must distribute
the film throughout our luggage, not keep it all in one big hunk. Since
he had now seen it, this struck us as wasted effort, but when I deal with
foreign officials my motto has always been "Do like the man say, soon-
est mended."

The doctor unfortunately chose this moment to balk. It was ridiculous, he said. All that repacking would make it very difficult for him
to find anything. White Wing, though not understanding the words,
sensed mutiny and glared at us balefully. *La policía* who had been
lounging in the doorway moved casually to his side. His rifle was not at
the ready, but it was in evidence. I gave my dear one a sharp, surreptitious kick. He looked at me like a fawn both wounded and outraged,
but we opened our other bags and started stuffing the film away with a

will. At last all was accomplished to official satisfaction. White Wing unbent, and *la policía* moved lazily back to his post in the doorway. We breathed a sigh of relief and were just starting off when our man observed casually that we were of course bringing the car back across the border?

Since this was not quite our intent, I gave him a dazzling smile, implying that he was so right. He was apparently reassured. Feeling like characters in an Alfred Hitchcock movie—only the suspense was killing us instead of the audience—Norton and I were about to step across the threshold to freedom when Peter, the dear, honorable child, piped up. So there should be no misunderstanding he explained that we were motoring through Spain, then back to Barcelona, where the automobile would be reclaimed by the owner and driven to Paris while we flew on to Majorca.

That did it. They were now convinced of what they had suspected all along: we were international spies and we had stolen the car.

It was some time later and only by dint of implying that the little boy was delirious and not quite bright at best—tapping of temples and shrugging of shoulders—and assurances that we would be seeing them within the week, that we were able to flee their scrutiny and hightail it out of the customs zone.

From there on Peter was instructed that whenever we met an official he was to wiggle his fingers and ears and pretend to be a deaf-mute. I don't know why customs are so nerve-racking.

Leaving the border, we drove south along the Costa Brava to Figueras. One of the first impressions one receives is that Spain is vast, arid, and, because of the aridity, desperately poor. It is also extremely mountainous, and any Americans who know our own Southwest and the West Coast are bound to exclaim as we did, "But it's Nevada, it's Southern California, it's the road from San Luis Obispo to Monterey." It's easy to understand why the Spaniards settled in California. The instant they struck it they must have looked at each other and said, "Home again." What is lacking in two thirds of Spain is the fertile valleys of California. The rain in Spain stays mainly in the plain, but the tragedy is that it stays sparsely. Irrigation is desperately needed, but even if they had the money for hydroelectric projects—which at that time they had not—it's hard to see where the water would come from. I suppose the mountains, but even on the mountaintops, in summer, there was little snow. Our most vivid memories of the Spanish landscape are the undulating plains, the great wheat fields of the central plateau, where we watched the grain being threshed by hand, the tumbled mountain ranges and the wide, eventful skies with their enormous cloud formations. At night they are higher, darker, more starfilled than any other skies I have ever seen.

Some of the national routes were in very good condition; over others let us draw a kindly veil of silence. Goat tracks wandering through the villages. It's only fair to say, however, that the Spaniards were thoroughly road-conscious. All along the way there were piles of stones and gangs working, if in pretty primitive fashion. The bulldozer was unknown. Men and women too would spread tar and then lug great baskets of crushed stone to pour over it. Where there was no paving the dust was bad and the potholes plentiful.

We arrived in Figueras in time for lunch and liked the town immediately. There are lovely old trees in the plaza and an excellent restaurant, the Durán, had been recommended to us.

As we had been at the border, we were again impressed by Spanish cleanliness. Everybody talks about how clean the Dutch are, everybody except those Europeans who followed them in Indonesia after the natives drove them out in 1949. Their tales of so-called Dutch hygiene are startling.

I have never been in Holland, but Spanish sanitation is impressive. They scrub from morning to night and in them such industry is even more praiseworthy than in the countries of the north where it rains for months at a time and water is no problem. In almost all the villages of Spain, including those adjacent to big cities, there was no running water. Over and over again we saw women carrying earthenware jugs to and from the village pump. They had to fetch it for every bit of cooking and washing they did, and we wondered how immaculate we ourselves would be under those circumstances.

We were charmed to find the washrooms of the restaurant spotlessly clean, and there was even free soap. A pleasant shock after *la belle France*, where, once out of Paris, hygienically speaking, you're on your own and where lavatories with holes in the floor rather than toilets are the rule, not the exception.

Oddly enough, it was in Figueras that I ate my first snails. Delicious, very like chicken. Even Peter tried one, which is saying a good deal, for the young are violently conservative in matters of taste and dress. Nothing that the other kids aren't eating and wearing, thank you.

The peseta is worth roughly two cents, and luncheon for three with hors d'oeuvres, cold lobster salad, wine, dessert for one, and coffee for two came to about $4.60.

Since it is painful for me not to be able to express myself, I usually travel with an arsenal of grammars and phrase books. Although not always able to cope with these keys to another tongue, I find them comforting. In Spain we had five and at Figueras we bought a Spanish-English dictionary. What I lack in skill I make up in audacity. Men, I think, are rather shy about making fools of themselves in a foreign language, but I have no shame and plunge in. The natives must have thought I was speaking gibberish but they were invariably polite and tried hard to decipher my meaning.

Our destination for our first night in Spain was Barcelona, but we stopped en route in the delightful old town of Gerona. A river wanders through it, and the stone and plaster houses go down into the water the way they do in the canals of Venice. The houses are old, gray and verdigris and earth-colored, and in front of almost all the windows are delicately wrought iron balconies with the characteristic bamboo blinds of Spain pulled down against the sun.

From years of hot summers the Spaniards are knowledgeable in the ways of shade. They either hang the blinds out over the balconies so the air can circulate, or when there are no balconies they build a kind of cage of iron ribs bulging out from the windows, and over this the blinds are lowered. From within, looking out, the effect must be rather like peering into a well-ventilated grotto.

Also hanging from the balconies, strung from window to window, was the laundry, opaque white against the old walls, a strong color contrast like that of some modern canvases. I always love the washing. All over the world my two favorite subjects for photography are washing and markets, possibly because they have been an integral part of human living since the beginning of time.

Seeing the world per se is marvelous, but I have found that one's enjoyment is greatly enhanced if it is focused, if one has a specific interest apart from what may be called the automatic sights—museums, churches, the countryside itself.

The quarry may be as humble as the markets and laundry. It may be animals or trees or restaurants, the theater or ballet, modern painting, porcelains, or hospitals, boats or carriages or pickle factories. The subject matters little; it is in the propelling collector's instinct that the reward lies. One need not necessarily buy. This kind of collecting is primarily furniture for the eye and heart and memory.

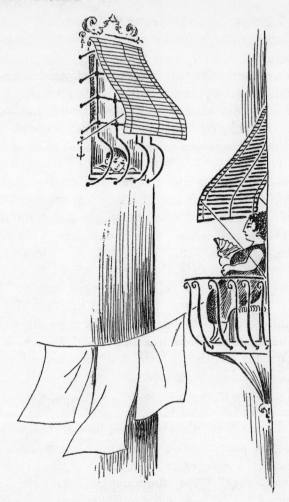

Traveler's Tip No. 6: Pack a hobby when you go.

There is a magnificent fourteenth-century cathedral in Gerona, and we visited the Arab baths that date from the twelfth century. They are charming, with a well in the middle from which they drew and can still draw water. Around the well's edge are the worn grooves formed eight hundred years ago by the ropes of the buckets. Stone benches where the habitués used to lie to be massaged encircle the walls, and there is a steam room ringed by delicate columns with Arabic carvings. They had everything the lads have in the Turkish baths of American athletic clubs, plus beauty.

We reached Barcelona a little after eight in the evening. The road skirts the Mediterranean and for miles the approach is lined by serried ranks of cabañas and small summer villas, rather like those of Malibu or Santa Monica.

The streetcars were filled with people going home from work, and it was in Barcelona that we were initiated into Spanish time.

In the summer they open up about nine-thirty in the morning and close at one. One to four-thirty, siesta. Sacrosanct. It is useful to remember that the museums reopen from four till six or seven and the shops from four to eight.

There is no use fighting the siesta hours of any hot Mediterranean country. Americans on short schedules begin pawing the earth, but the natives aren't going to change. In planning stopovers the thing to remember is that it may take two to three days to see what you feel you could encompass in one. Either take the time to rest yourself or use it for letter writing or reading. Don't try to buck it.

We discovered that in Spain eight-thirty is the correct cocktail hour, and between ten and eleven people start drifting toward dinner. The American ambassador at that time was Stanton Griffis, an old friend of ours. Some of the people from ambassadorial circles who knew him still talk about his unorthodox ways, but one custom he established and followed seemed to me rooted in common sense. He ate his dinner at an hour he was accustomed to, seven-thirty or eight, and went on to the tardy banquets well fortified.

One Sunday night in Madrid we were tired and asked wistfully if we couldn't get dinner at about eight, but a Spanish friend said, "Oh, I wouldn't try it if I were you, none of the good places begin functioning before nine-thirty." Weary and hungry, we stationed ourselves on the threshold of the Jockey Club and tumbled in headlong, the first customers when they opened the doors.

The Spaniards, perhaps, overdo it, but the customarily late hours of European dining seem, when there, natural and pleasant. The thing that baffles me is how the servants are persuaded to accept them as perfectly normal. Sitting down to dinner anywhere from eight to eleven, Norton and I would comment on the countless families at home who eat at six or six-thirty or the cook walks out. I suppose it's the magic siesta that turns the trick.

It was still too soon after the war for the quality of Spanish food to be first rate, and we had a pretty scrawny chicken for our dinner, but the skill, delicacy, and speed with which the headwaiter carved it were spectacular. The doctor observed that if ever he had to have an operation that was the fellow he wanted to do it.

We liked Barcelona. The *madrileños* look down their noses at the Catalonians, whom they consider mercenary, but Barcelona is a good city, a seaport of nearly a million and a half inhabitants, modern and progressive, with fine shops and restaurants, and I imagine by now good hotels, too, although the Ritz at the time we were there was not a shining example. Its manager, however, was a delightful man, Señor Albareda. He was remarkably good-looking, with a brown face and shining white hair and that combination of humor and virility that seems to be a prerogative of the Spanish male. There was no trouble to which he wouldn't put himself on our behalf, but his hotel, while not dirty—we saw no dirt in Spain—was sadly shabby.

The ceilings are very high, which is pleasant, but ceilings and walls were peeling in great strips like sunburned skin.

In the bathroom one poor little twenty-five-watt bulb blinked drearily down from its lofty perch about eighteen feet above the wash basin. I struggled to tilt my face to its etiolated rays, but I finally gave up and applied my make-up without even looking in the mirror. What was the use?

The bedsprings were broken and the mattresses sagged nearly to the floor, but the plumbing in the tub won our admiration. We turned the hot faucet on first, and then, after a few moments, the cold to regulate the temperature, and maybe that happened too, but the beneficial effect was lost because the cold-water spigot in the tub in some mysterious way released a scalding cascade from the shower head. We never did get that one figured out, nor could we ever divine why, throughout Spain, there were no shower curtains. We tried to be tidy, but inevitably the floor was awash. Maybe they think the moisture cools the air, or maybe the lack was, like everything else, due to the rigors of war.

The first morning in Barcelona we ordered breakfast in our rooms, and I asked for tea, an error I did not repeat. It was made out of old brown pine needles laced with pepper. I was glad we had dined sumptuously the night before at the Parallada, one of the top restaurants in Spain, if not indeed in Europe.

In many cities there are exceptional restaurants, and in many private houses the food is, of course, excellent, but I should say that Spanish cooking on the whole is like American cooking on the whole. Not good. Before I listen to any squawks of outraged patriotism, let me say I know whereof I speak. I have crossed and recrossed the United States countless times in the course of doing my job and I have had proven to me over and over again the sorry truth that our average fare is poor.

So often when we do get good meat, vegetables, and fruit, we massacre them in the kitchen and, since most markets sell by weight, with the use of chemical fertilizers we bring produce to giant size, only to discover that it has no taste. It's the same with those poor chickens who must spend their lives indoors on wire mesh and are never allowed to run. It's supposed to make them tender. All that happens is that it makes the flesh soggy and totally without flavor.

In Spain the indifferent quality of the food may be excused to some extent by the poverty of the soil. With so little land for grazing, dairy products are at a minimum, hence the use of olive oil in cooking; butter is scarce. The Spaniards drink wine, but it is not a religion with them as it is with the French. The waiter does not hover tremulously over the table as though you and the wine card were infinitely dear. He asks if you will have red or white, sweet or dry and lets it go at that. Vintage and vineyard make little difference.

A well-prepared *paella*, that casserole of rice, seafood, and chicken, is a delight and a Spanish favorite, and, though my friend Peggy Harvey is not Spanish, she is a great cook—her book *Season to Taste* should be in every kitchen—and I asked her to give me a *paella* recipe, and here it is. Good it is, too.

Have the butcher disjoint two broilers. Using two and a half quarts of water, make a strong broth from the backs, giblets, necks, wing tips.

Brown the rest of the chicken in butter in an iron skillet.

Grease a large casserole with olive oil and sauté one large chopped onion, one half clove shredded garlic (they use more in Spain), and twelve thick slices Spanish or Italian sausage (fresh, not smoked).

Pour off the fat when the sausage is quite done. This is very important.

Add the chicken, and if you have some leftover ham, chop up a cupful or so and add that. If you like zucchini, add a pound, raw, cut in chunks. If you don't, add a pound of fresh, cooked green beans at the point indicated later on. Season with salt and freshly ground black pepper.

Stir in two cups washed, raw, long-grain rice and cook over a low flame for two minutes.

Add five cups boiling chicken broth and save the remainder.

Bring a sixth cup to a boil and dissolve in it one teaspoon of saffron. Pour evenly over the rice.

Open twenty-four Little Neck clams and put them in a saucepan with their juice. Add twelve or more cooked shrimp and heat in the clam juice. When the rice is nearly tender, add the shrimp, clams, and the juice from the pan. Cook in a medium oven or on top of the stove until the rice has absorbed the liquid.

Now is the time to add the green beans if you use them.

One more point: most recipes call for pimiento. We are not pimiento fans, so we eliminated same. If you feel different, you may take your choice of the following procedures: (1) serve them whole, on the side; (2) lay a few strips across the top of the casserole; (3) stir in some, chopped, when you add the beans or at that point.

Serve in the dish in which it was cooked. For six to eight.

Another characteristically Spanish dish is the hot-weather delight *gazpacho*, the soup-salad combination. There are as many recipes for *gazpacho* as there are districts in Spain—sometimes, it seems, as many as there are Spaniards—so I shall not try to give one, but suggest that you will find an authentic version in Myra Waldo's *Complete Round-the-World Cookbook* written for Pan American. You can add variants of your own, and in summertime fresh herbs—tarragon, chervil, orégano —add piquancy.

Before starting our tour of the Spanish countryside we were told that we would do well to get our ration tickets for gasoline at the Banco de España, as all gas is state controlled. Every drop has to be imported, but they ought to make a mint, as in only a few places do you get top quality and the standard price is about sixty cents a gallon. Another reason, besides narrow roads, why small, non-thirsty cars are preferable. Today, although the price is the same, rationing is a thing of the past. Once out of the cities, one may drive for hours without passing a car, as few Spaniards can afford them, but they are proud of their busses, and we saw some behemoths trundling along that looked very comfortable. I hope they were, because while we did not experience the trains ourselves the Spaniards rolled their eyes heavenward when they were mentioned.

We went to the bank on a Saturday morning, armed, we thought, with every conceivable paper we could possibly need, including affidavits certifying to our mothers' maiden names. We walked jauntily up the steps but received a shock when, on entering, we discovered the

place manned with the military, rifles at the ready and bayonets drawn.
I thought of the fatherly gent in the gray alpaca who helps me out at
the Guaranty Trust and decided I liked him better.

We were directed to the proper window and found ourselves at the
end of a long line of French, English, and Spanish travelers. The bank
closed at noon and it was then about a quarter of. We began to feel
uneasy, and our apprehensions were well grounded. We were in a mo-
rass of European red tape and delay was inevitable, but although they
were allowing no one else in the bank they would deal with those already there. We drew a sigh of relief, as otherwise it would mean post-
poning our departure from Barcelona until Monday.

When our turn came, as we had at customs we whipped out our
winning smiles and with an air at once casual and reassuring deployed
our papers. The first hitch in international bonhomie occurred when
the man discovered that our name was Brown and the name on the car
papers was Ségur, the garage in Paris from which we had rented it. How,
or more interestingly *why*, did people named Brown have a car named
Ségur? As at the border our theft of the vehicle was all too obvious.
We pointed placatingly to our documents. The bank official spurned
them. We shoved our passports under his nose. He spurned those.
What he wanted was our money declaration. I looked questioningly at
the doctor, who gave a slight gargle. "Oh Lord, that must be the only
one I left at the hotel. But we have it," he said to the teller, "we have
it back in our room. It's just that we don't have it here." We could have
had it and the Gutenberg Bible; old poker face was implacable. Suddenly, though, there came a crack in the official armor as his eye lighted
on Peter. "Why doesn't *el niño* go fetch the paper at the hotel?" We
started forward en masse. "Oh no, two parents will stay here and wait
for him." So that was his game! Norton and I were hostages. Still, it
seemed a pretty good solution until we glanced at the face of *el niño*.
Since he and his father spoke even less Spanish than I, if that were
possible, he didn't fancy finding himself alone in the streets. We held
a brief council of war and decided that I had best be the one to cope
with the taxi.

The great doors of the bank were now closed and the chaps with the
guns and bayonets were leaning against them watching us, but with
courage born of the determination to start our touring when we intended to I approached one of them and attempted to convey our problem. He watched and listened laconically, and then opened the door
—just a crack—so I could slip through. In English, French, and what

I hoped was at least a Spanish inflection I explained that, like Mac-
Arthur, I would return and please, please to remember me. No lover
ever pleaded more passionately than I not to be forgotten.

I leaped into a cab, sped to the hotel, raced down the corridor to our
room, and rifled Norton's luggage, tossing what I didn't want to left
and right and feeling like Mata Hari. At last I found the precious paper
and fled back to the bank. The army was still on duty. "It's me, it's me,"
I cried. "Remember?" Franco's minions looked at me impassively, but
one of them opened the door and I slipped inside.

As soon as he saw the paper, the guardian of the exchequer relaxed
with a small gurgling sound like a baby who at last gets his bottle, and
after only another twenty minutes of tape unwinding, signatures, and
seals we were given our gas tickets and allowed to depart.

We went back to the hotel to lunch before starting off, and as we
sat in the lobby over an apéritif, we were amused to see two Spanish
men, with drinks before them, who from the way they kept glancing
toward the street door seemed to be waiting for someone. Sure enough,
presently two good-looking, well-dressed women, their arms full of
packages, appeared and joined them. Wives who had been on a Satur-
day-morning shopping spree meeting their husbands for luncheon.
Muy Americano.

Once fed and on our way, mindful of the morning's hazards and delay and safely out of earshot of authority, I mumbled and grumbled
about the tedious pettiness of bureaucracy, not to mention the slight
apprehension caused by all those rifles. "Force," I muttered, "the inevitable concomitant of dictatorship." The doctor agreed that the setup
was unattractive. "But," said he, "the dictator's position is precarious.
Both loud mouth and guns are essential to its maintenance. Also," he
added mildly—and that's where he's sneaky, coming in with the Sunday
punch when you least expect it—"supposing you were a visitor in the
United States and were driving along the road in complete innocence
when a husky guy on a roaring motorcycle with a revolver and bullets in
his belt herded you to the side, handed you a slip of paper, and ordered
you to show up at a certain place on a certain date where the munici-
pality would deprive you of funds. Wouldn't you consider that pretty
dictatorial?"

"Well, yes," I said, "I would, and motorcycle cops are my enemies.
On the other hand I suppose they sometimes have a point. Speeding
or going through stop signs or something. But we were innocent, we'd
imperiled no one, we'd just forgotten one measly little piece of paper."

"We're in Europe," said the doctor. "They don't have the forests we have and paper is precious to them."

This reasonable attitude, coupled with the passage of the miles and the fascination of the countryside, soothed my ruffled emotions.

We were driving inland over the great central plateau, the breadbasket of Spain. There is very little *mañana* spirit in the Spanish peasants. They are hard workers. Sometimes around noon we would see them sitting in the shade of the trees eating their luncheon of bread and wine, but we motored hundreds of miles and saw very little siestaing even during the blazing heat of the day. Men and women worked in the fields through the long hours of sunshine, and at eight and nine at night, as long as the daylight lasted, they were still harvesting the grain.

The wheat fields stretch on either side of the road, and over and over again the outdoor threshing floors are repeated, large round bald spots of baked clay. Men and women toss the wheat on three-pronged, peeled wooden pitchforks, the grain falls on the threshing floor, and the chaff is blown away. A sorrowful sight is the poor thin horses or donkeys, who, blindfolded, dragging behind them boards that press the wheat from the husks, tread round and round the circle from dawn till late at night.

This custom seems to me cruel, although the Spaniards will tell you that the blindfolds are actually a kindness; they keep the animals from getting dizzy. In more fertile regions where they have water, the donkeys endlessly turn the water wheels, some of which are primitive in the extreme. Earthen pots are strapped to them at intervals, and as the wheels dip they scoop up the water and dump it into conduits or narrow irrigation channels. In some places fortunately, Majorca for instance, there are windmills and the donkeys don't have to do the sorry job.

Spain is a land of proud and virile people. When one knows them and can appreciate the language, their humor, I should imagine, is both robust and subtle. History, beauty, courage abound among the Spaniards, and their treatment of animals is appalling. They keep small birds in cages against white-hot walls with no shelter from the grueling sun, and no matter how many thousands of people are thrilled by it, no matter how many persuasive and colorful books are written on the subject, I consider bullfighting a brutal sport. I do not deny either the skill or courage of the toreador, but I lament that these attributes are bent to such base purpose. An *aficionado* once explained to me that it has to do with mysticism, the Christian soul against brute force. A likely story. If the bulls roared in from the fields, trampling women and children, goring men, all of their own volition, I would be for shooting them in their tracks, but by way of Sunday-afternoon diversion, to stick innocent beasts full of spears and lances, to goad and weaken them, and to have men on horseback helping to break their strength and to have the horses gored, with their entrails streaming on the ground and their vocal chords cut so their screams will not disturb the squeamish—in the unlikely event there is any person of heart or stomach present—no, I thank you. When a bullfighter gets wounded, he damn' well gets his deserts. He isn't obliged to take up his profession. The bull is forced to.

More civilized flashes of Spanish color are to be found in the ambulatory population along the roads. Sometimes a whole family is on the move, but more often you see groups of women walking in the hot sunshine. They wear brightly colored blouses, straw hats, and white cloths across the lower part of their faces like sanitary bandits or the Turkish yashmaks of old, their dark eyes glowing above them. The cloths are to keep the wheat dust from getting into their noses and mouths, for they carry great bundles of it.

Once we saw a camel drawing a cart full of gypsies and frequently we saw men riding donkeys, their wives and mothers walking behind them. The eyes of the doctor and his son lighted up. "That's the stuff," they said, "woman's place. Those guys are smart." We sometimes asked people if we might take their picture, and always they seemed pleased and stood very still, looking seriously into the camera.

There is another common roadside sight, which we at first found baffling. Usually in the most deserted country, high in the mountains or in the middle of a plain miles from nowhere, we would come upon two soldiers standing at either side of the road silently facing each other, the butts of their rifles resting on the ground, the bayonets pointing skyward. They wore black leather hats turned up front and back, or else—more sensibly, because of the sun—round hats with brims and a green veil dropping down behind to protect their necks. At first we couldn't imagine why they were there and developed the interesting theory that they must be on punitive duty, the way we send cops to Canarsie, but further investigation revealed that they were the state police, but they don't patrol in cars because they have none. A truck takes them out in the morning and picks them up in the evening, and in between they stand around guarding the emptiness. In summer it is frightfully hot, and we felt sorry for them.

Out of Barcelona our target for the night was Zaragoza, a university town with about 225,000 inhabitants. We had some difficulty finding the Gran Hotel, as people we asked persisted in pointing up a narrow little alley, and we, having been informed that it was indeed quite grand, persisted in disbelieving them. As it turned out they knew what they were talking about. It fronted on the plaza but the most used entrance was on the alley.

After the genteel decay of the Barcelona Ritz we sparked to the fine modern plumbing of the Gran and were awed by the splendor of the bedrooms. The curtains might justly be described as gorgeous drapes; bright pink satin with yellow swags, bedspreads and couch covers to match. Marble-topped tables galore. Peter's quarters were a symphony of emerald green. The dining room unfortunately did not match the boudoirs.

Zaragoza has the dubious distinction of having been the seat of the Spanish Inquisition, and its cathedral is built around the first known shrine ever erected to the Blessed Virgin. The facet of the town that caught our attention the first night, however, was more secular. It was the telephone book. I do not know if Zaragoza is the telephone center of Spain, but the good doctor lay in bed perusing the directory with as much pleasure as if it had been an adrenal cortex.

"Look at this," he would say incredulously. "You can call the Union of South Africa for a hundred and twenty-eight pesetas, about two dollars and fifty cents."

"What about the Estados Unidos?"

"For two dollars and seventy cents. The Argentine for three seventy. The same for Japan."

We never did understand it but we decided it would be worth paying the fare to Zaragoza just to transact business by phone and agreed that we would have a little talk with American Tel and Tel when we got home.

The shrine to the Virgin was erected by St. James, the patron saint of Spain, forty years after the death of Christ. According to legend, on his missionary journey through the country the Lady appeared to him upon a pillar and told him to build a church on that spot. The pillar is still there, where it was placed nearly two thousand years ago, and the tiny chapel that surrounded it has grown into the great cathedral of Pilar, and the Virgin is referred to as La Pilarica.

We were in Zaragoza on a Sunday, so we went into the church during Mass. As we were about to enter, an old woman detached herself from a group of loungers and started a shrill tirade obviously directed at me. We stopped in amazement, not, of course, understanding a word she was saying, but we noticed that several bystanders seemed to be nodding in agreement. Puzzled, we again started for the door, but now the old woman came up to me and started clawing at my arm. I glanced down and suddenly realized what was troubling her. I was wearing a hat but had on a sleeveless black linen dress. She considered my bare upper arm immodest. Wishing to pacify her, for she was going on at a great rate in the hot sunshine and I had visions of stroke, I borrowed handkerchiefs from Peter and Norton and draped them over my shoulders, the wings of a pudic dove. She subsided muttering and we went into the cathedral.

It stands beside the winding, muddy Ebro and is a magnificent edifice, its many domes made of glittering colored tiles topped by cupolas and spires. Inside it is a vast square, with altars and small chapels around the sides and a great altar in the center. The Spaniards wander through it as though they were in an outdoor plaza and even at the most sacred moment of the Mass, the elevation of the Host, they continue strolling and chatting softly. The women respect the convention of covering their heads in the cathedral, but it is a token gesture, some using only pocket handkerchiefs, others brief mantillas. The mantillas are charming, and I bought several in black and white lace to wear in the evening. A long line of worshipers was passing the silver-mounted pillar upon which the Virgin stands and kissing an exposed portion. The doctor gently shook his head.

Over and over again in Spain and Italy one is struck by the enormous wealth of the Church and the poverty of the people, but it is their land and they apparently find consolation in the arrangement. The churches are a focal point in their lives, but it is not always religion or love of art that drives tourists to these magnificent buildings of the Latin world. They have another appeal. They are wonderfully cool sanctuaries from the blazing skies of summer, the season when most people travel.

The other most frequented sanctuaries are probably the *paradores*. The word means literally "one who stops." They are establishments that are a cross between a motel and a small inn and many of them are state controlled. Although the press, the gasoline system, and the railroads, state run, leave a good deal to be desired, the *paradores* are for the most part, tiptop. They are clean, the food is as good or better than average, and the people who run them we found to be unfailingly kind, helpful, and friendly.

Most of the *paradores* are modern in furnishing and similar in design. There's a square entrance hall, either to the right or left a comfortable lounge, and beyond that the dining room, with a big bay window. Since everyone except mad dogs, Englishmen, and crazy Americans takes a siesta after lunch, if you arrive in midafternoon the chances are you will find the couches and easy chairs filled with people napping before continuing their journey. The bedrooms and baths are upstairs and the furnishings, while simple, are comfortable. Prices are reasonable. There are also regular inns, *albergues*, but you can stay in them only overnight. A sojourn at a *parador* may be more protracted. One of the best of the *paradores* is on the way from Zaragoza to Madrid at Medinaceli. It is three or four miles off the main road, with a magnificent view of the undulating golden fields and distant purple mountains. We arrived at twilight. In a field beyond the garden men with easy grace were tossing wheat on their peeled pitchforks. The rhythmic, timeless occupation, the setting sun, the church bells tolling vespers on the still, cooling air made an idyllic scene.

The next day we reached Madrid at about half-past eight in the evening and after a good many wrong turnings finally arrived at the Ritz. Before the war the Madrid Ritz was considered one of the best hotels in the world, and when we were there, although it had perhaps fallen somewhat from its former grandeur it was still much grander than its Barcelona namesake.

Ours were by no means the most expensive rooms, but we did have splendid baths, sumptuous marble affairs with mirrors, stall showers, and two spacious washbasins. Those we appreciated and spent many fruitful hours over them chatting and doing our laundry. Traveler's Tip No. 7: Take along a small, stiff nailbrush. They are invaluable for scrubbing shirt collars and cuffs. Using ours, we felt like the women we had seen washing clothes at the river's edge and we scrubbed with vigor and sang at our work. We had apparently arrived at a fiesta period and service was sketchy—nothing back under a week or ten days—but also one likes to effect economies when possible. Why else drip-drys?

In our travels we have found washing to be more satisfactory than dry-cleaning, and this was definitely the case in Spain. Norton sent out a couple of lightweight suits, and they came back pressed to a razor's edge but with the grime around the collars more deeply imbedded than before. Spaniards at that period were innocent of the uses of carbon tetrachloride. We complained of this to the ambassador, who, as I have said, was our old friend Stanton Griffis, but he said, "Listen, you were lucky Norton could even get into those suits. Usually they come back shrunk to fit midgets."

Our ambassadorial contacts had started as soon as we arrived. We hadn't been in the hotel ten minutes when the phone rang and a man's voice said, "Is this Mrs. Norton Brown?" I said it was and he said, "One moment please, His Excellency the American Ambassador would like to speak to you." It had a rather grand ring and my snobbism was all aglow until the homey touch deflated it. "O.K., Stan," I heard the man yell, "I've got her, take the phone in the hall," and a familiar voice came on: "Hi, Queen, how are you and the boss?"

We chatted a while and it developed that His Excellency was full of beans, having just returned from the first baseball game ever played in Spain, an event he had initiated by bringing in some American Army players from Germany. "I'll be over in about an hour," he said. "We'll dine in the garden there at the Ritz." I have always warmed to ambassadors, theirs seems to me a glamorous life, but my admiration for them stems basically from the days when they were in far countries for long periods of time, cut off from their governments and obliged to rely on their own wisdom, knowledge and experience, when they had, in a word, to ambass. Nowadays they pick up the phone and the State Department for better or worse tells them what to do. It's not the same.

Our particular ambassador arrived shortly after our conversation, bringing with him the Angier Biddle Dukes. Mr. Duke was his assistant and right-hand man, and, Stanton being unmarried, Margaret Duke acted as embassy hostess. The Ritz garden is pleasant; we had an excellent dinner and chattered like monkeys, catching up on old times and asking questions about Spain. Our host felt that, although the Spaniards had lost their first *beisbol* game, as was only natural, the sport would do a great deal to build international sympathy and understanding. I said that I hoped so too, although the Japanese had always been great ones for the game and you could hardly call Pearl Harbor a sympathetic gesture. There was a slight chill in the garden, and my dear husband gave me that look best interpreted as "You and your big mouth."

The next morning we went across the street to the treasure house where all right-thinking travelers spend their time when in Madrid and where indeed one could profitably spend most of the mornings of one's life, the Prado.

Since my passions include Velázquez, El Greco, and Goya, not to mention Brueghel and Murillo, I hit the jackpot. Many of Velázquez's great canvases of the Spanish royal family hang there. Over and over again they confront the visitor, the long pale faces, the pale prominent eyes, the pendulous lower lip of Spanish rulers. There too hangs the renowned *Children of the Spanish Court*, also called *Maids of Honor* painted in the artist's studio. It is placed by itself in a small black-velvet-draped room, and a mirror angled in the corner reflects the canvas, giving it an extraordinary three-dimensional quality. There is something touching about the frail children in their magnificent architectural clothes.

In other galleries El Greco's flame-shaped ascetics soar and glow in their reds and golds, blues and grays and livid greens punctuated by the masterly use of white.

There is Goya, massive in his output and variety. The sketches, the war pictures, including the brutal butchery, *The Execution*, almost unbearable in its horror and tension, the dreadful and poignant *Madhouse*, and that soft lady the Duchess of Alba with and without her clothes.

Goya, El Greco, Velázquez we were prepared for; we knew they were there. The enchanting flower pictures by Brueghel came as a surprise. One views them without reservation; they create pure delight.

Apparently in art, especially that depicting the human figure, the quality of the painting and the composition counts for everything, and the expressions on the people's faces aren't supposed to matter; but they matter to me. Many's the masterpiece I wouldn't take as a gift because I don't care for the looks of the people. That which is admirable and that which is livable-with can be very different.

Today's visitor to the Prado will find many changes since we were there. Fifteen new rooms have been opened since 1956 and the old wooden flooring has been replaced with black marble. It's murder on the feet, but its great virtue, besides eye appeal, is that it is fireproof.

It does seem to me that there is one commodity museums might supply, an obvious convenience I have yet to find, and that is small, lightweight wheel chairs. If we could propel ourselves around without fatigue how immeasurably it would add to our delight in the masterpieces.

On our own visit to the Prado, when our feet got tired and our spines gave out, we went to call upon a gentleman who was eagerly cultivated by American tourists, Señor Luis Bolín, *director general de turismo*. Spain being a dictatorship, the bureau is part of the government, but Señor Bolín himself was a charming man speaking Oxford English and seemingly dedicated to making life pleasant for travelers. He invited us to go with him that night to a party that was being given by the mayor of Madrid to the Diplomatic Corps. Our acceptance plunged us into a project always referred to afterward as The Quest.

While still in New York we had inquired of our chum the ambassador, who, we felt, should know, whether Norton would need a dinner jacket in Spain. Since we were traveling by plane it made a difference. "Not at all," His Excellency assured us airily, "it's summertime, life is very informal." Informal, my foot. Until the Diplomatic Corps leaves the city, Madrid dresses to the teeth. Discreet inquiries revealed that such would be the case at the mayor's party. It was to be late, around midnight, and held in the Retiro, a large and lovely park.

I was not too badly off. A woman can usually manage a cocktail dress elaborate enough to serve for evening in a pinch. The doc had daytime lightweight suitings that obviously would not do. Our plight was acute, for I was longing to go to the party. The obvious solution immediately presented itself. Go out and buy dinner clothes. The doctor balked slightly at the expense, remembering the distinguished set of threads hanging in the closet in New York, but New York was a long way from Madrid. However, as we set out for the shop to which we had been directed, he cheered up. "It's probably just as well," he said. "I need some lightweight evening things and I'll be able to wear them in England when we stop off there on our way home."

It was then we discovered that the ways of haberdashers are not universal. Spain has excellent tailors; her ready-to-wear is nil. The shop owner to whom we explained our dilemma was courtesy incarnate, more than willing to make a suit and quickly, but not so quickly as tonight. He would happily direct us to another shop, although dubious that we would fare any better there. That was an interesting thing about the Spaniards. If they did not stock the merchandise you were seeking or if you were not pleased with what they had, they not only pointed out the competition, they left their own shops and accompanied you down the street lest you get lost on your way there. How rarely does Macy's escort one into Gimbel's.

We too were dubious of doing any better and must have looked dejected, for suddenly the man brightened. "What you will do," he said, "is to rent a dinner jacket. I have a friend, a theatrical costumer. I'll call him up." He did, and after specific directions we were on our way.

"It's an excellent idea," I told Norton, who seemed, I thought, a scrap lacking in enthusiasm over this brilliant solution to our problem.

"It's probably just like Moss Bros. in London, where peers of the realm go to rent cutaways and top hats for Ascot."

Peter, who was stage-struck, was enchanted. "Oh boy," he said, "a theatrical costumer's. Maybe we'll see some actors."

"The reason I do not spark more," said the master, "is because I am quite large. Even in Abercrombie & Fitch at home I sometimes have difficulty finding my size. So far I have not seen any very big Spaniards."

With Pete's and my urging him not to be defeatist we eventually arrived at the address, a little shop in a tiny winding street in the old part of the city. Inside it was dark, but through the gloom we could distinguish what appeared to be rows of suits hanging up. We tried to explain our need, or rather to explain who we were, as the tailor-friend had already described our plight over the phone, but all the proprietor would do was shake his head and mutter in a distracted fashion, "La luz, la luz." By this time we knew that luz meant "light," and it was obvious that there wasn't any. We didn't mind, we said, could we just look at dinner jackets? We could bring them to the door and look at them in the daylight. Again the man shook his head and volunteered the information that the luz would be fixed later, or maybe mañana. Mañana, we said firmly, wouldn't do. It was esta noche or never.

Groaning and muttering, he finally fetched a candle and disappeared up into a loft where, like an uncertain firefly, he flickered about among his ghostly inventory. He emerged triumphant, however. He had not only a dinner jacket but what appeared to be a large and brand-new one. We took it out into the street. The doctor stripped off his coat, handed it to Pete, and slipped into the other one. It might have come from Saville Row. By this time, having spotted us as foreigners when we arrived, a little crowd had gathered and was watching with interest. "Turn around," I said to Norton. "Let me see how it is across the shoulders." It is an audience that puts a performer on his mettle, and the doctor was no exception. He pirouetted to the right, he pirouetted to the left. He gave a little tug to the sleeves, and he fastened the middle button. He all but cut a buck and wing. The crowd broke into applause. He bowed. Taking the trousers on faith, saying that we would return with them mañana, we departed, the suit in a brown paper parcel.

Later that evening, at eight-thirty, the swank hour, we went to the embassy, or rather to the residence, for cocktails. A couple of Velázquezes hung on the wall, and there was a pretty garden. Mrs. Mc-Mahon, the wife of the senator from Connecticut, was there; and Ad-

miral Sherman. He was pleasant and interesting, and it was a shock
to read of his sudden death a few days later.

We stayed on at the cocktail party till it was time to rush back to
the hotel for dinner around ten. We then changed our clothes, the doctor impeccable in his rented finery, and were ready when Señor Bolín
came to pick us up at eleven to go to the mayor's party.

It was a garden party *cum* concert. The Retiro was discreetly
lighted and thronged with members of the Diplomatic Corps and such
society as had not already left town for the summer. The entertainers
were three singers and the chamber-music orchestra of Madrid, who
performed against a shallow shell hung with tapestries and bright with
roses and laurel.

I have never been able to feel that a grand piano was native heath
for a Spanish shawl and deplored the period when such was the fashion in interior decoration, but, put to more logical use, draping the
shoulders of pretty women for example, the shawl undoubtedly has
meaning. If there are two talents Spanish women have besides clicking
castanets and stamping the hell out of the floor when dancing, they
are shawl-wearing and fan-snapping. They move with grace and their
carriage is magnificent. The most elegant woman in the park wore a
black shawl closely embroidered in a white Chinese Chippendale design—birds, bridges, and pagodas. Watching her and others open and
close their fans, I was consumed with envy. A twist of the wrist and
they open with a little rushing sound, a snap and they are closed. Although God alone knows why any fans were in use that night. Sheer
habit, I expect. I thought it glacial. Madrid is at an altitude of two
thousand feet and even in July it can be cold. While I shivered, teeth
chattering in lightweight, easily packable chiffon, the doctor sat un-
feelingly in his rented suit as comfortable in the cold park as he would
have been in a steam-heated apartment.

Two or three women we saw I thought very beautiful, and I said
as much the next day to an American who had lived for some time in
Madrid but who took a dim view of Spanish femininity. "If you saw
a beautiful woman," he said morosely, "it must have been the wife of
the Brazilian Ambassador and she's a Dane." We did not know it then
but eight years later we were to meet Mme. De Mello in Djakarta and
become friendly with her.

Supper was served after the concert, and sitting with us was the late
Lucrecia Andujar, whom Señor Bolín had also invited. Her name, I
thought, sounded as Spanish as castanets, and indeed her father was

a Spaniard, but her mother was American and she was an American career girl working for *House and Garden.*

She was in Spain on a job, traveling around the country visiting ceramic and pottery and furniture factories, talking to rug weavers and meeting with manufacturers in an effort to get them to channel Spanish production into an output compatible with the American market and American taste. The Spanish workmanship was excellent, but their designs were pretty much where they had been before the war. Bullfighters, Don Quixote, and mantilla motifs were still going strong.

In the course of the evening Norton and I tried putting in our two cents' worth, along with those who had run that course before, in an effort to persuade the Spaniards to send a collection from the Prado on loan exhibition to the United States. We asked Señor Bolín if such a princely gesture of international good will would not be possible. "It would not," he said dryly and we felt that we had quickly reached the end of *that* road. Yet I could not retire without one last forlorn shot. "It seems a pity," I said, "when one thinks of the thousands and thousands of people who would derive enormous pleasure and education from seeing them."

"Let them come to the Prado to see them," said the señor.

"But they can't. They can't possibly afford it."

He shrugged. "Too bad."

He went on to speak at some length of the preservative qualities of the air of Madrid, and although I doubt that canvases would disintegrate if held at sea level for a few months—those in the Louvre, the Metropolitan, and the National Gallery do not seem to—moving those of the Prado would indisputably involve risk, and should anything happen to them all the insurance in the world would avail nothing. Still, such a loan is a pleasant dream and not pure fantasy, either, since the Prado collection *was* exhibited in Geneva in the autumn of 1939 just before the outbreak of the war. The Spaniards must think more highly of mountain air than of sea breezes for their treasures.

The next day we drove about thirty miles from Madrid to visit a work of Spanish art there can never be any question of moving: the Escorial. This monastery-palace-burial vault, a strange excrescence from the brain of the fanatical Philip II was begun in 1563 and was about twenty years in the building. It rises from the plain at the foot of a mountain, a mecca for visitors interested in history and not averse to the macabre. Beside the pictures, many of which are beautiful, there are three points of interest. One is the pantheon, or underground vault, where all the kings of Spain except two lie buried. The marble sarcophagi are all alike and are placed on marble shelves around the walls. A long corridor leads to the tombs of the princes and other members of the royal family. The natural son of Charles V, and half brother of Philip II, Don John, who won the Battle of Lepanto against the Turks, is also there. He is the one starred in Chesterton's ringing ballad; And Don John of Austria is going to the war.

The next apartment one visits is, if anything, less cheerful than the tomb. It was the private suite of Philip II, and it must be said that the monarch did not have the homey touch. No ruffled chintz at the window, no bright pots of geraniums. Philip, we know, suffered from gout; he must also have had a troublesome liver and dyspepsia. He sat walled up in a cell in the center of his vast empire, poring over papers and reports, no detail of administration too trivial for his attention while the land groaned in poverty and famine.

His narrow bed may still be seen. He would lie on it, gazing down through a window cut in the wall, watching Mass being said before the great altar in the palace chapel. The stone apartment has no fireplace, so that in winter it must have been bitterly cold, but possibly Philip was warmed by the smoke from burning books and burning flesh, for he was a holy man determined that his subjects should be brought to God, and if their approach to Him was more hellish than divine, they had the consolation of knowing that their king was sore burdened by their transgressions. His hard, straight chair still stands before his writing table, and one may also see the one in which he used to travel. We drove out from Madrid in about forty-five minutes. It took Philip seven days. He could have done it faster had he gone by coach or horseback, but gout made jouncing over the roads so painful he was borne the entire journey in a chair carried by two men.

Fortunately, as a change from such austerity and flagellation, there is also in the Escorial a suite of rooms deliciously bright and gay. They are hung with tapestries by Goya, scenes of picnicking, fishing, brawling before the village inn, a whole company of rowdy, happy humans done in warm and glowing colors. There is still some furniture about, straw matting covers the stone floors, and on the day we were there the sun was streaming in the windows. You wanted to laugh for sheer joy. Thank heaven Philip's descendants broke from the gloom and murk.

Yet despite the sunshine, the clicking of castanets, and the swirling skirts of dancers so much in evidence on travel posters, Spain is an austere land. One may have a "marvelous time" in France or Italy or Austria; one does not have the same kind of "marvelous time" in Spain. An interesting or fascinating time, yes, but trivia are no part of the land. There is something harsh and strong about it, stemming, I think, from aridity, poverty, and pride and possibly too from its ancient Moorish origins.

Both our time in Spain and the amount of territory we covered were limited, but Norton joins me in feeling that although the motoring was worth while and we are glad we went by car when we did, it is the cities that are the jewels of the country. Transport yourself quickly and spend time in the cities.

Spend time certainly in Toledo, one of the treasures of the land. About fifty miles from Madrid, it is a perpendicular silhouette built on rocks and almost entirely surrounded by the Tagus River. Because of its proximity to the capital many tourists do as we did; make it a day or several days excursion returning to their Madrid hotel at night.

We visited the Alcázar and I can still feel the intense heat as we crossed the partially ruined courtyard. Norton and I were at least dressed for it, but Peter poor child, for some abstruse reason of his own, chose to wear long hot trousers. I assured him that for a boy of his age in this place linen shorts would be quite correct but he remained immovable, proud and bakingly hot.

Speaking of the heat and sight-seeing this is perhaps as good a place as any to mention another vital tip. We will make it Traveler's Tip No. 8: *Wear comfortable shoes.* In theory everyone knows this is the thing to do, but we get seduced by the idea of chic or we refuse to believe that our feet can swell *that* much in hot weather. They can. We all have shoes in which we have confidence, but I have found over the years and in assorted countries around the world that for sheer comfort and dependability nothing matches the sneaker of my girlhood gym classes. Elegant you may not look, but comfortable you are. For traipsing through museums, scaling mountains, treading a promenade deck, or clambering up the Acropolis—sneakers! Also for walking around the Alcázar.

The Alcázar fortress—actually it was a military college—was besieged for two months during the Spanish Civil War in 1936, and it is one of the world's few contemporary ruins, ruins usually dating anywhere from Stonehenge to the eighteenth century.

The guide who took us around was one of the twenty-five hundred people who had been immured there during the siege.

They had only horse meat to eat and such flour as they could grind from the wheat they gathered in the surrounding fields when it grew dark. A rickety old motorcycle that somebody had to volunteer to ride out of the fort every night was their only means of transportation. They still have on view rolls made from that flour. They are now as hard and black as stone. Water was stringently rationed, they had no anaesthesia, and two children were born during the siege. When we were in Spain, they were both alive and well and wards of the state.

Probably the most memorable spot in the Alcázar is the room where the famous telephone conversation took place between the rebel Colonel Moscardo, the Franco man commanding the fortress, and the commander of the besieging guerrilla force of Loyalists, the Milicianos, who held Moscardo's son prisoner. The telephone is still there, and hanging on the wall is a transcription of what they said. The Loyalist commander said to Moscardo:

"It is your fault there is so much suffering and bloodshed. If you surrender the Alcázar it can be stopped. I'll give you ten minutes to make up your mind. We have your son here as hostage. Maybe you don't believe me. I'll let you speak to him."

"I believe you," the colonel said, and then the boy came to the phone. "How are you, Son?" he asked.

"I'm all right, Father."

"What's up?"

"Nothing. They say they'll shoot me if you don't surrender the Alcázar."

"Then commend your soul to God and prepare to die like a patriot."

"I love you very much, Father."

"I love you, Son."

The besieging commander came back on the phone and Colonel Moscardo said, "I don't need the ten minutes. The Alcázar will never surrender." Then he heard a shot. They had killed his son.

Although the truth was tragic enough, this particular tale of obstinacy and heroism is not accurate. The boy was not killed at that time and the father did not hear the shot. He was killed about a month later and for other reasons, but the story has helped to build the Alcázar legend and is, in essence, typical of war's horror.

One of the happy things to see in Toledo is the cathedral. It was begun in the thirteenth century and has a magnificent rose window dating from 1418. Architecturally the church is rich and luminous with superb iron and bronze grille work. It also possesses one of the most beguiling religious statues I have ever seen. Virgins usually looked pained, impassive, or matronly, and uprolled poached-egg eyes are considered pious, but this one is young and slim, with a darling little face and a sweet, secret merry grin. As she holds her Baby, whose hand reaches out to touch her chin, she is obviously bursting with pride. It's as though she were saying, "Whee! Look what I did!"

Another fascinating spot to visit in Toledo is the house of El Greco. The museum connected with it contains a fine collection of his later works and it is intimate and revealing: rather small, with a cozy fireplace for cooking. The kitchen must have been the heart of the house, and El Greco, genius and all, was quite possibly henpecked, a speculation founded on the information that not only his wife but his sisters and his mother also lived with him.

In one room stands an easel with an unframed painting propped against it. Any moment you feel that he may come and go to work. His bed is still there—he couldn't have been a very tall man; even living in Spain he probably didn't know the value of vitamins to be found in orange juice—and beside the bed is a washstand with a silver pitcher and basin. They are small, and getting the paint off his hands must have been quite a chore.

We returned to Madrid in the evening and were struck again by the primitive way of life of many of the people. Even two or three miles from the capital women draw water from the pump in the village square, for there are no running water and sewage disposal as we know them. In sharp contrast to such simplicity, however, is the pomp of officialdom.

The next morning I was waiting outside the hotel—Norton and Peter had gone back upstairs to fetch another camera—when suddenly I heard a clatter of hoofs. I looked around and there, galloping up to the door, came a troop of Saracen horsemen. They had dark Moorish faces, blue and white cloaks streamed behind them, their heads were wrapped in white turbans with silver points in the center, and they carried lances from which fluttered small pennants. They reined in their horses, which rose on their hind legs pawing the air, and pulling up smartly behind them came a magnificent coach, plumes swaying and dancing on the four corners. It was drawn by four horses and carried four men, two forward and two aft. The men leaped down, opened the door, and out stepped a slight figure in a tightly fitting, long black coat with a red fez on his head; the Egyptian minister come to present his credentials. He was followed by four or five high-ranking Spanish

Army officers very impressive in black court uniforms, their chests ablaze with golden oak leaves, rows of medals and braid, and red ribbons draped diagonally across them.

The few other simple American tourists who were standing gaping beside me were also goggle-eyed, and we bobbed curtsies and twisted the corner of our aprons as the quality passed. For one moment I thought we were going to see Franco, but we hadn't quite reached that altitude.

I spoke to the doorman of the Ritz, an imposing elder fluent in French, English, Spanish, and doubtless Swahili. "It's very impressive, isn't it?" I said as the horseman and the coach vanished around the curve of the road. He yawned. "They'll be back in half an hour with the Uruguayan minister. This keeps up all the time." And indeed it is just the Spanish way with diplomats, colorful but to them banal. Stanton Griffis proudly showed us a photograph of his own arrival equipped with credentials. He was in top hat, white tie, and tails in broad daylight and had been snapped stepping from the royal coach, Saracens in attendance, but it was the same vehicle and the same entourage that transported less glittering emissaries.

The grandeur ended soon, however. One afternoon we came back to the Ritz to find enormous moving vans at the door. That morning the Diplomatic Corps had left the city for the summer holiday. Only the personnel of the Chinese Embassy were sitting forlornly in the lobby waiting to depart. We studied them with interest, having missed out on a party that had a deliciously complex European flavor and that Stanton had asked us to accompany him to. The Chinese Ambassador to Italy, passing through Spain, was entertaining in Madrid. Later that same evening there was to be another party, for Admiral Sherman. I was eager to go, being one who enjoys high life in isolated patches, but alas, that was the night we were stricken. In nearly every trip I have ever taken there comes the moment of prostration when the food, the water, the olive oil, the green tea . . . something smites me down. The attack is usually brief, thank God, but completely annihilating while it lasts. Poor Norton experienced the same upheaval. We lay on our beds, pale and water-weak, while diplomatic festivities surged around us. We were doubly sad as it was the last gala of the season, and that was why the vans were at the door. When the embassies close, the Ritz quite literally rolls up the red carpet, and it was being carted away.

We ourselves were rolling south to Granada. The road runs through the heart of the country, and the distance is about two hundred fifty

miles. Some of the views were breathtaking, for the color of the land
is extraordinary. Against a sky pale blue and gray or brilliant blue,
heaped with tumbled clouds, tower brown and purple mountains, with
patches of raw earth red as Georgia and patterned with glistening green
groves, silver olives, and ocher-colored wheat.

In the valleys and along the roads in most of the villages we passed
the doors stood open, and as we drove slowly by, trying to do it tactfully, we would peer inside. To be tactful and snooping at the same
time is not easy, but all my life I have been curious and interested in
how other people live.

The Spanish households seemed humble; usually one room, with
possibly a bedroom off, the floor of earth, and the door opening directly onto the earthen sidewalk, which the women were constantly
sprinkling and sweeping. They are so clean in Spain they sweep the
ground itself. In the shadowy interior we perceived a table, a few
straight chairs, unexpectedly an occasional rocker; no couches, no
quaintsy cobblers' benches metamorphosed into coffee tables, no standing lamps, but always, inevitably, a sewing machine. The ready-to-wear
industry has penetrated to the rural areas even less than to the cities.
Spanish women sew their own.

The humblest house usually has a little courtyard or patio where
most of the family life is passed, but the women also sit out in front
of their houses a good deal, always with their backs to the road. I would
be curious to see the passers-by, but they apparently have inner resources, or they make lace. The pins and bobbins are attached to a sort
of small bolster, one end propped against the wall of the house, the
other resting on their knees.

We neared Granada at the end of the day and we were hot, dusty,
and weary. "The wine of the country is all very well," I said, "but oh
boy, what wouldn't I give for a bone-dry, ice-cold martini." The doctor
gave a brittle, bitter laugh. "We're in Spain, dear, remember? And
from here we go to England. You'll have to dream for another month."

"You should try Zimba Cola," said Peter. "I keep telling you it's
delicious." This eerie brew he had unearthed on his own. His doctor
father had at first watched him down it with misgivings, but as he
didn't stumble, break out in spots, or have any trouble with his
eyesight, he reconciled himself to the lad's lack of palate, and indeed
he was the only one of our trio who did not at one time or another
succumb to what was euphemistically known as Gippy Tummy.

It was dark when we reached Granada, and we asked a white-coated, white-helmeted policeman to direct us to the Parador San Francisco. From the waving of his arms and the fountain of information that gushed forth we gathered it was a far piece and complicated to boot. We were looking at each other in despair, when up from nowhere popped an urchin who spoke very good French and who offered to go along with us to show us the way. We were to thank God for this helpful moppet, as otherwise we would still be wandering the Sierra Nevada. We made our way up steep hills and along winding, heavily wooded roads, one of the few woodlands we saw in the part of Spain we traversed, and came at last to the *parador* in the gardens of the Alhambra.

The original building, the inn, that is to say, was very old and was destroyed by fire and rebuilt as a monastery in the seventeenth century. The natives refer to it rather slightingly—modern stuff. The front garden is filled with pink oleanders, and over the old walls grow thick vines starred with small pale blue flowers. The patio is engaging, with flower beds edged by low hedges and set with shrubs and great earthen jars of blossoms and overlooked by an upper gallery onto which the bedrooms open.

We were shown to our rooms, which had a monastic simplicity but which were as usual spotlessly clean and quite comfortable. We washed and went downstairs to dine, me still muttering and mumbling about the glories, the beneficence, of the martini. A broad terrace opens off the dining room, with tables set under the orange and lemon, fig and pomegranate trees. The terrace and walks are paved with swirling and geometric designs of pebbles and cobblestones, and below the terrace the ground drops away to a wooded ravine. To our left the town lay at the foot of another slope, the Albaicín, pitted with gypsy caves and scattered with houses and their small gardens, called *carmenes*. Carmen is a name but it also means a pleasure garden. At night in Granada under the stars the air is so clear you can hear voices from the town, the distant barking of a dog, and an occasional shower of guitar music. It is a romantic spot, next to Venice one of the romantic cities of the world, and the romance was to be intensified.

When she saw approaching her three people who were obviously Americans, the waitress had hurried away unbidden, returning shortly with a small bucket of ice, which, smilingly, she set upon the table. Also on the table by way of apéritif was a bottle of manzanilla, an extremely dry, pale sherry. The doctor tasted it. In his youth he studied chemistry and knows how solutions react upon each other. He delicately licked his chops, and a speculative look came into his eye. "What's that word again? The Spanish for gin?"

"*Ginebra*," I said.

"Tell her to bring us some. After all, gin's gin even in Spain. I may be on the verge of a great discovery."

"*Ginebra, por favor*," I said to the waitress. She brought a bottle and after a bit of pantomime and a minor struggle a glass pitcher. The doctor put in quantities of ice and poured a great generous dollop of gin. He made a sleight-of-hand pass with the manzanilla. He stirred. "Give me your glass," he said. I passed it over. He served me generously, and then himself. Breathlessly we raised our glasses, touched them together, and sipped. The greatest martini ever made by man! Husbands can be really darling. We gave some to Peter, for, young as he was, we felt he should share the Experience. He took a swallow, made a face, looked at us pityingly, and turned to the waitress. "*Zimba Cola, por favor*." But that was youth. We christened the martini Parador, and it was so fine that even after we got home for quite a time we made them with manzanilla from preference. We have since slipped back into the old Vermouthian ways, but the Parador, coming as it did at the low moment of a long hot day, was one of life's unforgettable blessings.

That night, exhausted by our motoring, we went to bed early to be ready for the next day's sight-seeing. In the month of July, Granada is cool in the evenings, but with early dawn the heat envelopes you. It is a physical sensation almost as if a blanket were being drawn about you. If you go in the summer, as we did, be warned and dress accordingly.

Our first goal was the Alhambra and the Generalife, the gardens that surround it, and of which the Parador San Francisco and its grounds form a part. We engaged a guide, a splendid fellow named Nicolás, with dark hair and long curly teeth. Good dentistry in childhood could have corrected them, but good dentistry was not available. He had them, poor chap, and so, perforce, did we, even finding a certain fascination in their wild and wandering ways. He spoke excellent English, and we learned in the course of our relationship that as a boy he had spent some years in school in England. For fifty pesetas—one dollar—he agreed to spend the day with us.

Nicolás was a fine guide in that he was knowledgeable and could answer our questions, but he also knew when to shut up, a rare talent. The Alhambra is so beautiful it is better to look and absorb in silence.

The exterior, the square towers topped with pinky gray tiles, and the connecting walls seem European. It is not until one gets inside that one is spellbound by the filigree work so typical of Arab architecture. The word Alhambra means "the Red [house]," but it is not red; it is tawny and amber and gold. The texture, because of the intricacy and delicacy of the carving, is like starched lace. The slender columns and airy domes carved like honeycombs give it an air of fragility, but it was begun in the thirteenth century, work on it continued for nearly four hundred years, and it stands today an enduring monument to the Moorish architects and Christian slaves who were its builders and sculptors. It was the palace of the sultans until they were driven out by Ferdinand and Isabella in 1492, which must have been quite a year for the royal pair, what with ousting Moors and financing Columbus. Ferdinand and Isabella were originally buried in the small chapel of the former monastery, now *parador*, but were subsequently removed to the cathedral down in the town of Granada. Their tomb is topped by two marble statues of them lying prone, their heads resting through eternity on marble pillows. That of Isabella is more deeply indented because, said Nicolás, she had more brains than Ferdinand. Also in the cathedral are canvases by Memling and Botticelli.

The Moors loved their palace passionately, and the mother of the defeated sultan is supposed to have said to her son, as he turned to bid a last farewell to the lovely structure, "You love it enough to cry like a woman but not enough to defend it like a man." Probably it was his mother-in-law who said it. That, by the way, is an aspect of harem life we hear little of. What about those rafts of mothers-in-law? Sultans must have been foolhardy as well as virile.

The delicious attribute of Granada, the one the Moors would have found irresistible, coming as they did from a parched arid land, is the water. Water flows from the Sierra Nevada, and the gardens spring green and fertile because of the liquid wealth. Everywhere, in the small patios, along the terraces are leaping fountains, dimpled pools. A stone staircase in the garden has narrow troughs running the length of the balustrade on either side, and down them slip ribbons of water. They have flowed for eight hundred years and it is delightful to trail your fingers in the shadowy, dappled stream as you go down the steps. The grounds, punctuated by cypress, abloom with orange trees, oleanders, and roses that fill the air with sweetness are a kaleidoscope of brilliant splashing sunlight and deep green shade. Unexpectedly one comes upon an enormous redwood, one of our own sequoias sent to Spain from

California more than a century ago. There is a small cascade in a grotto, and everywhere fountains and jets of water.

Within the building, in the Hall of the Ambassadors, is an oblong pool with narrow open gutters to channel the overflow. We were told that once in a flare-up of ancient days the gutters ran with blood. One of the most famous courtyards and one that curiously recalls the Victorian era, not because of its architecture but because it was so lauded and so popular in that period, is the Court of the Lions. It is circled by a cloister, the arches supported by alternating single and double columns. We glimpsed it first through a perspective of slender columns glowing golden in the sunlight. A circle of chunky, sturdy lions, maneless—they must be lionesses—supports a Byzantine fountain. From their mouths flow streams of water. When we were there the streams were only trickles, because, as Nicolás explained to us, the pipes were being repaired. We accepted this as fact, which indeed it was, and contentedly imagined beasts gushing instead of dripping. Not so a group of French tourists who straggled at our heels. "*Ah, ça alors, c'est du beau! Ça, pour eux ce sont les Grandes Eaux de Versailles, sans doute!*" And they roared with laughter. So all right! They were not the great fountains of Versailles, they were not supposed to be.

Tourists of France, despite the culture of the home land, can be just as obnoxious as any others.

More than once Peter and Norton and I felt deeply sympathetic when a waiter or waitress who, after all had not cooked the meal, was treated to the raised eyebrow, the curled lip, and a supercilious, "You see, *we* are French," implying that that was the be-all and end-all of civilization and how they happened to find themselves among these barbarians, the Spanish, they couldn't imagine. We could, though. The exchange was greatly in their favor. The Spanish Tourist Bureau was realistic and quite funny about them. All tourist money is welcome, but it is not the spendthrift ways of the citizens of Gaul that are going to enrich the Iberian Peninsula. More than once we saw a peseta, two cents, left as a tip. With prices the way they are in Spain it represents more than it would to us, but it still cannot be called largesse.

Another spot not to be missed in Granada is the sacristy of the Cartuja, the Carthusian monastery. It is a famous example of churrigueresque decoration, which means something infinitely elaborate as though squeezed from a tube; the absolute apex of the pastry chef's art. The sacristy is rich and fancy and gay, with tall slim panels of brilliant blue marble rising to the high vaulted roof and great columns

of twisted ice-cream plaster. The walls and doors are inlayed with silver, tortoise shell, and ivory. It is delicious, and, compared to it, the space and emptiness of modern décor seem singularly uneventful.

Granada boasts another claim to fame, too, as the home of the late great modern composer Manuel de Falla.

In sharp contrast to the richness and rococo elegance of the Cartuja are the gypsy caves of Albaicín. After our day of sight-seeing we asked Nicolás if he could come back after dinner and take us to see them. He agreed to do so, and Norton then offered him more money. This gave rise to quite a little contretemps. "You have already paid me," he said. "Yes," Norton said, "but that was for the day. We are now asking you to work longer. It is only fair you should have more money." "But the price was agreed upon," said Nicolás. "Our arrangement was made." "Quite," said the doctor, "but as I say . . ." It took real finagling and diplomacy on our part to get him to accept a raise. And I think this was done, not out of coyness or playing hard to get, but simply because an agreement was an agreement and the fact that the one rendering the service would profit by a revision was not the point.

The whole concept of tipping in Spain was interesting. Sometimes when we offered a few pesetas, no bones were made about accepting them, although always Spaniards were most polite in their thanks, but on more than one occasion there was a literal tussle before a bellboy or waitress would take a tip. And it was not because they were sumptuously paid. We were told that a top-flight cook might make around thirty or thirty-five dollars a month. When we gulped, our Spanish informant remarked, "But you must remember they are housed and fed." We thought of our treasures at home, rare as hen's teeth, who are housed, fed, clothed, and paid besides a monarch's ransom by employers who themselves slave like mad in order to support the Help.

I suppose eventually there will be a radical change in Spanish standards, some of it long overdue, but at present even with a small dollar income Americans can live in Spain not only in comfort but in luxury.

For the great majority of Spanish people, however, life is not luxurious. Nicolás and his wife ran a pension, she made lace, and he worked as a guide and radio repairman, anything he could get in order to eke out a livelihood, and certainly the gypsy caves dug deep in the mountains are not luxurious.

Hundreds of families live in them, yet even the caves are clean with black and white tiled floors and whitewashed walls. The walls are covered with copper pots and pans and ash trays the gypsies make, and family photographs and crudely colored holy pictures crowd the shelves. Each cave is electrified with a naked light bulb in the ceiling, and a curtained doorway conceals a deeper recess, the bedroom.

Truth to tell, and Nicolás had warned us, the gypsies' singing and dancing are primarily a stunt put on for tourists and not very good. The real artists among them have left long ago to seek fame and fortune in the capitals of Europe or in Hollywood. But the atmosphere is picturesque. You buy a bottle of manzanilla, which is drunk by the girls, and bring out cigarettes, which they whip from your fingers with alacrity and skill. The women, according to our standards, are mostly too fat. They are not conventionally pretty, but their faces have character; they are not the bland rice puddings of so much of America's dancing youth, and their dresses are gay, dotted and flowered, and flounced. They dance, their heels clicking on the tiles, the castanets chattering in their agile fingers, and the men seated on straight chairs behind them play the guitars. The singing we thought better than the dancing, for we are always moved by the harsh wild minor melodies of the flamenco songs.

Peter watched critically the whirling skirts, the flowers in the hair, the hands beating out the rhythm for the dancers. He looked like Sol Hurok on a talent hunt.

The stimulus, the romance, the beauty of Granada were too good to last. In any trip there is usually a low point. It may range from a day to a week or two, depending on season, place, and time involved; one rarely avoids an interlude when the whole premise of travel seems unsound. Our nadir was struck in our first twenty-four hours out of Granada. To begin with, the thermometer must easily have registered one hundred. True, it was a dry heat, but there was no shelter or surcease from the blazing sun. Also we were traveling a route that could be called a road only in the loosest sense of the word. A winding, mountainous dirt track traversing the most arid part of Spain. The very scenery had deserted us. Before we had seen mountains purple and tawny, their flanks checkered with wheat fields and olive groves, heights where the smallest pocket of fertility sprouted a vineyard. Now there was nothing but dreary, dun-colored monotony. The wide, eventful skies, with their high-piled clouds, were blanched of color and fanciful formation, and only the heat hammered down upon us.

We stopped for gas at a place called Baza. Any enemy you would like to consign to the nether end of hell . . . Baza. We had to sit in the baking car for some little time, waiting for the attendant, and a crowd of curious children and townspeople gathered around, staring at us. I suppose we did look like specimens from another planet—we were certainly unprepossessing, sweaty and rumpled, bored and cranky. Pete's Zimba Cola had given out, our bottle of water was uncomfortably hot to the touch, and the cool, fragrant terrace of the *parador* and the magical martini were far away. As the afternoon wore on, it became obvious that it would be well after dark before we reached our destination, the Parador Ifach.

At Murcia prudence dictated that we had better telephone to say we were on our way and please hold our reservations. In Murcia, too, although a much more sophisticated center than Baza, we drew our usual group of curious onlookers. Our viewers were invariably kind, however, offering in Spanish, sometimes in French, occasionally in English, to help us in any way they could. This time it was a French-speaking citizen who led us to the telephone building and helped us put in a call to the Ifach.

We concluded that outside of Zaragoza telephoning was not a familiar occupation with the Spanish. You do not just drop in your pesetas and let it go at that. You do not reverse charges. You have a long talk with an operator who sits behind a desk and whose attitude from the outset is that your delusion that you will get a number is purest moonshine. The operator is no fool. We waited well over an hour for a connection. We sat on a bench with other dreamers who would converse with distant parts, and, watching the women, I too drew from my handbag one of the fans purchased in Granada and tried to imitate the dexterous manner in which they snapped them open and shut. I improved slightly but I never did acquire the native skill.

Once in touch with Ifach a meeting of minds was still not easy. Chances of accommodations were poor, but come anyway—Señor Bolín had spoken to them from Madrid on our behalf and something would doubtless be arranged, just what they couldn't say. Under the erroneous impression that we had only sixty kilometers to go, we pushed on. When Mark Twain wrote down the title *Innocents Abroad*, he obviously had the Browns in mind.

The Parador Ifach turned out to be like one of those mirages in the desert seen by hapless travelers who, seemingly within arm's reach of the blessed shade and water hole, behold them dissolve into the air. Just as we thought that surely the next turn would bring us to it, just as it seemed to be advancing almost to meet us, the vision faded, receded another fifty kilometers. We began to take heart when we at last reached the promontory, jutting far out to sea, on which the inn is situated. Turning off the main road was a definite gain; we were entering upon the final stage. I suppose one may say that when we die we are entering upon a final stage too—eternity. That was the Ifach road. To complicate matters further, the night was now pitch-black, and we were navigating a precipitous mountain trail—solid rock on one side, a sheer drop to the sea on the other. We were also desperately hungry, and it began to dawn on us that even in Spain there must be some limit to the dinner hour. If we could corral a loaf of bread and a bottle of wine and spirit them off to our room, always supposing we had one, we would be lucky.

Finally we spied lights ahead. We blinked our eyes, yet it must be so—all three of us saw them. Incredibly, we had reached our goal. We drove into the courtyard, and two little maids in black dresses and starched white aprons came to take our luggage. Women do a lot of that work in Spain. We went into the hotel and were crossing to the reception desk, when we stopped dead in our tracks. It was then ten minutes to midnight, and believe me when I tell you that in this country inn, this remote provincial seaside resort, the dining-room doors were just opening for dinner. For my money that's sophistication!

The meal was not superb, but it was food and reasonably hot. The doctor materialized his Parador, and our spirits rose with nourishment. We didn't achieve Zimba Cola, but Peter made do with cambric wine, half wine, half water. In Spain even the natives drink bottled water, which is probably why tap water remains so vile. Since it never occurs to anyone to use it as a beverage, they do nothing to improve it.

Dining, we looked around at our fellow boarders. We had at least achieved the tourist's dream and ultimate snobbism: there were no other Americans. We noted, however, that Spanish moppets are not unlike their American cousins. They may become accustomed to the tardy dining hours in maturity, but when they are small at midnight they are sleepy. Two or three heads were nodding and one lay on the table fast asleep.

After dinner we spoke to the manager. As often happens in Latin countries where females don't have all those votes and independence, the boss was a woman and formidably efficient. As we had been told over the phone, they were full up but, she had made an arrangement: she had placed a cot in our room for *el niño*. For one night this would be all right, no? Indeed yes, who could ask for anything more and could we please go to the room, we were exhausted. When we got there we discovered that the arrangement was a *partial* cot, it was in fact a mattress on the floor, but it made no difference. Pete was so tired, poor child, he could have slept on boards. He had barely lowered himself onto his pallet when he was dead to the world.

The doctor and I were weary too, but slumber was briefly delayed while he experimented with the faucets in our bathroom. The hot water didn't work at all. The cold water trickled from the tap a rich burnt sienna and it was salt. Since the Mediterranean was five yards from the front door they presumably thought they might as well take advantage of it, but brushing one's teeth was a weird sensation and the condition of the pipes awesome to contemplate.

We slept like the dead until dawn, but not only did the dawn bring the sun—that wouldn't have bothered us much, as the venetian blinds were down for good, for the cords had worn away and never been replaced—but with the dawn came the usual onslaught of flies. They were indigenous to all Spain. Some hotels supplied mosquito netting, some did not, but we decided that the most vital lend-lease we could make was not destroyers or even fertilizers and tractors. It was screens and bug bombs.

At breakfast we noted with interest the costumes of our fellow guests. In our hemisphere we go in for exposure and daring colors on the beach. Not the Spaniards, at least not the group at Ifach. They were solid bourgeois and, like most Latins, in perpetual mourning. The men splurged a little, a bright tie, a colored shirt, but the women wore black. Black blouses, skirts, and jackets, black shoes and stockings. They wore it inside when they sat gazing through the archways at the sand and sea, and they wore it when they ventured onto the beach to lower themselves gingerly under the sun shelters, which were flat tops on four tall stilts like enormously high tables.

We bathed, as did a sprinkling of Spaniards, but the great rock of Ifach, which towers like a black and purple prow breasting the waves was obviously not the Roc of Eden at Antibes; no international sun worshipers sporting bikinis, toasting to a turn, no cocktails at lunchtime, no gala plans for the evening. Bathing at Ifach was a staid family affair.

The holiday spirit was more rampant at Valencia. Around Valencia, too, the country is fertile, and we saw for the first time growing rice, the brilliant, vivid green blades glittering in the sunshine.

Valencia is an ancient city, but of modern aspect. It was wrenched from Moor to Christian and back again until the thirteenth century, when it settled definitely into Christianity. Today it is full of hotels and tramcars and business. We were there on a Sunday, so unfortunately we missed the Lonja de la Seda, the Silk Exchange, with its magnificent Gothic interior, but we were told it is one of the fine sights of the city, and visitors should plan to see it.

Flamboyant posters splashed on walls and buildings advertised a bullfight, and I said, I hoped dispassionately, that Norton and Peter should go if they wanted to. Having seen my first and last bullfight on my maiden voyage to Europe when I was sixteen and having been led half hysterical and violently nauseated from the arena, I would, I said, forgo the slaughter. The gentlemen both declined. "We too are civilized," they said, and voted for the beach instead.

On a summer Sunday the Valencia beach, though smaller, resembles a luxurious Coney Island, but with real food, not just hot dogs and popcorn, and excellent wine and beer. Spanish families were out en masse, the older women attired as they had been at Ifach in immutable black. The younger element, however, was more emancipated, and a rollicking group was having a high time with a catamaran. It was my first view of the craft, and the twin hulls, lashed together on a light framework and scudding along under the billowing white sail, had a wonderfully free and festive air.

I recall that we didn't bathe at Valencia. I can't think why not, unless we had left our suits in the car, but we did have a dip in the big pool at the *parador* of Benicarlos, an especially good one where we spent the night. The next day we completed our circle and returned to Barcelona, leaving our trusty Ford Vedette in a garage where it was to be picked up by a man sent from the Garage Ségur and driven back to Paris, where, we had been assured, it would be waiting for us on our arrival a week later. Giving it a farewell pat, we boarded an Iberia Air Lines plane to fly to Majorca. It is a brief trip, only forty-five minutes, and there are eight flights a day from the mainland.

The Balearic Islands are a favored vacation spot, and Pan American has a direct flight, New York to Barcelona, where passengers change planes for Palma.

Our first night we spent in the city proper in the Hotel Mediterráneo, overlooking the harbor. Palma is a romantic old town with a lovely Gothic cathedral. The starched lace, the rococo and baroque grandeur of Granada we had found entrancing, but these soaring lines were by contrast calm and refreshing. Many of the streets are broad, shallow staircases, and we wandered up and down and sat at the outdoor cafés and drank Spanish beer—*cerveza*—and thoroughly enjoyed ourselves.

The Balearic Islands have been prizes throughout Mediterranean history. The Phoenicians traded there, and the Egyptians came ashore on the beaches. They are a spirited little archipelago, and many families whose names are associated with the island's earliest history still live there.

Nada Patcevitch, a friend of ours, once visited in one of the great old houses, and she said it was exactly like being back in the Middle Ages. In this particular family there were eleven daughters and four sons. The girls led cloistered lives, and whenever one of the sons left the house he went to bid his mother good-by, kissed her hand, and received her blessing. There were uncounted cousins and aunts and uncles, all with what would strike Americans as a claustrophobic sense of family life, and most of them sat down, a mob scene, at every meal. The eleven daughters may not have been career girls or had much high life in the sense of café society, but they could scarcely have been lonely.

After a couple of days in Palma we set out across the island in a rickety old taxi for Pollensa and the Hotel Formentor. Majorca is fertile, and in our two-hour drive we passed through wheat fields and olive and almond groves. The island almonds are famous, and in the very early spring when the bloom foams on the trees the sight must be unforgettable. I suppose the system of agriculture would be frowned on by the economically and progressively minded, for the land is divided into small fields, making the use of combines and tractors impossible, but it is picturesque and the beautifully built stone walls would win commendation from a New England farmer.

There is many a mountainous hairpin turn on the way from Palma to the Formentor, and the best way to relax is to keep the eyes focused far out to sea. The hotel, a long, low white stucco building, is situated on the side of a pine-covered mountain with terraces leading down to the beach. You walk through paths of pine and oleander to the cove and bathe in water like melted aquamarines. A sleek white British yacht lay for several days in the little harbor. We were told that it was the Duke of Westminster's, a craft that has been classic scenery in the harbors of the Mediterranean for years. We had some cool and cloudy weather the days we were at Formentor, a disappointment in the month of July, but when we did have sunshine the bathing was incomparable.

There are some enchanting drives around the island, especially to

Valldemosa and the Carthusian monastery where Chopin and George Sand spent so unmonastic a winter. Chopin's piano is still there, but he never played it, we were told. He had had it sent out from France, but it only arrived the day he left, a brand of snafuism from which others, less gifted frequently suffer.

Our own ordeal of snafu came about because of our conviction that we had reservations on the Air France Sunday flight that goes directly from Palma to Paris. So we had. Sunday, August 5, instead of Sunday, July 29, the date we had specified. On the fifth we were to be en route to New York and were eagerly anticipating a week in London before that.

No one could have felt worse about our plight than Señor Munar, the courteous chap in charge of the Air France office in Palma, but no one could do less about it, either. We were there at the peak of the tourist season and every seat on every flight was booked for weeks ahead. Our last day, instead of being spent in healthful relaxation, dabbling our toes in the crystal sea, was spent in frantic scurrying from the Air France office to Thomas Cook to the Spanish Tourist Bureau. We would have tried B.E.A., too, but, being British, they were respecting the weekend and were closed on Saturday.

Despair stamped upon our faces, we faced Señor Munar for the last time. We touched a chord. This fine man gave himself a visible shake, he grasped his spear for the final assault, one could almost hear, "Once more into the breach, dear friends," as with the light in his eye that has illuminated barricades he said, "There is one final hope, but I warn you! If they cannot come through we are lost." We hung upon his words. No White Russians escaping the bolshevik hordes, no refugees fleeing the madness of Hitler had ever listened to a possible deliverer with faster-beating hearts. It was crazy. We were only going from one holiday spot to another, but it was the kind of tension and frenzy that does overtake tourists. Oh, God, please don't let us miss this connection, we've looked forward to this so long, please call off the strike of the dock hands or the pilots for just this one trip! After us the deluge! "Yes," we breathed, "yes? Who are they? Where are they?"

"It is a small line but they exist, they may possibly have something but they don't go to Barcelona or Paris, they go to Marseilles."

"Marseilles!" It was Utopia, it was Shangri-La. We would go to Marseilles and eat bouillabaisse, and then, transported as by doves and a magic carpet, we would wing our way to Paris on an erring but still hospitable Air France.

The name of the company to which our savior directed us was
Aviación y Comercio, and they were Algerian. They were Algerian and
they had three seats left on their Sunday flight. We avidly snatched the
tickets and plunked down our pesetas. Panting, our prizes clutched in
our sweaty hands, we were about to leave, when the doctor, who had
learned to fly at Pensacola and gone through the Pacific war as chief
flight surgeon on a carrier, demanded casually what kind of a plane
they were using? It was, they said, torn between pride and dim awareness that theirs was not the preferred model, a converted British
bomber. "An old one," the man added helpfully. The doctor's lower
lip jutted out and he gave an almost Gallic shrug of resignation. It
could have been a converted trireme; it was all right with us. Theoretically it flew, and on Sunday—that's what mattered.

"Suppose it does come down in the Mediterranean," Peter said chat-
tily. "We can all swim."

I smiled weakly. "You and your father may be mermen," I said, "but
I'll thank you to remember I'm more the plummet type. If we do come
down, don't let go of me. I promise not to struggle and strangle you,
just let me rest a hand on each one's shoulder as you knife through the
gleaming waves."

"At this season of the year," the doctor pointed out reasonably, "the
sea is warm and pleasant anyway, and there are lots of boats about.
We'd be picked up in no time." It's remarkable how reassurance can be
so frightening.

When we got to the airport the next day, we had a little time to
wait before take-off so we sipped an apéritif. We noticed that the
Aviación y Comercio pilots were doing the same. I glanced at the doctor. "They're Europeans," he said, "they're used to it. It isn't whiskey
or martinis, after all. What are you nervous about?" But he left the
rest of his drink untouched and I could see his hands curving to the
controls. Doubtless he was thinking, In case of emergency, just in case.

Our apprehension was groundless. The British bomber was a lumbering old bus with bucket seats, but she sailed through the air like a
swallow. We had a lovely flight, two brilliant, sun-filled hours over
sparkling blue water from Palma to Marseilles.

Arrived at the airport, we discovered that we had a four-hour wait before our plane left for Paris, so we drove into the city. We snooped
around a bit, and then decided to make for the Surcouffe, a restaurant
in the Vieux Port that had been highly recommended by the man in the
Air France office where we had gone to get our tickets validated. Our

Algerian chums had served no lunch and we were starving, but it was only about half-past five, the twilight hour, between dog and wolf, as the French say. We reached the Surcouffe to find luncheon long over and dinner not yet ready. There was, however, one waiter in attendance and he came to our rescue. That's what I like about the French: they can cope. They won't always do it, but when in the mood there are few like them for converting an impasse into an occasion. We yearned of course for bouillabaisse, the great specialty of the city, but that wouldn't be ready for another couple of hours. However, they did have at hand a fish soup that was, the waiter felt, respectable, and if some broiled steaks and *frites* and possibly a little salad and cheese would sustain us until we could get a more substantial meal on the plane, he was sure that he and the cook between them could manage to provide it. We accepted this stopgap graciously and gorged with joy.

With a slight blush of shame I confess that we even managed to down a little something on the plane en route to Paris. How can one help it in France? The bread is so good and the little half bottles of wine automatically appearing on every tray so delicious. In these days when plane and pilot performance are taken for granted the companies serving the best food have an edge on the others.

Our flight from Marseilles was direct, and on that warm summer evening in no time at all we touched down at Paris, feeling very much at home after our Spanish holiday. We had only one regret. Elsa Schiaparelli had asked us to a dinner party, but we had had to wire from Marseilles saying we would arrive in Paris too late to make it.

We did lunch together the next day in the garden of the Ritz, and it was just like home, as all of Seventh Avenue was in Paris for the fall collections. There was only one sour note in the sweet harmony. We had no clothes.

The father of young Monsieur Jacob of the Garage Ségur had picked up the car we left in Barcelona with most of our luggage, according to arrangement. Instead, however, of speeding to Paris like a homing pigeon, also according to agreement, he had turned capricious and was at the moment lolligagging through Southern France. But we were not to worry: he had put our luggage on the train, and there was every reason to think, Monsieur Jacob assured us, that it would be in Paris Wednesday. As we were flying to London Tuesday morning and had with us what we wore on our backs plus a few Majorca play clothes, this disclosure left us less than enthusiastic. I could not feel that I would be at my best sashaying down Bond Street in a pair of green linen shorts.

I accordingly paid a professional call on my friend Elsa Schiaparelli and bought one of her handsome models. When the doctor saw it he raised a quizzical eyebrow. "You didn't by any chance have a secret agreement with Jacob that the luggage wouldn't get here in time, did you?" Honestly, husbands! *Riddled* with suspicion.

I wore the dress that night, our last evening in Paris, when we went to dine in the Place du Tertre on Montmartre. The waiters on Montmartre are special. Not only are they good waiters, they are sprightly athletes. In summer the tables are set out on the *place*, but the kitchens are in the restaurant, which is across a narrow little street thick with traffic so that your *poulet à l'estragon* or *bifteck* must survive a skirmish between a nimble waiter and a Paris taxi driver before it is set upon the table. This naturally enhances both its value and its delectability.

The next day's luncheon, aloft, was British: a couple of slices of greasy headcheese and some warm bitter beer. *Adieu, la Belle.*

We were met at the London airport by our friend Harry Yoxall, the director of British *Vogue*, who drove us to Richmond, where he and his wife, Josephine, had a beautiful old house, and we had tea with them in the garden. The garden was chilly, but the tea was hot and the scones and sandwiches and cake delicious.

If only the British had the same knack with lunch and dinner they have with tea and breakfast! If only the French . . . if only the Spanish . . . if only, if only—Heaven, I suppose, combines the climate of perpetual spring with French food, American plumbing and telephones, British coziness, oriental service, and Spanish prices. I will settle for it.

For the few days we were in London we stayed at the Connaught, to my way of thinking one of the best hotels in Europe, combining hominess with excellent service and exceptionally fine food. Do not be misled, however, by the slightly old-fashioned atmosphere. The prices are quite glitteringly modern, but one gets one's money's worth.

Today London is abloom with prosperity, but in 1951 meat was still scarce and the temptingly arranged hors d'oeuvres trays turned out to be mostly herring; fruit and vegetables were abundant, and the Connaught follows the pleasant custom of serving afternoon tea in the lounge. You do not have to call room service, wait an interminable time for an enormous table to be wheeled in on which, like a tiny settlement in a snow field, huddle a lonely cup, a few morose cookies, a pot of hot water, and, naked on a plate, one unspeakable tea bag.

Connaught teas invite relaxation and gossip and supply nourishment. Peter and I were enthusiastic consumers, and after our day's sight-seeing would fall ravenously upon the tea table, then spruce up a bit and get to the theater in time for the seven-thirty curtain. Unlike the bitter battle of Broadway, which Americans must fight nightly if they want to see a play, English theatergoing is delightful and leisurely. Here the first clash is over tickets. Try to get them. There, even for a solid hit, you can usually get seats within a few days. Here by the time a couple has paid for the tickets, hired a baby-sitter, paid taxi fare, and possibly had a snack, a good third of their annual income has been consumed. In London the biggest hit in town costs one pound, $2.80, instead of $8.60 and $9.90.

Also, the London theaters have bars where one may get drinks or coffee. We would have a cocktail in the intermission, eat supper after the performance, and be back at the hotel by eleven-thirty or twelve, all three of us ready for bed, looking forward to the next day's adventuring.

The season we were there Vivien Leigh and Laurence Olivier were playing their great dual bill, *Caesar and Cleopatra* and *Antony and Cleopatra*, and another big hit was *Waters of the Moon*, with Wendy Hiller, Sybil Thorndike, Kathleen Harrison, and Edith Evans in the cast. The play was a comedy, but there were a few touching moments and I cried. This disturbed Peter, who nudged me gently and said, "But Ilka, look, right here on the program, it says a comedy." When you are thirteen a comedy is a funny play and you laugh, for heaven's sake.

The year 1951 was the time of the big fair, or Festival of Britain, so we went to see it. It was impressive, the modern sculpture and architecture reminding me of the Glasgow and Oslo exhibitions I had seen in 1938, but somehow I do not spark to the history of a tractor or the intricacies of the most recent milker. I would be a dud in Russia. I liked better Hampton Court, with the twin octagonal towers and the old clock between them, and the mellow patterned bricks. Despite the courtyards and quadrangles Hampton Court seems intimate, and it is easy to imagine sauntering there Henry and Anne Boleyn and the toddling baby Elizabeth.

Some of the apartments of Hampton Court are still occupied today by Lady this and Lady that, usually aging gentlewomen, relatives of the royal family. The gardens are exquisite. I know there are enchanting gardens and parks the world round. Some of the loveliest are the azalea and dogwood and box enclosures of the American South, and the serene bowers of Japan, but an English garden touches the heart. The English *care* about flowers. When you think of the raw, Oxford-

gray winters of that fog-shrouded land, it is easy to understand Shakespeare and the lyric poets. "The darling buds of May," "The vernal
joy," "The cherry hung with snow," and the enchanting "A Garden is
a lovesome thing, God wot!"—who should appreciate them better than
dwellers in the British Isles?

Also at Hampton Court we saw the Vine. It is a grapevine that was
planted in 1768 and today it covers the entire glassed area of an enormous greenhouse. The leaves that form a vast green canopy and the
great clusters of purple grapes glowing in the sunlight are a shimmering
sight. The grapes are now grown and sold for charity and one pays a
pound for a pound of fruit.

Hampton Court is on the same sight-seeing circuit as Windsor Castle, so we went there late in the afternoon. It is fairy tale on the outside,
with its gray crenelated towers and the long road leading to it like a
yellow ribbon laid straight as an arrow for miles and miles across tree-
studded fields. The deer of Windsor are very cozy with tourists and
come up and try to poke their heads through car windows, their antlers
forming the only obstacle to familiarity. The town of Windsor is usually crowded with sight-seers and picturesque with guards in their
busbies and scarlet tunics, but the interior of the castle struck us as
dull. They do have some fine Rubens and Van Dycks, but the atmosphere is pompous, heavily Germanic in concept, the clasped hands of
dear Victoria and the Prince Consort heavy upon it.

An amusing exception is Queen Mary's doll house, to which the
manufacturers and artists of Great Britain contributed their best in
miniature. There are minute Rolls-Royces in the garage and the king's
study is filled with tiny, beautifully bound volumes especially written
by well-known British authors. And the royal cellars! What glorious
Lilliputian jags the doll family could go on, swigging from minuscule
bottles of real wine meticulously packed in hampers and cases.

Eton College is opposite Windsor, but by the time we got to it we
were so exhausted from our other sight-seeing and queuing up that all
we could do was stagger toward the quadrangle, lean against an archway, and mutter, "Look, Pete, Eton." No response. "Playing fields."
"Uh-huh," said the young master, and the three of us staggered back
to the car and collapsed.

Another must sight, and one we took in when more refreshed, is
Westminster Abbey. I know it was extensively restored in the nineteenth century but I don't care; it's still thick with history and still one
sees the stone so touchingly referred to by the beguiling diarist John

Aubrey, in his *Scandal and Credulities*. I quote a part of his account of Ben Jonson for the sheer pleasure of doing so:

Ben Johnson had one Eie lower than t'other and bigger, like Clun, the Player; perhaps he begott Clun. . . .

King James made him write against the Puritans, who began to be troublesome in his time.

A GRACE BY BEN JOHNSON EXTEMPORE, BEFORE KING JAMES

> Our King and Queen, the Lord-God Blesse,
> The Paltzgrave, and the Lady Besse,
> And God blesse every living thing
> That Lives, and breath's, and Loves the King.
> God blesse the Councell of Estate,
> And Buckingham the fortunate.
> God Blesse them all, and keepe them safe:
> And God Blesse me, and God blesse Raph.

The King was mighty inquisitive to know who this Raph was. Ben told him 'twas the Drawer at the Swanne Tavernne by Charingcrosse, who drew him good Canarie. For this Drollery his Majestie gave him an hundred poundes.

And Aubrey also says:

"He lies buryed in the north aisle in the path of square stone (the rest is lozenge) opposite to the Scutcheon of Robertus de Ros, with this inscription only on him, in a pavement square of blew marble, about 14 inches square,

O RARE BENN JOHNSON

which was donne at the charge of Jack Young, afterwards knighted, who, walking there when the grave was covering, gave the Fellow eighteen pence to cutt it.

Westminster Abbey is lofty, ancient, and imposing, but inside it has the cozy English touch: tombs and plaques, statuary and mementos, a jumble of British history in an old theatrical storehouse. Kings and queens, writers and artists, lie cheek by jowl in a companionable hodgepodge. When we were there, there was vague talk of spring cleaning—maybe some sort of reclassification and realignment might be in order. I prefer to think nothing came of it.

It's curious how the sheer weight of history forms one's impressions. Americans especially, owing probably to the vast areas of our own country—and, compared to Russia, we are small—tend to think that any spot or building that's all *that* famous must be big. It was a distinct shock to me when I first saw the tiny room in which Mary of Scotland and Rizzio were having supper the night he was murdered. I had expected a vast hall, men-at-arms, the Hollywood touch in Holyrood. I was equally surprised on my first visit to the House of Commons. The present building is spurious Gothic, having been erected between 1840 and 1867, but within modest dimensions a noteworthy Parliament has functioned on the same site for more than four hundred years. Childlike I had imagined something grandiose, resounding. And I remember my mother telling me that the first time she saw the Marne, after World War I, she exclaimed, "Why it's a stream." Mindful of its fame in battle, she had envisaged the Mississippi.

The London part of our holiday came swiftly to an end, and we returned to France for a final day or two in Paris and our flight home. Leaving Norton at the airport to cope with customs and return tickets, Peter and I hied ourselves to the Galeries Lafayette to buy bikinis. Everybody in the South of France and on the island of Majorca had been wearing them, and we'd felt frightfully dowdy, me in my one-piece suit, Norton and Pete in shorts, so we determined to insert ourselves into the fashion as well as the aquatic swim. I tried mine on. When I came out of the fitting room, my stepson gasped, but I promised him that I would wear it only on our own beach at Centre Island.

The next evening we left for home on the Pan American Clipper. We landed at Shannon, and everyone rushed to purchase his allowance of duty-free liquor. Everyone but the Browns. We are not averse to saving the stiff tariff imposed on every bottle of scotch whiskey imported into the States; our problem was something else again. We were short of your so fascinating American currency. We had cashed our last traveler's check and come down to the finish line with just enough to see us through customs and the cab fare home. Norton had cabled his secretary to be at the airport with funds, but just in *case* there was any slip-up he felt it prudent to be supplied with a little of the wherewithall, what an old French cook we once had referred to as *"la liquide."*

I regretted, though, having to forgo those lovely bottles of inexpensive scotch. When we passed through customs without having to pay a penny's duty, I was, if anything, irked. "You see," I said, "I *told* you it would be all right. We could just as *well* have bought the stuff, look at the money we'd have saved." Of all futile words of tongue and pen.

CHAPTER TWO

The Caribbean ✳ Monaco

Our next junket came about two years later, in 1953, and, while enjoyable, was on a simpler scale than our European vacation. We went for a ten-day cruise in the Caribbean on the *Nieuw Amsterdam*. She was a commodious, comfortable boat, but in ten days Dutch food grows heavy.

We joined the cruise because it was in effect a floating medical convention. A sort of good-will tour to consolidate the entente that it was hoped would prevail in Pan-American medical circles.

At one period of my life I received an impression of conventions, induced possibly by the wishful thinking of the men involved and also by unfortunate contacts with Shriners and Elks on the loose—an impression I had difficulty in shaking. It was simple: babes and booze. In recent years the realization has weaseled in on me that this is not necessarily so. At some conventions the men work hard. The doctors in fact overdid it. They met with Central American doctors and government officials when we were ashore, and at sea they held meetings in the ship's movie theater every morning and afternoon, engrossed in panels and discussions, papers and colored films of operations. We wives soon discovered we were along only for the sail.

Four of us became very friendly. Daphne Lyall, young and lean, with a turned-up nose and a sense of comedy and chic, the English wife of the surgeon David Lyall; Rosita Diaz, the small, soft-voiced Spanish actress who has worked a great deal in Mexico both in pictures and on the stage and is married to Dr. Juan Negrín, who calls her Microbe; Frances Berens, straightforward, warm, and friendly, with eyes as blue as the sea, the wife of the renowned ophthalmologist Conrad Berens; and myself. We would loll about in our deck chairs, occasionally struggling to rouse ourselves for a bout of shuffleboard, and once we took in a filmed operation. That is to say, Rosita and I did. Daphne and Frannie had more sense.

It was a warm afternoon immediately after a heavy Dutch luncheon. Rosita and I tagged into the theater in the wake of the flower of American medicine, and the ship moved to the rhythm of a gentle swell. The lights went out and an operating room flashed upon the screen in glorious color. The camera zoomed to a close shot of a hemisection of tongue and mandible. There it was in vibrant detail; flesh laid back, arteries and veins pulsating, gore galore. I began to feel very very unhappy. I glanced at Rosita. Her frail exterior is deceptive. She sat quietly, her eyes alight with interest, her blond head nodding accord with the doctor lecturing on the operation. "*Muy interesante, no?*" she whispered happily. The little iron girl. "Honey," I said, "if it's all one to you I think I'll slip out." Rosita was distressed. "You do not like it?" "I love every tendon," I said, "but if I don't leave now, I'll need the care of more quacks than we've got on board. Meet you later."

One of our ports of call was Cartagena, Colombia, a colorful tropical port where the black boys rowed out in little skiffs to dive for small change flung by the passengers. They laughed and shouted in the sparkling sea, their white teeth gleaming, rivulets of water slipping over the rippling muscles of their shoulders and thighs. I loved it, but exposure to my politically liberal friends has taught me that somewhere around in there an Indignity was being perpetrated. The underprivileged were indulging in begging—"That it's *aquatic* makes no *difference*, Ilka," and the moneyed classes were patronizing them. That sort of thing is paternalism, I believe, an amiable dictatorship, but a good living should be their *right*, not a *privilege* bestowed by us globe-trotting capitalists. That the diving boys and the tourists both seemed to be having a grand time was, it was explained to me, quite beside the point. It's very confusing.

Cartagena rises white from the brilliant blue water, her picturesque old fortifications feathered with palms and hibiscus. Sunlight and shadow make sharp patterns on the narrow street and on the rococo painted doorways rich with moldings, and the traffic is a clutter of jeeps, old cars, and donkey-drawn carts. We liked best the university, with its triple-tiered blue and white archways around an inner court, and the dark, ancient cathedral, with its deep, elaborately painted window embrasures.

We stopped at Panama and drove along the Cruces trail, the long, straight, never-ending road that cuts across the isthmus through the jungle. When we got out to take pictures we came upon a curious and sinister enterprise. A magnificent tall tree caught our attention, but when we looked closely we noticed tiny moving flecks of green on the trunk. Still-closer inspection revealed that two ranks of ants, millions of them, were moving up and down it. The left-hand file crossed the ground and started the steep ascent unencumbered. High over our heads they disappeared into the leafy branches, and when they started down again each one was bearing a tiny green triangle. It was awesome and sad to witness the implacable despoilment of so superb a giant.

Panama was hot, but we had a good swim and got on friendly terms with our very large, very black taxi driver, who urged us to write to his brother in the Bronx, telling him of our meeting, which we subsequently did.

The *Nieuw Amsterdam* touched at Haiti for a day of sight-seeing, and it had been arranged that the medical group would be received by President Magloire. For some reason we were held up at the pier, and our cavalcade got under way only after considerable delay. We wound up the mountain roads oohing and ahing at the scenery and drawing one another's attention to the picturesque natives, all of whom seemed to be lugging fighting cocks to what promised to be a spectacular bout. Since I don't think that cocks should be made to suffer any more than any other animals, I was in my usual doldrums over man's inhumanity to beasts, but the sympathy I got was sparse.

When we arrived at the presidential palace we discovered that Monsieur Magloire, having waited for us over an hour and having other fish to fry, had quite understandably gone off about his business. But, we were informed, he would be happy to receive us late that afternoon. Since it was then only eleven o'clock, there was nothing for it but to wend our way back down the mountainside. It reminded me of my nursery days: The King of France and forty thousand men marched up a hill and then marched down again.

We lunched and took pictures and poked around among the shops, which were not overly tempting except for mahogony salad bowls and duty-free French perfume, and finally it was time to return to the presidential retreat. This time we treed our quarry. Monsieur Magloire, a few government officials, and other assorted guests received us hospitably, and then came the moment for the little ceremony. One particular doctor was spokesman for our group and also presided at most of the meetings on board. In his capacity of chairman he had acquired a handsome gavel made of the various woods of South and Central

America and banded with silver. This he had proudly borne up the mountain.

We gathered round, perhaps fifty or sixty in all—doctors, doctors' wives, and Haitian guests. Our spokesman and President Magloire stepped forward, friendly gladiators meeting in the center of the ring, the referee-interpreter between them. The doctor explained how happy we were to be in this so beautiful country, which was duly translated into French, and President Magloire replied that he on his side was ravished to have us. A few more exchanges increased the glow of well-being. We all began to beam. How simple it was—race, color, language —there were no barriers that good will and kind hearts could not overcome. Then the doctor held out the gavel. Knowing his pride in it, we beamed even more. What a truly generous gesture! With a broad smile President Magloire reached out his hand to accept it, when our own smiles froze upon our faces, for as he did so our boy snatched it back with a squawk. "No, no," he said hastily to the interpreter. "Tell him I'm not *giving* it to him. I only wanted him to *see* it." When the president was apprised of this, his jaw fell open, his hand dropped to his side. I do not know to this day why there was not a mass descent through the floor. Embarrassment flooded the room like a pink spotlight.

It spoke well for the Haitians, I thought, that they didn't spike the drinks that were subsequently served, but a chill did settle over the house and grounds. Possibly it was the altitude. Later, on board ship and safely out of the harbor, we asked our leader what in God's name had possessed him; he seemed to feel injured. "After all," he said, "it's *my* gavel. I just thought he'd be interested in seeing all the different woods."

We stopped in Havana, too, but we were nearing the end of our cruise time and stayed only a day. Two or three years later, in 1956, Norton and I returned to Cuba to spend a little holiday with our friends the William Holcombes, who had a house on Varadero Beach, a superb stretch of sand where we went shell hunting. I brought mine home, each shell carefully wrapped in tissue paper and placed in a basket bought especially for the purpose, and put them away in the big upstairs store closet in the country until I should think up some imaginative way to use them. They are still there untouched.

The following month, April of 1956, I left without Norton for what was to be a memorable interlude in la belle France, or rather la belle

Monaco. I was writing a syndicated weekly newspaper column, so I went as an accredited member of the press. It was my first time at bat and an eerie experience.

In honesty I was motivated more by my love of travel than by any burning passion to bring news of the nuptials of Miss Grace Kelly and Prince Rainier to a waiting world, and, had the wedding been going to take place in Philadelphia, the bride's home town, the happy couple might well have got along without my co-operation.

As it was, the opportunity to travel lured me, but also other women newspaper columnists were doing it. Inez Robb was going to be there; the mother superior of the Hearst press, Dorothy Kilgallen, if she could bury the *faux pas* in which she had said that Prince Rainier was considering Marilyn Monroe as a possible bride, was going to be there; even Gloria Swanson was supposed to be reporting. Why not me? True, my column was new, it had been appearing only since the first of January, whereas the Misses Robb and Kilgallen were years ahead of me in experience, circulation, and fame in their fields, but I had put together enough words to make seven books, I had eyes to see with, and my French, though slightly rusty, still functioned. Under the circumstances was this last perhaps not an advantage? I discussed it with James Spadea, who was syndicating my column. He cogitated and said it would be all right with him. He questioned some of the papers that were using me, and they said it would be all right with them. I talked to Norton, who grunted and looked a little sour. He obviously considered the whole venture the apex of lunacy, but he finally said it would be all right with him if I really wanted to, though why in the world . . . I wanted to. I went.

He was right; the whole episode had an antic quality, and more than once I wondered what in heaven's name I was doing there.

Of course I didn't take off just like that; certain preparations were involved. Never having seen Grace Kelly in a movie, I felt that I should do a little homework, so I prevailed upon Paramount to run some of her pictures for me, *Rear Window, The Country Girl, To Catch a Thief,* and discovered what the rest of the world had known for some time: Grace Kelly was a beautiful young woman with talent.

My other preparations for the trip involved clothes. Hats particularly loomed upon my horizon, so I went to see Emmé and her Adolpho, the blond sprite who designs her hats, wears a cobbler's apron around the showroom to accommodate his shears, pins, ribbons, etc., and who pops his creations on his own head to see how they will look on others.

Almost without exception they are becoming to Adolpho and enhance the customers.

The *pièce de résistance* I selected was a broad-brimmed natural straw topped with a meringue of cunningly draped white chiffon. This was to wear at the marriage in the cathedral. Viewing myself in the mirror, I was very happy. I was very happy until Miss Emmé's voice fell upon my ear. "Miss Chase," she said, "what are you going to wear when it rains?" A dear woman but at times annoying. "Emmé," I said, "don't be silly. The Riviera in the spring! Rain! What nonsense." "Yeah, I know," she said. "I've been there in the spring. It rains." To placate her, I ordered a simple little gray straw banded with red and white polka dots. I would wear it for traveling with my gray flannel suit and discard it the day I got there.

My mother having been the editor of Vogue for thirty-eight years, the fashion world was, in my youth, inevitably my background. Today other facets of life interest me more, but some of Ma's training stuck and I have always felt, as I was taught, that a good 80 per cent of being well dressed was to be appropriately dressed for the occasion. If one is to proceed on that theory, I was the worst-dressed woman in Monaco. I don't know what happened to me. Having lived in France, having spent holiday weeks in the Midi, I should have known better, but enthusiasm overrode experience and common sense. I had some very pretty dresses; they were cottons and silks and would have been admirable for June and July. In early April they were completely off key. It was raw and cold and Emmé was right. It rained most of the time. I lived in my gray flannel suit, my red topcoat over my shoulders, my gray hat upon my head.

This ignominy however lay in the future. When I left New York the evening of April 5 on Pan-Am's glamour flight, No. 114, I was all aglow. By way of lagniappe one of our passengers was Porfirio Rubirosa. The darling of Doris, Babs, and Zsa Zsa was unaccompanied and spent most of the crossing relaxed in his reclining chair, deep in recuperative slumber.

Drue Parsons met me next morning at the Orly airport and we drove to her apartment. Geoffrey Parsons we have known for years, and Drue I have known for years *and* years. They have an enchanting flat on the Ile Saint Louis, overlooking the Seine, and, thanks to their hospitality, Norton and I think of it as home whenever we are in Paris. When I had written Drue that I would be there en route to Monaco, she had cabled that they were expecting me.

That night we retired early, and the next day, fortified by twelve hours of solid rest, I was able to lunch with joy and *bon appétit* at one of my favorite bistros, Raffatin et Honorine, on the Boulevard St. Germain. The only trouble with it is that the *pâté maison* and bread and *hors d'oeuvres variés* are so good there's little space left for the *grand plat*, the body of the meal.

That afternoon back at Orly, waiting for the departure of the Nice plane, I bumped into George Schlee, Valentina's husband, whom I have known for a long time but see only occasionally. George was flying down to his villa in the South of France, and we sat chatting and reminiscing through the short trip.

The swank place to stay in Monte Carlo was the Hôtel de Paris, but it was crammed as full as the small car in the circus that rolls into the ring and disgorges dozens upon dozens of clowns. Far bigger wheels than I had been unable to get accommodations there. I went to the Old Beach, a hotel four kilometers farther along the sea front toward the Italian border, and owed my comfortable quarters to Marcel Palmaro. Marcel and his American wife, Lucille, are friends and neighbors of ours in the country, and—things sometimes work out in very handy fashion—he is the consul general of Monaco in New York and a close friend of Prince Rainier. Marcel had to some extent expedited matters for me and had promised Norton that he and Lucille would keep an eye out for me once they arrived in Monaco themselves. Indeed before leaving home he had explained a good deal of the routine and ceremony we would all be witnessing, and the idea of having the *Constitution*, the ship on which Grace Kelly crossed the Atlantic, make a special call to the harbor of Monaco instead of docking at Nice as usual, so that her fiancé could meet her on his yacht, was of Marcel's conceiving.

I was comfortable at the Old Beach, but we were rushing the season and the restaurant was not yet open, so after I had deposited my luggage on the evening of my arrival I drove back to Monte Carlo to dine. I chose the Cancan, an indifferent restaurant, but one that looked like a place where a woman could go by herself. Much as I had wanted to come, I had been fearful that I might, at times, be lonely, but I squared my little shoulders and hoisted my little chin, firm in my determination that should loneliness be my lot I would accept it with dignity, philosophy, and humor, strong in the knowledge that my sojourn was to last but two and a half weeks and that Norton waited for me at home. I think I was wise to adopt this lofty attitude, but I am happy to say I did not need it. With the exception of that first evening and I believe one other, when exhaustion kept me by preference alone in my room, I always seemed to be a member of a friendly little cabala at mealtime. This was due, not to any irresistible magnetism on my part, but to the fact that everybody there was in the same boat and for the same reason: press coverage from one angle or another. The atmosphere was informal and friendly, but there was, I noticed, no great interchange of data or flow of wit, and many of the reporters, Art Buchwald, for example, and Ben Bradlee, of *Newsweek*, were bright buttons. This puzzled me at first, but then I began to suspect that the reason was that, friendly though they may be, on every story each member of the press is angling for an exclusive item for his own paper and is leery about dropping information inadvertently or otherwise. As far as wit was concerned, if anyone thought up a quip he hoarded it for his own dispatches, knowing full well that with the paucity of authentic material even reporters of integrity had to fall back to some extent on fantasy and witticisms. Larceny was not unheard of.

Since, as I say, this was my first experience as a news gatherer, for all I knew the procedure was normal, but those more experienced than I were frustrated and mad. They felt the whole affair was being handled in a highly unprofessional manner. Why no press releases? Why no briefings? Why no interviews? There was a real feud between the press and the palace, the latter to all intents and purposes having shut up shop just as the climax was approaching. I talked to some of the Monegasques and found their reactions mixed. They were fond of the prince and appreciated his attitude. On the other hand, because of the brutally cold winter that destroyed their crops and the elections that paralyzed business, they badly needed the trade the wedding and its attendant publicity would bring them. His reluctance to court it was annoying.

Things were at an impasse, but to some extent the press itself had brought it about by rendering His Highness and his advisers supersensitive. Many of the papers had accused him and Grace Kelly of being publicity hounds, but I could not in honesty see how it was their fault. If the press didn't want to give them all that space it had the simplest out in the world—just stop. The couple couldn't force the papers to print columns about them, but the reporters themselves had gone on a Cinderella jag—Bricklayer's Daughter Marries Prince—and were malicious when the daughter and prince co-operated and resentful when they didn't. I think the truth was that, despite the fact that his own true love was a movie star, Rainier and his advisers were simply not braced for the onslaught that overwhelmed them and their tiny principality.

With the passage of time His Serene Highness seems to be manifesting less reluctance to face the spotlight.

Things got better after the Kellys arrived, and for that Mr. Kelly *père* was probably responsible. I met him only once and we chatted only briefly in the lobby of the Hôtel de Paris, but he impressed me as a magnetic and able man. In an atmosphere taut as a fiddle string he had one of the best American qualities, that ease that sometimes accrues to men big in stature and, through the years, successful in their undertakings. It has no trace of smugness; it's just solid and sure.

In speaking of his daughter and future son-in-law he balanced neatly between discretion and candor, deflecting questions about her professional plans and launching instead into how maternal she was. "She's crazy about her little nieces. Any time there's a baby around Grace has to hold it. I think when her younger sister Liz got married first it worried Grace a lot. She was afraid she'd be an old maid."

"That isn't quite how it's worked out," I said.

"No," he said thoughtfully, "no, it hasn't."

Like many another father of the bride he was doing what the women of the family told him to. "But," he said, "I get out of that palace whenever I can." Accustomed as he was to American telephone efficiency, the palace switchboard was driving him crazy. He wasn't the only one. The phone service all over Monaco was lunatic. It was far quicker and surer to go in person to deliver one's message than to try to communicate by telephone.

One premarital festivity I went to, although actually it had no bearing on the wedding, being an old Monegasque custom, was the Battle of the Flowers. This is a widely touted tourist attraction, but despite its reputation it is a homey little procession not unlike a high-school festival. About twenty carriages paraded, and very pretty they were, with frames and superstructures set on open victorias abloom with hydrangea and stock, anemone, iris, and lilac, tulip and lily. It is better not to get too near them, though, as under the hot sunshine the blossoms fade quickly and the carriages have an air of being looked after by the maid rather than the mistress, the maid having yet to be born who will voluntarily discard dead flowers.

The parade is called the Battle of the Flowers because girls in the carriages toss posies at the spectators lining the route who toss them back again. In the atmosphere in which we live today that amount of antagonism is my ideal. The band played and the back streets were especially festive, hung with American flags and the red and white banners of Monaco and everywhere the initials "G" and "R" intertwined. The tiny city is picturesque, the houses standing, as it were, upon each other's heads as they clamber up the steep hillside from the inner harbor, alive at that time with pennant-bedecked yachts, a few sober gray American destroyers, and the lordly *Christina* of Mr. Aristotle Onassis presiding over the motley fleet like a gigantic mother swan.

April 8 was my birthday. I had been prepared to feel sorry for myself, alone on that so special day, but my sympathy was spared. I had met Julie and Clinton Sewell—he worked for Pan American Airways—and they had invited me for cocktails at the bar of the Hôtel de Paris, a location that quickly became headquarters for the press gathering from the United States and Europe to cover the wedding. The Sewells introduced me to Mr. and Mrs. Gerard Hale, Americans who lived many years in Monte Carlo and who were close friends of Prince Rainier. Learning it was my birthday—I do not remember what evoked this pretty confession unless possibly a cocktail—the Hales invited the three of us to dine at the Casino.

All my life I had thought the Monte Carlo Casino must be the essence of mad sophistication. If glamour, despair, and exultation didn't abound there, where *was* one to find them? I expected raddled old women with dyed hair, their clawlike fingers raking in the chips as they played their systems until three, four, five in the morning. I expected urbane men of the world whose only reaction, as the little white ball tumbled into the wrong section of the wheel, was a slight tightening around the mouth before they made their way quietly to the moon-flooded terrace and shot themselves. I expected beautiful and notorious *demimondaines* glittering with diamonds, laughing heartlessly as their lovers handed them a hundred thousand francs' worth of chips at a clip. I'd read books, hadn't I? I'd seen movies. Well, friends, that ain't how 'tis. The atmosphere of the Monte Carlo Casino is dreary and the lighting is a libel.

The lamps hanging down over the gaming tables are shaded with burnt-sienna silk, and this is no help to the complexion. The majority of the players have all the dash and romantic aura of small businessmen from Bridgeport or Canton, Ohio. This is probably truer of that quarter they call the Kitchen, where the stakes are low, but even in the steep department the great days of E. Phillips Oppenheim have gone. My impression is possibly jaundiced, for I am not a gambler. The ichor this pastime seems to send coursing through the veins of others has never pulsed along my arteries, setting me aglow. I have never won an automobile in a raffle or a quarter in the slot machine and I begrudge the disappearance of money when there is nothing to show for it. I understand that what others buy is excitement, but the few times I have risked my small stakes, my only purchase has been ennui and the morose sensation of being had. I am awed by the skill of the croupiers and baffled by the faith that moves mountains and stubbornly clings to "systems" right in the teeth of the adroit gentlemen hauling in the pelf with their little plastic rakes, and that about winds up my interest in the gambling hells of the world. The Casino food did nothing to convert me either.

The most winning aspect of Monaco actually is its geography. There are two central points, the Rock, on which stand the palace and the church and where, at the time of the wedding, the press bureau was set up. The Rock has a few narrow, winding streets, old houses, and cafés. The cathedral is uninteresting. It is of gray and white stone, was finished in 1895, and is more Romanesque than Gothic in architecture.

Leaving the Rock, one swings down the road along the Condamine, the flat land edging the harbor and up another hill to Monte Carlo, where the bisque-colored Hôtel de Paris and the bisque-colored rococo casino dominate the square. A long pretty stretch of grass, flowers, and trees slopes up to the Boulevard des Moulins, the town's main street and shopping center, and it is here that the dogs promenade. The Monegasque dogs are handsomely cared for, as are the cats, Mrs. Gerard Hale having contributed funds for a splendid cat asylum. Some people took exception to this, saying that money should be put to loftier uses, but the Hales also adopted an entire French village which they provided for after the war, so if they wanted to be kind to cats, too, that seemed to me their own business. These two generous people are dead now, but I understand that Prince Rainier carries on the good work.

From the Boulevard des Moulins, mounting a long steep flight of stairs, one comes to St. Charles, the church of the American priest Father Tucker, who was much in the news at the time of the wedding, and to the big square yellow house that is his rectory.

If ever a priest was in the middle of his flock, it is the good father, for the open-air market crowds against the foundations of the house, and the narrow street curls around it and clings to its back. Everything being on several levels, the street is even with the second-story windows, and the sounds of the parish and the smell of carnations and leeks, horse meat and fish come right in and blend with the odor of sanctity.

I had a letter of introduction to Father Tucker and called upon him to present it, but was told that he was in conference with Grace Kelly's spiritual adviser and I never did get to see him.

I had better luck with my old friend Mr. Willie—Somerset Maugham —when I went to call upon him at his villa at Cap Ferat about half an hour's drive from Monte Carlo. There were just three of us for tea, Maugham, Allen Searle, who is his secretary, and myself. In treating me to the *tour du propriétaire* he showed me a batch of communications from the palace inviting him to the wedding and assorted functions. It amused me to see the invitations because some of the members of the press, having nothing else to do, were whiling away their time making book on all the royal figures in the locality who had not been invited to the wedding—the Yugoslavs, for instance, who live just down the road—while others were polling who, besides Britain, Norway, and Holland, had refused.

Personally, having a crush on Mr. Maugham, I considered him as royal as any of them. He was grumbling a bit about having to put on a stiff shirt and white tie in the morning, but I took it with a grain of salt. I think secretly he was pleased to have been included in the festivities.

Not that he feels very out of things, I should imagine. At that time he was eighty-two, and hostesses were still clamoring for his presence at their dinner tables, and such obscure characters as Winston Churchill counted their day made when they lunched with him, although I understand that the great statesman observed that the stairs were a bloody nuisance and Willie should jolly well install a lift.

Lacking the age, achievements, and renown of Sir Winston, I can still agree. It is tactless of Willie to be so spry at his age. Not only are the staircases of his house long and steep, the house itself is set in a nine-acre property lavishly terraced, and the master sprints like a gazelle up and down the outside stairs as well.

His happens to be a face for which I have affection, but it can scarcely be called benign, and there is a detached, waspish satisfaction in his gaze as he watches a guest huffing and puffing at his heels.

His stammer is at moments intense but his conversation has the simple direct quality of his writing. Maugham himself has said he suspects that here and there a short story in an anthology is all of his that will survive, but to my way of thinking he is a great storyteller, and assured young authors who remark patronizingly that the old boy has had his day may find there is just the least bit of a trick to creating those characters, manipulating plot and suspense, and fashioning the prose that seems so facile.

Whatever he may think of his chances of survival, however, while he is still among us there would be small point in underestimating himself, and this Willie is not guilty of. He said frankly that his present to the happy pair was three handsomely bound volumes of his own short stories. "Less expensive for me than a jewel and more valuable to them."

Another spot besides the Villa Mauresque, Maugham's house, that I greatly enjoyed was La Tourbie, a restaurant high in the mountains with a boundless view out over the Mediterranean. I lunched there one day with Olga Curtis, of the Hearst press, and Berthe Pourriere, of Pan American Airways, and was introduced by a solicitous bartender to what has since become a favorite before-luncheon apéritif, Punt e Mes. It is a velvety, slightly bitter vermouth beneficent to the innards.

Whether it was a change of water and climate or the excitement of my first press assignment I do not know, but my innards were in turmoil. I was in Monaco for nearly two weeks and I don't think I slept more than three hours a night and I ate spasmodically. In the first couple of days a guardian angel whom I would not normally have anticipated appeared at my hotel in the person of Inez Robb, bearing paregoric. In France, oh, sensible land, one does not need a prescription for this pilgrims' balm, and thanks to the Robb solicitude I was able to get about. The Punt e Mes was a further benefaction.

One thing that set me atwitter was the fact that I would have to file my copy. This, to one newly come to a profession in whose service the only labor hitherto involved had been gathering the material, writing it, and dropping it down the mail chute, seemed a difficult and official step; the kind of thing that Mr. Harrison Salisbury of the New York *Times* was accustomed to, but that was terra incognita to me. It involved wire services. Where was I to find them? What, precisely, were they? Where were the others going? I did not wish to appear naïve but how, without asking, was I to find out? Despite Jim Spadea's reassurance and a cable credit card handed me before I left home, the hurdle had seemed formidable. Also, would I make my deadline? What happened to correspondents who did not? Their epaulettes and buttons were ripped off and in the space usually filled by their copy was a photograph of the shameful scene and that was the end of them.

One of the difficulties besetting all correspondents in Monaco was actual physical locations in which to write. I, for the most part, drove back to my hotel and portable typewriter. The difference in time between France and New York was greatly to our advantage, and in any event my reports were commentary rather than news. Correspondents with specific deadlines and editions to meet were harder pressed and set up offices wherever they could. The Hearst contingent was in a plumber's shop. Because this plumber's shop was French, among the fittings were bidets and upon these, as upon any other handy furnishings, the ladies and gentlemen sat typing the stories lapped up by millions.

Actually I need not have worried about my filing. Almost my first evening I met a savior, a pair of saviors in fact, Gene and Helen English. They seemed and were very American—Helen had once sung with a band, but they had gone to France, fallen in love with it, and made it their home. Gene's job was wire service; Press-Wireless. He took me under his wing and showed me the ropes; I filed with him and it was easy.

Normally my column was syndicated weekly, but for the wedding story I was filing daily. I began to get carried away by the whole idea. How the New York *Times* had managed without me all these years seemed mysterious. I yearned to make special editions like the established correspondents and cabled Jim Spadea asking if I could file more than once a day if something exciting happened. His reply was prompt and succinct. "No dear."

The Englishes and I became friends, and I saw them, George Schlee, George Abell of *Time*, and Ben Bradlee of *Newsweek*. The trip turned out to be a lot more fun than I had anticipated, for men are always at a premium and it is a delightful surprise when they are available and companionably inclined.

Interspersed with my coverage were teas at George Schlee's villa, luncheons and dinners with George Abell, Ben, and the others, a dinner to which David Schoenbrun, CBS's correspondent, and his wife kindly invited me—we were going across the border to Italy, but it rained, so we dined at Beaulieu instead—and there was a dinner party given by Julie and Clinton Sewell at which the King and Queen of Yugoslavia

were among the guests. The Yugoslavs were royal but they were out of a job, and there do not seem to be many openings for ex-kings. Later on I went to call on them in their small apartment in Nice. I gathered they were pretty much dependent on contributions from loyal royalist exiled Yugoslavs for their livelihood. They talked of the day they would be back on the throne, but Tito is awfully large and King Peter is very slight and the prospects look to me dubious.

The day following the Sewell dinner was a red-letter occasion because the bride arrived in Monaco. I had been invited to watch the arrival of the *Constitution* from the Onassis yacht, an invitation of which I availed myself promptly. The scene was very festive, pennants fluttering from every yacht in the harbor, and as the *Constitution* steamed slowly into view, dozens of tiny craft put out to meet her, while overhead four planes and a helicopter roared and circled. The people along the quais watched with interest but without much comment. As the big American ship drew nearer, I kept glancing over to the other side of the breakwater where Prince Rainier's yacht, the *Deo Juvante*, lay at anchor; there she lay, not a budge out of her. I was tempted to clear my throat and shout across to her, "Prince, dear, guess what? The *Constitution's* here," but then I decided that probably he and Grace had made plans about when he would set forth that he had not confided to me.

It wasn't until the big ship dropped anchor that the motors of the *Deo Juvante* started up. I ran back onto the upper deck of the *Christina* through the gaggle of press and friends of Mr. and Mrs. Onassis, and through the powerful binoculars mounted on the deck I managed to get a close-up view of Prince Pierre, the prince's father bedecked with medals, and of the bridegroom himself in conservative navy blue, dragging nervously at a cigarette as the yacht steamed toward the big liner.

The actual meeting of the happy couple took place on board, where they had a momentary surcease from prying eyes. Once the bride and her parents were safely transferred, the *Deo Juvante* pulled away and started back toward the little port. All that boat business made me think of *Tristan and Isolde*, but scored by Puccini, no heavy Wagnerian thumps, just rippling trills.

Miss Kelly and her beau stood forward waving at the cheering citizens, and I suppose screaming at each other above the whistling of the boats, the booming cannon, and the explosion of fireworks sent up by the *Christina*. The bride wore a navy-blue dress, a bunch of white flowers at her throat, and a large white hat, inappropriate for sea breezes. Her black poodle, Oliver, wore a white leash.

It took some time to berth the yacht, and there was about half an hour when we press could only lick our chops and hope for further crumbs. Officials were being received on board and, I suppose, indulging in a dash of whistle-wetting.

I did see Mrs. Gerard Hale, go up the gangplank—at the Sewells' dinner for the King and Queen of Yugoslavia she had told me she was going to present Grace with a bunch of orchids. She also imparted the information that she was an honorary private in Rainier's army, bringing the total strength of that indomitable force to seventy-one.

After a brief interlude Mrs. Hale returned down the gangplank, and there was another little space of nothingness and then suddenly the police on the quai snapped to attention, the corps of cameramen with one movement leveled their lenses, and the couple reappeared. Grace had switched from her white flowers to the orchids and carried Oliver. The three of them got into a closed green car—everyone said they should have had an *open* one so they could have been *seen* by their loyal subjects lining the road—and started up the winding drive to the palace, where shortly afterward, if they had any sense, they must have been lunching, laughing, and exchanging kisses.

I lunched at the Hôtel de Paris with the two Georges, Abell and Schlee, Ann McCormack and Millie Considine. We didn't kiss but we ate and drank and had a hearty time.

The next day the Georges, One and Two, and I went back on board the *Christina* for an afternoon's call. Gloria Swanson came along with us. Mrs. Onassis, Tina, was a charming hostess, as cordial as though I were an old friend, as thoughtful as though I were a new, offering to show us over the yacht. She is a small, thin pretty blonde who did not strike me as having an iron constitution. I do not know what difficulties caused her and her husband to split up but I should think that boat would have been one of them. She never had a moment's privacy and must have been exhausted much of the time, or if not exhausted certainly bored by the influx of visitors, many of whom they'd never heard of.

I noticed that the priceless jade *bibelots*, including a fat Buddha with ruby lips, in the big drawing room were cemented to the chests and tables on which they were placed. Tina giggled. "It keeps them from sliding off when the ship rolls," she explained, "but also it keeps them *here*." I gathered that some visitors, when their hosts were all that rich, held to the theory that the souvenir-hunting season was open and long.

I was impressed by the swimming pool although it looked more like a mosaic dance floor sunk an inch or two into the afterdeck, and such, we learned, was one of its functions, but by pushing a button the mosaic picture, a cavorting bull of Greek mythology, could be lowered several feet, spigots were turned, water gushed, and *voilà! la piscine, ze swimming pool.* It's not very big, but, like the dog who walked on his hind legs, remarkable that it happened at all.

The *Christina* also boasts a comfortable library with an open fireplace, a piano, a television set, and even a few books. There are eight double guest cabins, each with its own marble bath and each named after a Greek island. Since Aristotle Socrates Onassis (his parents were taking no chances) and his wife are both Greek, it was natural enough. There is also an extremely graceful circular staircase. This, it seems, is rather difficult to accomplish in nautical architecture, but, if one is given a blank check, it can be done.

There is a small infirmary in which minor surgery may be performed, and in view of the personnel on board, between thirty and forty, not counting guests and owners, it seems a prudent provision. The ship is capable of converting salt water into fresh, so sometimes remains at sea four to six weeks at a stretch.

The dining room is lined with pretty panels by Marcel Vertes, and in the master bedroom there's an open fireplace with an El Greco hanging above it. I dare say enough sea air and the roses come spilling back into the normally greenish-white complexions of even El Greco's characters. I asked Mrs. Onassis if salt was good for canvases and she said it was great. Her sister, Mrs. Stavros Niarcho, also owns a yacht and priceles pictures, and it seems it wouldn't occur to her or her husband to go to sea without their entire collection. What's the point of *having* things like that if you don't get any use out of them?

From the bedroom we strolled into the bar. The bar itself is semi-circular in shape and six or eight inches deep with a glass top. You peer down into it at a strip of curving blue cardboard ocean on which are set beautiful little models of real ships, and there's a crank you turn and the ships travel back and forth *sous cloche.*

I suppose the ultimate luxury on the *Christina* is the private plane that can fly the mail or any guest who becomes allergic to Neptune back to land.

We had finished our tour of the yacht and were sitting around chatting, when a steward announced that Miss Inez Robb had come on board and was asking to see Mr. Onassis. When told that he was not there, she was a bit put out since he had invited her for the time she arrived. Monsieur and Madame had got their signals crossed, so Tina knew nothing about her, but she asked George Abell to go out on deck and see if she would like to come in. She would and, hoping, I suppose, for some sort of exclusive story about the famous yacht, was understandably a little disconcerted to find Gloria Swanson and me already installed. Mrs. Onassis courteously invited her to make the tour we had just completed, so we all tagged along, we second-timers pointing out objects of interest with the possessive air of those who have only just beat the newcomer to the draw.

I believe Inez later told Cynthia Lowry of the Associated Press that covering the wedding was a wacky enough enterprise without competing with those who had never written before in their lives. It was reported to me that Cynthia said mildly, "Why, I thought Ilka'd written quite a lot, those books and all." "Well, Ilka, maybe," snapped Miss Robb, "but Gloria!" The ladies of the press are just like other ladies, but as a matter of fact the Robb annoyance, if it existed, was justified. Professionals are irritated by amateurs, and Miss Robb is a woman whose batting average in her column is high. Furthermore the lady has guts and is not afraid to espouse an unpopular cause if she thinks it's right.

Cynthia Lowry I also came to know and like. She had been one of the press corps who crossed with the Kelly family on the *Constitution*. I had sent Grace a copy of my just-published novel *The Island Players*, as it was about actors and I thought it might amuse her if she read it on the trip over. Since everything about the young lady was spotted and commented on, the book, too, was noted lying on her deck chair. "We gave you a little break," Cynthia said to me with a grin, "we mentioned what she was reading."

During the days, when everyone was marking time until the civil ceremony should take place, scuttlebutt was rampant, much of it made up out of whole cloth by people accustomed to writing and given nothing to write about, and who hoped rightly or wrongly that a waiting world palpitated for news from our tiny corner. Or possibly it wasn't so much the readers they were concerned with as it was their editors, who may have been sending out messages to the effect that, considering what it was costing the paper to keep its eyes and ears on the spot, the bodies to which they were attached had jolly well better come up with some copy.

Whatever the provocation, the stories swirled. "Grace slapped the Prince at dinner." "Did you know Rainier was so mad at Dorothy Kilgallen, because of what she said about him and Marilyn Monroe, she had to get the Pope to intercede for her before she could come here?" "Mr. Onassis is furious at the Prince because of that big ugly skyscraper right at the water's edge." "Why don't they complain?" "They do and all he says is it won't be noticeable when there are a whole lot of them." "How hideous!" "Of course, but what do you expect now that he's got a contractor for a father-in-law?"

President Eisenhower's somewhat pixie choice of Conrad Hilton to be his representative at the wedding added fuel to the flame. "He and Kelly have had a long conference. There's going to be a Hilton Monaco constructed of Kelly sand and bricks."

The report that Hilton was planning to tunnel the Monte Carlo railroad, which has always been air-borne, like New York's old elevateds, brought a tart reply from the Monegasques to the effect that theirs was one of the few budgets in the world with an annual surplus of two million eight hundred and fifty thousand dollars. If they wanted a tunnel they could finance it themselves. This surprised me. I wouldn't have believed that so much came from local industry: espresso machines and beer, spaghetti and candy. My naïveté was gently dispelled when it was pointed out to me that many great businesses are incorporated in Monaco for the same reason that the Du Ponts, who certainly have the fare out if they want to leave, remain embedded in the state of Delaware; an advantageous tax setup.

Things perked up considerably the morning the ballet held a dress rehearsal for its Soirée de Gala in Monte Carlo's rococo little opera house.

London's Festival Ballet, under Anton Dolin's direction, was a youthful, vigorous, and exuberant affair greatly surpassing what was considered the news event of the program, Stan Kenton's offering to Grace Kelly, written especially for the wedding festivities. I do not warm much to early-American Indians, and it occurred to me that the rhythm of the music and the tom-toms, the costumes by Levasseur, in red, black, and white, which were a combination of Sioux, bellhop, and space cadet, might well have baffled His Serene Highness of Monaco. His American bride might have had some trouble appreciating them too.

Another de luxe occasion was the Soirée de Gala at the Sporting Club. All day the principality had been in turmoil, the Hôtel de Paris in a ferment of titivation, the bar crackling with gossip and speculation as to what the entertainment would be and who would be there. At one moment there was a *susurrus* in the lobby, and as a messenger laden with a great carton hurried through, we all bent like wheat before the wind; Ava Gardner's petticoats had arrived from Spain!

A *soirée de gala* is a form of entertainment to which the French are singularly partial. This one was held on a Sunday night, it was the first big binge of the wedding week, and everyone was arrayed in full fig.

In accord with its usual slightly tangled procedure the palace public relations department didn't get out the invitations to attend the dinner until six o'clock that same evening. However, they had little to worry about; guests weren't so involved with other social engagements that they were likely to turn down any princely summons to festivity.

When the invitations had been delivered to me, I was in the usual feminine dilemma over what to wear, finally deciding on a slim Dior of yellow organza, as the rain was teeming in buckets and it would be easier to cope with than my printed paper-taffeta robe-de-style.

Driving myself was out of the question, but the hotel assured me I need not worry about ordering a taxi, as its own Volkswagen bus would deliver me to the door of the Sporting Club. For a description of the evening I resort to the column I filed at the time, as it seems to have retained a sense of immediacy. Since I had a lot to tell in a limited space, I adopted the stenographic method.

Explain to hotel must leave eight-thirty sharp as Sporting Club doors close at nine. Hotel says we're in accord. Descend at eight-thirty. Volkswagen in Monte Carlo four kilometers from Old Beach Hotel. Too late order taxi. Tell concierge what I think of him. Already strained relations now at breaking point. Storm upstairs to get car key. Storm down again. Volkswagen at door. Six French pile in, by barest fluke get last seat. Arrive Sporting Club plenty of time. Three footmen in knee britches and white wigs opening car doors. Go up stairs to long, narrow, elegant gallery. Slender white Corinthian columns down the sides. Ceiling midnight blue studded with stars. At intervals on balconies running around colonnade mannikin footmen in eighteenth-century crimson costumes hold candelabra. Candelabra on crimson cords swing from ceiling. Flowers everywhere. White lilac, lilies, red roses. On stage one end of room orchestra of twenty playing. Musicians wearing white wigs and white Louis XIV costumes sewn with silver stars. Look great. Room already crowded. Dais table opposite end of room from stage. Completely hidden behind flower-banked balustrade. With considerable difficulty get cocktails at own table. Now nine-thirty, when dinner supposed to be served. Room packed. No sign of Grace, Rainier, or friends. Reflect royalty never late. Reflect they are not royalty. Look about. Spot the Aga Khan and Begum, Randolph Churchill. The Onassis and Marcel Palmaro, Monaco consul to New York, not yet on deck. No star performers and no food. Rumbling sounds from American stomachs. Ten-past ten. There is a buzz, orchestra strikes up, room rises, and Grace and prince enter. There follows worst stage wait of decade. Orchestra stops dead. Five hundred people stand in complete silence. Grace and prince behind their chairs also silent with faint frozen smiles. Suspect violent stage fright. She looks very pretty with hair down around ears and full-skirted white gown with blue stole. Prince's family and Kellys file in. Mr. Kelly looks patient. Silence agonizing. At our

table Jinx Falkenberg whispers, "Oughtn't we to clap?" Men reluctant. We try it. A few tables take up applause but it sputters out. Dais guests now all in place. At hidden signal they sit and vanish from sight behind flower balustrade. No one emerges throughout entire evening. Dinner delicious, fresh caviar, clear turtle soup, *langouste* pilaff, duck, asparagus, ice cream, champagne, coffee, cognac. Overly-long vaudeville show opens with lady dressed in blue and green feathers explaining she is Mediterranean. Grace and prince mustn't complain when mistral blows and waves keep them awake. These are ramparts guarding Monaco, last oasis of peace and dreams. Rest of show nonpoetic, but George Matson comical in take-offs of Johnnie Ray and Yma Sumac. Jinx and I retire to ladies' room. Are strolling back along broad empty corridor when there is sudden quickening of tempo. Waiters, secret-service men, and *carabinieri* in blue uniforms with red and white plumes on hat snap to attention. Grace and prince appear, she going like bat out of hell. Lady in costume standing by wishes to give her flower. Prince makes a grab at her. Misses, calls Grace. She stops, takes flower, gives unenthusiastic smile, takes prince's arm, and sails out. Gala over.

A couple of nights later came the fireworks, supplied, I believe, by the ever-loving Onassis, and they were superb.

These formalities disposed of, the way was now clear for the civil ceremony, which took place on television at eleven o'clock the morning of April 18. It was televised so the citizens of Monaco could witness it and also because there wasn't enough space in the throne room for something like fifteen hundred correspondents. We watched it from the fish museum, which may seem a curious choice but it was roomy.

I was up early and drove along the bay into town, expecting there would be a special tension in the air, but the streets were nearly deserted except for little knots of people gathered here and there and a few local cops instructing the imported cops in matters of protocol. The flower shops were busy sending masses of blooms up to the palace.

I was drawn inevitably to the Hôtel de Paris, where I thought I might catch the virginal excitement of all the divorced and married bridesmaids on their way to the ceremony. The lobby, except for the gathering ladies, was deserted at the unholy hour of 10 A.M., and they looked tired. Indeed one or two of the maidens spoke quite snappishly to their husbands.

The civil ceremony program worked efficiently. Very nice opening; the camera panned over the harbor of Monte Carlo, gave us glimpses of the palace and a brief tour of the throne room, the sixteenth-century mantelpiece and a large portrait of Louis II, the prince's grandfather.

Two armchairs were set close together for the bride and groom. Gilles
Barthe, the Bishop of Monaco, who would perform the religious ceremony the next day, passed in front of the camera, and then Grace and
the prince came in and took their places. She was wearing a rose-beige
lace suit and a charming little bonnetlike hat. She looked calm but
solemn, Prince Rainier sat with one finger over his mouth. He looked
solemn. Monsieur Marcel Portanier, the president of the Council of
State, said it was a solemn occasion. Two of the bridesmaids who were
on camera looked sleepy.

Solemnity was later dispelled at a big buffet luncheon party on board
the *Christina,* to which many of us had been invited. Music was supplied by a handful of the Princeton class of '55, Stan Rubin and His
Tigertown Five, who rolled out a little number in honor of the Greek
host entitled "Acropolis You."

The following day was really *Der Tag,* the wedding day. After delays,
uncertainties, wildly fluctuating rumors, and exacerbated nerves, most
of the members of the press had received their invitations permitting
them entrance to the cathedral. They were sumptuous affairs in French
announcing that the daughter of Mr. and Mrs. John Kelly was marry-
ing Prince Rainier of Monaco, and there was another card, handsomely
engraved with a gold coat of arms, stating (in translation):

> "BY ORDER OF HIS SERENE HIGHNESS
> MONSEIGNEUR RAINIER III SOVEREIGN PRINCE OF MONACO,
> THE FIRST AIDE-DE-CAMP HAS THE HONOR TO INVITE
> MISS ILKA CHASE
> TO ASSIST AT THE MARRIAGE OF HIS SERENE HIGHNESS
> WITH MISS GRACE KELLY, WHICH WILL BE BLESSED
> IN THE CATHEDRAL OF MONACO,
> THURSDAY, APRIL 19, AT HALF-PAST TEN."

It was an assistance I was happy to give. After the spells of wretched
weather we had been undergoing, the sun came up on the wedding day
unequivocal and brilliant. The scene at the cathedral was brilliant too.
Graustark put on a fine show.

We were supposed to arrive at 8 A.M., and by eight forty-five a throng
was milling up the steps of St. Nicholas Cathedral, the great percentage of the men in white ties and decorations, if they had them; the
women in everything from suits to evening gowns. I wore my pet dress
from Harry Winston of white linen and linen lace and the large hat

with the meringue from Emmé. I was glad the weather was good for
the bride's sake; I was gladder for my own. It would have killed me
not to have worn that hat.

The writers Louise de Vilmorin and André Maurois were there, the
latter loaded with medals; the great English beauty of her generation
Lady Diana Cooper, a distinguished writer in her own right; fat King
Farouk, who the day before had had a rugged time, unable to snaffle
a top hat in all of Monaco; the Stanley Marcuses of Dallas, purveyors
of the bridesmaids' gowns; Mrs. Loel Guinness (big Stout); the Pierre
Cartiers (big jewels), and Her Majesty's representative, Sir Guy Salis-
bury-Jones.

The United States, Italy, France, and England had sent honor
guards, and a band of Chasseurs Alpins came swinging by, playing,
piquantly enough, "Swanee River."

The church was filled with white lilac and the altar was lighted by
eleven tall candles. There would have been twelve, but one had been
removed to make room for the television camera. Opening the ceremonies, an imposing major-domo in a Napoleonic hat, white knee
britches, green tail coat and crimson waistcoat, marched up the aisle
to escort Bishop Gilles Barthe in his beautiful robes and assisting
priests, in plum, to the altar.

The bridegroom's grandmother, usually glossed over due to a teensy-
weensy irregularity in the marital relationship of Great-Grandpapa and
Great-Grandmamma, was among the first arrivals followed by Princess
Charlotte, Prince Rainier's mother, Princess Antoinette, his sister, and
Mrs. Kelly.

A European wedding differs from an American, and Grace came in
on her father's arm before her bridesmaids and for some time knelt
alone on a red damask *prie-dieu* in front of the altar. She looked very
composed and seemed deep in prayer, which I thought was admirable,
as had I been in her place I would have had a small, uneasy feeling,
just a tiny prickling of the hairs at the back of the neck, that maybe the
bridegroom wouldn't show. The temptation to look around would have
been irresistible. I like the American way better, where the fellow gets
to the altar first and a girl is in no danger of disappointment. Not that
any bridegroom would have been likely to let Grace Kelly down, for she
looked very beautiful, truly a fairy princess.

Presently, and somewhat to my surprise, the music burst into a Hallelujah chorus. I have always associated Hallelujah with Easter and
the risen Christ, so it seemed quite ambitious for an earthly prince,

but anyway he appeared, preceded and followed by prelates and looking very handsome in his powder-blue trousers, his black jacket flourishing with oak leaves and spanned by a ribbon of red and white. He knelt down on a *prie-dieu* next to his bride, and the service began.

There were addresses by the bishop and the Kellys' parish priest from Philadelphia. Mass was said and a fanfare of trumpets accompanied the Elevation of the Host.

At the end of the ceremony, as the bride and groom turned from the altar and started down the aisle, the great doors of the cathedral were flung open onto a panorama of sparkling seas, blue sky, palm trees, and three helicopters.

Following the service came the big reception in the palace, at which point I began to take a dim view of the upbringing my mother had given me. Since I had not been specifically invited to the reception, only to the wedding, I didn't go, though I badly wanted to, both for myself and to be able to report what went on. Very few other correspondents had been invited either, but they barged in and were well received or at least not given the bum's rush. Apparently the palace staff either assumed that an invitation to the wedding automatically included the cake or that the members of the press might as well be there as off on their own inventing a party for their respective papers.

One may be well brought up or a good reporter, but there are times when the two are mutually exclusive. A few others of us unwanteds huddled together and wandered off to the gala luncheon at the Hôtel de Paris. It was all right, but it wasn't the reception.

I went back to my room at the Old Beach and around five o'clock, from my balcony, I could see the sleek little silhouette of the *Deo Juvante* slipping out to sea and bearing the honeymooners, to whom the peace and privacy must have come as a blessed relief.

Suddenly I felt deflated. I had been buoyed up by excitement and companionship and the challenge of a job I had not before undertaken. Now it was finished. I wondered if full-time professional reporters had that same sense of anticlimax once a story ended, or was there for them always the next one just over the horizon? There was no doubt that the feeling of being in the know was a heady brew even when, as in the present instance, the know was minor, confused, and implemented by generous dollops of imagination.

The next day I flew back to Paris. Driving from the Invalides to the Parsons' flat on the Quai d'Orleans I got chatting with my taxi driver and told him I had just returned from the wedding in Monaco. The wedding he took in his stride, what interested him were the jewel robberies that had had a big play in the Paris papers, several of the wealthy guests having been divested of costly bibelots. He asked me if I had been robbed. "No," I said, "but then I have no jewels to be robbed of." He looked at me in the rear view mirror. Under the walrus mustache his smile was gallant, "Ah," he said, "it is Madame herself who is the jewel." If the French are looking for an ambassador to a ticklish post my candidate is that taxi driver.

CHAPTER THREE

Italy * Portugal
Italy * Paris

ON A SUNNY Saturday afternoon in August some three of four months after my return from Monaco, Norton and I were in the garden trying, too late, to fend off the chrysanthemums. We had neglected the bud-pinching earlier, and now they were rushing the season. He was also debeetling the roses, a form of warfare into which he enters with venom and peculiar relish. The telephone rang. It was the overseas operator calling Dr. Brown. He went to the phone and had a long talk with a patient, a young American woman who had been in a shattering automobile accident in Rome, and the doctors were discussing the possible need of amputating her arm. She was desperate and wanted to know if Norton wouldn't fly over to see her and fend off the men she could think of only as butchers. Before he hung up he had agreed to go. Turning to me, he said, "How about it? If we can get off tomorrow, do you want to come too?" Well! Ask a foolish question, get a sensible answer. Of course I wanted to go. What did he think? Traveler's Tip No. 9: Always keep your passport up to date. Who knows when opportunity may knock?

There followed a wild twenty-four hours that were thoroughly stimulating. Our first problem was plane space, and we had a suspenseful interlude while we waited for Pan Am to cast about in the storeroom and see if they had an old pair of seats stashed away. Finally they phoned to say they had, we could leave the next day. There was then a frantic scramble, rearranging plans and appointments and long phone conversations between Norton and other doctors wherein he arranged for the care of his patients while he was away.

The moment we knew definitely we would be able to go, we walked across the lawn to Mother's house. We had lunched with her three hours earlier, and Italy had not entered the conversation. "We're going to Rome tomorrow," we said. "Ah? Didn't you make up your minds rather quickly?" "Yes," we said, "that's how we are, spur-of-the-moment types." We explained what had happened. "Have you any money?" said Mother. That dear, solid woman. "Now that you mention it, darling, that's what we've come to discuss."

Our problem was the weekend with the banks closed. We had a little cash with us, and by dint of a spate of checks made out to family, neighbors, and servants—Mother's cook was loaded—we were able to collect enough to start off in reasonably good shape. We packed and planned and organized, I drove into New York to appear that night on *Masquerade Party*, the television panel show of which I was a member, drove back to the country, and at 6 P.M. on Sunday we roared down the runway and were air-borne en route to Rome. The fact that I would have only about three and a half days there, since I had to be back in New York for my television appearance the following Saturday, intensified the sense of adventure.

We arrived the next day in the early afternoon. We had agreed that Norton would drive immediately to the hospital to see his patient, leaving me to cope with the luggage and customs. Having bought a Berlitz Italian phrase book at Idlewild and having applied myself to it at intervals through the night, I was set to battle heroically with customs, taxi drivers, and hotel clerks. What happened made me feel the way you do when, muscles tensed, you brace yourself to lift what you think is a solid load only to find it made of cork.

We were met by a friendly, sturdy girl who was working for Pan American. She smiled kindly at my phrase book and loosed a cascade of Italian that set the customs lads jumping. Her English was equally flawless, and as we drove along the Appian Way, I complimented her on her accent and vocabulary. She looked a little blank. "Oh," she said, "didn't you get my name? It's Nina Beckwith, I'm an American." I felt a fool, but the compliment still held, since her Italian was flawless too, and as she had dark hair and eyes even Romans took her to be one of them.

She frustrated me, though. Why had I sat up all night with that phrase book? Actually most of the Italians a tourist comes in contact with are eager to practice their English, but they are far sweeter and more co-operative about the foreigner's stabs at their language than are the French, who act as though you had insulted their mother as well as their mother tongue when your grammar and accent fall short of perfection.

I have just written: ". . . we drove along the Appian Way." It is a curious sensation to bowl along in a cab and to think, This is it! This is where the legions tramped. Furthermore many of the selfsame blocks they tramped over pave the route today. The Romans were indisputably the lads who thought up the little maxim dear to our grandmothers' hearts: If a thing is worth doing, it's worth doing well. They had their faults, but they weren't jerry-builders. That is to say, the road and aqueduct and temple crowd weren't. Others were.

In her erudite and beautiful book *A Time in Rome*, Elizabeth Bowen tells us that during the empire ". . . threatening glares . . . disturbed the worthy: houses were constantly bursting into flames. A dropped lamp or a kicked-over brazier could be enough; dwellings were easy tinder. Apart from Rome's major, historic fires, outbreaks took unreckoned toll of life and property. So far as I know, nobody was insured. And yet another reason to lie worrying was that the buildings were liable to fall down. Run up on the cheap by contractors to reckless heights of four or it might be five stories, the *insulae* (or tenement houses) were unsteady: thunderous glissading collapses, extinguished shrieks, might, any night, rend the ears of neighbours."

It didn't stop with Rome, Miss Bowen. Many a house in a hillside development in the twentieth-century United States has come careening and slithering down the sandy flanks in the first bad thunderstorm.

Because our dear friends the Reginald Roses had spoken highly of the Grand Hotel, Norton and I went there too. The Grand is not glossy and it is not commercial, it is old-fashioned and comfortable. We learned that the Italian word for room is *camera* and floor is *piano*. Our *camera* was on the third *piano* and very pleasant, too, albeit a bit noisy, for the street we overlooked was narrow and sound re-echoed against the walls. Our ceilings were high and our bathroom extensive, consisting of a suite of little rooms and compartments lined with what appeared at first glance to be chocolate ice cream, but that was just the color of the marble. We were also air-conditioned. I am always of two minds about air-conditioning: Mind 1, and by far the larger portion, loathing the system; Mind 2, accepting it when the weather is unbearably hot and sticky. Mind 2 had a slight edge.

On the afternoon of our arrival in Rome I hadn't been in our room very long when Norton returned from seeing his patient. "Well," I demanded, "how's the arm? It doesn't have to come off, does it?" "I shouldn't think so," he said, and that's all he said. It was enough, I suppose; he had answered my question and the lady never did lose her arm, but sometimes a person likes to chat a bit.

On our way out to dinner our first evening we discovered that our next-door neighbor on our *piano* was Marlene Dietrich, who was in Rome working on a movie, *Monte Carlo*. We knew Marlene, so it was pleasant to see her. She was more loquacious than the doctor and as we were waiting for the elevator she complained mightily, saying that the Italians were killing her. "My God, the hours they work here. No unions. You know when we stop at the studio? We stop when one of the workmen falls off a scaffold, unconscious from exhaustion. Look, I'm a skeleton." She grabbed her gray silk dress into a bunch at her waist. The shape looked pretty good, however, and the doctor, slow of tongue, maybe, but quick of eye, observed later over the dinner table that he was pleased to see the world's most celebrated gams were still intact.

We were dining outdoors at Passetto. In the summer in Rome one always dines outdoors, and, owing to the blessed dearth of soft coal, the linen remains immaculate.

Vittorio de Sica was at the table next to us. I longed to introduce ourselves to him and tell him how greatly I enjoyed his pictures, but, running ahead with the conversation, I could hear him saying politely, "Thank you very much." Then we would say, "This is our first evening in Rome," and he would say, "Ah?" And I would say, "I act in pictures myself but only occasionally." "Indeed?" "Actually I've never had a role I could get my teeth into." "Is that so?" I wasn't writing very good dialogue for Mr. de Sica; I didn't think he'd want the part. The doctor's example held. I remained silent, contenting myself with watching his lean, intelligent face, admiring his beautifully cut suit, and envying him his talent.

Leaving Passetto, we went to have after-dinner coffee in the Piazza Navona, surely one of the most beautiful urban spots in the world. Laid out originally about A.D. 85 as a stadium or circus, it is shaped like a race track, a long wide oval paved with the small, lozenge-shaped cobblestones characteristic of Rome and glorified by the Bernini fountains. At night the indirect lighting throws their baroque figures into fantastic shadowy silhouettes. The piazza is surrounded by lion-colored buildings, apartments, and little shops, and in the evening when the windows are lighted it is so incredibly like the setting of an opera that it would take very little *vino* or *grappa* to move even the most gravel-voiced to song.

It is the color of Rome, I think, that first strikes the visitor. Even in clear weather the predominating color of Paris is gray, the blue of her skies is soft, but in the southern city, in summertime at least, the sky is blazing blue and the golden light is itself an element. The wolf that suckled Romulus and Remus must have been a tawny beast, for the city is a blend of spice tones: nutmeg, cinnamon, and ginger, powdery yellows and deep earthy reds.

Our coffee finished, we hailed an open carriage and on our way back to the hotel got out at the Coliseum and stood for a while within its moonlit walls among the thronging ghosts.

The next morning, early, I went with Norton to visit his patient, to take her a few posies and wish her well. It was then that I met the young Italian who was looking after her, Dr. Frederico Caldiero. He was nice, no butcher tendencies at all, and eventually we came to think of him as a family friend, because three years later he married Micol Fontana of the renowned Roman dressmaking house of Sorelle Fontana, with whom we have a warm relationship.

Despite the fact that her crack-up had been vicious and that her arm and upper body were in a cast, Norton's patient was lucky in one way. The hospital where she lay, the Salvador Mundi, is a first-rate establishment. Modern, beautifully situated on a hill overlooking the city, it was spotlessly clean and run by white-robed sisters, many of whom were American. Indeed Sister Monica, the head nurse, came from Wisconsin.

Nina Beckwith had generously put herself at our disposal, and after I left the hospital she asked, "Which do you want to do more, sight-see or shop?" But I was like Jane in the nursery rhyme:

"Pudding and pie", said Jane, "Oh, my!"
"Which would you rather?" said her Father.
"Both", cried Jane, quite bold and plain.

I wanted to do both and I wanted also simply to wander the streets of Rome. Any wanderer in the Eternal City, however, runs one basic risk: annihilation. New York cops may think they have it tough. A day in traffic the way the Romans do it would send them to the booby hatch, white-haired and babbling. If they ever had to contend with the Japanese, whom we subsequently experienced, they would, I think, quietly turn their guns on themselves and end it all.

Here at home, especially over holiday weekends, newspapers and radios caution us to drive carefully. In Rome and in Tokyo they admonish you with sharp cries of glee to go out and get your man. Dr. Caldiero told us, not without a touch of pride, that he had sixty fracture cases in his clinic at that very moment. There are also a good many horse-drawn carriages in the city, and when I remarked on the animals' placidity in the midst of the horrendous traffic, the doctor said dryly, "Damn' right. Any horse who shied here would be sausage."

We fell in love with Rome, with its broad avenues, narrow, winding streets, and beautiful wide piazzas. Besides the Piazza Navona I had two other favorites. One was the Piazza di Spagna, with its fountain and the flower stand under two big white umbrellas at the foot of the world-famous Spanish Steps. Halfway up and around and down some other steps, one comes to the Galleria Schneider, a discriminating small gallery run by an American, Robert Schneider, where I bought a tawny abstract painting inspired by a Roman courtyard by the young Italian artist Buggiani.

My other favorite is the vast Piazza del Popolo, with its mackereled pavement and the twin domed churches, their pillared porticoes converging upon it and its sculptured groups on either side.

Open spaces in a city are a salvation. New York's canyons have a majesty of their own, but one must breathe, be able to expand and relax, to fill the lungs with air, the eyes with distance, to have areas where the air is circumscribed only by beautifully proportioned, widely spaced buildings such as in the squares of London, the piazzas of Rome, and the historic *places* of Paris: the Vendôme, the Concorde, the Etoile.

I feel compassion for New Yorkers in the spring when I see how eagerly they take advantage of Bryant Park behind the library at Forty-second Street—how they sit relaxed on the Central Park benches—how the little playground at the foot of East Fifty-seventh Street, with its few trees and minute sandbox, is alive with babies and young mothers. Were I Barbara Hutton or Doris Duke or Mr. Paul Getty, whenever I saw a block where a building had been demolished—and what blessings they are, those squares temporarily empty, allowing sun and air to circulate through the surrounding apartments and offices—before the cranes and bulldozers moved in, could I pay the taxes, I would buy it up and turn it into a little oasis of greenery where New Yorkers could sit and breathe and watch the leaves come out on the trees.

Nina introduced us to Via Veneto, a sort of small Champs Elysées, more intimate in feeling than the great Paris boulevard, but, like it, lined with outdoor cafés where the citizens spend hours sipping soft drinks and letting ices slip smoothly down their throats. There are chairs at the little tables, but also, along the curb, are swings like our porch swings, with white and crimson awnings. With parasols and pink tablecloths and bright lights at night the scene is wonderfully festive. When we dined one evening with Micol Fontana, she said, "Via Veneto is the living room of Rome." It is also the bedroom, for on a balmy starlight night it is so pleasant no one goes home.

I don't know why it made me laugh, since the pious must ride too, but somehow it seemed comical and gay when the monks ran to catch the busses, the Italian fathers with their long habits of black and white, the young German theological students with their crimson soutanes flying out behind them.

The American Embassy is on Via Veneto, and also the church of the Immaculate Conception, the latter a curious place to visit. We went in one afternoon, and slipped, in an instant, from the sunlit streets of today four hundred years back into time.

We approached a sound of chanting and there, gathered in a dim chapel, were six or eight monks wearing long beards and the brown, rope-girdled habits of the Capuchin order. There is a crypt under the church, a series of small, recessed chapels decorated with the bones and skulls of four thousand Capuchins who died between the sixteenth and nineteenth centuries. They were buried for a brief time in the floor in earth brought from the Holy Land and then exhumed and their skeletons disjointed to form the macabre but ingenious décor.

The arched ceilings are quite rococo, set with jawbones forming delicate circles, studded with great rosettes of vertebrae. There are niches of humeri and femurs and skulls, and tasteful little canopies of pelvic bones. Not everyone's dish, perhaps, but showing a nice sense of arrangement and a feeling for organization; all parts neatly assembled for Judgment Day.

It was a sharp contrast to go from the crypt to the Casa Silva, an atelier set in an old garden where they make beautifully embroidered stoles and skirts, distractions temporarily to enhance bones that someday will be as stripped of extraneous matter as are those of the long-dead monks.

Aware that my time in Rome was so limited, I determined to concentrate on two or three Greats rather than get cultural indigestion. With this in mind, although it will sound rather strange, I decided to forgo St. Peter's. From my girlhood visit, made the first time I ever went to Europe, I remembered it reasonably well and I made up my mind to go to the Sistine Chapel instead.

Seeing the Sistine Chapel once, however, is like nibbling only the first hors d'oeuvre of a long and delicious meal. One should make repeated visits, for its walls and ceiling boast a massive section of the world's great art, and to absorb it requires time and knowledge. In his beautifully presented picture book, *A Treasury of Art Masterpieces*, Thomas Craven, speaking of the Adam in the Sistine Chapel, remarks, "There are no weaknesses in Michelangelo's nudes. They are in truth of superhuman construction . . . it is not likely that the world will ever again produce the equal of Michelangelo in the painting of the nude." I fancy that most art critics would agree with Mr. Craven, but from the woman's point of view, if one accepts Adam as the father of the human race, one can't help wonder how he managed it. Craven goes on to tell us that the Adam was painted in three days while the artist lay flat on his back on a scaffold, and he adds, "One might think on beholding the vault of the [Sistine] chapel that he [Michelangelo] had exhausted every imaginable human attitude; but he returned to the room thirty years later, a tired old man, and painted on the back wall two hundred more figures in The Last Judgement without a repetition of posture!"

Bare statistic: The Sistine Chapel was built by order of Pope Sixtus IV. Frescoes by Michelangelo, Botticelli, Perugino, and others. Built in 1473.

It is of course impossible, unless one has very special pull, but the ideal way to view the Sistine Chapel is to be alone, accompanied only by a delightful art expert willing to share his lore. As matters are now, one pushes one's way in with a horde of tourists babbling English, French, German, and Spanish and stands closely packed with head thrust back staring up at the ceiling—*The Creation of the World*—and along the walls and willy-nilly moves on when the particular lump of humanity in which one is embedded decides instinctively, like the birds, that it's time to migrate.

As they had been highly recommended we went also to the galleries in the Borghese Gardens, the lovely wooded park of Rome. The building itself dates from the Renaissance and is imposing, but the art was not for us. Sculpture exclusively, and if there's anything that strikes me as dull it's masses of colorless marble statues, cold and noble with blank eyes. We much preferred the puppet show, with indestructible Punch and Judy, that was in full swing with a little crowd laughing and cheer-

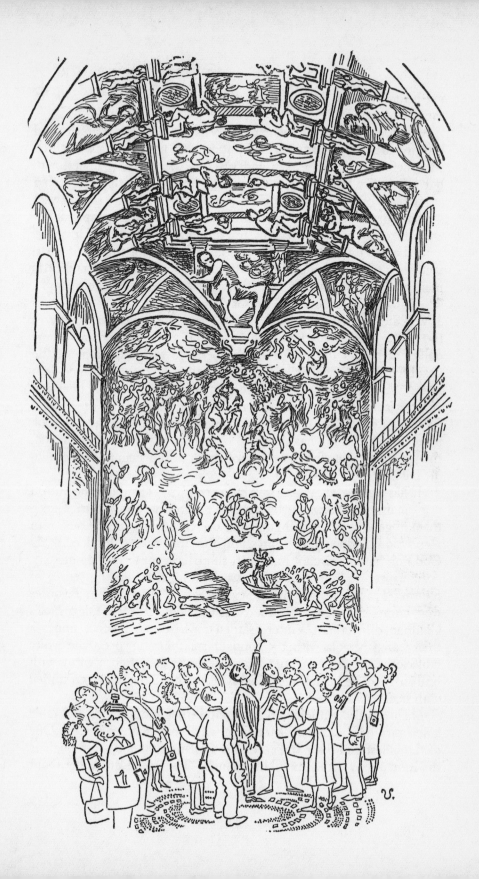

ing before it as we drove through the gardens in an open victoria in the late afternoon.

A museum that *is* a delight is the Villa Giulia, where are housed the treasures of an Etruscan civilization that flourished six hundred years before Christ. The jars and vases are beautiful, if impersonal, but things like safety pins and hairpins, mirrors and tiny sculptured animals are of human scale and endearing. There also we saw a sweet sarcophagus of terra cotta from the tomb of a married couple. They are half reclining and he has his arm around her shoulders. He sports a neat, pointed beard, their hair is beautifully curled, and she is wearing a long tunic with a pleated petticoat peeping beneath it and little pointed, flat-heeled laced shoes. Obviously they were a very chic couple. The Duke and Duchess of Windsor of their time.

We did a little shopping, but things were expensive, many of the shops frankly marking the merchandise in dollars and many dollars at that. I did persuade the doctor to take advantage of the beautiful Italian raw silk and a good Italian tailor who turned him into a veritable peacock, with evening clothes of midnight blue and an odd jacket of deep red. I considered he looked like the *Apollo Belvedere*, dressed, of course, and, being a man, though the trip took place in 1956, he still has the suits. I must say they look all right, too, though there is possibly a wee bit of strain in the vicinity of the middle button.

He has read the above and says rather coldly, "That about the button is a canard, but anyway, why shouldn't I still have my suits? I keep them in good repair. I still have that overcoat I bought in London in 1951, too." Suddenly an expression of alarm crossed his face. "My God, you haven't given it to a thrift shop, have you?" I have not.

An aspect of Roman life that we found a never-ending source of pleasure was the restaurants. They are *good*. Three of our favorites were unpretentious, but the food was delicious. One was Giggi Fazi's Giardino d'Inverno (Winter Garden), where one lunches under a thick-leafed pergola with the sunlight splashing down on the white tablecloths and flickering into a cage, against a great tree, atwitter with brilliantly colored parakeets. I highly recommend the tomatoes stuffed with rice.

Otello's is also outdoors under a grape arbor and has a central table laden with delicious fresh fruit from which one chooses dessert. One of the oldest and most Italian of the Italian restaurants—although as the Romans say with a rueful little laugh, "The Americans know about

this one, too"—we were taken to by Dr. Caldiero and Micol Fontana.
It is Trattoria Romolo, situated Trastevere, across or on the right bank
of the Tiber. On summer evenings one dines in the garden behind the
restaurant, and a gray cat gazes down unblinkingly from the old brick
wall, and when one comes to dessert, if the order is grapes, the waiter
simply reaches up into the arbor and cuts down a bunch of pale green
pearls. Followed by *caffè espresso*, it is an excellent way to finish a meal.

It is curious how quickly one can settle into a routine when traveling.
In the three and a half days that I could stay with Norton we found
immediately that one of the most pleasant times of the day came in
the late afternoon, when we returned from sight-seeing and shopping,
some of which I did without him, as he was spending a good deal of
time at the hospital. We would either arrive together or meet in our
hotel room to sort out and discuss our impressions. We would order
ice, pour long cool drinks, and he would devote himself to unloading
and reloading his camera, putting the rolls of used film into the little
yellow Kodak bags, and filling out the tags. Later we would bathe and
dress and go out to dinner. Very pleasant.

As soon as we arrived in Rome, I called Clare Luce, who was at
that time our ambassador to Italy. I had known Clare for a good
many years, for it will be remembered that she wrote *The Women*, a
play that was a much-discussed hit in its time, and I had a part in it.
She was away in Venice at the film festival. The day after she got back
to town I called again. It was shortly after noon and she asked Norton
and me to lunch with her. We would have done so with pleasure, but
couldn't make it, as we had already accepted an invitation from friends
who had rented a car and were downstairs waiting to drive us out to
Tivoli for luncheon and a visit to the Villa d'Este.

I was genuinely sorry to miss Clare, but the Villa d'Este can hardly
be called a punishment. The building itself is of little interest, but the
gardens, with the great cypresses and cool green shade, the ancient
moss-covered stone fountains, the cascades and jets of water plunging
and leaping in the sunshine, with rainbows shimmering through them
and the sweeping terraces overlooking *la campagna*, the Roman countryside, are unique.

We dined that night at the Osteria dell'Orso, a very swank restaurant
in a superb old house, part of which, so they swear, is a thousand years
old. Since this is Rome some of the stones may well have been there in
the year 900.

The next morning Norton drove me to the airport back along those other ancient stones of the Appian Way. He would be returning to New York in about ten days, bringing his patient when she had recovered enough to travel. There are tombs and statues beside the Appian Way, and as we turned off it to take the highway leading to the airfield, our driver pointed to a small villa and said, "That houses the most beautiful modern statue in Rome." "Oh?" we asked. "And what would that be?" He grinned. "Gina Lollobrigida lives there."

I thought that the doctor, who can't stand movies and frequently looks blank when a famous name is mentioned, showed a remarkably lively interest in this bit of information. "Of course," the driver continued, "she can't act. Still . . ." The two men looked at each other and sighed in fraternal unison.

As we were at the peak of the season when American tourists are thronging home, I was unable to get a direct flight from Rome to New York. Pan American was doing all in its power, even to trying to book me via Amsterdam, but Amsterdam would have none of me. Eventually the Rome office was able to get me on a flight to Paris. "Once there," they said, "something may break." I hoped that the "something" was not going to be my ardent belief that the wee people were watching over me. Saturday in New York was my deadline if I were going to make that night's broadcast of *Masquerade Party*. I liked to think I would not be fired, irrevocably, if I missed it; on the other hand I could not suppose that our producer, Herbert Wolf, would consider me the most darling member of the American Federation of Television and Radio Artists if I left him with an empty chair on his panel.

One reason that I was slightly smug in my conviction that a passage would be forthcoming was that David Parsons had said when we left New York and I told him I had to be back on Saturday "Go ahead. We'll get you home somehow." David is the brother of Geoffrey Parsons, head of the publicity department of Pan American and a singularly dependable citizen.

I arrived in Paris about two-thirty in the afternoon and rushed to the Pan Am counter at Orly. But of course! The diminutives had been at work, their little eyes snapping, the bells on their turned-up toes tinkling. There *was* a place on the 8-P.M. flight to New York, the company would put its lounge at my disposal for the afternoon. That was kind but dull. I telephoned the Geoffrey Parsonses. They had gone to Spain for the month of September, but Lutetia, their cook, whom I knew, was there. Would not Madame come to the apartment? Madame would with pleasure. I drove in from Orly through the pouring rain.

For once in my life I was in my adored Paris without the remotest desire to walk her inviting streets, sight-see, or shop. All I wanted was shelter from her cold streaming skies. In Drue's apartment I wrote her a long letter on her own stationery, smiling when I thought of the surprise she would get when she saw it. Lutetia brought me tea and a little later I asked for ice. Knowing Geoff, I felt he would not begrudge me a cold and warming martini before I set off on the trek back to Orly and the long hop home across the Atlantic.

I arrived at Idlewild Saturday morning with time to burn before showing up at the studio. When I walked into the make-up room that evening, the others looked up, Buff Cobb, Ogden Nash, Bobby Sherwood—"Hi," they said, "what kind of a week did you have?" "Oh, fine," I answered casually. "I've been to Rome." Their dropped jaws were very gratifying.

A year and not quite a month later we returned, but there was less of me than there had been. In July of 1957 my ulcer had become so fractious that Dr. Brown and assorted colleagues decided the best thing to do was to have a look at it. I was accordingly wheeled into the embroidery department of Roosevelt Hospital, and apparently what the gentlemen saw so entranced them they wanted it for their very own and a large section of my middle interior was removed.

Norton had been dear about the operation, but his apprehension was so apparent that his efforts to reassure me filled me with pity and furnished me, I'm afraid, with a little hilarity, too. He, obviously, was not going to do it. In the first place, he is not a surgeon, but a medical man, and in the second place, we all know the tradition that doctors never never take care of their own, don't we? Indeed it does sometimes seem that the dear boys overdo it when the little woman says wanly, "I don't feel so good," and the only reaction she gets from Hippocrates is either, "Well, take an aspirin, for God's sake," or possibly—and this when they are concerned—"Call up Bill or Tom or somebody," these latter being medical buddies on whom they are foisting the drag of an ailing loved one.

In my case one surgeon wouldn't do; we had a team of two from Roosevelt, the Doctors Sterling Mueller and Scudder Winslow; we had one from Cornell, Dr. Randolph Gepfert, whose interest lay in adjacent territory but who stood by just in case; and we had one, a trusted chum from the Rip Van Winkle Clinic in Hudson, New York, Dr. Caldwell B. Esselstyn, our dear giant Essie, whose function appeared

to be that of liaison officer. He would report to Norton on how things
were going, since my husband had said he would not care to witness the
proceedings. There were also of course to be a corps of anesthetists,
nurses, interested interns, and, as far as I could gather, The Man in the
Street if he happened to wander in. I assured Norton that I had no fear
of the operation itself, my confidence in my surgeons was absolute,
"But," I added, "I have a nagging little suspicion that I may be suf-
focated in the crush."

Apparently the police were on duty, firmly admonishing the crowd,
"Stand back, folks, back up there, take it easy, let the little lady
breathe." I came through all right.

When it came to a trip to Europe, which I promptly began nattering
for, that was something else again. Norton was dubious. The operation
had been of major proportions; did I feel well enough? Could we afford
it? Should he take time away from his office? Did I feel well enough? I
didn't feel superb, no, and rich we weren't; on the other hand, I'd had
my fill of abortive trips abroad. An offer to do a movie job in Munich
had had to be turned down because of an acute ulcer flare-up. An offer
of a role in *Ben-Hur* (nine months in Rome) had to be refused for the
same reason. When we'd planned to go to Europe on our own that
spring, a violent indisposition canceled our plans, and the nearest we'd
got to Dublin, our first proposed port of call, was the travel folders, because, "Supposing your ulcer ruptures in an Irish peat bog, what will I
do with you? Or Venice that you're so hell bent on. Peritonitis in the
Grand Canal, that's all we need!"

This time I was determined. The worst that could happen would be
that I'd feel awful, but any danger was past. And as the doctor said himself, he was between the devil and the deep blue sea. Travel is exhaust-
ing, and if we went I might have some wretched moments. On the other
hand, if we stayed home and I fretted and moped—and it was pretty
clear that the firm of Fretting and Moping would be in high gear—
that wouldn't be good either. There was a further point. None of us gets
younger and we live in parlous times. There is no guarantee that because a city has stood for a thousand years it is going to be there tomorrow. "See it now" is what I say.

I urged, I coaxed, I persuaded. I spoke glowingly of the beautiful
pictures he would be able to take in Venice—you guessed it. We left
on Friday, September 20, en route for Lisbon.

Our great Pan American bird touched down at 6:45 A.M. We had
been flying among the brilliant stars and toward a crescent moon, but

as we came down the sky was turning gray. The first sight we saw, after an amiable customs official who had no intention of opening luggage at *that* ungodly hour, was a stout woman in a faded blue smock, with small earrings in her pierced ears, and carrying under her arm a big bundle of morning papers, and we knew we were home again in Europe. In the U.S.A. I have never seen these old girls, but abroad they're familiar figures.

We went to our hotel, the Embaixador, for a few hours' sleep and found it clean, modern, and cramped for space. Before lying down we hung out the window to see what we could of Lisbon and at once noted an oddity. The building across the street seemed to be an apartment house in which there were also some offices. This was not too unusual, but what caught our attention was the fact that one floor was apparently a convent, for through the open window we could see nuns and young novices at prayer. If one must take the veil, that should be a good way to do it—more outside contacts. One would have to go out for marketing and errands of mercy and might meet interesting people in the elevator.

After a little rest we started our sight-seeing under the auspices of Albert, our guide, but how much more than that! Encyclopedia of Lisbon and the surrounding countryside, banker, historian, chauffeur, and bearer of charmed life.

With Albert at the wheel we did not drive along the roads; we flew three feet above the surface accelerating on the turns. The automobile was Detroit made, but obviously a special model: no low gear. Also the brakes must have been in A-1 condition, as they had never been applied since leaving the assembly line. We took every mountain road, and they were many and tortuous, on high and on the horn. It was quite stimulating. To my intense annoyance the doctor, who is an expert driver himself, except that I think he tends to ride too closely upon the tail of the fellow in front of him, was more fascinated than alarmed by Albert's excesses. When frightened, I tend to the profane. I fear that I let fly a string of expletives and asterisks, balloons and stars the gist of which was, "Tell this son of an unwed mother to slow down." My dear one patted my knee and said soothingly, "Now, now, take it easy. No point making him mad." No point making him mad! Norton claims it was the philosophical approach, but I suspected then and still do that it was craven. On the rare occasions when we fire cooks—usually they fire us—it is I who have to go to the kitchen to perform the grisly rite. "The home," says His Lordship expansively, "is woman's domain."

The few flat bits of Lisbon we saw on foot were lovely. I have seldom seen prettier parks or more colorful gardens, great sweeping expanses of bloom. In the Edward VII Park there is a lake with swans and a unique conservatory. One side is cut from a wall of solid rock, and from it extends an enormous lath house covering, I should think, several acres. The lath roof is high enough to accommodate palm and fern trees and is upheld by slender posts twined with vines. There are winding paths, waterfalls, and little streams, lovely flowers, and a ground cover between moss and fern, delicate, green and fresh. As part of the conservatory there is a spacious loggia open on two sides, with a stage at one end for concerts. We meandered through it for a long time, enjoying its fragrant coolness.

After the park we went to lunch at the Gondola, an unpretentious but good restaurant where we met by chance a charming couple from Boston named Wallis. In Boston they would never have spoken to us or we to them, but one of the pleasures of travel is the kind of free-masonry that springs up between Americans in a foreign land.

We went with them to see the ruins of the Moorish Castel de São Jorge, high on a hill overlooking the Tagus River and the harbor. It was taken from the Moors by the first king of Portugal with the as-sistance of a co-operative group of crusaders who, en route to the Holy Land, took time out to lend a hand before they sailed. One approaches the castle through the old part of the city, up and up through steep winding cobbled streets. The streets are so narrow and turn so sharply it is impossible to see around corners, so men with paddles in their hands, one side painted green, the other red, are stationed at intervals to signal the tramcars to stop and go. It's more personal than electric signals and quite as efficient. With the perpendicular streets and the marine view the city provides San Franciscans would feel right at home. Another fine Lisbon sight is the museum where they have the royal coaches, probably the finest collection on the Continent; carriages ranging from light, delicate, swift phaetons to the great, lumbering padded rooms on wheels that rolled along the roads churning up the mud and dust of Europe through many centuries. One of the most amusing and practical was a model, very like a sulky, that, small as it was, boasted a "convenience," a trap door that opened in the seat.

I should say the most striking feature of Lisbon is the color. The houses are shell pink and watermelon pink and a shade, forgotten since my childhood, ashes of roses. They are gray and slate blue and brilliant blue, ocher and umber and chalk white, with terra-cotta tile roofs and shining green shutters. Those that are not washed with color are faced with patterned tiles often two designs to a façade; the lower story one pattern, the upper another. There used to be a law about painting the houses every so often and tiles were cheaper. They are also marvelously decorative. Lisbon is a decorative city. Norton got a remarkable picture of a courtyard; of striped awnings over tiers of balconies, of clothes hanging on lines, and of a curving outdoor fire escape flung down the jutting side of the house next door. There are trees in the lower left foreground and the whole thing is patterned in squares of washed blue and mulberry, rose and olive green and powder yellow, like a cubist painting.

We did not think the Portuguese a handsome race, many of them are squat and swarthy, but they are picturesque, especially the women, passing through the streets bearing great brass water cans on their heads or huge bundles of greens or flat baskets piled high with asters and carnations and dahlias.

That is what I find so appealing about Europe, what we were to find so appealing about Asia. Life itself is in the streets. In France the children carry home the long delicious loaves; living kids about to eat visible bread. Here at home the cotton bread wrapped in waxed paper is shelved in supermarkets. In Portugal the women transport flowers that one can afford to buy. Here, with the rare exception of the few horse-drawn wagons laden with geraniums and tulips that illuminate the streets of New York in spring, the flowers are all behind glass in expensive shops. The human element is being abolished, and in every department.

There was a time when if we had to go to a public lavatory we went. If there was an attendant he or she was tipped. Today we have pay toilets, and God help the hapless citizen whose need is great if he has not got a dime in his pocket.

It is confusing and contrary to the American credo, but in backward countries where *people* function just plain everyday living can be very rewarding.

We were rewarded, our first evening in Lisbon, by dining at the Hotel Aviz. It has the finest restaurant in Portugal and one of the best in Europe. We had wanted to stay at the Aviz, for it is the most charming hotel in the city, but it has only twenty-five rooms, and the government holds a block of those and we were unable to get reservations. One thing that struck us was the small number of diners enjoying the excellent food. We counted only seventeen in the hour and a half we were there. Expense, I imagine, was one reason; while not exorbitant, prices were comparatively high, but there was another reason, too, which we discovered the following evening after our sight-seeing.

We drove in the morning to Pena, an old castle high on a mountain-top by way of Estoril, passing on the highway the enormous barracks-like Jeronimos Monastery, where Vasco da Gama is buried. Estoril is all right; Atlantic ocean, sand, a large hotel, casino, tennis courts, a typical European resort but nothing special that you'd travel miles to see. Pena is something else again. Perched upon its mountain with one of those classic, limitless views of the country and the sea, it has a golden onion dome on one turret and its stone- and tilework are superb. There is a stucco wall washed in lavender, and, upholding an archway, columns of carved, twisted stone rope. I fell in love with the urns bordering the mounting cobbled driveway. They too are stone, carved in a dozen different patterns of basket weave, and are filled with boxwood.

Winding down from the castle, Albert, the demon chauffeur, expatiated with gestures, both hands off the wheel, on where he was taking us for lunch. We went careening around curves at a mere sixty, the horn one untempered shriek; motorcycles and bicycles, children and chickens scattering before us like leaves before the gale. Since I am writing this book, we obviously survived, but there were a couple of moments when it looked like a near thing.

The place to which Albert shepherded us, however, if "shepherd" is the word for so precipitate an escort, redeemed all: the Seteais, the Seven Echoes. It is a hotel like a baby Versailles, done in exquisite taste. It has only eighteen rooms, so hardly anybody gets in, reservations are made years in advance, but we can all dream.

It is set in a pretty garden and the walls are painted with airy and elegant frescoes. Aubusson carpets cover the polished floor, the furniture is beautiful and the food superb. The reading room is paneled in white, has beige curtains and a carved crystal chandelier, while over the stair well hang candles in a brassbound crystal basket. The bedroom suites are done in delicate striped papers, and the place is run like a private villa presided over by a hospitable and sophisticated hostess.

Aside from its allure the Seteais does not have much to offer in the way of activities, but the thing to do would be to stay there if one were fortunate enough, and drive down to Estoril for bathing and the Whirl.

From this jewel we drove to Sintra Palace. The kitchens with the enormous ovens and domed and funneled roof through which the smoke escaped are curious and worth seeing; otherwise it is not particularly rewarding, with the exception of one of the great halls, which has a hundred thirty-six magpies painted on the ceiling. The guide told us that this was because the king was caught kissing a lady, not the queen, in that room and the palace rang with gossip. In disgust the monarch ordered the birds to be painted, signifying, "The ladies of this court talk too much." That cheer you hear is from the throats of ten million married men.

Returning to Lisbon, we passed two or three open-air markets and persuaded Albert to stop long enough to let us browse around. The fish market in the harbor, with its great cleaning sheds, the colorful boats, drawn up on the sloping, roughly cobbled mole, and the glittering silver piles of fish tossed onto coarse orange sacking, presided over by women in yellow skirts and lilac sweaters, men in brilliant blue shirts—all this had been picturesque and pungent, and so were the country markets. Under the trees the scene glowed with color, the women sitting beside baskets and sacks that bulged and overflowed with emerald peppers and golden onions, russet pears and flat green beans. They sold produce and pottery, china and gleaming tin and aluminum kitchen utensils.

We bought a little fruit to sustain us and at dinner that evening discovered where most of the Portuguese eat. We went to a *fado* and there they were. These are small restaurants, a cross between a French bistro and a Greek *taverna* frequented by the *fado* singers. The *fados* are infinitely "sad sonks" sung in a harsh, minor key, and in them lovers part, hearts crack and disintegrate, and as the evening wears on there is a gentle plop-plop of tears into the wine and everybody wallows happily in *Weltschmerz*.

I had one of my bad evenings, one of the times when the operation was kicking back at me that Norton had feared, but even through my malaise I was charmed by the atmosphere.

Our target had been Italy, and we went via Lisbon because we had never been there and it was en route, but the next day we took off for Rome. Nina Beckwith met us. We felt practically like returning natives as we drove along the Appian Way with happy exclamations of recognition. This time we stayed at the Eden Hotel and looked out upon a small formal patch of garden with vine-covered walls and a tall cypress sentinel.

As we were going to be in Italy for some little time, I went to Fontana's to order a few clothes. I could have a couple of fittings, and they would be sent on to Venice. Micol, as I have said, was already a friend, but there are three Fontana sisters in the business; Micol, Zoe, and Giovanna. There are also Mamma and Papa and Zoe's twenty-three-year-old daughter Gioia who designs for the boutique.

For two hundred years the Fontanas have been dressmakers and tailors, so they may fairly be said to have grown up in the business. They came originally from Parma, the home of violets, *prosciutto*—the ham so delectable when cut paper thin—and the world-famous Parmesan cheese, so delectable when freshly grated. Driven from home by the exigencies of World War II, they migrated to Rome, where, even with food at a premium, so strong was the family urge to stitch that they once bartered twenty-two pounds of potatoes for a length of magnificent embroidered blue fabric and started the dressmaking establishment that is today in the *haute-couture* group of Europe.

Between them the girls whip up six collections a year and boast some glittering figures among their clientele. Royalty is shrinking, but they have dressed Princess Maria Pia and Queen Maria Jose di Savoia. They enhanced Clare Boothe Luce when she was our ambassador to Italy. They have draped the notable physiques of Gina Lollobrigida, Ava Gardner, and Elizabeth Taylor. Mrs. John Cabot Lodge is a customer, and so is Lorraine Manville, sister of the Tommy who thinks so highly of the institution of marriage that he has had, as of going to press, eleven wives.

My order was far more humble than those of these glittering ladies, but, owing to our always-brief stays in either Paris or Rome, it was the first opportunity I had had in a long time to order and have clothes fitted in a first-rate European house. The pleasure was great. Even Norton, who in true American-husband fashion usually hasn't the foggiest notion of what I have on, behaved like a Parisian *boulevardier* and came and sat in the salon while I tried on various models and emerged from the dressing room to display them and await his pleasure.

I did my ordering in the morning. In the afternoon we went to visit the Forum. Would that Elizabeth Bowen had at that time written her book I have already mentioned. Through the magic of her pen the Roman world rises again. Her knowledge of historical facts is formidable, but upon them she has brought to bear her finely honed mind and writer's imagination, and the consequence is that the reader views the city on two levels, or perhaps it is better to say through two layers, ancient and contemporary. She also speaks highly of a guide book written by Dorothy Robathan called Monuments of Ancient Rome which is on sale in Roman bookstores.

The Forum is sunk lower than the present city so that it seems a cup brimming with history, although actually its shape is oblong. What appealed to me even more than the tawny moldering stones—and I am a great one for ancient stones, finding a blessed sanctuary in old graveyards—was the quiet that existed in the heart of the noisy modern metropolis. For most of the afternoon we wandered among the columns and tumbled boulders; where the marble façades had fallen away, noting the narrow, mellowed brickwork that has held through the centuries.

One can of course spend months in Rome, discovering her splendors for oneself, but I have never thought that limited time should discourage the traveler. Better a superficial acquaintanceship with the great art and monuments of the world attained through alert eyes, ears, and a sense of history than no acquaintanceship at all.

If neither money nor time were considerations I suppose the ideal way to travel would be to go all over the world sipping its wonders, deciding which appealed to us most, and then returning to those special favorites, staying long enough really to savor and to know them.

We visited the Coliseum again, too and as we stood there a jet shot across the sky, the thin white line of the twentieth century streaking across the first.

I was anxious to see the dressing rooms in which the Christians prepared to meet the lions, but they were closed to the public.

Having passed up St. Peter's the year before, this time we were determined on it, crossing the vast forecourt to the Bernini colonnade and the entrance itself. When Europeans were building their cities they didn't think of their countries as small; they thought they had space and accordingly built vast piazzas and splendid vistas and the whole world has profited.

As so many of the great Catholic churches are Gothic, the airy splendor and the light of St. Peter's come as a surprise, but it was built during the Renaissance, when magnificence and color were the idiom of the day. The construction took one hundred eighty-one years to complete, starting in 1445 and ending in 1626.

To me the treasure of St. Peter's is Michelangelo's *Pietà*, the poignant statue of Mary at the foot of the cross, the dead Christ across her knees. I care less for the imposing, seated statue of the saint himself, his big toe worn by the kisses of the faithful.

On one of our evenings we dined alone on the terrace of the Pallazi in the hills just outside Rome. Formerly the house Mussolini built for his mistress, Clara Petacci, who was killed with him as they were trying to flee Italy, it is now a delightful restaurant still owned by her family, who rent it to the present tenants. As a private house it is a bit overpowering, but I suppose the original tenants saw it as a trysting place for the world's leading politicians and diplomats for many years to come. It is certainly an excellent example of not counting your chickens before they're hatched.

Another evening we went to a performance given by Vittorio Gassman, the Italian actor who appeared in the movie *War and Peace*. The play was called *A Flea in Your Ear*. He was assisted by a company of vigorous young people and the scene was an after-the-theater actors' party where they discussed and illustrated various styles of acting through the years.

It was the first time we had been in a theater where some of the seats were equipped with earphones through which, as at the United Nations, one heard a simultaneous translation into English of what was being said on the stage. This was later done in New York when the Japanese kabuki players came over for a limited engagement.

The morning we left Rome bound for the hill towns and Venice, we had a slight domestic contretemps. The good doctor, our hired chauffeur, and our friend John Fornacca, manager of the American Express office, had decided on a nine-o'clock departure. Micol Fontana and I had decided on a nine-o'clock fitting for the clothes I had ordered from her. The irresistible force met the immovable object head on and there was a small explosion.

Actually our departure was delayed only forty-five minutes, but as we rolled away from the door of the Sorelle Fontana a few arrow-sharp family Looks shot around the car. In a few minutes, however, the doctor recovered his good humor and suddenly he began to chuckle. "What is it?" I asked. He shook his head. "When I was a medical student selling pints of my blood to get money for tuition I never thought the day would come when I'd be starting off on a tour of the Italian hill towns sitting in a car beside a dame wearing a mink jacket."

We decided that the blood-selling was probably the finer hour but the tour was more fun.

Umbria is beautiful. We drove through the hilly, meticulously terraced countryside under high, bright clouds, past olive groves and vineyards, the vines trained over stunted elms. From time to time as we bowled by them, herds of goats shoving and bleating compressed themselves along the side of the road like a stream suddenly forced into a narrow channel. We passed yokes of gentle oxen working in the fields beside the most modern tractors and we drove slowly by the women at the washing troughs in the public squares of little villages where, as they have done for hundreds of years, they still beat out the family laundry on big stones. It is a far cry from laundromats and detergents, and I should think rough on the women as well as the clothes, but on the whole probably a more sociable way of life. Machines have their place, but it's hard to enjoy a good gossip with the automatic washer.

Orvieto, where we were stopping for luncheon, breaks upon the traveler suddenly, crowning its steep hill that rises abruptly from the Umbrian plain. It seemed oddly familiar, but that is the quality of Italy; the country really looks like the landscapes in Italian primitives. It has followed the artists faithfully. I had been to Orvieto years before, the summer I was sixteen, and remembered that it was famous for its cathedral and its wine. When one of the popes—his name and number I have forgotten—went junketing through his realm, couriers went on ahead, advance men whose function it was, in the modern idiom, to case the joint. They sought out lodgings and sampled the food and wine. When the latter was especially good, they wrote upon the town wall, "*Est*," meaning "Is" or "This is it." After tasting the bounty of Orvieto, so runs the tale, in their delight they wrote in letters large, if possibly wavering, "Est Est Est." The wine of Orvieto does not travel well, but in its native habitat . . . how right the couriers were.

I remembered dimly that the cathedral was lovely, but I had forgotten its delicacy and shimmering beauty, its façade striped with black and pink marble glittering with colored and golden mosaics. Its only drawback for the tourist is the difficulty of photographing it. The square on which it fronts is not very large, and one must retreat up a narrow little street opposite and even then, unless one has a very wide lens, shoot at an angle to get it all in.

Refreshed by our good lunch and the delicious white wine, we set out for Assisi and the frescoes of Giotto. We spent only two or three brief hours there, and that was a mistake; Assisi merits longer. It also merits scrutiny early in the day. We arrived toward teatime, the high, bright clouds of the morning had lowered and darkened and in the church of St. Francis the great murals were hard to discern. To me those Giottos, so simple, so cunningly designed, so rich in color, are great art, but also they have a quality that much great art does not.

GREAT ART, in caps, tends to the monumental. Michelangelo, Tintoretto, Rubens, boy of bulge and burst, heroic in scale. Giotto is appealing. The frescoes are naïve and gentle and human. Since they glow today from the very same walls on which he painted them in the late thirteenth century and in the same climate, I suppose mere tourists should not complain, but it is nevertheless maddening that they are so hard to see. The church, especially on a cloudy day, is crepuscular. God forbid that the frescoes should be debauched by "effects," but a restrained lighting expert using the best modern methods could make them, quite simply, visible.

In the lower crypt of the church are St. Francis relics. One thinks of him as such a gentle soul, standing benign guard over countless bird baths in countless gardens from Italy to Santa Barbara, it comes as a disappointment to learn that he was a fanatic mortifying the flesh, wearing a hair shirt and a cruel girdle that pricked and chafed his body. The saint complex is demanding. I guess you can be a saint or comfortable, but you can't be a comfortable saint. St. Francis himself, as he lay dying, is supposed to have repented over maltreating his body, which he referred to as "my brother the ass," but as F. L. Lucas, in his book of brilliant essays, *The Greatest Problem*, so crisply observes, "He should have thought of it sooner."

The church and the Giottos are Assisi's fame, but in the upper square stands the small and exquisite temple of Minerva. It is the color of dark honey and built long before the birth of Christ, is today part of a convent housing a deeply secluded order of nuns. As we sat at a table in the square over our apéritif—I had tried for tea, but Latins do not take kindly to it—someone came up to a small wicket window. A nun's hand reached out and took a proffered envelope and was withdrawn again, its owner's face remaining hidden.

Strengthened by the apértif—I am aware there is a good deal of eating and drinking in this account, but it is a large part of touring; one requires frequent refueling—we rejoined Nello, our chauffeur, and headed toward Perugia. There are still many traces of the medieval fortress that the city was, but the old walls are largely obscured by modernity and it is very noisy.

We stayed at the Brufani Palace Hotel, with a magnificent view of the town, of the terra-cotta tiled roofs pink and copper in tone, with the bloom of velvet corduroy and of the plain and the mountains beyond. Unfortunately the church bells started before six o'clock in the morning, clanging without harmony, reverberating through the narrow streets and inspiring, I am afraid, not so much spiritual contemplation as irritation at having been awakened to godliness at an ungodly hour.

There is a lovely thirteenth-century fountain in Perugia and two superb interiors: the Merchants' Guild and the fourteenth-century stock exchange, with frescoes by Raphael and Perugino and magnificently carved panels and benches almost like pews—in those days too there was some confusion between God and Mammon—and a small adjoining chapel, its altar bright with painted bouquets. There is also a pretty parklike square where we strolled after dinner.

Of the hill towns of Italy, although choice is not easy, one may probably say that Siena, in Tuscany, is the jewel. Siena, with its spacious Piazza del Campo shaped like a lion's-paw shell—worn by the centuries to a mildly concave contour highlighted by its magnificent Gothic town hall and campanile.

For the *duomo* one rings out all the adjectives—superb, imposing, magnificent, colorful, yet while living up to them all it manages to achieve the seemingly impossible: intimacy. Its appeal is more personal than St. Peter's, its treasure of marble and mosaic richer than Orvieto's. Built in the fourteenth century, it has survived the ages to uplift the hearts and gladden the eyes of the millions of travelers who have gazed upon it as well as the lucky Sienese who live beside it.

We lunched in sunshine and shadow on the terrace of La Speranza, a restaurant facing the town hall across the piazza, and did the doctor have a happy time! He could hardly down his *pasta*, so busy was he with picture-taking. Three cameras, the Leica, the Minox, and the Stereo. My snapping turtle.

Great festivals take place twice a year in Siena on July 2 and August 16. The town relives its splendid past when the young men of its seventeen wards don costumes of the fifteenth century and march in procession in an agitation of whipping banners and martial music, afterward competing in a wild horse race down the square. The festivals are called Palio, which means "Prize," and some year we plan to be there. Will the doctor get pictures on that great day!

From Siena the road winds on to San Gimignano, where the patient oxen walk the furrows and the strange, silent, square towers, skyscrapers

of the Middle Ages, rise into the blue. Architecturally San Gimignano
is unique, but it is entirely a relic of the past. Other than coopers making great vats for wine we saw no signs of industry and a young man
leaning idle and sullen against a wall, dragging on a cheap cigarette,
seemed to symbolize what must be the moral climate of the youth of
the tiny community.

We wandered about for perhaps an hour and a half and then headed
for Florence. To readers contemplating an Italian trip: *Stay* in Florence. Stay several days. Remember it is a city in which many people
live permanently by choice. Again, as in Assisi, we were the too speedy
Browns. Florence is a rich and varied feast, indigestible if gulped too
quickly. We arrived toward evening and went at once to our hotel, the
Excelsior. Our room was pleasant, our bath de luxe, and the noise
frightful. My diary is studded with little yelps: "Noise terrible," "Noise
hellish," "My God, what noise." I feel like Jenny Carlyle, who had an
allergy to noise too and was forever complaining about the inns in
which she stayed, yet oddly enough, writing these words, I fail to re-
capture my discomfiture. If I had not recorded the offensive sounds, I
would not have remembered them at all.

I shall not try to improve on or implement the several tons of books
about Florence written by experts, residents, and the knowledgeable in
general. They are available in all bookstores. I shall simply say, What
a city! The shops! The good food! The art! *Molto bello, magnifico.* Go.

Our pleasure was heightened by a reunion with two old friends,
Gladys Swarthout and her husband, Frank Chapman, who have a
delightful small villa in the hills outside the city at Scandicci. On five
acres they raise not only their own vegetables and flowers but also vines
for the wine they drink as well as the Cranshaw melons Frank sells
to the big hotels. He's built them into quite a business.

The evening we dined with them was one of the pleasantest of our
trip. One item, although this was pure American, particularly sticks in
my memory. The before-dinner martinis mixed by the host were served
to each guest in little individual silver cocktail shakers and you could
pour your own dividend. They charmed me, and I have always meant
to try to find similar ones. I remember, too, the delicious string beans
served at dinner, the skinny little *fagiolini.* Frank came next day to the
hotel, bringing us some seeds, and we brought them home and kept
them all winter in a ventilated tin can and planted them in our own
garden next spring and they came up but were practically the size of
American beans. It must have to do with the soil, just as tarragon,

over which I strive most earnestly, still has a more pungent taste in
France and Italy than it does at home.

The Chapmans kindly listed for us the absolute Must Sees of art—
inevitably many of the Would Like Tos had to be eliminated, owing
to our curtailed schedule—and also guided us to the best shops, although I find that despite the fact that I have no bump of location at
all, geographically speaking—even when the sun is setting right in my
eyes I'm not sure I'm facing west—I can wing, unerring as a homing
pigeon, to the costliest shops in any given city.

We started on our sight-seeing with a bull's-eye, the Piazza della
Signoria, where stand some of Florence's most magnificent sculptures
and where a circle in the pavement marks the spot where the monk
Savonarola was hanged as a heretic in 1498. We also saw his cell in the
monastery of San Marco, where Fra Angelico painted his lovely
frescoes, including the tender *Annunciation*.

In the straw market near the piazza is a seated wild boar, a classic
bronze beast whose snout has been kissed to a brilliant patina by super-
stitious tourists who wish to come back to Florence. In Rome you
throw pennies into the Trevi Fountain; in Florence you kiss a pig.

We saw also the fountain of Neptune, with the lovely Diana slender
and smooth, curiously reminiscent of the sculpture of the modern Carl
Milles.

The campanile and duomo of Florence are world-renowned and need
small comment from me, but the interior I thought prosaic, or maybe
I had just had enough churches.

We saw too the baptistery of San Giovanni, with its doors designed
by Ghiberti. His authorship of these masterpieces is one of the few
lessons I seem to have retained from my school days, another being
that if you plaster a wet handkerchief on a mirror it will dry as smoothly
as though ironed. When traveling, this latter nugget is the more useful.

Standing in front of the baptistery, I was reverently focusing for a
photograph of what I believed to be the door that Michelangelo
had called the Gates of Paradise—artists spoke courteously of each
other in those days—when my dear husband pointed out that although
my door was a good one the Gates were on the other side. I was hum-
bled, but actually it didn't make much difference. There was such a
crowd in front of the right one I couldn't have got near it with my
camera anyway.

We visited the National Museum and saw the *David* by Michelangelo, and although what I am about to set down will cause me to

be stoned in the streets, I shall say it anyhow. To me David's head looks big. I would not have the effrontery to say *too* big, but *kind* of big. Yet the lad is still incomparable, a figure that, despite changing fashions in the medium, will probably always remain the quintessence of the sculptor's art.

Near him stands another piece, also by Michelangelo, an unfinished work. Emerging from the block of marble is the figure of the dead Christ supported by two disciples. The straining effort of the two men as they half-carry, half-drag the heavy, exhausted body, the body itself emptied of life, is deeply moving.

Relieving the sorrow nearby hang two enchanting tapestries: one the birth of Eve, in which the lady, with the most comical and anticipatory smile, stands waiting for Adam to wake up and see the tomato surprise that is his; and the other, of the animals going two by two into the ark. Beguiling beasties are a pair of porcupines abristle with excitement, the ham astronauts of their day.

Our last morning in Florence was memorable and shows what you can do if you rise with the dawn and release a burst of energy for a final onslaught on art. The treasures of Florence went down for the count. We first "did" the Boboli Gardens, very disappointing; dusty, dry, and bedraggled. The adjoining Pitti Palace is, however, a delight. I thought the rooms, with their damask-covered walls, rococo stoves, and elaborate fireplaces, more interesting than the pictures. The Medici Chapel is spacious, octagonal in shape, twilit in tone, and of green, rose, and gray marble. It houses a *Medea* by—you guessed it!—Michelangelo. Are there any other Italian sculptors? Well, yes—Leonardo.

From the Pitti we went to the Riccardi Palace to gaze upon a glorious achievement—Benozzo Gozzoli's presentation of the *Journey of the Magi to Bethlehem*. A brilliant company crowds the walls of the tiny chapel. The horses stepping proudly are magnificently caparisoned, there are leopards on leashes with jewel-studded collars, the crowns glitter, the opulent costumes are splashed with gold and crimson and emerald, and behind the thronging figures rise the terraced hillsides and the dark, pointed cypresses of the Italian countryside. The whole procession is coruscating and infinitely rich. There, by God, ride kings! And they ride in total blackness. How they were ever painted is a miracle, because today one views them by arc lights, and at the time they were done, the only possible illumination was candles, torches, or oil lamps, yet the work of this, so to speak, blind master sings as do the symphonies of the deaf Beethoven.

Drunk on the glory of the Gozzolis, we had a sobering cup of coffee and girded ourselves for the big push, the Lucullan feast; the Uffizi Gallery. The Uffizi Gallery is U-shaped, its contents definitely U. Since there are detailed guidebooks and books with costly colored plates and reproductions ad infinitum of the treasures of this vast palace, I will content myself by saying that it is there one finds Botticelli's *Venus* on her sea shell and the enchantingly lovely *Primavera*, her diaphanous gown strewn with blossoms.

One also may view Raphael's famed *Madonna of the Goldfinch*. From the testimony that endures on canvas it is obvious that very few ladies of that era went in for Metrecal. But although I prefer the lissome to the obese, I do think modern women are pushing to the point of absurdity their passion for the spare look.

One would assume that the great Da Vinci's *Madonna of the Rocks*, with its entrancing angel, one of the most exquisite female heads ever painted, would be found there on home ground, but it was scooped up by the Louvre years ago. There is, however, Leonardo's self-portrait of his old age, the very image of God the Father. There also is the Laocoön group—two of them, in fact, and you can have 'em.

In every gallery in Italy, indeed in all Europe, there are endless versions of St. Sebastian being pierced by arrows, and the good doctor finally bogged down. He really hated St. Sebastian. The skill with which the poor bloke was painted, composition, anguished expression, arrangement of masses and air space, underpainting, middle distances . . . it made no difference to my dear one that the masters of art had been moved by the possibilities inherent in the legend; he hated him. "Don't tell me he was a martyr," he snapped. "He was simply arrow-prone." He also got pretty fed up on bare feet. All those barefooted saints and apostles. "Didn't they have *shoes* in those days? They could at least have afforded a pair of sandals, couldn't they?" He took a scunner against the whole kit and caboodle.

An *objet d'art* that had caught his fancy was a modern bronze cat done by an American on exhibition at the Galleria Schneider in Rome. What with the cost of the trip, we felt we shouldn't buy him, and both of us have regretted it to this day.

By the time we finished with the Uffizi we were, shall I say, fatigued by the morning's work. We looked with some apprehension at our legs. Surely they were worn off to the knees? Even if they had been it was worth it, but that is *not* the way to see museums. As usual, however, the hounds of time were on our traces. After a revivifying lunch at

the Grand Hotel, where Frank Chapman came to bid us good-by, we set off for Ravenna. We stayed the night at Ravenna because it broke the long trip from Florence to Venice, but it's one of the dreariest spots on the map, and the Jolly Hotel is not. The whole town, in fact, is Dogpatch. That it is a strong communist center probably contributes to the over-all soul-destroying drabness; to make it at all palatable, one has to concentrate very hard on the fact that it was the last link with civilization before the Dark Ages set in in Europe. The food was indifferent and the beds of the hotel had been rifled from the baggage train of Attila the Hun.

Vasiliv

There is one lyric reason for going to Ravenna, but make the town a stop-over for a mediocre luncheon rather than for the night. The reason is the mosaics. They were done between the third and seventh centuries and are unique. The scenes from the Christian legend and the procession of saints in Sant' Apollinare Nuovo and in the house of the Emperor Theodoric, blazing with gold and color and a marvelously used white, are truly beautiful.

A delicious treat following Ravenna is Padua, where one thinks of Petruchio, and perhaps even more of Cole Porter than of Shakespeare because of the witty lyrics of *Kiss Me, Kate*—"I've Come to Wive It Wealthily in Padua." From there it is little more than half an hour to Venice. Two cities in which it is impossible to be disappointed are New York and the Bride of the Adriatic. In New York one expects sky-scrapers and gets them, the most soaring, imaginative, and beautiful in the world. In Venice one expects canals and crumbling palaces and there they are. Venice is the romanticist's dream come true.

We arrived by car, and just as years before, when arriving by train on my girlhood trip, I had been struck by the quiet of the city, so it was again; no roar, no honking horns. We got out on the pier, bade farewell to Nello, our nice chauffeur, had our luggage loaded into a gondola, and took off for the Gritti Palace Hotel. I can only say that it is a hotel to which we dream of someday returning, for Commenda-tore Masproni purveys excellent food, excellent service, and heavenly beds. It was the last day of September, and the weather was overcast and rainy, but the muted colors of those beautiful façades rising out of the water had an appeal all their own. We traveled by gondola for reasons of romance, but there are motorboats in Venice just as we have taxis, and the busses are *vaporetti*—ferryboats. Almost everybody uses them because they are very cheap and the private motorboat fares are high.

We had a corner room on the Grand Canal and on our first day—we arrived about four in the afternoon—very little of the tourist's house-keeping—unpacking, laundry, postcards—got done, we spent so much time hanging out the window. I did discipline myself to the extent of writing brief notes to accompany our several letters of introduction, which had been given us by our Washington friends, Alice Leone Moats and her mother. With one exception—and we learned later that the lady had been away—everyone replied with invitations to dinner or cocktails. Norton and I felt a little ashamed, remembering how a letter of introduction to us in New York has more than once elicited a rather irritable, "Oh, Lord, what are we going to do with these people?" I will say in our defense that usually at home we are both working hard, but just the same the attitude of Europeans, even those who do work, is apt to be more cordial than that of New Yorkers.

During our week in Venice we had some rain and it was pretty chilly, but we never tired of leaning over our balcony watching the life of the city floating and chugging and churning by us. We never tired of watching the slim black gondolas laden with produce nudge their way into the narrow canal that was the service entrance of the hotel. Sometimes in the evenings a boatload of singers would go drifting past our windows. They favored "Santa Lucia," largely for the tourist trade, I'm sure, but it was still nostalgic, still potent in weaving a web of memory for lovers.

Our windows overlooked one of the loveliest of Italian churches, the domed Santa Maria della Salute, and on our first morning we went through that other gem, San Marco. Our initiation into the vast piazza and the huge many-domed cathedral was, so to speak, a marine view, for the rain pelted down relentlessly, and we were happy to scurry into Florian's for hot chocolate and coffee. Except for a few hurrying pedestrians the great square was empty, even the famed pigeons having taken shelter. The upper façade and fretted silhouette of San Marco against the sky are incredible in their richness and variety. The arches, the glowing mosaics, the pointed cupolas sheltering statues, the famous four horses prancing, the winged lion, the haloed saint on top the six winged angels, the balconies, and the starry cross . . . they have left nothing out. It is exuberant, busy, yet somehow disciplined and marvelous.

Later we lunched at Ribotto's, where the food was delicious, and during our afternoon's shopping the doctor acquired another pair of binoculars. He had already bought one in Padua, where they are most reasonably priced. "One pair I am going to give away," he said virtuously. Furthermore he did. We went shopping, too, for Venetian glass, but there we were sorely disappointed. There are exceptions, notably the pieces turned out by the Fornace Venini, but though the objects are made with infinite skill the Venetians seem to lack good designers. Indeed some of the figures, clowns and hooligans, are so cheap and vulgar they look like the product of Coney Island.

I remember that when I went to the island of Murano, the great glass center, as a girl, they were making figures and small animals that had been designed by Claire Avery, one of the *Vogue* artists. She was a friend of my mother and when I was a child acted in an auntlike capacity and took care of me during the summer while Mother was in town editing the magazine. Some of Claire's designs are still among the most graceful and delicate the Venetians have turned out in recent years.

Our first afternoon, like all dutiful Americans we went to Harry's Bar for cocktails. It is owned by the famed Cipriani and merits its reputation, for its food and drinks are of the first order and it is justly crowded.

For has it not been ever said, that all the world one day
Shall pass before the terrace of the Café de la Paix?

I made up a companion jingle:

Travel near or travel far
Seek out commoner or star
You'll find them all in Harry's Bar.

That evening we dined at the Taverna de la Finice with Audrey Brokaw and her son Clifford. They were staying at the Gritti too, and we came together through our mutual friends the Reginald Roses of Oyster Bay. The Finice food was fine too. If the world's greatest chefs were assembled in tourney, the odds would probably be on the Chinese and French, but an Italian winner would be no surprise. The Swiss may be the hotelkeepers, but the Italians are the restaurateurs of the world. It was Marie de' Medici, arriving to wed Henry IV, bringing in her train her own Italian cooks, who originally introduced great cooking to France. It was an art the French were quick to appropriate.

One delicious Italian dish we did not have on that particular trip, but as we were introduced to it by our Italian friend Umberto Innocente, the distinguished landscape architect, I shall mention it in connection with his native land. It is fried squash blossoms. Pick fresh blossoms. Dip them in a very light batter and fry them in hot oil. Tender, crisp, succulent. Watch your guests pounce for the recipe.

The next day the weather cleared, but it was cold enough to need a sweater under one's coat. The Piazza San Marco, however, was in full fig, alive with people and pigeons. We bought little newspaper cornucopias of corn to lure a quota of our own and Norton got a very funny picture of me, my arms weighted with pigeons, a pigeon on my head. Those birds are inexplicable. One would think, considering the centuries they've been there, that the entire Piazza San Marco would be armpit deep in guano. It is, on the contrary, spick-and-span. Whether the pigeons are trained to fly out over the canals I don't know, but, even passing through the square late at night, we never saw anybody around with brooms, so they must in some way be house- or piazza-broken. Many people, even those who are bird lovers, cannot stand pigeons, but I think they're nice. I like the cooing sounds they make, and their plumage is beautiful, especially that lovely sheen at the neck.

The Doge's Palace is of course a Must, but as we were traipsing through the great halls, Norton suddenly balked. I wanted him to go and stand in one corner while I whispered to him from the other end of the vast room. He would, I assured him, hear the whisper. This,

owing to a fantastic twist in acoustics, is true, but he didn't believe me
and would have none of it.

In imagination one peoples the enormous chambers with the glittering figures of the fifteenth and sixteenth centuries, when Venetian influence and power were at their height, yet the morbid sections of the
old homestead exert a horrid fascination of their own: the Bridge of
Sighs, over which the hapless prisoners crossed, and the black and fearful dungeons where they rotted. Civilization and the concept of progress are confusing. Just as we are saying to ourselves that man's
inhumanity to man is a thing of the past, that today more Christian
precepts prevail, along come Hitler and Stalin and their ilk and we are
plunged once more over our heads in barbarism. Were the dungeons of
Venice any more appalling than the gas ovens of Buchenwald? Than
the torture chambers and concentration camps of Siberia? It is a nice
decision.

Among the delightful people we met in Venice were Marjorie and
Antonio Lucarda. Marjorie had an American mother and speaks fluent
American English although she has never been to this country. Tony is
an artist and sculptor, his specialty small portrait busts. They are
charming. As he said, "The taste for the heroic has passed. Who lives
in great halls any more where they can have life-sized statues?" His
work is reduced in size, ten to eighteen inches high, but the busts are
truly portraits rather than miniatures.

We bought an ink-and-wash drawing of his in white and tones of
gray, Venice swept by storm, and he gave me a beautiful old gilt frame
to put it in. The picture lay flat in the bottom of a suitcase and seemed
safe enough, but I was so fearful of something happening to the frame
I handled it gingerly as eggs, and when we disembarked from the *Queen
Mary* on our arrival in New York, I stepped off the ship with it hung
around my neck like a horse collar.

Antonio Lucarda is a true Venetian, with a long, narrow head, an
aquiline nose, and a nervous, vivacious manner. He knows the history
of his native city as well as that of his own family and is an active
member of the city planning board. A pressing problem is how to preserve the old *palazzi*. Since the advent of motorboats the pressure and
vibration of the waves against the foundations are much greater than
the gentle lapping caused by gondolas, which have served the city some
thousand years, and the piles and foundations are loosening. Tony's
concern lightened for a moment and he laughed with pure pleasure.
"Imagine how it was in the great days," he said, his eyes alight with

visions of past magnificence. "Venice had fourteen thousand gondolas
and eleven thousand courtesans. That was what you call it, Living!"

He and Marjorie took us to dine one evening at La Carbonerra, an
excellent and typically Venetian restaurant. It had at one time been
a stable, and we sat in a stall. No different from a booth. Another evening they dined at the Gritti with us, and we went back home with
them for coffee, crossing the Piazza San Marco by moonlight.

They live in a very old building in a roomy, top-floor apartment on
two levels with a bird's-eye view of the city, but for those not hardened
to it the ascent to the eyrie was formidable: ninety-five steep stone
steps. Their two small children apparently skipped up and down like
chamois, but the Lucardas admitted that the tradesmen took a dim
view of delivery. The postman had long since gone on strike. In the
morning he would blow a whistle, they would lower a basket on a long
cord, rather like Rapunzel letting down her golden hair, the mail would
be placed in the basket, and they would haul it up hand over hand.

We went to cocktails with the Contessa de Robilant in her flat on
the Grand Canal. It was picturesque, but she had no fireplace and admitted that in winter it was a bit shivery. We had also been invited
to call on the Prince and Princess Clary in their enormous old *palazzo*,
in which they rented apartments, occupying the top floor themselves.
Their fortune in the Sudetenland had been expunged by war, and two
of their three sons had been killed, but their spirit, vigor, and charm
survived, and their courtesy to a pair of strangers was memorable.

The most luxurious house we visited belonged to the Contessa Anna
Maria Cigone, who sent her beautifully appointed private motorboat
to fetch us at the hotel, just as an American hostess might send her
car. She gave a dinner party for ten, and I have rarely seen so many
flowers so beautifully arranged. I think she warmed to the doctor, but
I would rather not dwell on what she must have thought of the doctor's
wife. It was one of my bad evenings, following a stormy night before,
and as course after delicious course was passed to me by white-gloved
footmen, I sat fasting and mum, my teeth tightly clenched for fear of
what might happen were I to open my mouth, with the rioting that
was going on in my interior. I hope that she and the guests charitably
put down my nonparticipation to lack of Italian rather than to lack of
gray matter. It's a dim hope, however, for they nearly all spoke admirable English and out of courtesy to Norton and me conducted most of
the conversation in our native tongue.

When the evening was over and as we were bidding them farewell on the stone landing, I forgot for a moment that the asphalt pavements of a lifetime were not behind me and came within a hairbreadth of stepping off into the canal. I should think that at merry parties where the *vino* has been flowing it would happen all the time.

Another friend in Venice was Her Royal Highness the Princess Aspasia of Greece, the mother of the Alexandra married to ex-King Peter of Yugoslavia, whom I had met the previous year on the Riviera. The princess had been married to the king of Greece who died so tragically of a monkey bite in 1920. She asked us to luncheon in her tiny house on the Giudecca, set in the midst of a lovely nine-acre garden. In Venice nine acres of solid land is the King Ranch, and with only one gardener to help her the princess does all the work herself.

She is a nice woman and a great dog fancier, so we took to each other at once. Indeed her love of dogs nearly did her in during the war when the British were evacuating Greek royalty from the path of the advancing Germans. Princess and pup were members of the party and the British authorities said she would have to leave him behind. This she flatly refused to do, saying she preferred to stay and face the Germans rather than desert little four-foot. The authorities then allowed grimly that she could bring him, but every island they went to was British-controlled, and every one of them held to the rule, today with reliable anti-rabies vaccines, totally unnecessary, that no dogs are allowed ashore without six months' quarantine. Still, Aspasia was a princess, and, more important, her dog was healthy. The outlying territories bowed; she was allowed to land and depart, hound in tow. When they hit home port, however, Britannia put her foot down. The little animal was sent to quarantine with foreseeable results. It sickened of loneliness and shortly died. When we were in Venice, her dog was a dachshund named Jasmine, who was very jealous of an older dog named Tulip. To spare her feelings, the princess always spelled out Tulip's name when speaking of her in Jasmine's presence.

Norton was able to render one small service in return for the royal hospitality. He is a marvelously handy man around the house; indeed it's lucky for plumbers and electricians that he devotes himself to medical practice, or they would find jobs hard to come by, and after luncheon he installed the princess's new steam radiator that had recently arrived from London. I was glad for her sake, as October in Venice was proving reasonably crisp, and I should think the winter months in her little house and in the old damp *palazzi* would be a real hardship.

We made a few brief excursions away from the heart of Venice itself. One when Marjorie Lucarda took me to Murano to watch them
blowing glass at the Fornace Venini. There, as I mentioned before, they
had some lovely designs, modern and imaginative. Figures, bottles,
vases, lamps, glasses, countless beautiful and useful objects. The Venini
now have a store in New York, and I wish them well, for they deserve
it. We came back with Signora Venini in her gondola, slipping under
the bridges so thoughtfully arched for their passage, and I found her
a fascinating woman, lean and beautiful, with the dark, brilliant eyes
one finds so often in the intellectual Latin. We drew up at the door
of her great house, and as the gondolier held the bark steady, she
stepped up to the threshold more nimbly than the pavement-bound fare
steps from a taxi.

One morning we went through the Accademia di Belle Arti and
gazed upon acres of Tintorettos, and although I appreciate that he is
a great artist he is not for me. We had a better time at Torcello, a remote, peaceful little island. Small parties set out for it in a motor launch
from the landing of Harry's Bar, for the island inn is also owned by
Cipriani. It is tiny and enchanting. In the boat we met Bill and Barbara
Lowe. He was at that time the editor of *House and Garden* and, recognizing me as a kind of alumna by proxy of the Condé Nast organization, he introduced himself and his wife. We lunched together on
the terrace under a pergola and regretted not being able to see the rooms
of the inn, for they were occupied. There are only six, but we were
told that they all have open fireplaces and are furnished with great
taste.

Torcello is much cherished by writers because there is little to do but
concentrate, and the quiet is broken only once a day by a couple of
small boatloads of tourists who arrive as we did to lunch and visit the
squat octagonal Byzantine church and view its mosaics. The late Er-
nest Hemingway and Nancy Mitford have both found inspiration in
Torcello, though in the case of the former it was perhaps temporarily di-
luted, for the book he wrote there was *Across the River and into the
Trees*. Another good thing about Torcello is that the tranquillity *can*
be broken by a motorboat spin into Venice for a little night life and a
nightcap at Harry's Bar.

Before we left home Bertha Rose had said to me, "If you're going
to Venice don't miss the theater at Vicenza on the mainland, it's fantastic." When it turned out that Vicenza was the birthplace of Antonio
Lucarda and that he too highly recommended it and its theater, we

decided to go. Apparently it is a site that spawns artists, for it was also the home of the great architect and sculptor Palladio.

He built exquisite villas and a basilica, and we went to see the Villa della Rotonda, which served as inspiration for Jefferson's Monticello. He also designed the Olympic Theater, and it is unique. The seats are curved benches rising tier on tier, finished off by a row of columns on which rests a balustrade topped by sculptured figures. There is a pit for the orchestra, and the stage is a permanent set; a sort of great hall with columns, statues, and arches, and through the arches, extending back some thirty feet on a slightly raked angle, are streets lined with Palladian houses made of wood, papier-mâché, and stucco. They are built in diminishing perspective, and the illusion of distance is extraordinary.

The theater was completed in 1583 and the first bill was a performance of *Oedipus Rex*. In 1953 Laurence Olivier gave his *Oedipus* on the same stage, and it must have been an evening long to remember. The theater is in constant use, and the day we were there a good deal of hammering was going on, as there was to be a concert that night. Some of the audience was bound to be American soldiers, as at that time there were about seven thousand of them stationed in Vicenza. The service club was housed in a sixteenth-century building, and our morale builders, a pool table, leatherette chairs, and Coke machine, were all in evidence.

Led by a chauffeur guide we had engaged on the pier, we entered a house he implied was a national monument. There was a good deal of chat between him and an elderly maid in attendance, and when we mounted the staircase we found ourselves in a large drawing room-dining room, with a luncheon table set for four, complete with cheese and a carafe of wine. That seemed a bit *intime* for a national monument, and we looked around at the beautifully proportioned old room with interest but distinct uneasiness. Norton was just muttering something about, "I can't believe this is a public building," when in came a gentleman who seemed surprised to see us but who bowed politely and looked at us questioningly. We bowed back and with simpering, deprecating smiles edged toward the door, murmuring a few broken apologies to the effect that there had been some misunderstanding. As his Italian reply was mild in tone we hoped that he was not outraged and we skedaddled out of there. Later we extracted from the chauffeur via broken English-broken Italian and gestures the news that the place wasn't *exactly* a national monument. *Exactly* it was a private house, but an authentic old one, and as we seemed so enthusiastic about the other antiques, he had thought that we might like to see it. We concluded from the manner of our unwitting host that something of the kind must have happened before. I suppose if one lives in a Palladian masterpiece, within limits one accepts intruders gracefully, but Norton and I housebreak rarely and we lacked his aplomb.

Driving back along the *autostrada* to the gondola dock, we learned of a custom interesting to tourists. The toll is doubled on Sunday.

In Venice we stopped for tea in the Piazza San Marco and listened to the band playing, and Tony Lucarda, unexpectedly strolling by on his way home from his studio, sat down and joined us. We said a regretful good-by to him, for the next day was our last.

Since the Lido is such a famous beach and so much *the* place for the so-called international set in August, we decided that we ought to see it. Accordingly we took a *vaporetto* over the next morning and walked along the streets from the dock to the shore, but the Lido is like any seaside resort in the late fall, and in October the great hotels were shuttered, the deck chairs piled under canvas and the whole atmosphere bleak and forlorn. An air of desertion per se, however, is not always unattractive. There is something a little formidable about the Season anyplace great wealth and sophistication gather. On the few occasions I find myself in the midst of it I feel like an interloper, and it seems to me remarkable that there is an element of society that can pass its whole life involved eternally in dinner parties, bridge and canasta games, racing, skiing, sun-bathing, and similar so-called entertainments and recreations. I don't think it's sour grapes—who doesn't relish an occasional holiday?—but as a way of life three hundred and sixty-five days a year—well, I don't wonder the alcohol consumption is high. How, stone sober, could they stand it?

Our last bit of sight-seeing was a trip up the campanile to look out over the city spread below us like a map. It is a lovely, lovely sight and the best way to get an impression of the geography of Venice. I am happy to say that the campanile, unlike the apartment house of our dear Lucardas, does have an elevator.

At six o'clock that evening we left Venice for Paris on the Simplon Orient Express. Times have changed. I remember it as one of the de luxe trains of the world. Today it is a far cry from luxury, but the dinner was excellent: spaghetti with sauce *pomodoro*—golden apples to the Italians, tomatoes to us—a choice of chicken or veal, spinach, roast potatoes, a *good* tossed salad with *real* dressing of oil, vinegar, salt, and pepper freshly made, cake, *real* cheese, not pasteurized blotting paper in the handy pack, fruit, coffee, and naturally, with the meal, wine.

In Paris we went directly to the Parsons apartment. Geoff was a cordial host, but we missed Drue, who was en route back from New York. Our schedules, alas, overlapped, and we were to pass like Evangeline without seeing each other.

For once we were coming home by ship instead of flying, and our return journey really began as our train rolled through the beautiful cultivated countryside of Normandy to Cherbourg, where we boarded the *Queen Mary*. The *Queen* is a buxom girl, eighty-one thousand tons, and we had a comfortable cabin and found ourselves at the captain's table, a mixed blessing, I always think. The first evening the captain dined on the bridge. We had cocktails at the bar and introduced ourselves to our fellow guests, among them Kate Graham, a pleasant, forthright woman who was the British consul general in New York, and the atomic physicist Sir John Cockcroft.

The next day there was a swell and I was deathly sick. I have ever been a poor sailor and with my recently reduced interior I was even worse. Norton could hardly believe his eyes and ears. He adores the sea and kept insisting it must be psychosomatic. How *could* the glorious bounding main have that effect on anybody? The thing to do was to distract my mind. With that end in view we accepted an invitation to cocktails in the captain's cabin. I again played the mute wife, behaving as I had at the Contessa Cicone's dinner, terrified to unclench my teeth. I finally staggered down and got into bed. The instant I didn't have to make an effort I felt much better. I had been able to touch nothing *chez* the captain, but, cozily ensconced in bed, I downed a stinger and dined very well. The stewardess eyed me with disapproval. "It used to be," she said, "that when our passengers were seasick they didn't eat. Very relaxing for us. Now they get seasick and they take a Dramamine. It makes them drowsy, so they stay in bed, but they eat like horses. Big trays all the time."

Tony Curtis and Janet Leigh were on board with their little daughter, Kelly. Tony and I had played in a picture together called *Johnny Dark*, not a major Hollywood achievement, but he was a nice and friendly fellow and we saw quite a bit of the Curtises as well as of Donald Klopfer, Bennett Cerf's partner at Random House, and his wife, Pat.

This pleasant relationship at sea was the kernel in which was imbedded a curious accident that befell the doctor some weeks later. One evening in the following December the Klopfers asked us to dine. The dinner was excellent, the company cheery, and we left the party only because good manners demanded that the host and hostess be given a break should they want to go to bed. It was a bad night, sleeting and snowing, so when we got downstairs Norton said to me, "You wait here in the lobby. I'll go get the car." He was parked in the next block. I waited four or five minutes, eight or ten minutes. I was beginning to think that something must have happened, perhaps the motor had frozen, and I was just starting in search of him when he reappeared looking rather white. "What is it?" I asked. "Anything the matter?" As it turned out, yes. Crossing the street, he had slipped on a sheet of ice and crashed his full length on his back. He had a pipe in his mouth and he bit through it, knocking out a tooth. He was terribly upset over the loss, but I could have shouted with relief. A missing tooth was a bonanza! It was a legacy from that rich uncle in Australia! He might have cracked his skull open and been lying dead on the pavement while I waited in the lobby. Nothing serious developed, but he was badly shaken up, and it was the kind of occurrence that causes me to go about muttering biblical imprecations: "In the midst of life we are in death."

CHAPTER FOUR

Paris ✳ Austria
Greece and the Islands

WITH THE exception of a brief trip to St. Croix in the Virgin Islands over New Year's, we hibernated, geographically speaking, through the first half of 1959. We stayed at home, dividing our time between the apartment in town and weekends on Long Island, but our plans were going forward, we were plotting our big push, our trip around the world. Paris, Vienna, Istanbul, Athens, Bangkok, Singapore, Indonesia, Cambodia, Hong Kong, Taiwan, Japan. Doesn't it sound great? It was.

The doctor once saw a sign on a trailer with a Florida license, "Have Wife Must Travel," which he thought very funny—personally I can restrain my laughter—but now he always pretends that our junkets are my idea, and sometimes they are, but who *extends* them? Just a wee bit? Sometimes a day, sometimes a week, and then another day or two? *He* does. "When I think of the condition of our bank account, sweetie, why quibble over a few days?"

June 1 was our actual departure date, but as I say, long before that we were laying our pipes, making preparations. It was in these preceding weeks that I abandoned my impression of a sieve as an inanimate object. A sieve can be a human being, living, breathing, talking. I know. For a while there I got so punched full of holes you could have strained soup through me. This was due to shots. Typhus, paratyphoid, cholera, yellow fever . . . you name it, we had it. To me, though, the unexpected treat was the fact that with the exception of sore, stiff arms for about forty-eight hours after every injection there were no ill effects. No chills, no fevers, no shivers, no misery of any kind. Modern science is nifty.

I once read an account of the items Sir Edmund Hillary stored up in preparation for his ascent of Mount Everest. We were going into tropical climes, so our goodies were in reverse, but in variety and comprehensiveness we matched him.

My husband charmed me. He spoke severely and I fear with some repetition of the limited amount of luggage we would be allowed. The words "sixty-six pounds apiece" tolled like curfew through my dreams, yet every night he came home with a new gadget he claimed was absolutely indispensable if we were to be comfortable and healthy en route. For a while I began to fear we'd have so much equipment that the only clothes we'd have room for would be those we stood up in.

I pass over the rolls of colored film. The lesson learned in Spain eight years before had faded from memory. You'd have thought we were being sent on a mission by the combined picture magazines of the world instead of being two tourists taking snapshots for home consumption. Number of cameras, four: Leica, Stereo Realist, Bell and Howell, Minox.

Since this was a doctor and his wife making preparations for a trip, the greater part of which would be spent in the Orient, we took a pharmacopoeia that would have given the Mayo Clinic pause. We also had water purifiers; two kinds. Halazone pills, excellent but rather bourgeois. *Lots* of people have those, but we had a *special* device: a blue plastic bag with crystals in it and little tubes and nozzles sticking out from it, the idea being that you pour in water from the Ganges if so inclined, passage through the magic crystals purifies it, and it comes out sparkling clear as a mountain stream and eminently potable. We did not have a still for converting salt water to fresh; it was the one contrivance we lacked. We were rich in converters to tap European and Asiatic electric currents, we had inflatable horseshoe-shaped pillows to put around our necks to make us confortable in the plane—planes supply small pillows in large quantities, but we were to be beholden to no one—and we had a wee transistor radio that came from Japan in the first place and was going home again via Southeast Asia. The doctor's theory was that it would be pleasant to relax in our hotel room after sight-seeing and listen to sweet music. Also, I assumed, to Thai and Cambodian commercials. We had my typewriter and two brief cases. Those sixty-six pounds apiece were beginning to strain at the seams.

In order not to miss out on some essential I indulged an old weakness of mine and resorted to Lists. I am sometimes so encumbered by great sheaves of them I am a real fire hazard, but they bolster my flagging memory. Traveler's Tip No. 10: Make lists. People to call; man to take down, clean, and store curtains; man to shampoo rugs; man to restore and repair hall cabinet; head off milkman; stop papers; car dead-storage; suspend insurance; . . . the thousand little domestic chores familiar to any housewife.

Probably the most comprehensive list, and I offer it as Traveler's Tip No. 11, is the aid-to-packing one, starting at the top of the head and going to the soles of the feet, the list of supplies to take for the care of the person. Set down on paper, it looks formidable, but it is vital: brush, combs, hand mirror—take your own or you'll never know how you look in profile for the duration of the trip—curlers, spray net, cleansing cream, nourishing cream, lotion, cosmetics, toothpaste, sewing kit. Every woman will have her own indispensable treasures, but a systematic checkoff at the start of the journey will save many moments of anguish later on. One doesn't need masses of these things, in most places—possibly excepting the African veld and Russia, where I haven't been—supplies can be replenished, but that is prosy shopping when one wants to devote one's usually limited time to rooting for such truffles as antiques or clothes or *objets d'art*.

Besides lists there was the matter of renting the house in the country for June, July, and August. We would rather not rent our house to strangers, but a little question of economics was involved—the rent money would help pay for the trip. Even I, who am not astute about finances, could grasp that one.

Then there was Thor, our beautiful taupe boy, our Weimaraner. There we were shot with luck as well as with antibiotics. Our dear friends David and Daphne Lyall, who had been on the Caribbean cruise with us, were summering in Martha's Vineyard; they would, they said, be happy to take care of him. Games with their young son, the companionship of Brunhilda, their female boxer, swims in the Atlantic Ocean, romps around the yard . . . we bade him farewell with tears in our eyes, but we could not bemoan his lot.

We turned our attention to the garden. I had planted ethically for our tenants, they were entitled to flowers and, the wife being English, I assumed that through the summer she would nurture the blooms with pleasure and that on our return the first of September there would still be autumn glory left for us. It was a pretty conceit and it might have worked had not the lady got involved nurturing twin sons who were born to her early in July. Also our part-time gardener went awry. He gave at the head and knees, and we returned home to a wilderness. But if you're going to let those things scare you . . .

The moment of departure finally came. The luggage, weighed and checked, was just at the limit, one hundred thirty-two pounds for the two of us. There remained cameras and coats, my typewriter, brief case, and office. This was an Air France bag with supplies of paper, pencils, and general equipment, since I would be keeping a diary and writing my syndicated column. For these necessities their bags are best, they are flat, light, and hold a lot.

We arrived at Idlewild to find the Air France personnel the soul of courtesy and vastly indifferent over our piddling pieces of hand luggage. The question of weighing them never arose. Norton and I smiled at each other, breathed a sigh of relief, and set ourselves to counting them for the final time, and my blood froze. The pharmacopoeia, the depository of the combined skill and experience of Dr. Brown and the drug houses of America, was missing. The blue plastic bag and the halazone tablets were *missing*. We would have to drink ordinary water just like everybody else. We would die! The doctor looked at me, and his very eyes were pale. "*You*," he said, "*you* were going to be responsible for that. Just that and your own camera. I am carrying your typewriter, your office, and *all* the other things. I don't even mind wrestling with the coats but I did think—"

"I know," I cried, "I know. It's inexcusable, but it isn't too late. I'll phone Elizabeth, she can send it. We may even get it in Paris. Vienna certainly, long before we'll need the stuff. We were only counting on it for the Orient anyway."

"You'll do better," he called after me as I ran off, "to tell her to send it to Athens. It'll have plenty of time then and be sure to reach us."

I ran to the telephone booth and dialed our apartment. My secretary picked up the receiver. Without waiting to hear my voice she said calmly, "You forgot the drugstore. I'm wrapping it up now. Where do you want it sent?"

Everybody has his favorite air line, and today the safety record of all the great companies is impressive, but when going to foreign parts one gets the flavor of a land more quickly when traveling on foreign carriers.

For this reason I would suggest that Americans, on a maiden trip, book on European lines, just as I would suggest that foreigners coming to us should by all means travel with one of the great American air or steamship companies.

As for Europe, where the French are concerned, we are apt to overlook that they have been air-borne longer than any other nation. Excepting Icarus, the first man to leave the earth was a Frenchman when, in 1783 the Montgolfier brothers sent up a paper-lined cloth balloon, its orangelike sections buttoned together, elevated by the heat from a fire of straw and wool. The basket swinging below it contained a rooster, a duck, and a lamb that reconnoitered the atmosphere for breathing possibilities. They returned alive and the lamb lived out his days in Marie Antoinette's Petit Trianon, meeting, let us hope, a more tranquil end than his hapless queen. History doesn't say what happened to the duck and the rooster, but as they were French fowl, suspicion is strong that they ended up *en cocotte*.

Later in that same year, encouraged by the success of the air-borne livestock, two intrepid gents, Jean Pilâtre de Rozier and the Marquis d'Arlandes severed the cords that had hitherto held trial balloons captive and rose in free flight. The first men to soar above the earth. We weren't in balloons but Norton and I still fared well on the journey. We dozed sporadically through the night, and arrived the next morning to find Drue Parsons waiting for us at the Orly airport. The drive into Paris, like the drive from most air terminals, is ugly, but once one enters the city proper, ah! how lovely it is. There are people, the good doctor is one of them, who are not in love with Paris. I try to understand this idiosyncrasy as I try to understand all his little ways, and indeed on occasion I swing over to his camp. Parsnips, for example; I never used to be able to abide them, but now, thanks to perseverance and his tutelage, I appreciate their subtle flavor. I have, however, no intention in persevering toward not loving Paris. In this instance it is he who is missing something, not I.

Our first French luncheon was with our friends Claude and Esther Lazard at their house in the Rue de Varenne. One enters the courtyard and the courtyard is austere. Well proportioned, correct, impassive. One enters the house. Downstairs it is formal, discreet, a little severe. Then one enters, or rather exits, onto the terrace and a soft explosion of pleasure. In the heart of Paris an enormous garden; flowers, trees, a great expanse of exquisitely manicured lawn.

The luncheon was as delightful as the setting. Esther is San Francisco born and Claude is French, so they are aware of food. We started with fresh, succulent crayfish followed by a delicate mixed grill, a green salad, cheese, and a strawberry tart, cherries and green almonds, the whole accompanied by a light Austrian May wine and finished off with black coffee. It was good.

That evening Geoffrey Parsons was out of town, so Norton and I took Drue to dine at Maxim's. Since we were to be in Paris only two or three days, we felt that we should live it up.

Maxim's looked just as it did in *Gigi*—our clothes were different—but we were disillusioned. We had built up a glow from its reputation, which, when confronted by fact, faded. The food was nice but unexceptional, and the service was poor. Dinner for three with three cocktails and wine came to about thirty-two dollars.

As we were eventually going to Japan, a chum in New York, Jane Grant, had given us a letter to Madame Tetsuro Furukaki, the wife of the Japanese ambassador to Paris. Jane felt that we should get our oriental licks in early, begin to acclimate ourselves, as it were. She had also written to Madame Furukaki, and when we arrived at the Parsons apartment, I found a card inviting Drue and me to tea at the embassy. We went with pleasure, and I was able to deliver some stockings Jane had sent her. They must have been Size 1, for Madame Furukaki is a beguiling, doll-like creature who speaks perfect French and English. It was quite a large tea party—I should say more than a hundred wandering through the spacious rooms—and, to entertain her guests, the hostess had engaged Sofu Teshigahara, the master flower arranger of Japan.

The master can take three bare branches signifying sky, earth, and man, a rose by way of lagniappe, and the result is Art. After one particularly skillful arrangement there was a gasp from the assembled ladies and a little flutter of approbation. Mr. Teshigahara waited a moment and then said delicately, "In London they applauded me for that one."

He showed us two tricks worth following. By skillful cutting of the bark it is possible to bend branches any way you like without breaking them, and, to preserve flowers, cut their stems underwater to seal out the air, and afterward dip them in alcohol.

The night Geoff and Drue Parsons gave a dinner party for us I went down stairs with Drue to *les caves* to bring up the wine. The house in which they have their apartment was built in 1640, and the deep cellars are cut from the bedrock of Paris. The lighting, until one gets into the wine bin, is virtually nonexistent, and I hung on, childlike, to Drue's skirts for fear I should get lost in the wandering catacombs. Sometimes, when the Seine rises, the cellar floods and the labels are washed off the wine bottles, and then are the men separated from the boys, the poseurs from the connoisseurs! One must really know his vintages.

That Drue, she mothers the world. During the war she mothered many fliers and resistance fighters. She never refers to them, but today, on a table in her drawing room are two small boxes. Once, when we first stayed in the apartment and I happened to be in the room alone, I opened them. I refrain, with an effort, from reading other people's mail, but I tend to open their small leather boxes. In one lay the Legion of Honor, given her by the French Government, in the other the Medal of Courage, awarded her by King George VI.

Drue is practical as well as brave and was distressed when she discovered that although lifesaving drugs and water purifiers were winging our way we were planning to circle the globe without a personal supply of toilet paper. "I never *heard* of such a thing," she cried, "you *must* have paper, you're going to the *Orient*." The result was four rolls of Scot tissue, which she insisted on packing in my bag. They made a good nest for my orange velvet pillbox hat acquired from Sally Victor. I carried them around the world, and when we got home I put them in the supply closet in the apartment. I believe it was necessary for the wayfarer to transport this particular kind of stationery during the war, but you may now count on finding it all over the world.

We were sad to leave Drue and Geoff and the apartment we cannot help think of as our own particular *pied-à-terre* in Paris, but the next stop was Vienna and we had never been there. Vienna was new and the idea was exciting.

That, I think, is something to consider when planning a trip. Once we had decided to go, basically it made no difference to us whether we went from east to west or vice versa. Distance and cost would be the same. The deciding factor in the end was novelty. Europe we knew reasonably well. If we went to Japan first, then Hong Kong, Bangkok, and so on around, finishing up in Europe, much as we love it, familiarity would be bound to make it something of an anticlimax. For that reason we decided on Europe first, with the Orient to follow. If we pushed into the unknown, anticipation, we felt, could only build. It turned out to be a good idea for other reasons too, as I shall explain when we get there.

Leaving Paris, we had the delay at the airport that was to be the first of many. It is for these occasions that the traveler does well to take along in his luggage a little lightweight drip-dry sense of sportsmanship and some portable Val-a-pak humor. It enables him to accept philosophically plane and train schedules encountered en route that for the most part seem to have been arranged by trolls. It was frightfully humid and sticky at Orly, and the wait was tedious; it was, however, only one hour. We were destined to *far* worse than that. We arrived in Vienna around nine in the evening and were met by our friends Paul and Minx Fejos. Years ago Paul was a wild Hungarian director in Hollywood. Today he is the dignified, immensely knowledgeable Hungarian director of the Wenner Gren Foundation, a learned society of anthropologists. He is also the most generous and thoughtful of men, and it's fatal to admire anything in his presence, as he either insists upon giving it to you instantaneously or, if you hold him off at gun point, he suddenly capitulates almost indifferently and a few days or weeks later either the original or an exact replica of that which you admired is delivered to your door. He is *very* difficult. His young wife long ago gave up the struggle of trying to keep things on an even keel. "You know Paul," she says, and indeed once you do there you are; indebted to him for the rest of your days.

We breezed through customs; anthropologists from all over the world come to Burg Wartenstein—the old fortress-castle where we were to stay, owned by the foundation—for summer seminars, and the customs officials are used to strange specimens both human and inanimate.

We drove through the darkness for about an hour and a half, the road winding ever upward like excelsior, and came at last to the darker mass of the *burg* silhouetted against the night sky. We sat chatting for a while over drinks and a cold supper and were then shown to our rooms. It is an amusing spot to stay in, for it is a castle *cum* college. There is no proper living room such as one finds in a private house, for any of the larger apartments that might serve that purpose are used for lectures and conferences. Although they prefer smaller groups for flexibility, they can accommodate as many as fifty-six scientists at a time. The dining room is a huge enclosed veranda with what Dr. Fejos refers to quite accurately as a "faboolus" view of valleys, mountains, and the little town of Gloggnitz, which is the local metropolis and the fez capital of the world, manufacturing the red felt flowerpots for Egypt and Algeria and other Moslem lands. In the long corridor leading to the dining room is a bar that becomes the social center when the learned are gathered together. The summer term didn't begin for another week or ten days and that was how the Fejoses were able to have us for a visit.

Two large rooms had been put at our disposal, an anteroom and a bedroom. The foundation has done extensive restoration, and the bathroom facilities were modern and comfortable. We had prettily painted peasant beds and sheets buttoned to the blankets with big blue buttons. There was only one slight inconvenience—no washcloths. Bath towels, hand towels, no washcloths.

We were in a delicate position. Had it been Paul's and Minx's own house, we would have assumed that they had simply been overlooked by the maid who prepared our rooms and we would have asked for them. But although Minx is a distinguished anthropologist in her own right and was our hostess in a sense, she was not running the house. That was being done by Herr and Frau Haupt, the caretaker and cook who had been there for thirty years, long before the Wenner Gren people bought the place. We did not like to imply criticism of their arrangements. The hitch about taking the matter up with Frau Haupt herself was that we didn't speak a word of German. I had recourse to the ever-present Berlitz German phrase book and a grammar, but apparently in Germany one either has one's washcloths, as the ladies of Boston have their hats, or the hotels never forget or one does without. It wasn't until we got down off our mountain a day or two later and took our first sight-seeing trip around Vienna that I was able by dint of eloquent pantomime to make the salesgirl in a drugstore understand what I had in mind. Pantomime and the word *bitte*. In Austria, and I suppose in Germany, *bitte* is invaluable. It means please, I beg your pardon, don't mention it, not at all, how's that again, quite all right, come in—good serviceable word.

We had arrived in Austria Friday night. Saturday was our first tour of the *burg*, or castle. The oldest part, the tower, was built in 1100 and the structure has been added to every century since. About the middle of the nineteenth century it was bought by Francesca, Duchess of Liechtenstein. Francesca was a Tartar. She decided that the magnificent old beams didn't look "woody" enough, so she had them painted a sort of mud brown to simulate grain and painted knotholes were applied to heighten the realistic effect. They were then edged with lines of blue and red. She painted the stones in the chapel, too, to look stonier. The foundation is gradually erasing these desecrations but had to devote time and money to basic needs first.

Francesca was followed in the twentieth century by more deliberate vandals, the Russians. They swept in during the war and stayed until 1955. When they came Herr and Frau Haupt fled to the forest. Two little dachshunds were left behind. When the Russians got there the dogs were on the terrace barking. They machine-gunned them, doubtless in self-defense. There used to be a lovely old marble balustrade with marble busts edging the moat. This the Russians hacked to pieces and in its place installed pine logs that they used as latrines. They tore the plumbing fixtures from the walls and, when asked why, said it was because they would take them home and stick them on their walls and then they too would have running water. They were, among other things, naïve. They took hand grenades to a bas-relief in the chapel because it was covered with gold leaf, which they thought signified hidden treasure. They didn't find any treasure, but the destruction of the wall was satisfactory. One thing they did leave, probably an oversight, was a very old, almost life-sized carving of Christ on the cross with a spent, agonized face, one of the most moving portraits I have ever seen.

In the courtyard is a pretty flower bed, and in it is placed a bust of Maria Theresa that used to adorn the balustrade. Her nose is broken, but otherwise she looks quite regal embowered in tulips and petunias.

We walked in the surrounding countryside, which was lush and lovely, the fields filled with wild flowers: Queen Anne's lace, daisies, and mustard, buttercups, clover, and wild sage. The pine forests marching up and down the mountains, for we were in the foothills of the Alps, smelled delicious.

The household consisted of ourselves, the Fejoses, a young Dr. Honea, an American, Mrs. Mohling, who was Minx's secretary, a very intelligent and amusing colored girl, May Alice, who was the librarian, and another pretty girl, a Greek, I think, who was the accountant. When we waxed ecstatic on the fairy-tale architecture of Burg Wartenstein, Dr. Honea told us that there are hundreds of old Austrian castles for sale. They can be picked up for around a thousand dollars. The headache comes later, restoring and reconstructing. Very costly.

One evening Paul decided that a little festivity was in order, so we had an especially good dinner and Herr and Frau Haupt joined us. She was pretty and buxom in her dirndl, her lovely white hair shining, and he was very correct in his green wool uniform with knickerbockers and long black hand-knit socks. Two musicians had been engaged to play; an accordionist and a chap who played a devil's violin. I had never seen one before and I was bug-eyed. His was a homemade instrument, like a very long-necked banjo on a rubber-tipped peg leg that rested on the floor. It had two projecting wooden pegs and a boat-shaped piece of wood screwed onto the back. On top was a small carved wooden head topped by a tiny pair of cymbals, the whole edifice, including the banjo strings, was struck in rhythm by a drum stick. Busiest musician I ever saw.

We drank light, delicious Austrian wine and slivovitz, the famous plum brandy, and sang old songs including that local favorite "Happy

Days Are Here Again." The Austrian way of life looked pretty good. But beware the slivovitz, my friends, the white-hot firewater that leads to *der katzenjammer* for the unwary.

Another evening was more cultural and austere. After all, you can't just laugh and live it up the *whole* time. Dr. Fejos is a gentleman devoted to the classics and hi-fi. We returned from Vienna late one afternoon to discover that he had decided on an outdoor concert. The tower is partially ruined but still usable, and in it Paul had installed his hi-fi equipment. We were to lie on deck chairs on the greensward under the stars and be treated to an opera. It sounded idyllic. It didn't work out quite that way, but as Browning so sagely observed, a man's reach must exceed his grasp. One difficulty was the weather. Unco-operative. The month was June, but the night was cold. Ever the gracious host, Paul arranged for blankets to be brought and wrapped around us. This was fine, but I suspected that the maids, in their picturesque dirndls, doing the wrapping had been trained in the stern school of the sanitarium or the spa where they went in for wet packs. We were wrapped tight as mummies, our arms at our sides, and couldn't move. Willy-nilly we were prisoners of song. The selection was Maria Callas in *Tosca*. That would have been all right, but Paul's hearing is slightly impaired, so Miss Callas's already-muscular tones were amplified a good ten decibels larger than life and boomed and echoed and bounced within the topless tower walls. Also it began to rain. Paul, busy inside with his knobs and controls, was blithely unaware of our plight, so there we lay for the entire opera, the rain sprinkling our faces and soaking gently through our thick, imprisoning cocoons. He was so happy giving us happiness, however, we didn't have the heart to disillusion him. We didn't have the mobility, either.

When not wrapped literally in music, we went about Vienna loving it. We loved especially the Volksgarten, an enormous, beautifully tended rose garden that wafted its fragrance over the city and the two swank shopping streets: the Graben, which means "Ditch" and which was formerly a moat circling the town, and the Kärntnerstrasse. The merchandise was tempting: beautiful ceramics, china, table linen, fabrics and leather. The good doctor bore up pretty well under the ordeal of shopping, as we stopped for frequent restoratives—*Kaffee mit Schlag,* a sweet cloud of whipped cream, and little cakes and tiny roll sandwiches and wild-strawberry tarts. The two most famous coffee shops are Demels, in Kohlmarkt Strasse, which also serves a delicious *smörgåsbord* luncheon, and the Konditorei Lehmann. After a pick-me-up in one or the other we thought we'd never be hungry again. An error. We were always hungry and we were always ready for the delicious Austrian beer. The place to diet, we decided, would be the Orient, all that green tea and rice. Austrian water is especially good, which may have something to do with the quality of the coffee and beer.

We had taken a room at first at the Hotel de France, but later moved to the Imperial, which is considered the best hotel in Vienna and which functions in the great hotel tradition. Our bathroom was a many-splendored thing, with radiant heating in the floor and hot nickel pipes for warming the enormous bath towels. Draped in one, the doctor would stroll about the room in lordly fashion, a Roman senator giving the Forum the once-over.

The Imperial was once a private palace when the Austrian court was one of the most luxurious in Europe. Paul Fejos told us that in the great days noblemen had their valets spray their golden ducats with cologne before they started out on a spending spree.

My old friend from Hollywood, George Cukor, was in Vienna directing the picture about Lizst, *The Magic Flame*, and he was also stopping at the Imperial. He took us to a cocktail party where we met the gentleman who, now seventy, still is the great magnet for feminine affection, Maurice Chevalier, and also Miss Sophia Loren, in black and white polka dots glittering with diamonds. I have read someplace that she puts all her money in jewels. Is that wise? Surely investments that bring in an income are better? It's none of my business, but I'm a snob, I worry about the rich.

Libations and food at the Imperial are very good, and the dining room is charming, like a room in a private house, the walls stretched with striped silk. The Drei Husaren, an excellent Viennese restaurant, is of the Theodore Roosevelt era, easy chairs around the tables and standing lamps with fringed silk shades. The barman is tutored in American cocktails, and dinner for two with cocktails, beer, steak, vegetables, cheese, and coffee came to two hundred seven schillings, or a little over eight dollars. No complaint there.

At the Deutches Haus, not particularly swank but gustatorially rewarding, one may lunch outdoors under a red- and white-striped awning, and the *Göss Bier* is tops. An amusing restaurant to go to, although the food is unremarkable, is the Lindenkeller, a cellar establishment that, incredible though it may seem, has been functioning as a restaurant since 1435.

One thing we noticed in Vienna was that all waitresses wore black stockings and high black laced shoes. Seems it's a law or something, has to do with sanitation. Actually many of the clothes have a slightly native flavor that is amusing and attractive. The dirndls—those full skirts and square-cut bodices—are very much worn in the country, and one sees them occasionally in town, too. Also in town a great many very large men wear very short pants, way above the knees. Some wear knee-length hose; others effect short ones and sandals like those for kids. We tend to think of this costume as strictly for hiking, but apparently gentlemen go to their offices and conduct their daily lives in these comfortable, *dégagé* outfits, and no one glances twice.

The children's outfits are adorable, especially their rainwear, which we were able to appraise pretty thoroughly, as it rained most of the time we were in Austria. They wear gray woolen capes and little green hats with feathers and look like pixies.

One rainy morning, our ardor for the outdoors once more dampened, we decided to go to a museum. There is certainly nothing like travel for bringing out one's ignorance. My humble pride is an acquaintance with museums. The Metropolitan, the Louvre, the National Gallery, the Prado, the Uffizi and the Pitti. I may not be able to point, unerring as a bird dog, at a specific picture, but I've been in those great storehouses, I've seen their treasures, and, sight unseen, I know that the Hermitage exists. I had never heard of anything in Vienna, but I said to Norton, "We're in a European capital, they must have something." They have, they have indeed. They have the Künstlerhaus. Its scope and riches are world renowned, but, living as I do in the bottom of a well, word had not reached me. They have Brueghels, an enormous gallery full of them, and Cranachs and Rembrandts. Right there I'm happy. They have the great Vermeer, the artist in his atelier, back to camera, painting the girl in blue. They have Rubens, Franz Hals, one small Bosch—at least one was all we saw—Memling, a charmer of whom I had never heard called Savery, and the giants from the south, Titian, Tintoretto, Veronese. Nor do they overlook Velázquez. Go.

The Hofburg, the imperial palace, to which the Viennese are devoted, impressed us on the whole as a big bore, but Schönbrunn is a delight. It had for me a special interest because in my youth, when going to school in Paris, I discovered Edmond Rostrand's *L'Aiglon*, played, in that particular production, by Vera Sergine. My youthful enthusiasm for L'Aiglon's father has given way to keen distaste: the mania for power leading to mass slaughter strikes me no longer as brave, romantic, and enterprising. But as a young girl I warmed to Napoleon's fame and to his pale, tubercular son, coughing out his life beside the Gloriette, a sort of colonnade on a hill. Yearning, although living in halls reasonably vast, for the still-vaster ones of Versailles seemed to me poetic. Now I think he was just spoiled. Schönbrunn is no hovel. Fourteen hundred rooms, forty-five state apartments visitable.

In the endless series of white-and-gold rooms repetition is inevitable, but about four small salons are so enchanting they revive flagging interest and weary feet are forgotten. One is called the Millionen Zimmer and must certainly have cost a million of something to build. The walls are paneled in a superb satiny wood, walnut, I think, inlaid with exquisite irregularly shaped Persian miniatures each framed in rococo, gold-leafed carving. A couple of rooms are delicate explosions of *chinoiserie*, lovely Chinese panels and brackets and ornaments; there is a joyful affair lined with blue and white porcelain and the walls of another are bedecked with embroidered medallions done by the daughters of Maria Theresa, of whom she had eleven, including Marie Antoinette. There were also five boys. Nobody pays much attention to Pa; he is rarely mentioned, but I can't think why. Surely he deserves some kind of medal, *nicht wahr?* He was from Lorraine and his name was Franz Stephan, and Franz, old man, I salute you.

Another Viennese delight is the Redoutensaal, surely one of the most elegant concert halls in the world. It is in the Imperial Palace and was once a ballroom—fancy-dress balls were held there until the mid-1800's. It is an enormous room seating about a thousand, oblong in shape, over two stories high, with the stage and orchestra pit at one end, and lighted by magnificent crystal chandeliers. The lower parts of the walls are hung with tapestries, the upper sections are divided by tall curtained windows and flat pilasters, the whole painted the customary white and gold.

There are screens rather than enclosed sets, and a kind of traveler curtain. They play only Mozart and the evening we went the opera was *The Abduction from the Seraglio*. Konstanze was sung by Mimi Cortese, a pretty woman with a lovely voice. Rita Streich sang Blondchen, and the Pedrillo was Murray Dickie.

We went for supper afterward to the Drei Husaren. When the hotel operator had tried to make a reservation for us over the phone they had said Nothing Doing, but we went anyway, firm and proud, and said they *must* have our reservation, and sure enough we got an excellent table. Faint heart ne'er won good meal.

Access to most restaurants and theaters was difficult because we were there at the festival season. It is a sorry admission to make, but in the interests of honest reporting I must confess our shame and bitter disappointment. We did not get to the opera. To go to Vienna in June and not go to the opera is a little like saying, "Yes, we were in Athens but we didn't see the Acropolis." God knows it was not for lack of trying. Our loss was rooted in ignorance. If you think there is a possibility of your being in Vienna next year, make opera reservations now. We did not appreciate the reputation and magnetism of the Staats Oper, so we were left out in the cold, empty-handed, irresponsible grasshoppers, while all the foresighted thrifty ants who had stored up tickets in advance streamed through the glamorous portals.

We offered fat bribes to the hotel concierge if he could get us in, but either he was a man of granite integrity or the house was sold out. I even tried calling the head of the press department. I murmured that I was a writer, that I had a syndicated newspaper column, that I was doing a book—the Vienna opera, I implied, would become a household word in the remotest American hamlet. I could hear the press man yawning over the phone . . ."Madam," he said, "there are no tickets." Maybe there weren't.

We added unnecessarily to our woes, however, by an evening at the Volks Oper. The bill was *Wiener Blut*, by Johann Strauss. How could we go wrong? With the greatest of ease. *Wiener Blut* and the performance thereof were dogs. As we spoke no German, the intricacies of the plot escaped us, but ham, Austrian, German, Polish, French, Italian, is still ham, as were the sets and direction. We left after the first act. Unable to find a taxi, we rode a streetcar back to the hotel. I don't know why riding the streetcars or subways of foreign countries always makes me feel so triumphant, but I get a sense of splendid accomplishment. Giving the conductor the right amount of money—this is usually accomplished by holding out a fistful and letting him take what he wants—getting off at the correct station—Well, I think to myself, I'm not an idiot after all. This reaction is probably caused by the fact that in the city of New York, where I was born and have spent most of my life, I am an imbecile where transportation is concerned. I will spend a small fortune on taxis and eat meat balls for a month rather than enter into the interstices of the I.R.T. and the B.M.T. Busses I'm not quite so allergic to, as I can see where I'm going. The minute I come to a corner beyond familiar territory I get out and take a cab. Granted that I am mentally deficient in these matters, I still feel it should be possible to simplify the New York subway system.

In Vienna we had better luck with other enterprises than we had enjoyed at *Wiener Blut.* On Sunday morning, the sixth day of rain as I noted in my diary, we went to the chapel in Josef Platz to hear the boys' choir. The chapel is small, there is only a center aisle, and throughout most of the service we stood packed in with other tourists and worshipers. Toward the end we were able to slither our way into a couple of seats when their occupants abandoned them, but even under these adverse circumstances I was glad to have gone. Between shoulders and under ears we could glimpse the golden vestments of the three priests glinting and sparkling in the light of the tall candles and the crystal chandeliers. The young boys' voices were pure and lovely, especially that of the child who sang the Hallelujah. The doctor later claimed to have heard a couple of cracks, but he was in a bad mood, induced by the crowding. It is true, however, that he is more tutored in music than I am.

We left before Mass was quite finished that we might be in time for the performance of the Spanish Reitschule next door, also a part of the Imperial Palace, as is the chapel.

The Reitschule, the only *haute école* of equestrianism in the world, was founded in 1562 by the Hapsburg Emperor Maximilian II, who first brought Spanish horses to Austria. Between 1729 and 1735 the Emperor Charles VI ordered the erection of the magnificent riding academy in which they perform today. It is an enormous oblong hall almost three stories high with great double rows of windows one on top of the other down both sides and around the end. There is also a double row of balconies, the upper level supported by high columns, and it is lighted, as is the Redoutensaal, with glorious crystal chandeliers. The fill of the ring looked like soft brown cork or peat moss.

The white horses are called Lipizzaner after the village in Spain where they were originally bred. They are born dark-skinned and turn white only as they grow older. Their riders are unparalleled, true centaurs, slim, erect figures in tight-fitting maroon coats with a double row of brass buttons down the front and tails that lie on the horses' backs. Their white breeches are skin-tight; their high black boots gleam. They wear chamois gloves and black bicorne hats with a cockade of gold braid.

With no word of command, only the pressure of knees and reins, the horses break from one gait to another. They create diagonal and herringbone patterns, but there is almost no swift action, only one brief trotting sequence. The only sound is the off-stage music, the snuffling of the animals, the creak of saddles, and the clapping of the spectators. Beside the open patterns they do dance steps, and at a given moment the reins are dropped and they leap straight into the air from a standing start. The house leaps too in a burst of applause. Their precision as they work together challenges the demoiselles of the Radio City Music Hall, but from the point of view of a nonequestrian American, each act, although beautiful, is a little too long.

Supposedly a Lipizzaner never errs in the ring, but one was a human horse and did. I was pleased for the sake of the hungry little sparrows flying about the upper reaches of the hall.

The story goes that during the war both the Russians and the Americans had their eyes on the horses, but our General Patton got there fustest with the mostest and one dark night spirited them out of town under the otherwise-occupied noses of the opposition, so they were saved, thank heaven, for decadent capitalism.

A less regal but still-entertaining occasion was our visit to the Moulin Rouge, a famous Viennese night club. As one sits down at the table a bottle of champagne is plumped upon it and there is no other liquor. The champagne is obligatory and costs five hundred fifty schillings, about twenty-two dollars, drink it or not, but that is the only charge and under the circumstances can hardly be considered exorbitant. The show runs for over two hours and it's good. There were magicians, jugglers, Spanish dancers, French singers, and, its *raison d'être*, les naked girls. But naked. In Vienna it's not a strip-tease they give! No beads, no fans, no doves, no bubbles do these fair maidens wear. As they were born so do they appear, and it must be said that most of them had lovely bodies. The act that made us laugh was one in which the turntable revolves bringing into view an all-girl naked orchestra holding cardboard instruments, lutes, flutes, and violins. There's something very funny about everyday pursuits pursued in the nude.

There were also more suggestive acts, ze naughty games played against a lamppost and a lady returning from the opera. You knew that she'd been to the opera, because she had on pearls and a cape of which she was quickly relieved by her maid, identifiable by her cap and minute, transparent apron. The lady then relaxed upon a couch and indulged in imaginative pastimes with her rope of pearls.

It is perhaps redundant to add that the Moulin Rouge does excellent business and the night we were there there was a large party of middle-aged Middle Western American women chaperoned by a couple of

travel-agency guides dutifully absorbing the folkways of an ancient culture.

Parting from friends is hard, but at least when we left Austria we knew we would be seeing the Fejoses in New York in the fall.

We left them and charming, rainy Vienna and flew by Caravelle to Athens. The flight was two and a half hours, smooth and delicious, a bolt of silk unrolling. We arrived at night to find that the American Express man had goofed. As we learned the next day, he met a later plane. We managed to get our luggage through customs, get to the Hotel Grande Bretagne, tip and pay the cab, without a drachma to our names, by the judicious application of an occasional dollar bill. Things cost more this way, but in a pinch the extra expense is justified.

Traveler's Tip No. 12: Keep a little American money in small bills in an inner section of your billfold. You'll need it anyway when you arrive back home, and it's always negotiable in emergencies.

The next morning we were up early to greet nearly our first rain-free day since we had been in Europe. We breakfasted on the terrace of our room and decided that if Greece could export her climate she would be the richest nation on earth. The sunshine is hot, the air dry, the breezes cool, and this for eight months of the year. Because of the lack of rain the great Attic plain is bare and dusty, but the climate does much to preserve the incomparable ruins and to encourage foreign travelers.

In Greece we had decided to splurge and to engage a car with chauffeur and an English-speaking guide. The latter is a real necessity. The myth that a winning smile and a smattering of French can take you around the world is not accurate.

Our guide was Mando Aravantinou. She had soft brown eyes and was intelligent, informed, and pleasant. She spoke fluent English and only occasionally did we encounter a little semantic confusion. The first day she suggested going to the Benaki, a small museum in Athens that she said we might find interesting, as it showed contemporary Greek art. I am interested in modern art and always like to see the work currently being done in any country. There were indeed some treasures in the Benaki, but the most contemporary piece was a fourteenth-century icon. We decided that Mando was using the word in its broad historic sense, and after all, when your history goes back three thousand years before Christ, the fourteenth century probably seems fairly recent.

Besides the icon there were three exquisite necklaces made of leaves

of pure gold. They were not quite so contemporary, dating, I think, from the great days of Cretan civilization, around 1600 B.C.

Before absorbing culture in the museum, however, we had had a more earthy experience in the post office. When we arrived at the hotel we had found a notice from them saying they were holding a package for us. The pharmacopoeia I had so inexcusably forgotten the day we left New York had arrived. Our first trip in our rented car with Mando and Panyotis at the wheel was to pick it up.

It was fortunate we had Mando, as we certainly had nothing else. The concierge at the hotel still held Norton's passport, and he hadn't thought to ask for it back, yet he had in some way to prove to the satisfaction of the Greek postal authorities that he was a doctor before they would hand over to him what, as far as they were concerned, might be a couple of pounds of heroin. Mando felt that a prescription blank with his office address on it might help. At least it would look professional. My dear quack didn't have one. Well, then, did he have a card? To be sure. American Express cards, Diners' Club cards, Texaco cards for charging gasoline, even, for auld lang syne, a couple of greasy, disintegrating speak-easy cards. Professional calling cards, no. By this time the postal clerks were tapping their foreheads and snickering behind their hands. A doctor, eh? That was a hot one! A dope smuggler and they were right the first time. Well, said Mando, and by now she was getting desperate, did he have anything with numbers on it? The Greeks were great ones for numbers; maybe something of the sort would impress them. Numbers we had! Norton pulled out his driver's license. There they were, numbers in a great gorgeous string and, better still, the magic letters "M.D." tacked onto the end of his name. Mando translated what they meant. The clerk still looked skeptical, but he must have been impressed to some extent, for he beckoned to her, she left us at the counter and followed him down the hallway. It was then that another little fellow who had been hovering at the perimeter of all the pourparleying seized his chance. He was convinced of Norton's au-

Vasiliv

thenticity. Mando, pleading her cause, must have said that Dr. Brown was the most distinguished physician in the United States of America, for our man poured out his symptoms and drew a madly waving line indicating the irregularity of his pulse. "He's got high blood pressure, too, and bum kidneys," the doctor said to me. "Transparent look, waxy skin—could well be uremia." He looked disapprovingly at an ash tray piled high with cigarette stubs, shook his head, and moved his hand back and forth in a strong negative gesture. The little official hung his head in shame. Seeing this, his colleague at the next desk gave a short, contemptuous laugh, pushed forward his own ash tray, innocent of a single butt, thumped his chest to show his excellent condition, and looked proud. The doctor gravely nodded approval.

At this moment Mando came hurrying up to announce that the problem was solved and all Norton had to do was to sign a sheaf of papers. We went out of the office and down the hall to a window where documents and more officials awaited us, the rest of the office personnel hot upon our heels. By this time word had got around that an American doctor was on the premises. One fellow who had liver spots held out his hands to the great healer. It was funny but it was also touching. "You know," Norton said to me later, "I am thinking of setting up the Klinico Brownapopolus. I might not make any money but I'd sure have patients."

After luncheon we took advantage of the siesta period to try to get in touch with a few people to whom our dear friend Deppy had written. Deppy is Despina Messinesi, a long-time member of the Vogue staff who, although born in Boston, was born there of Greek parents. Several years of her life have been spent in the homeland, and she had written to friends to alert them of our coming. "All you have to do, Ilka dear, is to phone on your arrival. They are longing to see you." The wear and tear of life have taught me that very few friends of mutual friends long to see foreign strangers, but I planned on being the soul of tact, of giving them plenty of outs was there the tiniest implication that their cups were already running over without us. My diplomacy was needless. Greek phone service is worse than French, so that it was to be some little time before contact of any sort was established.

In the late afternoon Mando came back to fetch us, and we drove to the Acropolis. We stopped first at the amphitheater that lies at the foot of the height crowned by the Parthenon. The curving benches are broken, chipped, tumbled, but still in place, as are the marble chairs, the seats of honor for the legislators. The carved statues of the frieze against the low wall are for the most part headless, but their exquisitely graceful nude and draped torsos and the kneeling Atlantes are well preserved in their perfect proportion.

Having completed our camera work, we started our climb. I suppose the same emotion holds, if to a lesser degree, with any famous monument. Will it live up to its reputation? The weight of fame and history is formidable, and dreary steel engravings in schoolbooks do little to quicken interest and imagination. Uh huh, we think, looking at them, so that's the Parthenon. And then perhaps one day we get to Athens. We are here! We've come a long way and spent a lot of money. It had better be good. Don't worry about the Acropolis. It is awe-inspiring. Probably every visitor has a favorite time for his first sight of it. We saw it frequently afterward, but our suggestion for the very first encounter is near sunset. The light at that time is a benediction. The serene, majestic columns of the Parthenon, tawny in color against the pure deep blue sky, frame incredible vistas. All we wanted to do was to stand very quietly and look and look and look.

More than twenty-four hundred years old, bruised, battered, worn and partially destroyed, combining to an astounding degree solidity and grace, it still stands, incomparable testimony to man's aspiration. In 1687 the Turks, who had been in control of the city since the fifteenth century, with a truly shattering lack of prudence used the Parthenon as a powder magazine. It was hit by a shell fired by the bombarding Venetian army and the great central portion of the temple was blown to smithereens.

Nearby is the temple of Athena. The architectural feature, the caryatides upholding the portico, famous around the world as the Porch of the Maidens, was referred to airily by Mando as the Girls' Place. Another beautiful building is the Propylaea, the entrance gate of the Acropolis.

My other nugget of art and architectural knowledge—besides remembering that it was Ghiberti who designed the doors of the baptistery in Florence—is the three styles of Greek columns. For some happy reason Doric, Ionic, and Corinthian have always stuck in my mind. Furthermore I can identify each design. It remained, however, for Mando to teach me that Doric symbolized strength, Ionic wisdom, and Corinthian beauty, the three pillars of the ancient world. The columns of the Parthenon are fluted Doric.

Another classic sight that gave us considerable pleasure was the evzone sentry, in his ballet skirt with great pompons on his shoes, who was patrolling up and down in front of the palace. Gun on shoulder, he would march smartly for a few yards, bring his heels together with a click, make a brisk pirouette, skirts flaring, and march back to his point of departure. We did not dare speak to so exalted a being, but Norton aimed his camera and shot him, so to speak, on the rise, the split second between the halt and the turn.

The evening of our first day we drove with Christopher and Judy Sakellariadis, who were friends and patients of Norton, to dine at a restaurant on the shores of the Aegean. On the way out Mr. Sakellariadis detoured up a special hill from which one may obtain a matchless view of the Acropolis lighted by night.

The great spectacle was a source of rancor, and Son et Lumière, which the French were trying to promote with the Athenians, was the reason. These performances were being staged at historical monuments throughout Europe. By a combination of music, lighting effects, and narration, famous events that have transpired in these locations are evoked and re-created for large audiences usually to considerable acclaim. The Acropolis had been scheduled for the treatment too, but apparently it was to take place at the time of the full moon when the Athenians themselves, out of respect for the natural beauty of the occasion, were wont to forgo their own usual nocturnal illumination.

Athenian society was split into two factions, the Philistines and the Artists. The Artists contended that the Philistines, gross of soul, were all for having Son et Lumière, since the French were footing the bill and the attraction, wherever it had been done, had proven popular. This was the crassest kind of materialism and they, the Artists, would have no truck with it. The Acropolis was unique in the world and if that incomparable work flooded by moonlight wasn't enough for both natives and tourists, then they were quite simply barbarians and the hell with them. It was very stimulating.

The restaurant to which the Sakellariadises took us on this night of controversy was the Asteria, on Asteria beach. This is a public bathing beach, easily accessible by tramway from the center of Athens. Office workers frequently go out there to lunch and swim during the siesta period, which, during the summer, lasts from two until five in the afternoon, when shops and offices are again open for business. They close sometime after eight. Nine o'clock is the rush hour, when the busses are jammed, and by nine-thirty the restaurants are beginning to fill. Bedtime is late, for the balmy evenings are delightful and everyone wants to linger under the stars.

The sand is fine and pleasant, the cabañas are clean, and the parasols, green, raspberry, and butter yellow, are very gay. Although open to the general public it is not overcrowded; the atmosphere is that of an attractive private beach club at home. We went there a couple of times to swim and enjoyed ourselves thoroughly. This agreeable state of affairs is explicable, I think, on two counts. One is Greece is not yet suffering from overpopulation. The public may still find pleasure in public places. The other is that the charge for cabañas and parasols, though modest from an American point of view, still is a little high for many Athenians. We were struck by the notable absence of banana skins and beer cans, but just so that we wouldn't go overboard on Greek refinement, perfection was side-stepped by a couple of braying portable radios. Greek boys and girls also go for rock-and-roll, and the stations most tuned to are those carrying United States overseas programs. A good deal of English was spoken on the beach, most educated Greeks learn it in childhood, and there were also American wives and children of our overseas servicemen.

For a delightful drive out of Athens I should recommend Sounion, at the end of the Attic Peninsula. The road, a comparatively new one, is very good, winding along inlets, coves, and bays of deep and brilliant blue. I suppose the day will inevitably come when the area will be encrusted with developments, but at present it is deserted and seductive. Three beneficial hurdles to progress are the lack of water, electricity, and telephones.

At Sounion there is a group of beautiful columns, the ruins of a temple to Poseidon, of particular interest at that time, as active reconstruction was in progress. Gaunt scaffoldings adjoined the ruins, and on the ground segments of columns two and a half to three feet in thickness were being fitted with sections cunningly chiseled to match exactly the fluting and proportion of the original. Later they would be hoisted into place.

There is a mediocre restaurant at Sounion and I fed a thin little Grecian cat and gave it two saucers of water—there was no milk— which it lapped up as though it were nectar. I think its thirst had never been assuaged before.

Norton and I dined one night in a sea-food restaurant in Piraeus right on the water's edge. To enter it, you go down five or six steps from the road. Across the road is the kitchen, and waiters bearing great trays of dishes dodge traffic as nimbly as their French colleagues at the restaurant in the Place du Tertre in Paris.

This restaurant, too, had a cat, a dusty, thin little creature. How *can* a cat be thin in a fish restaurant? But this one was. When offered a morsel it glanced right and left and winced, obviously frightened and expecting a kick, but too hungry not to snatch the tidbit. Greece was one of the highlights of our trip, but beginning in Greece and continuing around the world throughout Southeast Asia the treatment of animals was horrifying, ranging from callous indifference to active cruelty. This of course was not true of the educated and sophisticated people we met, who loved their pets, but kindness is not a basic human instinct.

We met some charming Athenians, and among them our chauffeur Panyotis ranked high. His English was limited, and the little he knew he found irritating. A particularly galling phrase was "O.K., Panyotis, we have time at our disposal." This he claimed was the favorite refrain of the English. They would be lolling under a tree sipping Ouzo, relishing the leisurely life, assuring him that the day was yet young. "No hurry, old boy, none at all." "And," he exclaimed, sputtering with indignation, "this always when we had to be hurrying to catch train or plane."

Anyhow one fine day with Panyotis at the wheel and Mando beside him we set out for Delphi, about a four-hour drive from Athens. On the way we passed through Thebes, once a great city, the home of Oedipus and his complex, today a lively small town through which the tourist busses roll. Those busses, incidentally, are commodious and comfortable. Thebes confused me. Having seen Sir Laurence Olivier's unforgettable performance of Oedipus, I kept thinking he must live there. Maybe we could call?

The home of Apollo was Mount Parnassus. The Muses dwelt on Mount Helicon, nearby. Whenever Apollo was feeling giddy he lighted a candle, and the girls, spotting this invitation, trooped over for a bit of a chat and a wing-ding. Delphi, Mando explained, means Delphine or Dolphin, who was the God of the Cretans. He came to the Greek mainland to this location high in the hills above the Bay of Corinth and found a shrine already established to the earth mother, but he didn't mind, he moved right in beside her and changed the name of the place to Delphi. The way the Greeks talk about the ancient gods you find yourself beginning to accept them as picturesque, not too remote ancestors and after a little time you're not at all sure that they didn't exist. Who's to guarantee that they were mere figments? Their temperaments, their characters, their exploits, they're well known. Where there's all that smoke . . .

Delphi is fascinating, but the site of the oracle is now no more than a few revered stones. What is charming is the little one-room marble house that was the Athenian treasury and also the refuge of the ambassador when he was there. The city-states sent their envoys to Delphi to consult the oracle and to spy on each other. Politics apparently were much the same in those days. Questions had to be submitted in writing and the oracle actually was the mouthpiece of the priests, who were politically powerful and had all ten fingers in governmental pies.

The Platonic philosophers somewhat queered the business by favoring realism over mysticism, but for many hundreds of years the priestesses or Pythias, as they were called, did a brisk trade handing down predictions, making decisions, and peddling influence.

The stadium carved out of a hillside is a long, narrow course, the tiers of stone seats in a surprisingly good state of preservation. It could accommodate several thousand people, and it is curious and exciting to visualize the stream of chariots and horses galloping along the dusty roads, pounding up the steep hills, bearing the throng of spectators who had undoubtedly been gouged by speculators for their seats, bearing too the highly keyed, highly trained, perhaps occasionally apprehensive athletes.

One may still see the ruins of the brick shops installed by the Romans, and lower down the hillside the beautifully proportioned columns of a lovely little temple. Delphi is a site rather than a city really, for everything is close at hand and intimate in scale. The museum boasts the famous statue, the *Charioteer*, one of the most perfect relics of ancient times. It is a bronze standing figure of a boy, a bandeau around his head, wearing a long, simple, pleated tunic, and in an excellent state of perservation, with the exception of a small hole in his garment.

The night of our Delphi visit we spent at a nearby mountain inn, a modern tourist hotel, somewhat larger but not unlike the Spanish *paradores*. Before dinner with cocktails and afterward coffee we sat out on the terrace gazing at the mountains and far below the Gulf of Corinth and the twinkling lights of the little villages hugging the shore. The moon rode high, and Venus, or, to give her her Greek name, name, Aphrodite, never shone so bright. The day had been hot but the night was cold, and no gnat or mosquito disturbed the nocturnal paradise. Alas, it was a different story in the morning, when the first light and the flies arrived together. This is not true of Athens, but in country villages food and donkeys are close at hand.

In the mountains the farmers are either so lazy or so indifferent that they leave the harsh, high wooden saddles on the donkeys all night so that they cannot lie down or roll. I kept inveighing against the cruelty; Norton kept saying, "It can't be cruelty, that would be idiotic, they must have a reason." What reason? The few lucky donkeys that were owned by decent people had had their saddles removed and were able to rest. If there were any valid reason for keeping them on, presumably all the peasants would do so.

Fortunately we did meet people who were not only kind to animals but eminently bright, among them the vivid and highly successful Helen Vlachos. I had first met her a year or two before when she was on a visit to New York, and it was pleasant to see her again. She asked Norton and me to lunch with other friends, Mr. and Mrs. Argyropoulos.

Mr. Argyropoulos is a diplomat. He has been Greece's ambassador to China and Italy and was a member of the Greek delegation at the establishment of the United Nations in San Francisco.

Helen Vlachos is feminine, small-boned, and delicate—clearly a believer that woman's place is in the office and the world at large. This doesn't mean that her apartment is not charming; it is furnished in great taste, with an enviable view of the Acropolis; but most of her day is spent at the office, for she is the publisher of *Kathimerini*, which was founded by her father and is the most widely circulated daily paper in Greece. She also runs a monthly and a weekly illustrated magazine, is, or was at that time, president of the Publishers' Union and the Movie Critics' Circle, vice-president of the Hellenic Society for the Protection of Animals—I planned to bring the cats and donkeys to her attention—and vice-president of the Association of Greek Chess Players. In speaking of her various interests she laughed, "You find me everywhere, like catsup in America."

Helen Vlachos has traveled widely throughout Russia, Europe, and the Orient, as well as the United States, and is a great New York fan. "Extraordinary city, a continuous world's fair. You have the best gathered from all over the earth. The best makers of music, the greatest pictures, your stores carry the finest that is designed in clothes, furniture, everything. Your architecture and your weather are the most stimulating!"

I reminded her that we had met in New York on a sweltering July day and said that on occasion our climate left something to be desired. "Not at all," she said firmly, "it was summer. I expect to be hot in summer but New Yorkers I have noticed are always surprised by their weather."

When on that first meeting we had spoken of the war and the frightful hardships her country had endured, she observed that the first year was the worst. "After that one becomes accustomed. War is classic, one accepts it." I suppose that to the Greeks classics are second nature, even grim ones. She added that the Greeks felt the aftermath to be far more dreadful than the war itself. "We thought it was over, you see, we thought we had won. Our frightful struggle was with the communists between 1945 and 1947. Thirty-five thousand people were killed in Athens in one month. Over a thousand a day, it was appalling."

It is strange to meet people who are intelligent and well bred, witty and gay and in their lives are experiences, behind their eyes are memories of some of the most savage butchery in history.

Norton has told me that he is never quite braced for the shock he feels when sometimes, asking a new foreign patient about his background or whether his parents are dead and what they died of, he learns that they were never ill, that they died in a bombing or in a nazi gas chamber.

At luncheon Alexander and Kaity Argyropoulos, more succinctly known as the Argys, offered to act as guides for a trip around their city. We accepted with pleasure. The gentleman Argy was most anxious that we see Mount Hymettus, which was fine with us, what with its being so historical and the source of that delicious honey, but we discovered he was interested in it for reasons other than history and *gourmandise*.

During the war, in their desperate need for fuel, the Germans and the Greeks themselves had cut down every tree on the mountainside, and Mrs. Argyropoulos almost singlehandedly had reforested it. Aided by only a small committee of women, she had planted one million, three hundred thousand trees. To see them is to appreciate the truly gargantuan effort of these women, because while the planting is not so difficult, the terrific aridity of the country makes survival almost impossible. All Greeks that summer were worried about the drought they were undergoing, and Kaity Argyropoulos had obtained aid from Greek army soldiers who drove around in trucks watering the young trees.

Besides her reforestation project our hostess had also done a great deal of work on the Byzantine monastery of Kaisariani, dating from the eleventh century. The frescoes in the chapel, sixteenth century, are lovely in color and in excellent condition. "When I first took over there were big conferences on how to restore them," she said. "I thought maybe just washing them would work, and do you know, it did."

The view of the city from Kaisariani is magnificent. There are only eight million Greeks in the whole land and nearly a million and a half of them live in Athens. There are those Athenians who would have some return to their villages and farms, but it is easy to see that the life of the city is more tempting when meanwhile back at the farm nothing much is going on. The country produces wheat and olives, tobacco, wine, cotton, citrus fruits and goat cheese, and most of it, I should say, is produced by women. Driving through the villages, one is struck by the life of ease pursued—if that is not too active a word—by the men. Greek men in the country sit at little tables in front of the cafés and under trees doing absolutely nothing. They don't read the papers, don't drink coffee or wine, they don't even drink water, although, for the reassurance of timorous tourists, Greek water is excellent. They just sit. The women work in the fields, the lower part of their faces swathed in the black headcloth typical of the Greek peasant.

After we had seen the museum our friends took us back to their house. Kaity Argyropoulos is a connoisseur of art and a determined, efficient, patriotic woman. She drives a car with determination, too. We were both shaken and impressed when she turned into a one-way street heading firmly in the wrong direction. All those drivers going the other way made her very mad.

Her house is the style found on the Greek islands, white, part Arab, part modern, situated in the heart of Athens with a lovely garden and a mouth-watering collection of jade that Alexander Argyropoulos gathered together when he was ambassador to China. They also had a small, yapping white poodle, the gift of Clare Boothe Luce.

As we sat in the garden over our drinks they told us a little of their war experiences. Kaity and their child escaped; her husband was captured by the Germans and held for a year in solitary confinement. Looking at him, frail of frame, patrician in bearing, with a face wonderfully sensitive and intelligent, one wondered how he had retained his sanity. I expect a well-furnished mind and a dauntless heart are sources of strength under a terrible ordeal.

Thanks to the good offices of our host, when we went to the Acropolis Museum we were permitted into rooms that were at that time closed to the general public. I can't imagine why, for there were some extraordinary sculptures admirably arranged, but Mando said wearily that things had been like that for a year. Politics. The Archaeological Museum is another gem, with a fabulously beautiful gold death mask and delicate, embossed golden cups. They are Mycenaean and date from about 1500 B.C.

As always sight-seeing seemed to work upon our gastric juices, and in the course of our stay we frequented several *tavernas*. Tavernas are fun, in the spirit of the French *bistro*. The food is good and the atmosphere informal. You make your way to the kitchen and snoop about to see what's cooking and make your choice. While waiting for the meal to be ready you relax in the garden over a carafe of Greek wine, coarse good bread, olives, cheese, and cucumbers. French wines are the world's greatest, but for daily drinking the light white wines of Austria and Greece are little loves. They make you feel happy and relaxed. You don't get drunk and you don't get sick.

One of our favorite tavernas was the Old Palm. There was no palm in sight but there was a flourishing young fig tree and great hogsheads of wine set on the white gravel of the garden. Dining there one night, we saw a very old man with skin like brown parchment, a patriarchal nose, and silky white hair, long as a woman's bob, clustering in rich curls about his ears. He was beautiful.

Greek delicacies that particularly appealed to us were the pistachio nuts. They hawk them in the streets, big rolls of them wrapped in cellophane. They cost two or three drachmas, about eight cents, and are delicious.

Since we could not pronounce the names of streets and stores, the doctor and I spoke to one another in the grand and classical manner rather like a badly translated play. "One finds those woolen skirts in the shop enjoying the patronage of the queen," I would say, and one morning, speaking of the drugstore, he informed me that, "It is at the foot of the street at which Panyotis waits." That was the street we came to know best. It was around the corner from the Hotel d'Angleterre and every morning the sleek black Cadillacs of the American Express would be lined up waiting for the patrons to start on the day's sight-seeing.

In Athens the offices of the American Express are not large and usually they were jammed. I myself thought of it as the great father image. From it flowed cars and guides, tickets and chauffeurs and—oh, fatal blessing—the credit card that so gently hypnotizes one, inducing a sense of euphoria and the delusion that though low in traveler's checks there is cash galore in the bank at home. If I was able to use any will power at all and apply the brakes before irreparable damage was done, it was due not so much to prudence and a sense of thrift as to a deep-seated aversion to paying the piper long after the dance is over. I prefer to feel that such pennies as do remain in the bank at the end of the month are mine all mine.

One hot and sunny Sunday we drove from Athens to Corinth, traveling over the bridge that crosses the great trench separating the Peloponnesus from the mainland, the Corinth Canal. A new café had just opened, and we were frightfully thirsty and longing for beer, but it was a very new café indeed and the proprietor was waiting for the priest to come and give it his blessing. Apparently selling anything before he got there would be jumping the gun and might bring bad luck. By fetching it herself from the inner depths Mando was able to get us a glass of water, but it was obvious from his expression that the boss took a dim view of us and our requirements.

The ruins of Corinth spark the imagination. It must have been a marvelously colorful port, welcoming sailors and traders from the entire Mediterranean world: Egyptians, Phoenicians, Ionians, Syrians, they swarmed into the city bawling and trading and peddling their wares. A thousand courtesans trafficked in the market place. They wore nail-studded sandals, and as they walked the dusty roads the nailheads spelled out "Follow Me." They would send their slaves to post their names in the market. Beneath it a man would write his name and the country of his origin, and it was up to the lady to decide whether or not she would accept him.

Still easily discernible are the ruins of the public toilets. The old two- and three-holers of a rural America of an earlier day, but made of stone instead of wood.

From Corinth it is not far to Nauplion and one of the romantic inns of Europe, Bourdzi. Bourdzi is an island in the gulf. Originally a fifteenth-century Venetian fortress, it was later turned into a prison, a dear little Alcatraz. Later still the Greek Government let it out as an inn. You get to it from the mainland in a putt-putt and tie up at the long stone jetty. The first afternoon we arrived we thought the place was run by children. Two little girls and a little boy scampered down to meet us and toted our bags back along the jetty and up the stone steps to the courtyard, where we were turned over to an adolescent damsel with her hair down her back. Baby-sitter *cum* manager, we decided. The infants—they couldn't have been over twelve—besides acting as porters waited on table and made up the rooms. We later discovered that there *was* a more mature element in charge: a large taciturn man with a head like a cannon ball and his mountainous wife, who did the cooking but who was not, unfortunately, a cook. Indifferent food was the one blemish, otherwise the place was a delight. Depending on the sun and moon, tables were set on different terraces and one night after a performance at the drama festival we sat at supper under the stars, watching the fireworks on the mainland.

They were not the fireworks of Mr. Aristotle Onassis of Monaco, but, like drops shaken from a celestial salad basket, the sparks cascaded down the sky in shining rivulets, making us very happy.

The Bourdzi terraces are at various levels, set at different angles, and abound with hollyhocks and fig trees, and the central patio is abloom with carnations. Plants have to be staked, as there is a good deal of wind, but the bathing pool is to leeward and the swimming is delicious. So is the sun-bathing.

Some of the walls of the fortress are four feet thick, but those are the thin ones. Others are *much* thicker than that. The rooms—most of them I believe were cells during the prison period—are grouped in turrets and open off terraces. They are whitewashed, there is electric light, and the beds are reasonably good. There are showers and wash-basins in the rooms, but no private toilets. The facilities, however, are spotlessly clean, well organized, and adequate. As far as the child labor was concerned, if it can be condoned at all, one may say that it was not too arduous and that it was based on the profit motive. Fortunately it was the children who profited. The patrons, beguiled by the small fry and troubled by a slight feeling of guilt, tipped them heftily and the money went toward their education. Theirs were summertime jobs and they returned to school in the autumn.

The inn accommodates twenty-five people, and if one is planning to be there at the time of the drama festival, it is advisable to make reservations well in advance. We had not done so, but thanks to Mando Aravantinou's skillful machinations we were able to get in. There was no room for Mando herself; she stayed in a hotel on the mainland on the water's edge.

Both in Greece and Japan, the only two countries where we had personal guides to look after us, we found the business very well organized. Their accommodations and meals are not the tourists' responsibility. If you like your guides and want them to eat with you, you are of course free to invite them; otherwise they assume that you prefer being by yourselves and go off to eat the meals and sleep in the

rooms all hotels provide for them. They probably like it better that
way too, as the employers must sometimes get on their nerves, and it
is a relief to be among their own friends, other guides shepherding
other trying parties through the beauty spots of the homeland.

As far as Mando was concerned the food situation was reversed. It
was she who was forever staying us with homemade cookies and tea
and coffee from the thermos bottle she carried with her.

I have mentioned the drama festival. This is an annual affair that
takes place at Epidaurus about a forty-five-minute drive over winding
mountain roads from Nauplion. The setting is extraordinary, the great
amphitheater cut in the hillside where Greek plays were first presented
2400 years ago. In an excellent state of preservation and undoubtedly
some restoration, it seats about 14,000. When we were there we estimated there were between 7500 and 9000 people in the audience. The
performance was the trilogy of Aeschylus on two successive nights. The
first evening as we were driving over Mando told us that Panyotis was
sunk in remorse because he had forgotten the permit that would enable
us to park close to the path up which one must climb to get to the
amphitheater. We laughed it off like the splendid sports we were, saying
a bit of a walk would do us good.

As we drove into the great parking lot, our progress was inevitably
slowed by the stream of cars all converging on the same place. The
policemen were wearing white uniforms with belts to which were attached small flashing electric light bulbs. It was early evening and still
light, but it would be dark by the time the performance was over. As
we drove along one policeman after another stepped forward to demand
our pass, but we did not stop. Always Panyotis shouted something
quite loudly, the policeman snapped to attention, and on we rolled.
We could make out the word "Amerikanoi" and nothing more. Only
too eager to hope our great nation was beloved by one and all, we nevertheless thought it odd that the mere mention of its name should call
forth such respect. Still we swept forward, Panyotis shouting, Mando
in the front seat beside him laughing her head off. Finally we could
bear it no longer. "What goes *on?*" we demanded. Between gulps and
giggles she told us. "Panyotis found his forgetfulness about the permit
too humiliating," she explained. "He's determined you shall get the
good parking space so he's telling all the policemen that you and Dr.
Brown are the American ambassador to Japan and his wife who have
come all the way from Tokyo to absorb Greek culture. As you see, they
are much impressed."

They were impressed and we were awed. Ambassadors yet! This in itself was inspired, but from Japan! How shrewd of Panyotis, what a diplomatic coup! Who would bother checking anything that remote! We swept with a glorious flourish and a smashing of brakes practically onto the stage itself. For the next three days the doctor answered only when addressed as "Your Excellency."

Our seats were reserved, but there was some difficulty about obtaining cushions, highly desirable in view of the fact that the tragedies of the fifth century are very hard upon the fannies of the twentieth. They are *long* and the seats designed by Mr. Polycletus, sculptor and architect, are *hard*. Mando was a veritable tigress fighting for her young when it came to getting cushions. She snatched them from under the very posteriors of those who had got there ahead of us.

We gathered that when the theater had been designed it was part of a center. Nearby had been a shrine to Asclepius and a temple to Hygeia, but they were destroyed long ago by an earthquake.

Norton and I had done our homework; we had bought a Penguin edition and read the trilogy: *Agamemnon, The Choëphoroe,* and *The Eumenides,* and we settled down, using our pocket flashlight as it grew dark, to follow the dialogue like Wagner lovers following a score.

The tiers of seats forming a semicircle rose up from the stage, which was walled on the far side by a permanent set, the façade of Atreus's palace. The first night I was very disappointed. Though spacious the façade was unadorned, a drab, tired brown far from regal. The next morning we went to see the ruins of Mycenae, and that's how the buildings were in that era, primitive and simple in the extreme. The costumes we thought only fair, but that part was unimportant. There was something strangely moving in seeing the same play that had been performed in that same theater 2400 years ago. The first night they did *Agamemnon.* We discovered, to our sneaking relief, that the script had been cut considerably, so the play moved at a brisker clip than we had anticipated. The principal players seemed lacking in voice and emotion for so formidable an assignment—remembering Judith Anderson in *Medea,* one could only wish that Aeschylus had been as lucky as Euripides had been in obtaining her services—but the chorus, which I had been looking forward to with some misgiving, was excellent. They had been admirably coached and chanted and danced and lamented with enthusiasm. As I had come late to many of the classics, it was instructive for me to learn that red carpet was not something thought up by Mrs. Vanderbilt's butler for New York's 400 to advance across when they slipped from their broughams to attend one of her dinners, but dates from the Greeks.

Clytemnestra rolls out this red carpet for Agamemnon—a subtle dig since he is abrogating to himself credit for the victory over the Trojans, which rightfully belongs to the gods. She has dirty work in mind, and it is a blood-chilling moment, but I could not help noticing that the carpet was of several strips sewn together, each from a different dye lot.

We returned to Epidaurus the next night for the double bill *The Choëphoroe* (The Libation Pourers) and *The Eumenides* (The Furies). This time we felt like habitués and went at once to the restaurant pavilion to get coffee and sandwiches to sustain us through the performance, and afterward strolled up the winding path to the theater. That night the Greek prime minister was there, seated not far from us, among his compatriots. His compatriots, we discovered, are impatient audiences. The performance was scheduled to start at seven-thirty. At seven thirty-one they began pounding and applauding, expressing their displeasure at the delay. They should attend a few New York theaters! Norton and I thought the Furies were convincing, but they were certainly a tatterdemalion crowd, wearing long, tangled wigs, and their agonized groanings and swayings evoked titters from the customers, followed by shamed shushings.

We read the reviews with interest. One Greek critic, writing in English in the Athens *Post*, observed that the actress who played Clytemnestra was a fine woman with an uneven physique. He also remarked of *The Eumenides* that the Athena was the black spot on the performance. There, unfortunately, we had to agree. The Greeks have the scripts, other countries have the actors.

Epidaurus, besides being the site of the theater, is also the site of an enormous beehive tomb built of stone and shaped like a gigantic Eskimo igloo. It was built into and under a natural mound about 1700 B.C., and one may still wander around inside it. The architecture in that part of Greece and in that era was primitive in the extreme, yet in the museums are the most exquisitely refined masks and objects of gold, molded, carved, and embossed. It is thought likely that sometime during the never-ending wars and conflicts among the Greek states the Mycenaeans subdued the Cretans and brought back their artisans to work as slaves. Such a speculation is probably correct, for, as we were to learn later on a visit to their island, the Cretans were sophisticated and enormously skillful.

On the afternoon of the day we returned from Nauplion we boarded the *Aegean* (ship) for our cruise of the Aegean (sea). There are two steamers, the *Aegean* and the *Semiramis*, that make the cruise of the Greek islands, and my advice is to take one of them, for this is an enchanting experience. We had become devoted to Mando and would have liked to have her with us, but the boats have their own guides, who are included in the cost of the trip and do not welcome outsiders, so we had, reluctantly, to part with her. One can, I believe, take more time and visit more islands, but our own journey lasted five nights and four days and was one of the highlights of our trip around the world.

It isn't that the boats are de luxe; they're not. The *Aegean* is no floating palace with Ritz restaurants, *soirées de gala*, bars, swimming pools, nurseries for the children, and runs for the dogs. The *Aegean* and her sister ship, the *Semiramis*, were English-built toward the latter part of the nineteenth century and used to ply Puget Sound. Eventually they passed into the Greek maritime service and are today sturdy and beloved craft, sailing in their declining years the wine-dark sea of Homer, and a real change it must seem from Clydebank and the western coast of the North American Continent.

Some of the cabins are infinitesimal—our first assignment was such a one—but via outraged bellows from me and a torrent of Greek rage released by Mando, who had come to see us off, we improved our lot. The second cabin was also small, but at least we could both stand upright at once, whereas in our original slot that would have been impossible. It is obviously desirable to have space to expand your rib cage, but after all, the staterooms function primarily as sleeping quarters and the berths are quite comfortable. There are no closets; you keep your clothes in your suitcases.

The bathing facilities are limited too, but you can swim every day in the Aegean so the deprivation is not acute. As a matter of fact we had a private bath consisting of washbasin, toilet, and a hand spray, and just across the hall was a quite large stall shower. You went in and closed the door, but as there was no curtain to draw, a dressing gown hung on a hook got sprayed along with the bather, and the only place I could find to put my slippers to keep them from getting wet was on my head tucked under my shower cap, but as the water trickles rather than gushes, no great damage is done.

Of the food I can say that it began fair and got better and better as the cruise progressed, and I have been on far grander craft than the *Aegean* and have experienced exactly the reverse. The local Ouzo is the best apéritif, and the table wines are good.

The cruise for two came to ten thousand drachmas, or about three hundred dollars, and that was for the better accommodations. There are some staterooms, food is included, for about seventy-five dollars a person. The management suggests tipping 5 per cent of the cost, certainly a reasonable amount.

The first night out, tired by all our gallivanting, I went to bed early, but there was a fashion show of Greek clothes held in the lounge, and the doctor decided to stay up to watch it. He arrived back in the cabin considerably stimulated by the exhibition and gave me an imitation of the way he fondly believed the models walked. Considering the floor space in which he had to cavort, he put on a spirited show.

On that first evening also we discovered that we were wonderfully lucky in our table companions, two delightful English couples, the Frank Hoares, from Wimbledon, and the Philip Tallents, from Cheltenham. There was also a pleasant young woman, as well as a monosyllabic South African from Rhodesia. His job was prospecting for oil in Persia and he was on holiday. He was allergic to neckties, wearing his shirt open with shaggy tufts of chest hair sticking out, and he hated everything from the moment we raised anchor till the moment it was dropped in the harbor of Piraeus on our return.

From the first the English and ourselves hit it off very well and went together on all our shore excursions. Mindful of our manners, we tried during the first few meals to include the girl and the ambulatory mattress in our conversation, but it was obvious we were not the most sympathetic creatures they had ever met, so our efforts petered out, and in a curious way they did too. It was as though they were photographic negatives fading from view, and one meal we discovered with a real start of surprise that they were no longer with us. They had asked to be moved to another table, and they were quite right.

The cruise, as I have said, was an unforgettable experience, but there were no long lazy days at sea. They worked us! Every morning we were up, had breakfasted and were off the boat by eight o'clock, following in the wake of one of the guides. They were three Greek women who spoke excellent German, French, and English. The first morning I naturally went with Norton, the Tallents, and the Hoares but our lady was of a skittish coquetry I found hard to bear. When viewing historic monuments I want the facts ma'am, just the facts. No reminiscences about, "When I was a little girl reading Greek mythology I used to think . . ." the whole served up with arch glances and fluttering pantomime and deliberate, appealing little mistakes in English.

Many of the tourists didn't feel as I did, they thought her cute, but those Greek ruins don't need any personalized icing, and after the first morning I deserted my husband and new-found friends to tag along with the French group. Their guide had a Gallic sense of discipline and restraint, and also there were fewer of them.

The first morning was Crete and the palace of Knossos, and very happy I was to have read Mary Renault's beautiful book *The King Must Die*, with its brilliant re-creation of the Minoan era. Incidentally there are two excellent little guidebooks, obtainable in Athens, that I heartily recommend. They are "Athens from the Acropolis" and "Crete, Delos, Rhodes," by Maria Alexandrapis and Cleo Mantzoufa. I believe them to be historically accurate and they are succinct and informative.

The island of Crete was inhabited as early as 5000 B.C. The first palace was thought to have been built about 2000 B.C., but it was destroyed, possibly by the earthquake that had demolished the shrines at Epidaurus on the mainland. The "new" palace, and it is the ruins of this one that the traveler visits, was constructed about 1700 B.C. and destroyed probably by another earthquake and fire in 1400 B.C. There has been a good deal of reconstruction, some of it unfortunate —the concrete beams and columns painted to simulate wood are pretty awful—but it is a fact that wooden beams were placed between the stone walls and the ceilings to offset the movement caused by earthquakes. The columns of the palace are tapered toward the bottom, a device that served two purposes. It was thought that that form better supported the great weight of the roofs and upper stories and it incidentally provided more standing space on the floor. The palace itself is enormous, covering between five and six acres, but the rooms, though numerous, are not very large. Even the throne room, with the original stone throne, is of modest proportion.

The two most striking features of Knossos are the frescoes and the plumbing. Most of the frescoes today are reproductions, the originals having been removed to the museum of Herakleion on the island, but they are exact reproductions and the color, beauty, and gaiety of the drawings are wonderfully fresh and modern in feeling.

The plumbing is noteworthy. The copper conduits constructed in 1700 B.C. are still in place and were never copied and never equaled until the twentieth century. The queen's apartments boast a handsome bathtub and a very practical flush toilet, and in the magazines still stand enormous earthen jars for storing oil and grain and dried fruits.

Inner windows look into open shafts that are in effect wells of light admitting sunshine and air. There is a staircase called Grand. It has not the sweep of the staircase of, let us say, the Paris Opera House, but it is still impressive. It is hollow underneath, and Sir Arthur Evans, the archaeologist who began excavating the palace of Knossos in 1900 and worked at it for thirty years, was obliged to import mine workers to keep it from collapsing as it was being uncovered.

We went from the palace to the museum of Herakleion in the town. They have there an exquisite little faïence statue of the snake goddess, with her exposed breasts, slim waist, and long, flounced skirts, holding in each hand a small, writhing serpent. She is wearing a flat hat with a bird perched on top of it and has a rather wild look in her eye, which, under the circumstance, is understandable.

There is also a glorious small sarcophagus and a fresco head of an extremely modern-looking girl with made-up eyes, a painted mouth, and long, curling hair. Because of her elegance she is known as La Parisienne. The frescoes of the men show them to have been equally elegant, with jeweled collars and curled hair, their slim waists wrapped with tight girdles, their heads crowned with lilies and peacock feathers.

Their bodies are painted red to indicate that they were hunters and athletes browned by the sun. The mainland Greeks had nobility, purity of line, the classic approach, but the Cretans were chic and gay.

The bull was their animal, and the athletic, frequently mortal bull dance and bull games are vividly described in Mary Renault's book. The museum has a marvelously spirited fresco of this sport and a fine sculptured bull's head, but I prefer the incomparable one and the golden masks and cups of the Archaeological Museum in Athens. They also have the Disc of Phaestus, inscribed with a spiral on both sides with little figures and signs pressed into the soft clay. This was fired, in the pottery sense, at the time of the earthquake and fire and has been preserved through the ages, so it may be considered the first printed plate in the world.

The second morning of the cruise Rhodes was on the agenda. Norton and I had thought to wander around by ourselves, depending on the guidebook for information, but in the end we got sucked into a guided party, and although I always feel slightly mesmerized when in a group of that kind, it is probably the most concise way of receiving concentrated information.

The largest of the islands is Crete, but Rhodes is no pin point. It is fifty miles long, twenty miles wide, and the port is dramatic. It is a flowery land bright with roses and hibiscus, bougainvillaea and azaleas, and, according to mythology, Poseidon, the god of the sea, fell in love with Halia, the sea goddess of the Telchines, and their daughter, Rhodes, gave her name to the island. Just as every small town in colonial America claims to be a spot in which George Washington bedded

down, so do most towns on the Greek islands claim to have been the
birthplace of Homer. Rhodes is no exception.

Myth inevitably swathes these ancient lands, but the huge statue of
the sun god, the Colossus of Rhodes, one of the seven wonders of the
world, is no myth. He did stand a hundred five feet high for fifty-six
years, but he did *not* straddle the harbor. He was knocked over by an
earthquake about 225 B.C., and the enormous fragments lay about, clut-
tering the landscape, one would imagine, for 830 years, when they were
removed by an ambitious junk dealer, a Saracen, who hired nine hundred camels to cart them away. They were lost forever in the deserts
of Asia Minor.

Today the notable site is the town itself, the most perfectly preserved
medieval city in Asia Minor, crenelated, moated, and highly romantic,
founded by the Knights of St. John. The straight, picturesque street,
the Street of the Knights—also known as The Street of Tongues because members of the order from all over Europe lived there—is lined
on either side by ancient houses decorated with carved coats of arms,
and the great hospital built around a courtyard, now a museum, is in
a state of excellent repair. The central hall is enormous and beautifully
proportioned, with a row of columns running down the center, and,
opening off it, small cells where the very ill and those with contagious
diseases were lodged.

The modern town lies on the small harbor of Mandraki. At the entrance are two columns topped by delicate bronze stags and there are
round towers—windmills—along the quay. A long, tree-lined avenue
runs the length of the harbor.

There is also a huge palace, built by the Italians in the current century, in which Mussolini once stayed. It is hideous, with shiny wood,
bulbous Chinese vases, Roman and Byzantine columns, alabaster windowpanes, and electrically wired Venetian chandeliers. A real fright.
Skip it.

Exhausted by sight-seeing, exhausted by the ugliness of the palace
as much as anything, we refreshed ourselves at a pleasant American
sort of delicatessen and went for a swim. The beach of Rhodes is not
sandy, it's made of trillions of tiny stones, but the water is delicious,
cooler and more refreshing than the water off Crete had been and with
a sharply shelving beach.

Back to the ship for luncheon and after a brief rest ashore again
for the trip to Lindos, another of the island towns. One goes by bus
and the drive takes over an hour. There are olive and apricot groves

along the way, and great walls and hedges of purple bougainvillaea.

By now we were so immersed in antiquity that the acropolis of Lindos seemed fairly recent, only 700 B.C. It is also virtually impossible of access but that is what the Hellenes love. I made up a poem. "On an inaccessible mountain peak, there you'll always meet a Greek." No one can guarantee whether the Russians or ourselves will get to the moon first, but I'll guarantee that whoever does will find a Greek well established. The more outlandish the location the better they like it.

The intrepid spirits of our party clambered up the mountain on foot. I rode up on a donkey that went full gallop and scared me to death. Once you achieve the summit there are a few columns, the remnants of a temple, and the view out over the Aegean is meltingly beautiful and the place is marvelously peaceful when the voice of the guide is stilled. I rather enjoyed her version of the Trojan legend, however. "Rhodes sent thirty ships to the war, and," said the guide, "bring Helen back. Menelaus was about to slaughter her. Sensing this, she dropped her garments. Such was the dazzling beauty of her naked body that this discouraged Menelaus and he dropped his sword."

Having lost faith in the donkey, I walked down the mountainside to the little village clustering at the foot. It is picturesque but achingly poor. The steep streets are actually staircases up and down the mountainside, somewhat like those of Palma in Majorca, but not so broad. They are set with black and white pebbles in charming geometric designs. The guide was supercilious about these, saying they lacked imagination, but I thought them most imaginative and pretty.

The next morning we dropped anchor off Cos. Cos is not so dramatic as some of the other islands, but in a way it was our favorite. It seemed to be more fertile than the rest, and in the big square was a colorful market place where we bought ripe figs and tiny plums. We also cashed some traveler's checks at the bank. Greece is not expensive, so I cannot explain how money seemed to melt away. Norton referred to this phenomenon as the Flight of the Drachma, and I could see them on swift, white little wings disappearing into the blue and golden air of Greece.

Owing to its more fertile soil, the struggle for survival doesn't seem quite so acute on Cos as on some of the other islands. There are lovely flowering trees of delicate pink and white oleander blooms and, as on Rhodes, foaming waves of purple bougainvillaea.

We viewed the usual hilltop ruins of what had once been a temple to Asclepius and where it is thought Hippocrates may have taught. He must have been a very good doctor, for, born around 460 B.C., he lived to be well over a hundred. There is a gigantic plane tree on the island under which, they claim, he definitely did teach. That the tree is of such great antiquity is fame enough whether the master expounded the principles of medicine there or not. It is nearly hollow in the center, and the huge, spreading branches now rest on iron supports, but its leaves are green and flourishing and good Dr. Brown stood proudly under it while I took his picture.

The island of Patmos was another delight, and I again accepted the mountain challenge on another donkey, this one so small I should have been carrying him. The wooden saddle and rope stirrups were uncomfortable, the white cloth they throw over the saddle for the sake of cleanliness was rumpled, and my chum placed his wee hoofs at the road's edge, from whence I obtained a dizzying view of the sheer drop to the sea. Coming down was worse, as he was heading for the stable and went at a spirited clip, loose stones flying and bouncing along our path. Surely, I thought, the creature is going to turn his ankle and topple me headlong into the sea. Were mountain ponies as sure-footed as mountain goats? I could only pray.

On top of Patmos there is a Byzantine monastery built in the eleventh century, with a small, dark, ornate chapel containing frescoes, carved wood, icons, a heavily embossed silver chandelier and many incense burners hanging from the ceiling.

The library is fascinating and boasts a fifth-century manuscript, the Gospel according to St. Mark in ancient Greek, wonderful embroidered vestments, and a crown of gold set with turquoise, emeralds, and diamonds given to the monastery by Catherine of Russia. A sweet old monk showed us around. He had long hair done up in a bun under his black chef's hat, and a sister in Houston, Texas.

On the way down the mountainside we stopped to see the grotto where St. John wrote the Book of Revelations in A.D. 95. It is curious to realize that events that seem apochryphal, lost in the mists of time, actually took place and that the people involved in them were once the normal people of their era and not strange historic characters so elusive to the youthful student who must memorize them.

Outside the grotto I had my big fight with a donkey driver who was beating the small animal unmercifully. There was something maniacal in his rage, and I regret to say it made me a little manic too. I admire the cold and controlled visitation of just wrath upon the transgressor, but I never seem able to manage it. I screamed at the man, slid from my own donkey, and went for him. He stopped in sheer astonishment at seeing an American woman furiously bearing down on him brandishing a stick. I don't suppose the surcease lasted long, but at least it gave the little beast a breather.

Before we climbed the mountain the Hoares and Tallents and ourselves had decided that we would dine at a small *taverna* on the quay that had caught our eye. Back on the level we went to select our menu from a table under a tree and on which were displayed all kinds of fresh fish but only six lobsters. We glanced quickly at each other. We wanted them. Apparently two or three other couples did too. Our boys started forward, pretending not to see the competition but all the time imperceptibly accelerating their pace. It was like trying to get a taxi after the theater on a rainy night. Loma and Joan and I held our breath. The others were gaining, when suddenly Philip leaped forward with a shout. "I'll take all six," he cried in Italian. Having spoken to the waiters earlier in the day, he knew they understood it. One of them darted forward, scooped up the beauties, and departed for the kitchen, winking at Philip over his shoulder. The enemy dropped back, muttering and tossing us lethal glances.

That meal was a bucolic idyll. We sat at the water's edge under the pepper trees in the starlight, sipping an excellent Ouzo while we waited for the lobsters to broil. With them we ate olives and tomatoes and cucumber and a delicious coarse bread. We drank white wine and had the figs I had bought at the market for dessert. We sent carafes of wine to the three fiddlers and watched the children and some of the boys and girls from the village dancing around the big tree that sheltered the *taverna*. It was an enchanted evening, and when the three men came to pay the bill they discovered that it amounted to a little over a dollar apiece. Once in a blue moon the best things in life *are* free.

We went back to the ship and sailed at 11 P.M. for Delos. Delos has exquisite mosaics, an avenue of marvelously engaging stone lions, and a high wind. Traveler's Tip No. 13: Dark glasses and a shade hat are musts, but be sure that the latter will stick with you. I took along what I thought was a dream. It had a brim, not too wide, just enough to shade my eyes, it was natural straw, so it would go with everything, it weighed nothing, and it was becoming. How could I miss? With the greatest of ease. It flew from my head at the first zephyr. I even had a comb in the headband to anchor it to my hair, but the winds of Greece merely puffed out their cheeks like the cherubs on old maps, blew a lusty gust, and my hat went sailing through the air. My gyrations getting in and out of the motor launch in which we plied between the ship and the islands could have pleased only a contortionist, as I was obliged to clutch my hat with one hand while clutching the rope railing of the steps that went down the ship's side with the other.

While on the subject of clothes I would also caution lady tourists to be sure to take bags with handles rather than the envelope variety, as you will want to keep your hands free for hanging on to things and taking pictures. I learned this elementary lesson only after acute annoyance caused by having either to put my bag on the ground or grasp it between my knees—a remarkably unappealing pose—when working with the Stereo.

Of all the islands we visited, Delos, the birthplace of Apollo, is the most arid and most devoid of life, the ground littered with stone, marble fragments, and broken columns. It is an enormous outdoor museum where nobody lives. They did, though. Once upon a time they lived there in splendor with great festivals and a heavily patronized slave market. Merchants of the Mediterranean world, attracted by its trade possibilities, established themselves there by the thousands. The crowd of dizzying color and variety must have been worse than Times Square on New Year's Eve, for Delos covers an area of about one square mile.

Today its lovely lions are one of the sights of Greece. There are five whole ones and nearby fragments of four relatives. They sit on pedestals on their haunches. The detail of their carving is worn away, but their mouths are open in defiance and their fading eyes gaze, fearless, upon the passing centuries.

The ancient underground water cisterns of Delos are still in good condition, and the houses are in good enough repair to give one a feeling of the daily life in the island's great days. There is an open-air theater, built around 300 B.C., that held about 4500 spectators, and a large, three-story building with many rooms and a big cistern of its own. It is thought that it was a hotel where people who came to the festivals and merchants who came to trade stayed.

In the house that belonged to a sea captain there is a small, well-preserved floor of inlaid mosaic with a center circle in a key-and-wave design and gay dolphins in the corners of the outer square. The color is lovely, tiles of black and white, beige and pink. Norton got a very good shot with his Leica, but it is funny to see it surrounded by tourists' feet as they stood gazing down at the picture. There is another marvelous mosaic, of Dionysius seated sideways upon a fierce and elegant panther that is wearing around his neck a wreath of ivy leaves caught by an elegant Cartier brooch, and one of a vase, a laurel wreath, and a palm, indicating that someone in the house won the Panathenaic games.

That day we lunched on shipboard and afterward went by launch to Mykonos. The sea was wildly rough, but Norton and Philip Tallent had the inspired idea of continuing in our cockleshell to St. Stephanos beach. We could just as well have got out at the little port, which was a much shorter haul from the *Aegean*, and gone to the beach by cab, but no. The boys had suddenly got a jolt of Vikings' blood and nothing would do but that we must breast the waves. The Hoares were no fools. "We will take a taxi," they said, "and meet you there." With only the skipper, Loma, myself, and our two gents aboard we bobbed over the white water like corks, but, once washed upon the rocks, as I was sure we would be, I could not think we would prove so buoyant. Romantically speaking, the ideal way, one hears, to cruise the Aegean is in a chartered schooner, either honeymooners alone with a crew, or two or three congenial couples sharing the expenses and the exhilarating work of the running wave. For them as likes it, O.K. It would not be my choice. The *Aegean* and the *Semiramis* are quite small enough, and if anything bigger made the cruise I would be happy to be on it. At that we were lucky to get to Mykonos at all. The captain told us that very frequently they approached the island only to find the water so rough they couldn't drop anchor in the harbor.

I have to admit, however, that St. Stephanos beach was a delight. We bathed and lay on the sand and much later went back to the little town of Mykonos itself. This time by car. The shops, widely touted, proved disappointing, but I did manage to find a bag of hand-loomed fabric and a red velvet eyeglass case sewn with gold. Norton bought a linen pullover of black and white horizontal stripes. It looked all right on Mykonos. When he got back to New York he gave it to his elder son.

The extraordinary thing about the town is its dazzling whiteness. The square houses look as though they were made of salt, and the crooked, winding little alleys are blindingly white. The wooden balconies are painted green and blue, and some of them are roofed with vine leaves.

The well-to-do Greeks have country places on the islands and many others of the Dodecanese that we did not see. They go by boat or more easily and swiftly by plane. They love their island houses, but they all wrestle with the lack of water. Baths are curtailed, gardens a serious problem.

Mykonos was our last port of call. Knowing we would be docking at

Piraeus very early the next morning, we said good-by to the Tallents and the Hoares the night before and exchanged addresses over the after-dinner coffee. Both couples turned out to be the shipboard acquaintances who endured. From time to time we write to each other, and when Norton and I were last in England we saw them both again.

CHAPTER FIVE

Istanbul ✳ Bangkok
Singapore ✳ Djakarta ✳ Bali

FROM ATHENS to Istanbul by French Caravelle the flight is a dream; quiet as sail, faster than the wind. One hour flat from door to door.

The customs procedure was mysterious. All the luggage was brought from the plane, placed in a gigantic pile in the middle of the floor, and left to mildew. There seemed to be no attendants and no plan for speeding the travelers on their way. After a little while we began to mutter and point to our bags. A couple of lackadaisical chaps arrived and, scenting mutiny, began in leisurely fashion to sort things out. There was a Turkish woman next to us who had to unpack every single item in her suitcase, open boxes, unroll laundry, turn dresses inside out—the whole process accompanied by whimpers, tears, and what sounded like muffled Turkish oaths. Norton and I were getting a little worried. We had nothing to conceal, but the nuisance value would be considerable if we were subjected to the same merciless search. Fortunately by the time he got to us the customs inspector was bored with the procedure and chalked our bags without opening them. We concluded he must have been tipped off that the woman was a jewel smuggler, but as far as we could see no diamond glittered among her rather pathetic and threadbare effects. We fell with relief upon the frail and aging American Express man who had come to meet us and who led us to the Istanbul-Hilton.

Even when traveling around the United States I prefer small, noncommercial hotels, and certainly, when abroad, staying in inns or in hotels run by the natives of the country one is visiting would seem to make more sense. I mean, I don't see the point of traveling halfway around the world to sleep with Mr. Conrad Hilton. But everyone of experience had said to us, "Listen, in Istanbul don't crowd your luck. Go to the Hilton. It's the only place you'll be comfortable." Well, it was comfortable, and we might as well have been in Pittsburgh. In Pittsburgh the view from the Hilton out over the river is good. In Istanbul it's better because you have the whole sweep of the Bosporus and a balcony, but the atmosphere indoors is American Commercial.

On the whole I think they manage hotel life better in Europe. It's a little more human. Here, once the snappy bellboy has set down your bags, flung open the window, for the room is usually at the boiling point, held out his hand, and departed, you're all alone with the Serv-A-Dor, the glasses shrouded in cellophane, and the antiseptic paper band around the toilet seat. Kind of bleak. In Europe and Asia they don't so automatically take it for granted that the guests are diseased.

Istanbul is magnificently located, lying as it does along the Bosporus, bifurcated by the Golden Horn. Driving in from the airport, one passes through the outer walls that were the old fortifications, and then up steep hills and along narrow, winding streets. Many of the houses have big square bay windows enclosed by fretted woodwork. They have a shabby, rather picturesque charm, but if anyone hopes for yasmaks, Turkish trousers, and fezzes—and I had hoped—he is in for disappointment. Turkish dress is as Western as our own, and fezzes are forbidden. Kemel Ataturk handed down the ukase when he was in power, and it has never been rescinded.

We arrived in the late afternoon and decided that our first evening we would dine at the hotel. The food was good, the atmosphere dreary, and the drinks terribly expensive. The Turkish currency at that time couldn't run to the importation of alcohol or even of coffee. Hotels and restaurants had them, but few individuals did. We were told that in the next two months the government was planning to import 500,-000 pounds of coffee from Brazil, and the Turks were hoping that the following year they might be able to import or make whiskey.

Our first full day in Istanbul was a Sunday. Since we were in a Moslem country I had assumed that everything would be open. Not at all. Turks observe the Christian day of rest along with any of their own.

Sight-seeing, however, was permitted, so we took a bus that was making a tour of the mosques. The driver started off in fine fettle, but his concert pitch was somewhat queered by two ladies who gave shrill little shrieks of dismay when they heard the word "mosque." "This is the mosque tour?" "Yes, ladies, it is." "But our tickets are for the Bosporus tour. Do stop, hurry, they'll go without us." The bus obligingly grinds to a halt. The ladies descend. We start off again.

Our first mosque was the loveliest, the one known as the Blue Mosque, although the Turks themselves usually refer to it as that of Sultan Ahmed I. It was built in 1616. The great dome is supported by four huge pillars. There are no pews, the floors are covered by prayer rugs, mostly crimson in color, and the whole effect is marvelously spacious and airy. The décor is blue and white tiles flecked with green in exquisite patterns, geometric and floral. The Moslem religion forbids depicting animal or human forms, for Allah, they say, is a spirit, not a person. There are fine stained-glass windows, the lights are small glass cups set at close intervals on low-hanging iron hoops. Today they have electric bulbs in them, but they used to be filled with oil in which floated lighted wicks, and a charming sight it must have been as they twinkled and glowed in the diaphanous gloom.

Altars are not as they are in Christian churches, they are niches in the wall in which the *hoca* (priest) stands facing toward Mecca. The mosque at Mecca in Saudi Arabia, as the mother church of the Moslem world, must always have the most minarets. Two, three, or four are usual, so when the mosque of Sultan Ahmed put up six, Mecca was obliged to add one. Although no infidel eye may gaze upon Mecca itself there is a model of it in the mosque that all may see.

The slim minarets of Istanbul pierce the sky, and five times a day the muezzin appears high on his little balcony to call the faithful to prayer. One can see him, one knows that he is speaking, but he is inaudible. The product of Detroit and the general cacophony of twentieth-century life blanket the holy words. The peculiar holiness of Friday noon however is still observed. Shops close and everyone goes to one of the city's 453 mosques. Yet, numerous as they are, the temples of Mammon outnumber them. I've never seen so many banks. They dot the streets of the city the way bars and drugstores do at home. I do not think Turkey is all that rich, but perhaps they have ambitious plans and want to have the depositories ready when their ships come in.

On entering a mosque you either go in stocking feet or keep your shoes on and slip into the big old scuffs that the caretakers provide. It is considered disrespectful to wear shoes in a holy place, but it's good housekeeping, too; preserves the handsome carpets. Really pious Moslems wash their eyes, ears, and nose, hands and feet at the running taps and fountains set in the outside walls of the mosques before entering. One would think that with so much westernization going on all over

the world the custom would fall into desuetude, but time after time we
saw adult men performing these ablutions before going to pray.

Traveler's Tip No. 14: In Eastern countries be sure that whatever
comfortable footwear you use does not have laces. Gentlemen especially, please note. You will be slipping in and out of your shoes a
dozen times a day, and having to wrestle with knots and bows is a
nuisance.

In front of some of the mosques heavy iron chains are looped across
the forecourt. We thought perhaps they were like the red rope in a
crowded restaurant, indicating to the faithful that they should come
back for the second service, but on inquiring we learned that they had
simply been left there from previous centuries when worshipers tethered their horses and camels before entering.

Our second mosque was St. Sophia, the third- or fourth-largest church
in the world. It was Christian from the sixth to the fifteenth centuries and Moslem from then until today, although now it is used
as a museum rather than a place of worship. There are no carpets and
no slippers. The doctor was relieved. The mosaics are superb; Christ,
Mary, the saints, but they have only recently been revealed. When
the Moslems took the church in the fifteenth century, in accordance
with their policy of never depicting the human figure in their places
of worship they covered them with plaster. It seems curious in a way
that they did not destroy them, but in our travels we were to learn that
an altar, a temple, a grove sacred to one sect was usually kept as the
holy place of another. The conquerors of the inheritors practiced their
own rites, they made changes but they rarely destroyed the edifice or
the site itself.

The mosque of Suleiman the Magnificent is large and imposing but
lacks the quality of the other two. By pure chance, however, we found
an enchanting little hidden-away one that we adopted as our own.

One day at home, riffling through some magazines, I had come upon
an article by Leslie Blanch on Turkey and learned about the lovely
little mosque of Sokollu Mehmet Pasha. We had some difficulty getting
there, our taxi driver seemed irritated by Americans asking for a mosque
of which he himself, had never heard, but he persevered in his inquiries
and our acrobatic little cab, fueled by goat's blood instead of gasoline,
having scrambled up and down steep, winding cobbled streets and in
and out of archways, eventually deposited us at the gate.

It was a deserted, dreaming place with grass growing between the
stones of the courtyard and two little boys in pajamas playing quietly

around an old covered well in the center. The cloister was roofed with a series of small domes typical of Turkish architecture, and after a while the guardian came and unlocked the door, and we took off our shoes and went inside. There were the usual prayer rugs and stained-glass windows and on the walls delicate and pretty blue and white tiles. Blue is the color of heaven and that is why in many Mediterranean countries they use blue beads to ward off the evil eye. The Moslems have prayer beads as the Catholics have rosaries. On the first thirty-three beads they invoke the name of Allah, on the next thirty-three they ask pardon for sins, and on the last thirty-three they give thanks.

After our mosque work we lunched, and very well indeed, at the Divan Oteli, a hotel down the street from the Hilton. We entered by a wrong door and had to go through the kitchen to reach the dining room. I can report that it was immaculate. We had pilaff and cold lobster and, thus fortified, set off with another girl guide, Selma Akday by name, for a drive along the Bosporus. The better way to explore the Bosporus is by boat, and I am depressed when I read other people's travel books by the skillful manner in which they unfailingly achieve the apex. Always they have the best tickets to the best entertainments —they would never have missed the Vienna Opera—and their sight- seeing is always done in the preferred way. Norton and I sensed the boat ride would be more picturesque than going by car, but our guide discouraged us, saying that on Sundays the boats were terribly crowded and we would be uncomfortable.

Anyway we had a good time and we learned from our little red book, "Encyclopaedic Guide to Istanbul," with its sometimes confused but debonair use of the English language, that "Bosphorous means 'Bull's Passage' taken from the Greek mythology according to which goddess Io transformed by Jupiter into a cow swam across the channel."

Bull or cow, it has the quality I most admire in a body of water: limited size. Furthermore, I have had a love affair with the Bosporus since my Paris school days, when I read Pierre Loti's *Les Désenchantées*, the nostalgic, melancholy tale of the frail and lovely harem lady who dies for love of a European. I imagined this broad and beautiful chan- nel lying between Europe and Asia Minor connecting the Black Sea and the Sea of Marmara as lined with exquisite marble villas and palaces of alabaster set in profusely flowering gardens. To be sure, there are a few marble terraces—we had tea on one in the village of Yenikoy on the water's edge—but the houses are mostly enormous old ramshackle wooden structures called *yalis*, bedecked and bedizened with gingerbread, yet not without a certain rakish appeal. They were the summer homes of the rich in the old days and many of them still serve as summer embassies. The diplomatic corps winters at Ankara, the capital.

We were blessed with a lovely day, sunny and cool, and our guide told us that April, May, and June, September and October are the best months. This came as no surprise. In the Northern Hemisphere where are they not? The doctor was pleased by the delightful weather because he was keeping a record. "Do you know," he said, "both in Greece and here our rooms have never been above seventy-five degrees."

I was happy for his sake. He never travels without a thermometer and a compass, and it was nice to know they were functioning so equably.

There is a delightful park in Istanbul called Yildiz, meaning "Star." It's big and quiet and shady, more rural than Central Park, and many families were enjoying it.

Not far from it is the romantic Rumelihisar'dan Palace, a fortification built by Sultan Mehmet II. Although it was built in 1452, practically everything one sees today is restoration, but they've done an authentic job, and from the crenelated towers and walls one gets a superb view of the shores of the Bosporus. Within the walls are green sloping lawns, and families sunning themselves on a Sunday afternoon are treated to spirited spurts of martial music by the military band.

We dined at a Turkish restaurant, the Facyo, near the hotel. It was not very crowded, and I counted eleven men sitting either with each other or at tables by themselves, and there were no women. They may have abolished the yasmak and the harem, but apparently Turkish females are still fairly cloistered. We had fresh mullet that was delicious, tomato and cucumber salad, cheese, and wine, and the bill for two came to a little over three dollars. We also tried Abdullah's on Istiklâl Caddesi, the main street. It has a big reputation, but we thought it overrated both as to food and service.

An excellent restaurant, however, is Liman Lokantasi in the customs building on the harbor. It is open only for luncheon. One goes up in an elevator to an enormous, airy L-shaped room. The side overlooking the water is entirely windows with arched red- and white-striped awnings fresh and gay. Unfortunately the day we were there the view was blocked by a large, solid United States troop transport, the *General Maurice Rose*. We wished the general no harm, but it would have been nice if he had weighed anchor and we could have admired the Golden Horn.

A buxom, smiling lady in a flowered dress and pink organdy fichu took our order and translated it to the waiter. Roast chicken, medallion of beef, salad, beer, wine, raspberries *mit Schlagobers* and coffee. Including the tip, the bill came to just under four dollars.

Turkish exchange is highly advantageous to Americans. I had my hair done at the Divan Oteli, and the service I pay eleven dollars for in New York I got in Istanbul for two dollars and twenty-five cents. The premises were small and crowded, but the job was expert.

A dank yet fascinating spot in Istanbul is the subterranean basilican cistern near St. Sophia, built by the Emperor Justinian in the sixth century. It covers more than 105,000 square feet, and the vaulted roof is supported by a forest of Corinthian columns. In the days of the Byzantine Empire it was fed with water by underground pipes and aqueducts and was always kept full against attack by the enemy. There is still some water in it, and you may paddle about in little boats if you want to. We didn't want.

A more bustling locale is the Great Bazaar, the tourists' joy. The original building, erected in 1461 and used as the royal stables, has been damaged and destroyed through the centuries by a series of earthquakes and fires. The present building dates from only 1898, and in 1954 a large part of it, which has since been rebuilt, was also destroyed by fire.

Encompassing about a square kilometer, the Bazaar is a vast, sprawling rabbit warren, a covered arcade. Its dozens of vaulted streets crisscrossing each other at every angle are lined with three thousand shops. It's the easiest place in the world to get lost and the hardest place in which to find your way back to a shop where you had lingered only minutes before. The merchandise is divided into sectors: shoes, bedding, luggage, carpets, jewelry, all clustering together in their own streets or corridors.

The shops and stalls are small and for the most part wretchedly lighted. They were cool enough, but the air was stale, and Norton said he imagined the tuberculosis count must be high. One has to believe that their tenants exist on a pitiable take.

The display is infinite, but to an American eye the merchandise is sleazy. There is, to be sure, an enormous selection of copper and silver, but the objects are mostly massive, great platters and braziers, the kind of thing nobody uses any more.

There were some extremely pretty pieces of embroidery, charming in color and workmanship and not expensive. I was tempted to buy them, but then I thought, What on earth will I do with them when I get them home? As I'm not a needlewoman myself, there was nothing I could convert them into, so I resisted temptation and have not regretted them, which is rare, as usually the only purchases I regret are, like sins, those I don't commit.

One of the tantalizing aspects of travel is that it's hard to know where one will find the most worth-while shops. Should one buy a lot in one city only to discover more glorious merchandise in the next when low in funds or should one husband resources now in anticipation of greater treats to come and then realize, too late, that in the last place one passed up the chance of a lifetime? As regards Istanbul I think it's fair to say that it is a fascinating city but not a particularly rewarding shopping center. You will almost certainly do better elsewhere.

Like the Bazaar, the cisterns, and the mosques, the Topkapi Saray, or Palace and Seraglio, is also situated in the old part of the city across the broad and busy Galata Bridge. A great compound of buildings set around three courtyards, it was built in 1468 and added to by succeeding sultans until 1853, when Abdul-medjid I built Dolmabahçe Palace farther out along the Bosporus.

Probably the most popular apartments are the kitchens, a whole series of them, where eleven hundred eunuchs prepared meals for the three to four thousand people who lived in the palace. High funnels, the chimneys, rise from mushrooming domed roofs constructed of narrow bricks, and displayed in the kitchens today is a unique collection of Chinese porcelain, over seven thousand pieces, mostly Ming, and supposedly the finest in the world.

Another bit of enchantment is an enormous woven rug, in shades of softest green, on which the dancing girls of the harem used to perform. The harem quarters themselves were unfortunately closed for restoration.

The Pavilion of the Treasure is another series of apartments. Restraint and discretion do not seem to have been qualities of the Ottoman Turks, but in going whole-hog the other way, they were masters. Lushness and luxury they understood and reveled in. There's a great big throne of tufted gold, buttoned with emeralds, and a little old unostentatious one of tortoise shell, mother-of-pearl, and turquoise, with an enormous emerald hanging from the canopy. There is a darling *bibelot* in enamel and jewels of a sultan sitting under a canopy, his body made of a great fat baroque pearl. The most exquisite object we saw was a Chinese piece, palaces on a hill with figures and trees made of gold, jade, and precious stones. That one I'd like to have.

The lads went in for elaborate jeweled and embroidered velvet quivers for their arrows and fancied chess sets of crystal, the knights and bishops and pawns topped with great blobs of rubies and emeralds. They were delectable toys, but as one New England tourist in the party said with a sniff, "Didn't make them play any better."

To me the loveliest of the treasures were in the gallery containing collections of calligraphy and manuscripts with delectable miniatures and illumination. The guide was a bit brusque about those and hurried us through. We wanted to go back the next day to linger over them and also to see the carriage museum and the tomb of Alexander the Great, which weariness prevented us from seeing the first time, but the next day was Tuesday and on Tuesdays the museum was closed.

If one has only three or four days for Istanbul, I would suggest trying to arrange the schedule so as to be there Wednesday, Thursday, and Friday and possibly Saturday. We had only three days and a late afternoon. Four days, I think, would be better. That is brief but still allows time for the finest sights with a little rest in between.

The doctor did not regret our departure. He had had mosques. He enjoyed the palace, but mosques were St. Sebastian all over again and enough was enough.

On learning that our plane was due to take off for Bangkok at 4 A.M. our reaction was bitter, but experience taught us that such mischief is not necessarily deliberate. It is simply that no matter where one is the point of departure is elsewhere. The distances are great, the air lines can't control the rising and setting of the sun, and some hapless wights have to settle for the tiny hours. Send not to ask for whom the bell tolls. It tolls for you at 2 A.M.

We arose groggily, fumbled into our clothes, and set out bleary-eyed for the airport, shepherded by a wizened little Turkish American Express courier. As we passed the city boundaries we looked back. In the indirect lighting the ancient walls glowed like a dramatic stage set and a slim crescent moon rode the sky. It seemed a fitting farewell to Istanbul.

Our courier deposited us in chairs at the air terminal and went away to reconnoiter. He returned with the gladsome tidings that the plane would be two hours late. If you think there are heaps of things more fun than nodding in the Istanbul airport in the predawn darkness of a hot July morning, you are quite right.

Air France came at last, however, and by six-thirty we were winging our way over those countries I am always at a loss to place, Syria, Iraq, Iran.

We came down at Teheran for luncheon, and I was grateful to be dressed as I was. I am not always secure about my clothes. Sometimes I feel I haven't done badly, at others it is obvious that the Duchess of Windsor and the other nine women on that list are brighter, but this time I was all right. The little beige suit, the traveler's stand-by, would have been too hot, also the trip was a long one, nearly twenty-four hours, and any suit skirt would be butt-sprung on arrival. Besides a constricting waistband was no good. I had chosen a washable, ironable, sleeveless blue wrap-around. It was simple, comfortable, and cool. The first leg of our flight was the first time we experienced the pleasant oriental custom of cologne-drenched towels. The stewardess sprinkles you with cologne and hands you a fragrant, tightly wrapped, moist linen roll. You wipe your face and hands and it's very refreshing.

If Greece is arid, Iran, at least the part we saw, is a desert, a vast flat land of dust and stone and blasting heat. As the air is bone dry in the shade the heat seems tolerable, but in full sunlight one can hardly breathe. The terminal building was a welcome asylum, well designed, modern, and air-conditioned. We lunched there at the expense of Air France instead of on the plane and fared very well on sumptuous Persian caviar and wine, among other fine comestibles, and with an interesting companion in the person of an Indian eye, ear, nose, and throat man who had studied at the Mayo Clinic. The lady with him we assumed to be his wife. He said no. Ah, we thought and, being sophisticated types, would have passed on to other topics, but the Indian wanted to set the record straight. The lady, he explained, was his secretary and was traveling tourist class, but she'd been let out to eat like everybody else. Having assured himself that we understood the relationship, he ignored her for the rest of the meal.

Through the long afternoon we flew over Iran and western Pakistan, landing at nightfall in Karachi. We regret that our glimpse of Pakistan and India was no more than that. People who know that we went around the world raise their eyebrows when we say we didn't stop in either country, but in three months one cannot see everything. We didn't go to Egypt, either, or to the great game preserves of Africa or to the South Seas or Australia. A person has to have something to look forward to. We did get out at Karachi and walked around a little and drove in a bus to the Hôtellerie de France for refreshment, and, driving back to the airport, we passed several women draped in saris walking quietly along the road, the first truly Eastern silhouettes we had seen.

In front of the airport building there was a large grass turn-around. Several men were kneeling on it and touching their foreheads to the ground in prayer. Afterward they adjusted their garments and stretched out to sleep there for the night. The night was hot, so they didn't suffer from exposure, but they had no place else to go. It was a small sample of the terrible poverty of the land. It was strange to board the plane and to realize that those few steps brought us unto an *ambiance* as far removed from the men on the grass as though we had been on another planet.

We are told that it is a shrinking world, but one does not have to travel far to appreciate that although this may be true of space it is certainly not true of time or of economy. There the lag between East and West is startling.

We thought soberly of our less fortunate brothers, but were able to settle down to our generous French dinner with unimpaired appetites. What a pleasure it is when the steward rolls up the little wagon and there is real, savory-smelling food served from real casseroles onto real plates instead of the preset, molded papier-mâché trays we are usually handed in our own air, when frequently it is hard to tell the difference between food and container. When I have asked why we so rarely use china, usually cardboard or plastic, I've been told it's a question of weight, but Air France must have that problem too. I suspect fundamentally it's a question of one's attitude toward food rather than of gravity.

Taking off from Karachi, we flew straight across India, landing at Calcutta around two or three in the morning. Although conscious that we had touched down, we were able to see nothing in the darkness, so, heavy with sleep, we continued dozing in our seats. We flew on across the Bay of Bengal, across the southernmost tip of Burma, landing finally at Bangkok at half-past nine in the morning. It had been raining and the sky was cloudy, the weather warm and humid but with a good breeze.

We were in the Orient at last! The drive from the airport to our hotel was about eighteen miles, and Norton and I hung out the car window all the way. There we saw our first water buffalo, the gentle, patient gray beasts pulling the little plows of the rice paddies. Norton was puz-

zled by the plowing when he first saw it, and several weeks in Southeast
Asia still didn't convince him of its necessity. "They've done it for
thousands of years," I said, "they must know what they're about."

"But plowing up mud under the water, that's not the same thing as
earth." Anyhow, necessary or not, they do it and it seems to work, as
Asia produces 95 per cent of the world's rice.

On either side of the Bangkok road run miles of canals—*klongs*, they
are called—with small, shacklike houses set along the opposite banks,
each one reached by its own small bridge. Standing against the houses
are great jars for storing rice, and we saw our first Buddhist monk, with
his shaved head and brilliant saffron yellow robe. There are four hundred temples in a city of nearly a million.

There was a disappointing amount of Western dress, a condition we
were to find all over the Orient. In another few years, I imagine, the
native costumes will have disappeared entirely, one more casualty to the
standardization that is sweeping the world. Here and there, however,
some women were wearing the typical Thai straw hat. Straw hats are
worn by all Orientals, but they are so distinct in shape that, once
familiar with them, suddenly unblindfolded, one could tell what country one was in simply by the millinery. Some women wore sarongs, the
long, narrow wrapped skirts, a few of the older men and women were
in trousers, and the little children ran naked.

We saw our first bicycle rickshaws the *somlars*, but by now I imagine
they have been largely abolished all over the Orient. The Thais told us
that the following year, as far as they were concerned, they would be
forbidden. For men to pull other men was degrading. When they
learned about degradation the rickshaw folk naturally rebelled. Why
should an ancient and honorable profession be insulted? Furthermore
that's how they earned their living. What were they supposed to eat,
how were they to shelter themselves without the rickshaws? That many
taxis weren't going to be available all that soon, and when and if they
were the men would have to learn to drive them and to cope with their
mysterious, alien innards. The do-good authorities found themselves
confronted by a hostile minority.

The rickshaw models change from country to country, but the basic
idea is the same. In Bangkok the rickshaw men, most of them barefoot,
pedal bikes, drawing behind them small three-wheeled carriages. The
carriage has a top like that of a Victoria and is very comfortable for
one, and two can squeeze in if the ride is not too long.

The two big hotels in Bangkok are the Oriental and the Erawan. The

Oriental is the older of the two, has more charm, and, as it claims in its brochure, "the location that comfort the tourist," but the food we found to be much better at the Erawan. Both there and at a small dazzlingly clean restaurant nearby, the Palms, it was excellent. We went also to the much-touted Golden Dragon, but didn't think the Chinese food as good as that served in the best Chinese restaurants in New York.

Then there is Nick's Number 1. Nicholas de Gero is a colorful Hungarian with a beautiful young Thai wife named Sue. We did not care a great deal for the décor—cheap Americanized murals and wine bottles spattered with wax instead of more conventional holders for the candles, but the food was quite good except for the coffee, a powdered American brand that covers Europe and Asia like dust, and although many Americans seem to be inured to it and even claim to enjoy it, we were embittered and asked to see the manager, who turned out to be Mr. de Gero. Having vented our spleen, we found him so amusing we had a long and pleasant chat. He has another popular restaurant called the Casanova.

Our room at the Oriental was split-level and overlooked the broad, muddy Chao Phraya River, the great artery dividing the city. We were air-conditioned, but we also had cross-ventilation, a vital necessity in hot countries before air-conditioning came in, and, as far as I am concerned, still a boon.

The room itself was amusing. You entered on the sitting-room level, which opened onto a balcony and which contained a couch covered in black, with rust and yellow cushions of Thai silk, a round table, two comfortable modern wicker chairs, a writing desk, and low bamboo racks for luggage.

Six steps led to an upper platform, or balcony, that was the bedroom. Twin beds, a narrow dressing table, and the bathroom opening off. The bathtub was split level too, with a shelf you could sit on. At night we drew a gaily striped curtain of black, pink, red, yellow, and green along the edge of the platform—there was a little railing—so that if the room boy came in or there were any guests privacy could still be maintained. Our room boy was Ah King (Ah, there, Mr. Maugham!). He was small and brown, with a glistening white jacket and trousers and little brown toes peeping out from under them. We got very fond of him. He was a diminutive Mr. Clean and saw to it that we remained as spruce as himself.

Traveler's Tip No. 15: Wear cotton underwear in the Orient. Nylon is far too hot and sticky. You can also economize on nylon stockings, which in muggy weather embrace the legs like leather puttees, and use instead the blessed Ped. Cotton underwear does not have the advantages of drip-dry, but the laundries of the East are quick and efficient. They've been at it for a long long time.

Now we were in full Orient, but even so we didn't need our blue bag with the crystals for sterilizing water. Ah King kept us supplied with Polaris, bottled water with a label proclaiming that it has been Treated, Filtered, and Polished. We used to speculate on how this last might be accomplished.

Neither of us is what could be called demon fight fans, but the wonder and mystery of Thai pugilists had seeped through to us, so our first afternoon after a nap we set out for the arena. The fights take place at five-thirty. The arena was big and airy and about half full. We were a little early, so we settled down to read the brochure, which for the benefit of visitors described in English, sort of, what they would see. That afternoon it was to be Saknoy Charoenmeuang pitted against Rungsak Singh-Isan, and we gathered we were in for a humdinger. Of Saknoy we learned that he was "colorful, dangerous and forcible, a lickity-split kid whose assets of bursitis of elbow punch and kick which provide sensation for fans to their hearts' content completely from going to the home stretch." Well! His opponent was no less formidable. "Super star of Singh-Isan camp, Rungsak is terrific rooted deed and brainy, a fighting machine with special knowledge of high kick worshiping the 'Do or die' motto. Once in the ring it is either his opponent is carried down or he is to be carried out to the hospital. Win or loose Rungsak promise a fistic treat for fans to be long remembered."

As it turned out the most bloodthirsty part of the contest was the blurb. The two champs, each one hundred and twenty pounds wringing wet, spent most of their time jigging in the center of the ring, refraining from bodily contact.

On entering the ring they kneeled, touched their foreheads to the ground, and prayed for a couple of minutes. They then indulged in a little ritualistic dance, posing and gesturing like figures on a screen. On their feet they wore white socks of what appeared to be surgical elastic, without toes or heels, and on their heads were braided chaplets with little tails. These were removed by the seconds before the slaughter started. The actual fight was orchestrated. A four-piece band kept up a kind of rhythmic, thumping jingle-jangle but halted, out of delicacy, we assumed, when one of the heroes hit the canvas, where he was instantly joined by the referee. The gladiators stabbed at each other with their gloves, but they really put their soul in the high kicks. The idea is to kick the opponent's head as frequently as possible, though a boot to the kidney is not to be sneezed at. As the rounds ended the seconds whipped big square tin trays into their man's corner, trays that caught the water they poured over him, as well as his spit.

The main bout was conceded in the first round, one of the menaces stalking from the ring with an unmistakable, the-hell-with-it expression on his face. We gathered he must be the other one, not the exponent of Do or Die. *Mai pen rai* was his philosophy. *Mai pen rai* is a recurring phrase in the Thai language meaning "Never mind, don't fret, and everything will be all right."

A more exalted spectacle, although it too has certain elements of lunacy, is the king's palace. After the sophisticated elegance of seventeenth- and eighteenth-century European architecture, the purity of classic Greece, and the airy domes and soaring minarets of Turkey, the king's palace at Bangkok is like an inspired Disneyland. The effect is one of nonsense, magic, and fairy-tale beauty. The peaked tiered roofs of the palace and temples are of brilliant multicolored tiles, blue and orange, red and green and gold, each peak tipped with a flirty little tail, pointing skyward, that wards off evil spirits. The palace was built by the prince who was the pupil of Anna Leonowens made famous in the story *Anna and the King of Siam,* later popularized in movies and in the wildly successful musical *The King and I.* Magnificent as were the sets and costumes of that enterprise, they are outshone by the original temples and shrines. The palace itself, however, gives one pause. Mrs. Leonowens' pupil went to Europe and on his return home erected a huge raspberry and buff edifice in more or less Renaissance style. It has columns and a sweeping staircase and arched doorways, iron grilles, marble pediments and balustrades. It has two great blocks topped by bronze elephants from which the king swung aboard his own elephant. One may fairly say it has impact, but the viewer gets a slight jolt because this great chunk of European municipal architecture is topped, incongruously, by the green- and red-tiled peaked roofs of the homeland.

The palace is set in a compound about a mile square where there are rows of cone-shaped tamarind trees and shrines, all sorts of pavilions and temples made of concrete, broken china, broken mirrors, and gold leaf. The Thais manufacture cups and saucers of flowered china, then they break them up and imbed the fragments close together in

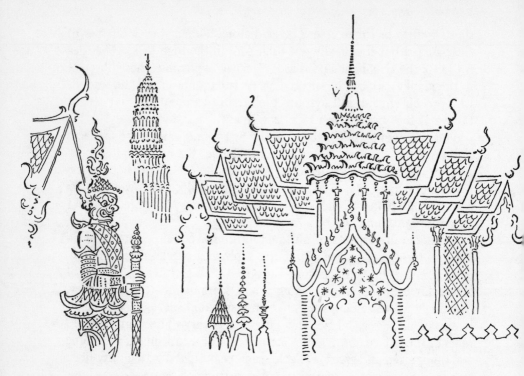

concrete. Perpendicular strips of gold are inset with bits of mirror. Porcelain flowers are superimposed upon the façade, and there are whole walls of incredibly intricate carving in glittering gold leaf.

Demons abound. Huge ones of painted concrete and gold leaf stand guard at the portals, small, fat, fiercely ferocious ones painted purple and blue and ocher and studded with jewels uphold the temple walls. They leer so frightfully they would strike delicious terror to a child's heart. Slithery dragons of stone and gold leaf, the Naga, terminating in fan-shaped feet, snake their way down the stone banisters of the temple of the emerald Buddha. Normal Nagas have five claws, senior Nagas seven. The Buddha himself is carved from a block of solid jasper emerald-green in color and tops a magnificent tiered golden altar flanked by golden figures.

When there is a service in the temple the priest sits on a small throne on which there is a little cushion made of patchwork just like Grandma's quilt. The congregation sits about on the floor sipping tea and smoking. Their Bible or Koran is called Samud Khoy and is not a bound book but long, narrow palm leaves strung together. There are some beautiful objects in the temple, but there is a lot of junk, too, statues

and screens and vases, tasteless "official" presents from foreign courts and governments.

The throne room of the palace is magnificent. The riotous taste here encounters a little discipline. The tiles are of palest blue-green and gold, the scarlet and gold ceiling is upheld by square tiled pillars, and between them hang superb golden curtains. Over the throne there is a nine-tiered canopy representing the Buddhists' nine heavens.

Much in evidence around the palace compound are statues of the Garuda bird. They are of stone or gold-washed metal or plaster. The difference, I think, is one of class. Apparently there are aristocrat and peasant Garudas. The former have vaguely human legs with claw feet and a kind of wattle mounting the calf and ending in a spur behind the knee. Their long, thin tails curl upward, they have hands and arms, a woman's torso, and a human head crowned with the typical Siamese headdress topped with the little spire. The peasant fellows are more gross. They are squat, carved out of stone, unadorned. Their short, chunky legs end in claws too, but they have no spurs, the torso is human, with heavy female breasts, they have wings instead of arms, and a human head with a round cap, round eyes, and a snub nose. The Garuda is a speedy one. Summon him or her and he or she arrives in the wink of an eye. It—this seems simpler—has given its name to an Eastern air line that does not always arrive at its destination in quite such jig time, but even Garudas nap now and then.

The Thai appreciation of and creative genius with color is focused in their world-famous silk as well as in their architecture and in the life along the Chao Phraya River.

By the time World War II came along, the once-vivid but always-limited silk industry had been almost smothered by imported textiles. It was an American, James Thompson, who sensed its quality and revived it singlehanded. He arrived in Thailand in 1945, a member of the United States Armed Forces. It was a fortuitous post, for his family had been in the textile business at home, and young James sparked to the world-wide marketing possibilities of the lovely silk if a system of durable and standardized dyeing could be introduced and American distribution methods applied.

He brought back samples to America and designers raved. He established contact with an importing company and then returned to Bangkok, where with a capital of $700 he set up shop. The sales in 1948 amounted to $36,000, in 1957 they topped $650,000. Today Mr. Thompson employs some two thousand Thais in the growing, weaving, and dyeing of silk. The only problem a lady faces in visiting his shop in Suriwongse Road is how to get out of there with enough money to pay the passage home. The merchandise is irresistible. There are scarves, shirts, blouses, neckties, evening bags . . . one gets drunk on the colors and textures whether they be the luminous glowing plaids, blue and green, pink and gold and scarlet, or sheer or marvelously soft, heavy, monotone silks in beige and sand and tawny tones. The difficulty is that the prices are reasonable, so that one is swiftly seduced into taking advantage of bargains. Who would miss this unique opportunity? Then comes the moment of truth, when the bill is presented. It's fantastic, the sums that can be dispensed saving money.

There is, however, this to be said in defense of disbursements *chez* Thompson. If you travel around the world as we did, pushing east all the way, you can either take fabric with you or have it sent to Hong Kong, where skilled tailors will make it up into dresses and suits. As it is silk from Thailand you do not need a certificate of origin to bring it into the United States, which is the case with clothes made from Chinese silk. The certificate of origin states that the material does not come from communist China. Also, and this is a delightful thought, once you have established contact with Mr. Thompson and the ladies who work in his shop, you may write from home and have things sent to you. It is no longer true that if the value is under ten dollars merchandise may be imported duty-free, but in the case of silks or leathers the saving is still considerable.

My one great regret was that I did not meet Mr. Thompson himself. When we were in Bangkok he was on a brief trip to the United States. Thanks to the intercession of friends I did have the pleasure of visiting his unique and beautiful house. I hope he does not mind. Built on a *klong*, it is a composite of several old Thai houses. They are mostly teakwood, and one of them came from upriver several hundred miles away and was transported in sections on big barges. The exterior is painted dark red, the interior walls are paneled in wood, and there is a lovely open gallery-drawing room. The life of the city passes in small boats up and down the *klong*, and on the opposite bank live some of the Thompson weavers and dyers, so he may watch the bolts of delicious color coming into being before his very eyes. The upholstery and cushions in his house are, not surprisingly, the product of this industry and they are mostly in solid color; purple and plum, crimson and bronze-green, gold and oyster. His collection of oriental art is mouth-watering and bespeaks a disciplined, discriminating taste.

We unfortunately missed Mr. Thompson, but one reason we enjoyed Bangkok so much was that we met a good many local folk. One day at luncheon we were invited by a Chinese merchant to a dinner party he and his wife were giving that evening. In Bangkok many houses are located on lanes running parallel or at right angles to the main road. Our destination was such a one. We drew up under a porte-cochère and stared about in some bewilderment. The place was so enormous we thought at once, It's a hotel. We had understood our host to say "house" and concluded we had made a mistake. It was easy enough to see inside, for the façade was mostly big windows without glass or screens, the shutters standing open to the hot night. There was a main lobby in which the guests seemed to have congregated, to the right we could see the dim dining room with several tables, and on the left a big lounge. They've commandeered the whole downstairs for their party, we thought. We thought wrong. It was a private house on a grandiose scale, but once inside the hotel atmosphere prevailed: a great stairway sweeping to the upper floor; heavy plush-upholstered chairs and sofas and golden oak tables. The hostess was a delight. She looked to be in her middle thirties although she was the mother of five children, including a son of thirty-four who was working in the movies in Hollywood. She also had the sorrow of one daughter with polio.

We had been invited for seven-thirty, but it was nine o'clock before dinner was served. I thought that possibly the movie-actor son had come home for a visit and had introduced Hollywood folkways. I was served one Chinese martini, which is really all a person needs, and then our hostess took us across the garden to her studio, for she was a painter and several of her pictures, dark and strong, hung on the walls of the house. She sculpted as well and showed us a large clay figure in work. It was a male nude, and she told us she impressed her gardener into posing as a model. The figure was notably sexless but we didn't know whether it was out of respect for the gardener's modesty or whether she hadn't got that far yet.

When dinner was finally announced we went into the high, airy dining room, where welcome ceiling fans were whirring, and sat down at two tables. We were fifteen in all, four women and eleven men, and that is my idea of a dinner party! A charming young Dane sat at my left, and when I commented on this happy state of affairs he assured me it usually was that way in Bangkok. "Of course," he added, "not all these men are bachelors. Several of them are married but they go out a good deal without their wives. It's an oriental custom. At some dinner parties the percentage of males is even higher." I thought of the squawk that would go up from American womanhood if the boys tried to instigate any such custom at home. "And you," I said to my Dane, "are you married?" "No," he said, "I'm out here in the rubber business, I haven't had time to get married."

Besides this delectable Norseman our table boasted our affable, roly-poly host and an American lady whom Norton knew slightly as the patient of a colleague. She had passed us the day before in the street, and as she went by he murmured, "Hysterical stomach." A doctor's wife picks up unexpected little insights into people. Also at our table was a young Thai musician who wore glasses, said little, studied his nails, and fell asleep.

The man on his left, the Dane informed me, was a very successful businessman, whether Thai or Chinese I could not tell. From time to time he pursed his lips and looked supercilious and rich, as a successful merchant should. He also looked clean and comfortable. All the men did, for it was a very hot night and the hostess had insisted that they remove their coats, for which she was heartily blessed. On my right was the village cutup, a young Thai with hair *en brosse* and an awesome thirst for liquor. His capacity apparently matched it, for he remained conscious and was not sick, maudlin, or belligerent. Merely exuberant, mixing whiskey, beer, and Chinese wine, reaching across me to lift the drink of the Dane if service slowed and he found himself temporarily empty-glassed. He also gave the Thai greeting by way of a toast. This consists in placing the hands together as though in prayer and inclining the head just a little when you first address someone or are introduced. It is graceful and at a cocktail party highly practical, for you can mind your manners still holding a glass or cigarette between your joined hands.

Not to be outdone by his antic neighbor, the Dane pulled a trick of his own. He extended his hand, fingers together, thumb straight up, and in the L thus formed balanced his glass of beer, tilted it back to his mouth, and drained it, never spilling a drop. It was an intellectual evening.

The dinner was long, starting with a crab-meat and shark-fin soup, one of the great dishes of my life, and continuing through course after delectable course. It was then that we learned about rice and the Chinese.

We have always enjoyed Chinese food, but our experience with it had been limited to the best Chinese restaurants we could find in America, and in the restaurants rice is automatically brought with the first course and accompanies every dish throughout the meal. Not so in the East. At an elaborate dinner it is served once and is the penultimate course. When it finally does appear you know you have only one more to go, and usually it comes as a relief, since, no matter how superb the repast, satiety is reached at last. When it is served in that fashion it is light and dry, each flake separate, the novice's dream, but we found to our bewilderment that when it is consumed as a staple the Orientals prefer it in a glutinous mass. They relish a result for which, were she confronted with it here at home, an intrepid employer would fire the cook. The oriental view, however, is that it is more nourishing that way and sticks to the ribs.

Dinner lasted two hours, ending with an ambrosial fruit, mangosteen, a fruit rounder than a fig but about that size with a hard, rough skin the color of eggplant. You cut a ring around it and remove the top half of the shell. Inside is a white pulp scored like an orange and something the consistency of lichee-nut meat with a taste indescribably subtle and delicious. A little peach, a little nectarine, a little pear . . . whatever fruit you love, this is it raised to the nth degree.

Since the other guests left immediately on rising from table, we did too, assuming it to be the native custom, but it did seem rather rude, gorging and running that way.

The next day was Saturday and the Fourth of July. Whether it was the splendor of the previous evening's repast that did me in I do not know, but I had a slight fever and experienced one of the few days of misery of the entire trip. It wasn't grim enough, however, to keep me out of the shops. We had met a charming woman, Mrs. Kamala Sukhum, who took us under her wing and recommended shops and restaurants. The two most reliable jewelers, she said, were Alex and Ainslie.

The stones of Bangkok are a joy, and Ceylon, too, I believe, is famous for fine ones at possible prices. Riffling through them, I began to understand how those maharajahs could have themselves weighed in emeralds and rubies. Very pretty cone-shaped rings, called princess rings, of small rubies and diamonds set in gold may be had for as little as thirty-five dollars. Bigger and better ones obviously cost more but are not exorbitant. Norton bought some unset black star sapphires, enough for four evening studs and a pair of cuff links, and planned to have them set in Hong Kong. Another reason for circling the world our way. Buy your raw material en route, have it processed in Hong Kong; far cheaper than Europe or America. One is happy to effect economies where one may, as the price of liquor, for instance, is grisly throughout the Orient. Scotch over eight dollars a bottle, wine over three. Thai money is the *baht* (or *tical*), and there are twenty to a dollar.

In the afternoon Kamala Sukhum came by the hotel to pick us up to drive us to the Fourth-of-July cocktail party at the American Embassy. The residence is a big, airy house set in a large garden. It has an enormous loggia where the several hundred guests, Thais and members of the American colony, congregated. This was the rainy season, which meant that at intervals throughout the day there would be heavy showers of five to ten minutes' duration, after which it cleared and activities temporarily halted swung back into action. Frustrated in their first attempt by the elements, the Marine band eventually got in its licks, and the lads went through their precision drill. Ambassador Johnson came to the microphone and proposed toasts: first to the President of the United States, then to the President of the Philippines, since July 4 is their independence day too, and then to the King of Siam. I know that is the correct protocol and it always seems rude. I should think it would be courteous to drink first to the host country, just as when foreign dignitaries visit us in the United States I should think it would be polite to raise their flag first, but no, it must always be us. I believe it has to do with sovereignty, but I should like to feel we were so strong we could afford good manners.

Mrs. Alexis Johnson, the ambassador's wife, was charming and asked us to come to tea a day or two later, when the official entertaining would be over. She must be a woman of steel, for that morning she had received eight hundred Americans, including the crews from three American ships in the harbor, and gone to the races in the afternoon before bracing herself for the cocktail party.

We had met an attractive American couple, Major Stephen Welsh and his wife Lorna. He was air attaché at the embassy. A couple of days later Lorna, Norton and I went back to tea. That time it was very peaceful and Mrs. Johnson talked about the various posts to which they had been assigned, all of which apparently she had enjoyed. Her husband had also been our ambassador to Japan and Czechoslovakia. "We've had a really wonderful life," she said, "we still have. The only thing is, I miss my daughter." Her daughter had married and was now living in the United States.

"Where does she live?" I asked. A puzzled look came into Mrs. Johnson's blue eyes. "Well," she said, "for a girl who's traveled all over the world . . . Omaha." The power of love, I reflected, is strong indeed.

Mrs. Johnson thought Bangkok was fine. She didn't even object to the tokays, large lizards that are called that because they make a noise that sounds exactly as if they were saying "tokay, tokay" and who like to live behind pictures on the wall. They are harmless, and I suppose a person could get used to them if he knew they were there, although I think it would be a shock to look up and see one leaning out, his elbows on the picture frame, surveying the company. I would never get used to the pythons and cobras that, we were told, occasionally wander out of the *klongs* and cross the lawns, but Mrs. Johnson didn't wince at those, either. Nor did Norton, who went unaccompanied by Madame to visit the snake farm where they extract the venom for laboratories around the world. In case a prospective visitor cares, the snakes are fed on Mondays at two o'clock, and venom is extracted Thursdays at 10 A.M. "It is," said the good doctor, "extraordinary to see how nonchalant they are about the whole process." The snakes are kept in a huge round pit. There are low trees on which they festoon themselves, and when handling them the boys, seminaked with no covering whatsoever on hands, feet, and legs, jump in and out of the pit, grabbing their coiling charges behind the jaws, squeezing out the venom into little cups, and kicking them out of the way with airy disconcern.

But then the Thais are not a worrisome people. Thai is the Siamese word for "free," and they have always been free and the rice crops are plentiful. As a missionary said to a friend of ours with a deep sigh, "It is very difficult to instill a sense of sin into these people." The Buddhist God is serene. Many Buddhists are amazed and appalled by the Christian symbol, the crucifixion, with its implication of agony and bloody murder rather than benignancy and peace.

The Thais, we found, take a very no-nonsense attitude toward communists, one of whom they had recently arrested. A Russian agent, he was tried, a collection of papers and arms that had been found in his possession was displayed in the public park so people would understand why he was being accused, and he was hanged with dispatch.

One night we went to see some Thai dancers. The performance was given in the high-school auditorium, which was immense and differed from other high-school auditoriums in that it was wide open on both sides. There was only a small troupe performing, and the music, to our Western ears, had a monotonous, tinkling, nasal twang. The dances were attitudes, slowly arrived at, held, and slowly dissolved, but it was fascinating to see the dancers' fragile, supple, bent-back hands and turned-up feet so familiar from pictures, and the costumes were magnificent, the upper part of the body glittering with gold and silver, encrusted with jewels, the legs tightly swathed in rich brocade or flaming vermilion and emerald-green silk. They wore round caps and glittering, tapered headdresses, and the most active dance was done by a green-faced demon, whose costume was the most splendid and blazing of the lot, and by his partner, costumed as an agile white monkey. There was also a brisk bout between two warriors, each brandishing two swords; long wooden poles painted silver.

One of our most colorful memories is of the day we spent on the Chao Phraya with two French couples, the Ramond Canns and friends of theirs, Monsieur and Madame Félix. Monsieur Cann used to be a colonel in the French Army, but there came a time when he decided that his future as an army man would lack elements of stimulation, so he bid the motherland adieu and joined the Shell Oil Company. At the time we were in Bangkok he had been with them for eighteen months.

We boarded the company launch at the hotel pier at nine o'clock in the morning and chugged up the river to Wat Arun, the Temple of Dawn. It is a lofty tower, 243 feet high, with a cone-shaped top rising from a square terraced base. One can clamber up and down steep steps and get a close view of the millions of bits of broken porcelain thickly embedded in plaster and of the demons and monkeys supporting the structure. A smaller tower is set in each of the four corners of the square surrounding the big one. Wat Arun is of the same bizarre texture as the temples in the palace compound, but it has mellowed through the years and the effect is one of shimmering beauty punctuated by the acrid yellow robes of the temple priests.

A network of hundreds of canals branches out from the main channel of the river, and after our visit we started a leisurely trip along one of them, watching the life of the country pullulating on the banks as we glided past. Although we were theoretically in the rainy season, there hadn't yet been enough to do much good and the river level was very low. The houses—they are really shacks with roofs of corrugated iron or occasionally palm fronds—are built on stilts driven into the gray-green mud and backed by the jungle. At high tide the water comes up almost to the thresholds, at low the householders scramble up and down rude ladders. Everywhere we saw children, three to six or seven naked little kids waving from every veranda. They looked happy and seemed healthy, which to Westerners conditioned to hygiene and antisepsis and don't-breathe-on-baby-without-a-gauze-mask seemed a sheer

miracle, for the river in which they pass their lives is filthy. It is mud brown and filled with mud, but in it they bathe and wash their clothes and dishes and cooking utensils. They brush their teeth with its water and into it are dumped all refuse, garbage, and sewage. The mortality rate below the age of two is shattering, 50 per cent, but if they get beyond two and survive the river through childhood, they are immune. Nothing can kill them! And the fantastic thing is that as a race they are notably clean; a fragile filigree people yet obviously resilient, beautifully clean in their persons and their clothes. We saw babies being bathed, women washing their hair, even a dog getting a bath. His mistress had soaped him thoroughly and was sluicing him off with water from a tin can dipped in the river. Many of the old women wore their hair cropped as closely as a man's, and one very old beldam had naked

breasts but she apparently was a rugged individualist; the other women all wore jackets and blouses.

One thing that fortifies the Thais is their food supply. Their diet is simple but sufficient, mostly rice and fish, which are plentiful, and all day long the market boats ply the river and the canals with their cargoes of melons or vegetables, hot soup or rice fritters, occasionally piles of sun-dried meat and always fresh fish. For a few cents a family may be fed. Because of the boats not much cooking is done in the houses, although we did see coal being sold for the small stoves on which they boil water or prepare an occasional meal.

We also saw a floating hardware store, the lady proprietor in her round straw hat hawking her wares. She was shaded by a parasol of ultramarine blue, and, punting along with a load of green melons, another woman wore a mustard-colored sarong topped off with a black jacket. In a gray boat cruising the brown water sat a monk in saffron yellow. The Thai color sense is infallible.

With enough to eat and enough to wear—in early childhood they are naked, and later trousers and a shirt, the simplest blouses and skirts suffice—their economic problems are not acute. One can only pray that they will have the common sense to limit their birth rate so that this desirable state of affairs may continue.

Primary education is obligatory in Thailand, but as we cruised the canals, waving back at the hundreds of laughing youngsters, we couldn't help wondering how many of them actually did get rounded up and set down to the rigors of book learning.

Their laughter was infectious. All through the long day we never saw a child crying. They are petted and loved and surrounded with affection from the time they are born and they thrive on it. If it is a life admitting of little or no privacy, its practitioners, one would think, must be equally immune to loneliness. The whole canal is home, the family next door is one's own.

Furthermore the universal nakedness of childhood, sensible in a climate where the thermometer habitually hovers around ninety-five, can only make for a healthy attitude toward sex. The mystery, the fear, the "dirty" aspect simply don't exist.

The majority of pets seemed to be edible; chickens, ducks—one house kept three rabbits in a cage, but there were also dogs and monkeys. The dogs running and rooting in the mud were lean but not emaciated—they were probably reasonably well provided for, but the fate of homeless animals is heartbreaking because the Thais, being Buddhists, won't destroy them, but they won't feed them, either, and the wretched beasts die slowly of starvation.

The life of the canals is primitive, yet they are not totally without the amenities of civilization. There was an outdoor movie theater on the riverbank, the screen stretched between two trees, and people gathered in boats to watch the picture just as we at home gather in cars. We passed one house with a veranda on which a crowd of musicians was rehearsing for some sort of festival, and in another we counted about sixteen sewing machines going full blast, the *haute couture* of Bangkok. Several families apparently were in the shrine business. These are rounded, tapering towers—they may be any size from a few inches to a few feet—made of plaster and painted ice-cream colors. They are not pretty, but every house has at least one, as they are mandatory for keeping away evil spirits. We went so far up the canal that mud finally made the water unnavigable and we were obliged to turn around and head back for the main channel of the Chao Phraya.

In the afternoon we pulled alongside the sheds where the royal barges are kept, and got out to look at them. They are spectacular affairs, shallow, narrow, and long enough to accommodate sixty to eighty rowers in scarlet robes. Their prows are soaring golden dragon heads, and one is the seven-clawed foot of the senior Naga. Thick golden tassels drip from the dragons' mouths, and on state occasions the high-roofed thrones of the king and queen with their needle spires are set like small pavilions in the rear, and the royal couple, followed by the royal children in their own barges, are borne down the river to the tumultuous cheers of the populace lining the banks. Today, since the court is monogamous and there are only four royal children, I imagine the lesser barges are used to transport government dignitaries. We were told that the last time they had been exercised was when Mike Todd was in Bangkok filming *Around the World in Eighty Days*.

In the mud under the racks in which the barges are berthed we saw our first walking fish. They were little fellows about three inches long with two front feet, burrowing into the mud like gophers into a prairie. Margot Cann told us that her chauffeur picked one up in their driveway one day that weighed three pounds, and they had it for lunch. I'd have been a bit leery myself, but she said they were very good.

From the point of view of a weary Do It Yourselfer, life in the East is pleasant. In Bangkok a good cook makes eight hundred bahts, or about forty dollars, a month. Servants are not awfully efficient, but they're plentiful and pleasant.

Near the place where the barges were dry-docked I bought a pair of rubbings: Thai dancers and a Rama monkey courting a maiden. Rubbings have interested me for a long time, and in Thailand and at Ankor Wat we found some charming ones. They are made by stretching rice paper—I believe it is usually dampened—over a bas-relief carving and rubbing it with a heelball, a composition made of wax and lampblack or colored inks or chalk. The design of the raised and indented surfaces is transposed to the paper, and the result is highly decorative.

In the East rubbings can be bought for very little, but they are fragile and I did not want to tote them the rest of the way around the world so I took them to Jim Thompson's to have them matted and sent. They were beige-sanguine in tone. The mats were to be made of natural-color raw silk, the narrow bamboo frames gilded. Restrained, elegant, chic. "Nothing to worry about," the little old Chinese in his freshly laundered blue and white striped pajamas assured me, "we wrap, we send New York." It was done. The pictures were laid face to face without so much as a layer of tissue paper between them. In their journey halfway around the world the glass in the frames splintered into a million pieces. It was virtually pulverized. As I scanned my pretty treasures fearfully, I could detect two or three tiny cuts in the rice paper, but I was lucky, they might have been shredded.

Back again on the river proper we passed colonies of boats with curved iron tops like Quonset huts where families passed their whole lives, similar to the sampan families of China, but the marine architecture of Thailand is less picturesque. There were a few log jams, too, along the banks, but the river is so broad they did nothing to impede its flow. They seemed to be relatively permanent, for here and there small shacks had been erected on them. One young householder, I should say he must have been ten or twelve, stark naked, was joyously jiggling up and down exhibiting himself with rooster pride, whooping and waving at us as he did so, hoping, I think, to shock the prissy Westerners, but he was so comical we could only laugh, and Norton snapped a very funny picture of him.

Mixing business with pleasure, the doctor went one day to visit the hospital where the opium addicts were confined. There was a big drive on against the habit, in fact on June 30 at midnight all known opium pipes had been seized and burned by the government, putting a stop to the traffic that up until that time had been legal, but the problem of the addicts remained. The period of cure and rehabilitation was ninety-five days, after which the patients were released on parole but had to report for regular checkups. Norton said the hospital was a reformatory setup fenced by barbed wire, no recreation halls, and the whole place inexpressibly dreary and bleak. Medically, he felt, they had not made any advances we did not know about at home.

On one of our last days in Bangkok we went back to lunch with our Chinese hostess who had given us the delicious man-encrusted dinner. This time the sex ratio was reversed. The food was just as good, but there were eleven women and two men. For the most part they were duck-bottomed little female Thais in sports shirts and slacks, and they were going golfing after lunch, but it poured and I doubt if they got much of a game.

Our one regret in Thailand was that we missed the elephants. I have always loved the great beasts, and ever since reading *The Roots of*

Heaven I have had a special kind of devotion to them. The place to see them working, we were told, was Chiang Mai. This is a city in the north, and they work in the teak forests about fifty miles outside. The only day we might have managed it, if we had gone by air, was a Sunday, but the travel bureau advised us against the trip, saying that in the first place the elephants didn't work on Sunday and that we should have at least a couple of days' leeway because sometimes, if they weren't in the mood, they didn't work on Monday either.

It's comforting to think that they weren't driven against their will, but when elephants are valuable to you as hired hands you respect their feelings, since, if ever Oliver Herford's famous "a whim of iron" is applicable, it must surely be to creatures of such bulk and solidity. Without resorting to brutality, not respecting their whims would be physically impossible.

The morning we left Bangkok we drove through the streets to the airport at half-past seven. Thais subscribe to the British left-hand drive and traffic was heavy and the streets crowded with children on their way to school, boys and girls neat as pins in their white shirts and blouses, and blue, black, and khaki pants and skirts. This was July, but the schools were open.

We were en route to Singapore, flying by the Indonesian line named after the famous bird, Garuda. The plane was perfectly good and the pilot was able—but the lunch! Theoretically a hot meal, the component parts were cold. There were fibrous carrots and a dish captioned chicken that I think was scrambled dragon with bits of black intestine hanging out, the whole floating in greasy red gravy. The little heap of tired worms was, so they said, spaghetti. There was a roll of uncooked dough, and a glutinous tart climaxed the yummy spread. We were hungry when we arrived in Singapore.

Our arrival was enough to turn our heads. A veritable delegation was at the airport. A couple of members of the press and representatives from the American Express and Shell Oil companies. These last were present because we were en route to visit our friends the Astley-Bells in Djakarta, where Leonard had been stationed for a couple of years as the company's representative, and he had alerted his colleagues in Singapore to do whatever they could for us. It was delightful, but with everyone gallantly contending for the honor of driving us to our hotel and sorting themselves into various cars and assuming that someone else had looked after the luggage we very nearly lost all five pieces.

The Raffles has long been a famous hotel and it's easy to understand why. It's picturesque and very well run. It was built about 1880 and rambles around a big beautiful patio planted with grass and fan-shaped traveler's palms, so named because they grow in the desert and spent wayfarers may refresh themselves with coconuts and the fluid in their stalks. The frangipani trees, a cross between a magnolia and rubber tree, with a waxen-white fragrant blossom, meant a lot to me. Ever since I first read Somerset Maugham I longed to see them. I was happy about the banyan trees, too, with the gray branches that go down and become rooted in the earth so that every tree becomes a small individual jungle.

The hotel is a quadrangle, one side having three stories, the other three sides two. The roof is very pretty, of irregular earth-colored tiles, and the second-floor rooms where we were open out onto a long gallery overlooking the patio. There were ceiling fans and token air-conditioning but it was comfortable, and from our point of view very "local color."

We were glad of the hotel because Singapore itself was in a way a disappointment. I had dreamed of it as a teeming oriental city, a sink of iniquity, the crossroads of the world. Malays, Indians, Chinese, Indonesians, Japanese, the babble of a hundred different tongues, thronging allies, the padding of the rickshaw boys, opium dens, the clinking of coins, a scream in the crowd, a knife dripping crimson, and somewhere a great gong. J. Arthur Rank. So much for romance. Founded in 1819 by Sir Thomas Stamford Raffles, who, in effect, conjured it from a tropical swamp, it is today a large modern city, very clean, with a beautiful harbor, broad avenues, and big, English-looking municipal buildings. Robinsons is a modern department store, famous all over the East, where salesgirls with cockney accents and clerks with Scottish burrs will sell you merchandise ranging from yard goods to liquor. Nice but scarcely exotic.

There was one exotic street we finally did discover where we spent most of our time. This was Change Alley. We heard of it because I had lost my extra passport photos, which, we had been told in New York, we must be certain to have, as Indonesian immigration laws were quirky and I wanted to get new ones made. In Change Alley we would find a stall where this could be done. Here at last my novel-fed, movie-fed imagination found a certain solace. Winding between the tall buildings was my narrow, thronging thoroughfare, a kind of perpetual bazaar through which we elbowed our way among crowding pedestrians. Overhead wires stretched from one side to the other, so we walked and were jostled under a canopy of handbags and scarves, dolls and dangling slippers. Here, too, the peoples of the Orient converged: Chinese, Malayans, Indians, this was more like it! There were men in white suits, swathed from waist to knees in bright sarongs. There were turbans and some men wore tightly wrapped, ankle-length plaid skirts, the long sarongs. There were Chinese pajamas and girls in *cheong sams*, their narrow skirts slit up the side to within kissing distance of the hipbone. There were even a few dhotis, the white baggy pants of India with the diaper-like drapery we had also seen in rich silk in Bangkok. The East was picking up! The passport photos were just as grim as the ones at home.

We were invited to a cocktail party in the lounge of the hotel, a spacious marble area where we again had the pleasure of seeing some of our American Express friends from the New York office and where there was a hearty Englishwoman, a true colonial straight out of a Noël Coward comedy, who, no matter what I said, replied, "I say, jolly good show." I'm afraid she must have thought me very rude, as she struck me as too good to be true and I am not the inscrutable oriental type. My face, I fear, is scrutable as all get out, so that my incredulity must have been writ clear for her to see. When she learned I was in the middle of a novel—it was *Three Men on the Left Hand*—there was no holding her. "I say, *jolly* good show! *Do* tell us the plot." I spared her. One of my sparse virtues is that I have learned that there are few conversations more lethal than those devoted to the plots of books, plays, and movies. In Hollywood some of the dearest people have not yet caught on to this, and when you are yearning to learn the latest gossip or possibly how they have braced themselves for the space age, you are liable to be handed instead, line for line, the sequence they have been shooting that day at the studio.

Following the larger cocktail party, Franz Schatzman, the manager of the Raffles, asked us to his suite for a more cozy drink. He is, I believe, a Hollander, but his suite was the oriental McCoy. A real ding-dong affair of black and gold with light switches he could control from behind the bar so that with the hi-fi adjusted, the third martini coming up, and the lights dimming down he had the nicest little quail blind you could find east of Suez. Another time, Mr. Schatzman hospitably invited us for luncheon. It was a curry spectacular, and curry is my dish, but this was not the debilated yellow concoction sold in bottles in the supermarkets at home, so tasteless you might be eating talcum powder. The Raffles curry was the concentrated fire of the Orient, and for two days afterward my mouth felt like the gates of hell and ice-cold beer did not prevail against them.

We dined one night on milder fare at Princes with our chums Eleanor Williams and Cal Palmer. The food was not memorable, but the band was fine: Eurasian drummer, Ceylonese fiddler, Chinese guitarist, and an Australian girl singer.

Another amusing restaurant is the Chicken Inn at the Sea View Hotel, set right on the water. The waves lap against the foundation and a moist warm wind blows constantly.

It was in Singapore that we made our finest purchase of the trip, but it took a little budget searching. Priscilla Astley-Bell had told us of a friend of hers whom she had known years before when she lived in Shanghai, Helen Ling, who had a shop in Tanglin Road. "Go in and see her and say hello from me," Priscilla had written. "She's a darling and won't care if you buy anything or not but some of her stuff is lovely so look around." I have heard that "they don't care if you don't buy" routine before, but what I say is, why open a shop if you're not expecting turnover? Still, as I understood from Priscilla that Mrs. Ling's inventory was wide, ranging from brocaded spectacle cases and straw slippers to fine oriental art, I thought we couldn't get too badly burned. We'd settle for minor merchandise; a courtesy purchase. Accordingly when on our way to the Botanical Gardens we passed Tanglin Road, I said to the doctor, "Since we have to come back this way we might as well drop in and say hello for a minute, Priscilla will be eager to have news of her old friend." The doctor didn't say anything. I occasionally call him Ug, great silent Indian chief, because he is a man capable of making no comment at all on burning issues like the shop, and it is a characteristic that can drive a wife quite crazy. I suppose he was gathering his forces.

The Botanical Gardens are a good place to do it. Spacious, airy, meticulously manicured, with lakes filled with chalk-green water from which rise little islands planted with lush foliage and tall, feathery palms. The paths and roads are beautifully kept, and little gray monkeys race across the lawns to snatch peanuts from your hand the way squirrels do at home. I had quite a tussle with a very fresh minute party who wanted the entire cornucopia of nuts for himself. When we had nourished our furry friends, the doctor persuaded me back into the car, which, via the long reach of Leonard Astley-Bell from Djakarta, had been placed at our disposal by his company. Getting me to leave had not been easy.

"Come on, sweetie, those monkeys are bursting. Let's go."

"I want one."

"I know, but some other time."

"I want one now."

"Dear, it isn't practical."

"But, he's so cute and he loves me. See how he's clinging to me."

"Ilkayoucan'ttravelaroundtheworldwithamonkey*comeon!*"

I went. Sniveling. "Well, if I can't have the monkey at least let's go to Tanglin Road. Huh, Pappy? Can we go to Tanglin Road? Can we?"

When we arrived at the shop Mrs. Ling was busy with a customer in an inner room, so we contented ourselves with snooping around and

picking up a few inexpensive oddments that would make gay Christmas presents. We were about to go, leaving behind regrets at not having met her and warm messages from Priscilla and ourselves, and the doctor was looking quite lighthearted, when the extremely pretty little Chinese assistant came hurriedly from the inner room and said, "Won't you come in? Mrs. Ling is so sorry to have kept you waiting but the other lady has just left and she is most anxious to see you." What were we to do? Say, "Phooey on Mrs. Ling?" We went in. We saw Mrs. Ling and a moment later we saw *him*. "Who ever loved that loved not at first sight?" Ah, Marlowe, broth of a boy. It is rare that man and wife fall simultaneously in love with a third party, but Norton and I did. There he stood, fifty-five inches from the base of his pedestal to the tip of his flame-crowned head, an elegant, slender standing Gautama Buddha in glowing golden bronze. "Oh," we said. Mrs. Ling smiled. She was used to his effect on people. "Yes," she said, "he's a good one. He comes from Thailand, not awfully old, around 1825, but I like him as well as anything we've ever had in the shop." We priced him. "That's what we were afraid of," we said. We looked at other things, we looked back at our boy—"Honey, we really can't"—we chatted about Priscilla and garnered all sorts of good wishes to take to her and finally we dragged reluctant feet past Buddha for the last time.

The doctor is a chap who knows what he likes in art, but he doesn't follow the art world as a matter of course. Fine machines, scientific tidbits are more his dish, but Gautama had got to him. In the car he kept murmuring things like "Handsome piece, no doubt about it," and back at the hotel, "If the trip weren't such an expense we might consider him but it would really be foolish." "Maybe she quoted us the price in Straits dollars," I said. I knew she hadn't, but I've been wrong before, and three Straits dollars are only one American. If it was Straits dollars we were home. I called her up. "Mrs. Ling, was that American money or Singapore money for Buddha?"

"American."

"That's what I thought you said. Thank you, good-by."

As we were dressing to go out for dinner the immovable object budged. "Oh hell," he said, "this is a once-in-a-lifetime trip. The statue doesn't cost *that* much after all. You're crazy about it, we both want it, let's go ahead."

Cheers! Hugs and kisses! I fall upon the telephone. The shop was closed for the day and we were flying to Djakarta at nine o'clock the next morning. I was panicky for fear we'd lose him, but in a crisis the doctor is calm. He cerebrates. He's Kipling's man . . . "If you can keep your head when all about you . . ."

"Relax," he said, "we're seeing Cal Palmer at dinner. That's what the American Express is *for*. To help the clients. We'll use our credit card, he'll get to Mrs. Ling first thing in the morning, Buddha will be packed and shipped to us in New York."

And that is what happened. The actual trip didn't take too long, but there was a maddening period after we got home and after we had received the bill of lading, or whatever his notification of arrival was called, when he lay on the docks for a solid month due to a strike of longshoremen. It's good he wasn't fish. Every two or three days I would call the import firm and raise Cain. I was in fact beginning to feel a little ashamed of my tirades, when one golden day the girl told me over the phone that Buddha had been picked up, he should be at the house the next day at the latest. I apologized for my testy behavior and felt pretty small when she said wistfully, "Oh, Miss Chase, you've been nice. You should have heard some of the other ladies."

Here I will insert Traveler's Tip No. 16: If on a journey you see something you long for and can afford it at all, BUY IT. If you don't you'll regret it all your life. I don't even hedge this advice by suggesting that you find out what the shipping charges are going to be. Had we done that, they, coupled with the price, would have scared us off, I think, and we might not have got him. We certainly wouldn't have had we foreseen other unexpected disbursements. We discovered that it isn't the initial cost of an object; it's the other things you have to get to go with it. I once knew a woman who had to redo her entire house because of an Oriental Export Orange Fitzhugh sugar basin.

When we finally got Buddha uncrated we stood him in a corner of the drawing room. He looked beautiful but he looked bare. I bought a young bamboo tree to frame him. Bamboo is graceful but in New York it is expensive. Then, too, it didn't thrive. Although the room is flooded with sunshine, not enough penetrated to that one corner to keep the flora of the East flourishing. We therefore had to remove the bamboo and set it nearer the window, where it would be bathed in sunshine. Now *it* was happy but beauty boy was on his own again. One day I went to an antique show and saw some delicate artificial greenery in a pot. It had rather an oriental look and needed neither sun nor water. I got in touch with the artist who could make a tree. Could he make one to specifications? Height? Shape? With pleasure. He'd bring his materials and do it before my very eyes. Well, we all know what handwork costs today. We now had our man enshrined, but we were still one step short of perfection. In the daytime we were all right, but we needed a couple of special lamps so that at night his contours might be highlighted, so that the soft gold color and subtle modeling might be picked out and admired in all their simplicity and splendor. We had to get those and we had to get specialists to install them. By the time we got through with that boy we could have bought an annuity for our old age, but we love him and every time we look at him we are happy and satisfied. At Christmas time he holds in his hands a little wicker tray of holiday ornaments, small glittering birds alight on his shoulder and cluster at his feet, and he becomes St. Francis.

Having given detailed instructions for acquiring him, we left Singapore for Indonesia via Malayan Airlines. An Australian pilot was at the controls, and during the four-hour flight tea, coffee, and delicious little sandwiches were served. A far cry from the scrambled dragon of Garuda.

At the Djakarta airport we were met by Priscilla and Leonard and were relieved to see them strong, smiling, and able, as on the plane we had had a bad moment. In Athens we had received a letter from Priscilla warning us to bring no currency. They made you convert it into rupias at the official rate, and you were stuck if you had anything left over, Indonesian money not inspiring confidence outside the country. Traveler's checks were what we would need. These we had, but we also had between us $128 in American money, which we wanted to hang on to for emergencies. It didn't worry me particularly, Norton could keep half in his wallet, and I would keep half in an inner compartment in my handbag, we would declare our traveler's checks and that would be that. So I thought, which only goes to prove that women never learn one of life's basic facts: men are the world's worst smugglers. How they did it in the old days—running blockades, and those chaps who coped with the twelve-mile limit during prohibition, or the wreckers who set lanterns on jagged rocks and lured storm-tossed vessels to their doom and then made off with the loot—I'll never know. Today if it comes to one bottle of perfume or $128 they are craven.

"I don't think keeping money in my *wallet* is a good idea," said the man who in sixteen months in the Pacific, much of the time under kamikaze attack, had established something of a record for *sang-froid*. "Supposing they ask to see it?"

"All right, then, keep it in your shoe, why don't you?"

"What you don't seem to appreciate," he said patiently, "is that

we're going to a part of the world which is unsettled. Papers and passports are in constant demand, there's considerable political unrest.
They may very likely *search* us." I tried not to giggle. "Oh, come on,
you mean to tell me they'll make us undress and everything? Search us
the way they do the Kaffirs coming out of the diamond mines?
What'll Leonard and Priscilla be doing all that time? Standing around
letting them? We're only tourists, for heaven's sake!"

I was a summer shower spattering against Gibraltar. "I think what
we'll do," said the master, a cunning gleam in his eye, "is put our
American dollars in our camera cases. You know, down the back.
They'll never *dream* of looking there." *That,* if you like, seemed to me
chancy. Machinery, cameras, typewriters, such things are always suspect, but in the end I took half the wealth of the Indies and squeezed
it down behind my Stereo Realist and packed it in our big suitcase,
and Norton put the other half in with his Leica. Cherub-faced and
only slightly shaky-hearted, we boarded the plane. En route some fellow traveler broke the news. "In Djakarta, you know, they make you
register all cameras. They're very strict about them, go over them very
carefully." For a man of normally deliberate motion the alacrity with
which the doctor transferred his pelf from camera to watch pocket was
notable. All we had to worry about now was my Stereo in the big suitcase, which was in the luggage bay and unreachable.

Whether or not our Shell Oil chums made a judicious application
of the controversial product to officials I do not know, but we rolled
through customs on greased wheels, although it was true that our
cameras and my typewriter were duly recorded. Our persons remained
inviolate.

Norton was right, however, and so were our hosts, who had cautioned
us about passports' being in constant demand. The first diplomatic
cocktail party to which the Astley-Bells took us, and it was only around
the block and we went in their car, was an occasion for breaking them
out of the bureau drawer and securing them in pocket and handbag.
We weren't asked for them, but one never knew and it was more prudent to have them available. Another time when we drove to the weekend cottage in the mountains, the car was stopped by a soldier in green
uniform and businesslike rifle. "Get out your passports, kids," Leonard
murmured as he approached, but that time too we were lucky. The
military only wanted to bum a ride.

Our first view of the Astley-Bell château fair stunned us. Right in the
city of Djakarta, it is set well back from the street in a spacious gar-

den. Owned by the Shell Oil Company, it was built many years ago
by the Dutch and floored throughout with white Italian marble that
the ships used to use for ballast when they returned from Europe
emptied of their cargoes of spices and rice, copra and oil. The house is
only one story, roofed with beautiful old velvety tiles, but it is enormous and airy with high ceilings eminently desirable in that climate, a
broad entrance porch, a very big drawing room, and a wide gallery one
hundred twenty-five feet long opening onto the back veranda, which in
turn gives onto the garden and swimming pool. There is a huge dining
room for formal parties, a guest room and bath in the main house,
and a big library opening off their bedroom, where Priscilla and Leonard dined when alone or with a few friends. These two rooms were
air-conditioned, as were the quarters assigned to us: bedroom, sitting
room, bath, and another bedroom beyond. This apartment formed a
wing joined to the main house by a porte-cochère, and its counterpart
across the garden housed the kitchens, laundry, and servants' quarters.
Priscilla had done a major job of redecoration, replacing the Dutch
heritage of rich chocolate brown, crimson velvet, and thick wool rugs
with comfortable cushioned rattan and cool pink and gray chintz. We
were amused by the shower fixtures in our bathroom: the faucets had
tiny little handles like those in a doll's house, but the water gushed
hot, cold, and plentiful. Apparently it had not always been so.

The Astley-Bells told us that when they first arrived there was running water throughout the establishment, but only cold. This they set
about remedying at the first opportunity. They called in plumbers, explained their need, and, upon assurances that it would be arranged,
departed for a brief trip to Singapore. On their return they found a bill
and a letter from the contractor saying the job was completed. They
hurried to the bathroom, turned on the hot faucet in the washbasin,
gingerly inserted fingers in the resulting stream, and found it cold. They
tried the tub with the same results. Where oh where could "the benison
of hot water" be? Research eventually disclosed it, with a scalding
shock, in the most unlikely appliance in the bathroom. Matters were
finally adjusted, and the day the words "hot" and "cold" on the fixtures
actually meant something, Priscilla and Leonard and the servants
raised heartfelt cheers. They were quite a little crowd, for there were
twenty-one servants for a household of two. Even in the East this was
considered reasonably de luxe. However, although not part of the diplomatic corps, because of Leonard's job they led a semiofficial life and
entertained a great deal.

Norton and I were properly awed by the battalion of help, and Priscilla and Leonard laughed and said, "Yes, remember Scotch Wilson, who used to come to us on Long Island and how lucky we were when we could get her?"

Somewhat to our surprise, hours of work in Indonesia were pretty much down to union standards. There were three chauffeurs; his, hers, and a relief man for night driving, and six gardeners, but when some of the magnificent old trees were uprooted in a hurricane just before we arrived, they had to get in extra men to saw them up and cart them away.

They kept chickens and ducks, a resplendent red parrot, and dozens of parakeets, and three dogs, a boxer, a Belgian bouvier, and a ten-year-old What-Is-It. There was also a chap with whom I fell in love, a gray monkey named Ciro, who had a little black leather triangle of a face and wore a belt on his hipbones like a cowboy and, on a very long chain, swung and clambered around in an enormous tree.

There were two houseboys (middle-aged), picturesque in their white uniforms and batik sarongs. They wore turbans or the little black boat-shaped hats that are affected by Moslems and are never removed. One of them, an excellent servant, was deaf and dumb. The Sukarno government tapped the telephone wires of foreigners, censored their mail, and, in the guise of servants, planted spies in their houses. The embassies and the oil people were accustomed to it; you just got to know which one was the spy and conducted yourself accordingly. Leonard at first thought there was something fishy about the deaf and dumb man, so to test him out one day he walked quietly into a room, when the man's back was turned and he thought himself alone, and suddenly dropped a heavy silver tray that made a great clatter. Leonard said it would have been impossible not to react if you had heard the sound unexpectedly, but the man neither jumped nor turned. Leonard was satisfied that he was deaf. The other houseboy could speak a little English and he was the one who read the mail. He was nice about it and would grin at Priscilla in the most friendly way if she came in and caught him. The Astley-Bells were fond of them both.

Presiding over the men, the cooks, the maids, and laundresses was the Number One, Ah Chai. Height about four feet eight, age indeterminate, nationality Chinese, uniform black trousers and white kabaya, the jacket or blouse widely worn throughout the Orient, Ah Chai had been sold by her father in Singapore at the age of twelve. She escaped to one of the islands and went to work for a European family. Today she

is one of the celebrities of Djakarta and the embassies, and the Shell
people are in constant battle for her services.

She longs to leave Indonesia, she wanted desperately to come with
the Astley-Bells when they left, but her passport situation is murky.
Nationalist China was not recognized by the Communist Chinese Embassy in Indonesia. She couldn't get a passport from them and if she got
one from the communists there were many countries, notably the
United States, she would not be allowed to enter. From the point of
view of normal innocent people who only want to mind their own business and live in peace, politics are really maddening. Ah Chai had a
reason, however, for not pushing too hard for a passport, much as she
wanted one. The reason was a minute female creature two years of age
with long pants, and black hair parted into pony-tails sticking out from
either side of her head tied with bright red bows: Ching Wah by name.

Ching Wah was Ah Chai's darling. She was neither her child nor
grandchild, but the woman's life revolved around her and she was in a
literal sense a godsend. Ah Chai had been returning to the house one
night after her day off, when, passing a pile of garbage, she heard a
whimpering sound. She hesitated a moment, thinking it must be a kitten. The sound grew louder. She approached the garbage and saw on
top an untidy bundle of newspaper. She opened it up and there lay a
naked baby girl only a few days old. Ah Chai picked her up and carried her home. The baby had been placed there by her father but not
entirely abandoned. He was lurking in the shadows, waiting to see
whether any passer-by would relieve him of his importunate burden.
Ah Chai was the hand of providence. He followed her to see where the
baby was being taken. One can only suppose that, seeing her enter the
large rich house, he rubbed his hands in glee. Heartless he may have
been, harassed no doubt by an already excessively large family, he was
also an opportunist. Storming after Ah Chai, he shouted that his child,
his wee one, had been kidnaped, but he reversed the usual procedure,

demanding ransom from the kidnapers instead of offering it. The Astley-Bells are human, but their guff threshold is low. They weren't having any. They called in lawyers and it was agreed that the Shell Oil Company would be responsible for raising and educating the child, Ah Chai would mother and care for her, and the father would receive the sum of two dollars and fifty cents American. He settled.

The little creature was enchanting, a funny bright little thing who could understand and speak a few words of English, who followed Ah Chai about like a puppy, and who spent a good part of her time hugging Ciro the monkey. They were the same size.

When she is seven she will be issued an Indonesian passport, and possibly then the situation will have changed enough for her and Ah Chai to leave Djakarta and come to America or go to any other country of their choice.

Priscilla bought her charming little dresses, but I thought she was her most beguiling in her Chinese pants or infinitesimal rolled-up rompers. She adored Leonard, who roared at her fearsomely and romped with her all over the house and grounds, and when the time came for her to have a European name she made it quite clear that she wanted to be called Leonora after the Tuan Besar, the big boss or headman.

The language problem in the household would have been acute had it not been for Priscilla. Her American father had gone to China on business when she was a child, taking his family with him, and Priscilla learned Mandarin Chinese so well that on deciding she wanted a Cambridge degree she took her junior entrance examination in that language.

While Ah Chai might have fathomed a little of this aristocratic tongue, although her own language was Cantonese and they are as different as French and German, it would have got the mistress no place at all with the Indonesian servants. She therefore became proficient in their own language and ran the big house in a seemingly effortless fashion but with marked efficiency.

The Indonesian language has a certain simplicity about it which is appealing. *Tuan*, for example, means "master," or "gentleman." When they want to use the plural, they say "tuan tuan" or put a small figure 2 in the upper right-hand corner the way we write "X^2". *Tukang* means "artisan" and a *tukang gigi* is an artisan dentist. It must be a popular profession, because one street in town was lined with dentists' offices, each with a sign on which was painted a set of ferociously gnashing false teeth.

We were walking across the lawn near the swimming pool one day, when one of the women servants started to come out from behind the hedge. When she saw us she ducked hastily back again. Priscilla called to her to come on out. "It's really too awful," she said to me. "It was the Dutch who did that to them. It was absolutely incredible the way they treated servants. They were beaten and kicked if they spoke above a whisper and they had to come into a room on their knees. They did it to us when we first came here. Leonard and I were never so shaken in our lives. I grant you some of the things they did to the Dutch in retribution before they drove them out were pretty terrible, but they had provocation. They'd had it for three hundred and fifty years."

The Dutch did some good things too, of course. They built roads and installed electricity and they were clever at trading and building fortunes for themselves, but when they were booted out of the country they left a population that was 90 per cent illiterate. Whatever the shortcomings of the present administration, and from the point of view of more sophisticated governments they are not inconsiderable, it is doing a good job stamping out illiteracy. Education is compulsory, schools work in shifts fifteen hours a day, and illiteracy is now less than 50 per cent and decreasing all the time.

The ordinary Indonesian seems instinctively gentle and friendly, but their experiences with foreigners have ever been stormy. When the Japanese came in during the last war, they rounded up all the men and women they could find who could read and write and killed them so that they should not incite the populace to revolt. Experiences like this make you leery of strangers.

If it were possible to get honest hard working men in government it should not be too difficult to stabilize the shaky economy since the land is rich in rice, rubber, tea and of course oil.

The Indonesians are full of pride and nationalism but lack a certain sophistication. The government has had to put soldiers on the trains to collect fares, as, having run out the Dutch, the natives blithely assume that the railroads are now theirs and payment is unnecessary.

Also Priscilla told us that shortly after their arrival in Djakarta she was overjoyed when she found a good Dutch butcher shop. It was scrupulously clean, the equipment modern, and the knives sharp. The fresh meat was well hung, and frozen meat was available. She went home gloating to Ah Chai. Two weeks later she went back again. The Dutch butcher had been forced out and the place was being run by his Number Four boy, a filthy little chap who stood surrounded by

squealing pigs, waving a rusty knife, and wildly at a loss as to how to
proceed.

Indonesians are to some extent still infants and not only economically and politically. Toilet training also seems to have lagged. Their
habits are, to say the least, untutored, but this we learned to our great
surprise had also been true of the Dutch. When we inquired why there
were wooden racks beside the toilets, with big round holes in them, we
were told that they were for the carafes of water that the Dutch used
to wash their hands, which were all they did use. When the Europeans
who followed them into the country learned about this and realized
that the natives who waited on them at table were continuing the custom, they were appalled, but there was little they could do other than
supply paper and carbolic soap, issue instructions, and pray that they
were obeyed. About these functions, which we feel should be carried
on in the utmost privacy, Indonesians are casual.

A large canal running through the center of the city is used by men
and women as a public toilet. Whatever needs to be done is done quite
unconcernedly in broad daylight in full view of passers-by. The incidence of tuberculosis in the country is high, as is the mortality rate
among babies. On the other hand there are no ulcers, no high blood
pressure, no alcoholism, and no mental hospitals. Now let's all try for
a nice middle ground, shall we?

Aside from our pleasure in being with old friends we realized how
lucky we were to be staying with them when we saw the Hotel Des Indes. There was a time when Des Indes was famed throughout Southeast Asia as Shepheard's of Cairo used to be known in the Middle East.
Those days have gone. Currently those who must put up at Djakarta's
best hotel are viewed with compassion by their fellows, who speak of
them as of those who support the fell visitation of leprosy, and they
are invited out for as many meals as possible, since eating at the hotel
is tantamount to a passage across the River Styx. It seems that even
Sukarno complained about the dirt in the kitchen.

Leonard, en route one night to visit a hapless business associate quar-
tered there, told of going to his room on the second floor when, in the
semiobscurity—one twenty-five-watt bulb in the corridor was the management's idea of a blaze—he stumbled over something that moved!
Yes, I know. This being the Orient, our own thoughts flew to pythons
too, but fortunately the livestock was domestic; a mother goat and two
kids.

One Sunday we drove with Leonard and Priscilla into the mountains to spend the day, passing a rubber plantation shortly after we left the city limits. I had always fancied a plantation as a sort of jungle growth, but on the contrary. The underbrush had all been cleared and stretching for miles were row after row of slender tree trunks rising into high, light foliage.

Although the modern capital of the country is drab, dirty, and uninteresting, Java itself is a magnificent land of rolling mountain ranges, terraced rice paddies, and tea gardens; row upon row of low bushes, their leaves like laurel but softer and more pliant than laurel, climb the steep slopes.

The clouds shred over the mountaintops, and delicate, tall fern trees throw their shadows against the drifting mist. When the clouds and mist disintegrated, we looked back over the dark, winding road we had traveled, through the Punjak Pass, to the green of the tea bushes, on down to the rice paddies glinting silver and blue on the lower slopes across the valley, and to the distant purple mountain ranges beyond.

Our destination was a small cottage where the Astley-Bells sometimes went for weekends. Most of the embassies and the oil companies maintained these houses for their personnel so they might occasionally have a breather and escape the heat of sea level. The settlement is managed by a Dutch woman, but the various houses have their own staffs. The Shell house had three in help who lived there the year round. They were the tiniest adults I have ever seen: a youngish man, an attractive young woman, and an ancient infinitesimal crone Cookie. Such teeth as remained were stained black by betel nut, her sparse gray locks were drawn tightly back into a small gray bun, and she was a sixty-five-pound bundle of concentrated essence of charm and personality.

Cookie wore a sarong and a red kabaya, and down her front marched four twenty-dollar gold pieces sewn on like buttons, gifts from directors of boards who had fallen under her spell. She was perhaps not a *cordon bleu* at the pots, but she was invincible and during the war had held the cottages singlehanded against the Japanese. She did it, I am sure, by a combination of fortitude, sex appeal, and the sheer charm of that black snaggle-tooth grin.

At the time we were there rebel bands called D.I.'s, for Darul Islam, roamed the mountains. They were religious fanatics who were opposed to the government and who were agitating for a pure Moslem state. They were a nuisance and could be alarming. They would invade the cottages of the Westerners and take what they wanted in the way of food, but they rarely did any actual harm. They made a clean sweep of the larder of one British family, but left powdered milk for the baby and enough tea for one meal.

On our way down from the cottage we stopped at the village of Megamendung, which means Misty Mountain, and Priscilla did a little marketing. She bought tiny potatoes, beets, and three cabbages grouped in a bouquet. Lettuce was taboo, for the Indonesians still use night soil by way of fertilizer and everything has to be cooked. She also got an orchid plant, a tall spear about three feet high hung with small exquisite blooms, for less than fifty cents. Travel is expensive, but you make it up on the necessities.

The market was under a great shed, the red and white pennants of Indonesia hung from flagpoles protruding from the roof, and horses and carriages and cars were lined up in front of it. Women in sarongs and kabayas, with turbans on their heads and great baskets atop the turbans, although small in stature, walked like queens along the road.

Along the flat streets of the city the pedi-cab was the common means of transportation as it had been in Bangkok, except that there the driver had ridden his bicycle in front, pulling the light carriage behind him, and in Djarkarta he peddled from the rear, pushing the carriage ahead of him.

We rode in one or two but were mostly whisked about in the car by one of the three chauffeurs. The distances were small, but between our schedule and the heat we were glad of the transportation. The only time we seemed to ride forever was the day we went to watch them make batik, and even then it wasn't that the distance was so great but that we were so lost.

We learned then, and it was further emphasized in Japan, that the street and number system of the Orient is loaded with originality. Two or three streets may have the same name, and the numbers don't do anything so archaic as to follow in sequence. No indeedy. That's for squares. The whole arrangement is far more larky than our way of doing things and spiced with uncertainty. You may get to your destination, you may not. Kismet. That we eventually did find the place we were looking for, was pure fluke.

An Indonesian woman ran a small private batik business in her own house. She had about sixteen men and women following her designs, and we watched them working on pieces of cloth stretched on the floor, the design outlined in pencil. One portion would be covered with wax while color was applied to another part. Then the wax would be

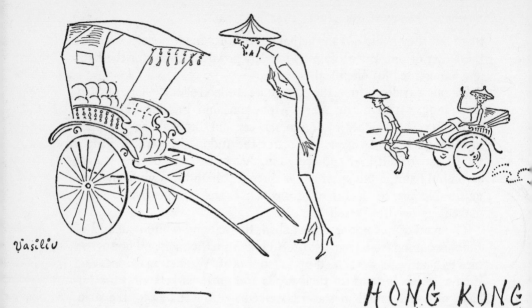

removed and the section thus revealed would in its turn be tinted. In
a shed out back were the dyeing vats. The work was slow and meticulous, and they told us it can take as long as eight months to complete
an intricately patterned length of cotton. One they were working on
would cost 3500 rupias, or about $35. We bought a couple of lengths,
enough to make slim summer dresses for about 700 rupias each. In
my youth I always associated batik with Greenwich Village and artsy-
craftsy, but some of the patterns we saw in Djakarta were lovely, of
muted colors and sophisticated design.

During our stay in Djakarta we went to several embassy parties,
which we enjoyed, but we quickly came to realize that the diplomatic
world in dictator-ridden countries is a small one. Over and over again
one saw the same people. Our first entry into diplomacy was a farewell
cocktail party at the Swiss Embassy for Ambassador and Mrs. Arnold
Sonderegger, who were being transferred to Copenhagen. They were
elated.

There we met Madame de Mello, who was the Danish wife of the
Brazilian Ambassador and who eight years before had been identified
by our disillusioned chum as the only beautiful woman in Madrid.
We met Madame Harsleman, the Rumanian wife of the Dutch chargé
d'affaires, and watched the papal delegate in his white robes and crimson skull cap chatting with the wife of the Vietnamese Ambassador,

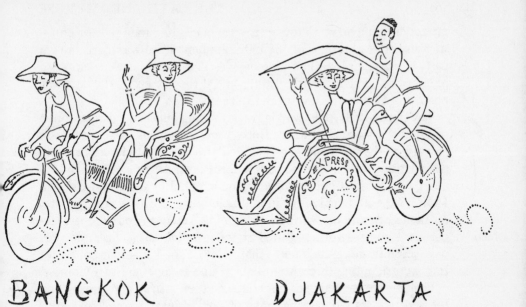

BANGKOK   DJAKARTA

charming in a brilliant pink gown, her dark hair looped with a scarf of mustard yellow. Madame Harsleman, while vivacious, was not altogether happy. She had escaped from the communists in Rumania, and her brothers were being held in prison in retaliation for her act.

The beau of the ball was the Italian bachelor ambassador, Duca Roberto Carriciolo di San Vito, who, like Ambassador and Mrs. Sonderegger, was thanking his stars that his term of duty in Indonesia was coming to a close. When he heard that Norton and I were going to Angkor Wat, in Cambodia, he said that he was planning the trip too on his way back to Europe, and we agreed to go together.

The rooms of the Swiss Embassy were bright with familiar flowers, and when I asked Priscilla how, in that tropical climate, they managed to get such beautiful dahlias and gladioli, she said they were grown in the mountains, where it is cool, and brought down for festive occasions. The drinks, though generously proffered, we found dubious. Europeans are not very successful with hard liquor anyway and in Moslem countries, where they don't believe in alcohol, matters are only aggravated. The mixed drinks are like a brew served on Walpurgis night and, the trays are awash with Colas and alarmingly colored juices. Traveler's Tip No. 17: In the Orient stick to gin and tonic. Scotch whisky is available but costs the eyes in your head.

There was a law in force at the time we were in Djakarta whereby any private citizen who was a foreigner was obliged to obtain police permission and state the time of the entertainment if he wanted to give a party and invite more than nine people. The festivities were supposed to last only a certain length of time, and if they exceeded the limit the police might come in and break things up.

The Astley-Bells gave two big parties during our stay, a garden lunch party and a formal dinner. Both were delightful. The luncheon focused on the pool, and guests started arriving about eleven, bringing their bathing suits in air-line bags. On the lawn Air France and BOAC and Pan American jostled together, punctuated by CAT and Garuda. I think we were twenty-four in all, including the British Ambassador, Sir Leslie Fry, and his wife and a charming American couple, the Flannagans. He was with the United States Information Service, and they were certainly doing their bit to maintain the good-neighbor policy, for they were adopting three Asian babies: one Indonesian, two Chinese.

People were greeted with hot coffee on their arrival, and about noon the servants started passing trays of cold drinks: tomato and fruit juices, beer, gin and tonic. Also superb little hot crispy hors d'oeuvres. The base was shrimp and from there Priscilla's and Ah Chai's imaginations took flight.

At one-thirty the buffet luncheon was announced, a groaning and delicious *rijstafel*, meaning literally "rice table," a combination of Indonesian and Dutch food in the face of which, I am afraid, we behaved more like gourmands than gourmets, but was it good!

Feeling that his effete house guests should rest and recuperate, Leonard shooed the transients home shortly after lunch, but, replete and having to shoulder no responsibility, Norton and I would have happily continued babbling with the Shell doctor and a couple of nice young chaps from the company for the rest of the afternoon, settling for relaxation later on.

The other party, the formal dinner, was more corseted but also memorable. We had an Idonesian doctor and his wife, a lady member of Parliament, and we were thickly encrusted with ambassadors: Italian, Australian, Brazilian, and our own Howard Jones, American.

At this dinner, for the first and last time on our trip around the world, we wore evening clothes. It is nice to have them for an occasion as special as that one was, but on the whole I should say, as Traveler's Tip No. 18, if going to Southeast Asia in the summer don't take evening clothes unless you know in advance that you will positively need them. For a woman it doesn't matter so much. A summer cocktail dress that can double at dinner weighs little, but for a man the extra paraphernalia is burdensome and may be costly in excess-luggage charges.

The morning after the dinner we took off at 8 A.M. in the Shell Company plane for Bali. We were learning oriental ways. The Moslems are early risers, and so is Christian Astley-Bell. By first light Moslems not only are up, they have performed their ablutions and breakfasted. Their dream is to get offices to open at 7 A.M. so they may get off in the afternoon. Norton and I are reasonably early risers ourselves, he especially, but we were beginning to find the life of pleasure and adventure fatiguing. Eager though we were to see Bali, we wouldn't have minded leaving, say, at ten-thirty.

On the plane Priscilla, used to her general and his hours of reveille, simply stretched out on the plane's broad, comfortable couch, motioning me to lie down beside her if I felt inclined, and went to sleep. After a fruitless attempt, however, I gave up and sat chatting with the two or three company people who were making the trip with us, and absorbing tidbits passed by the Indonesian crew. It was a beautiful flight that could have been made in three hours but it took us four, owing to a government pronunciamento. No planes were to pass over Surabaja, where certain secret maneuvers were going on. The constant state of siege under which dictators feel it necessary to function is trying.

Bali has been called the Last Paradise, and although I have never been to Tahiti—from what I have read I think I should prefer it for retirement purposes—it is not hard to see how Bali got its name.

On either side of the narrow but excellent roads rice paddies glinting green and yellow reflect the sky, giving rich sustenance to ducks. There are thousands of coconut palms, groves of delicate bamboo, and distant purple mountains.

The dogs rooting about and lolling along the roads are heartbreakingly thin. On the other hand, the long-snouted, sway-backed gray pigs, half brother to the wild boar, are reasonably plump, at least the sows are, for they are perpetually gravid or moving in the midst of litters of piglets like an ocean liner among tugs. The gray water buffalo turned their benign, mildly curious glance upon us as we passed and the brown cattle turned their white, heart-shaped behinds. We saw fighting cocks in bell-shaped baskets, and brown men and women moving with infinite grace under their loads of ripe rice the color of ripe wheat. They bore the sheaves on their heads, and the bundles looked like the heavy, elab-

orate millinery of around 1912 or like something that would have
brought a gleam to the eye of the late Flo Ziegfeld.

Being but venal tourists, we were naturally interested in seeing
whether what they say about Bali and indeed what we have all seen
photographed in the *National Geographic* was, in actual fact, the case.
Were the women naked from the waist up? Well, Junior, Mother will
tell you. It's yes and no. About a year before we were there Sukarno
had issued a decree: Everybody cover up. Indonesia was beginning to
play a political role in the world; the traditional free display of charms
was no longer appropriate. There was a great scuttle and bustle as the
local females broke out kabayas and homemade bras. Both the bras
and what they supposedly concealed would give the Bali Bra Company pause. The copy writer who dreamed up that name has obviously
never visited the Last Paradise, but anyway the ladies were covered,
formal as penguins. This went on for several months, then, gradually,
the old customs, so to speak, began to reappear, and during our sojourn
it seemed to be pretty much a matter of personal taste. One thing we
did notice, however: along the roads or in the market places the women
very definitely objected to being photographed. After one or two at-
tempts Norton gave up, although by surreptitious use of his Minox he
managed a few souvenir snaps. The most popular fashion was a swag

of material draped across the throat and collar bones. The area between it and the waist was exposed, but it could be pulled down like a shade against the too curious glance of any tourist. Otherwise both men and women were unself-conscious and at twilight both sexes bathed naked and openly in canals and pools along the road. It was a purely practical matter. Denpasar is electrified to a certain extent, but the countryside is not. Candles and primitive kerosene lamps are the principal means of illumination, and the great majority of the population lives in mud huts in compounds formed by walls of sun-dried mud bricks. They work throughout the day in the mud of the rice paddies. They have no running water at home, so that outdoor bathing is the only way they can keep clean, and they are very clean. In the warm air, at sunset the groups of brown bodies, the splashing water, the flash of white teeth and the sound of laughter were gentle and curiously nostalgic. When they had finished bathing they would wrap their sarongs around them, tuck a hibiscus flower behind their ears, and wander off down the road.

The compounds are small and life therein is intimate. When young boys reach the age of puberty, they are banished during the night from the vicinity of the girls and go off to sleep in the communal dormitory, which is primitive but where they probably have good times, manly stags together. The dormitory actually is no more than a huge platform by the side of the road roofed with palm thatch. There are wooden benches on it and there the boys sleep. It didn't look particularly cozy, but the climate is so warm there is little chance of them suffering from exposure.

Although we stayed in a delightful spot, our beds were pretty Spartan too. There is a Bali Hotel and one called the Segara Beach, but we were at Jimmy Pandy's. Mr. Pandy is an Indonesian, small, rounded, extensively traveled, and speaks perfect English. The ways of Hollywood are not unknown to him, and Connecticut is the state of his dreams. He opens his house to paying guests, and as it is charming his two double rooms and one single are always in demand.

Situated directly on the beach, it is set in a grove of palms, casuarina trees, and hibiscus bushes. In the garden there are curious lichen-covered limestone sculptures of animals and demons, the latter garlanded with flowers, a hibiscus blossom behind the ear. Jimmy Pandy, an artist himself, runs an art gallery where for thirty-five and forty rupias each— a rupia equals roughly one cent—we bought several small, amusing wood carvings: a water buffalo couchant, a duck with his nose buried in a water lily and a strange little kneeling beast with a long neck, round ears, and a snout raised to heaven. We had intended them for gifts, but they are beguiling and friendly to the touch and we have kept them all. The wood is pale and satiny and with caressing develops a lovely patina. The best pictures in the Pandy gallery ran to eight or nine thousand rupias, eighty or ninety dollars. There is a good deal of carving for sale in the shops of Denpasar, notably the lean, elongated figures that are a speciality of the native artists but that we did not find appealing. The best of the island art is privately owned and not on sale in shops catering to tourists. We were shown a thick book, an illustrated catalogue of pictures and sculpture belonging to Prime Minister Sukarno. He is a connoisseur with a means of acquisition not always open to other art lovers. If he goes into a house and sees an object he likes, he commandeers it, a refinement of collecting that was not unknown to England's great Elizabeth in the course of her progresses through her realm's stately homes.

The Pandy house is built almost entirely of bamboo thatched with palm, the walls—movable to accommodate every passing breeze—are stretched with woven grass cloth, and the main room is filled with books and *objets d'art* and was patronized by a fastidious cat family, a mother and two kittens. There are kerosene lamps with delicate shades of rice paper and wicker work and the dining room is a small, airy, pavilion where Mr. Pandy served food good by any standards and by Indonesian (at least from an occidental point of view) quite extraordinary. There was an especially good vegetable dish made of fern flavored with spices and coconuts. Luncheons were Eastern, dinners Western. We had taken the precaution of bringing our own liquor, although the house provided beer and a light Italian vermouth for martinis.

Tacked over the doorways were small bits of fluttery, tattered cloth. When we asked about them Jimmy Pandy told us they were tacked up there by the priests when the house was built to bring good luck. One must not take them down, but allow them to rot away in their own time.

Our rooms, although very simple, were adequate, as were the baths, which boasted a washbasin and toilet, both manual. There was a tiled square tub in one corner full of water and a pail. You soaped yourself and sluiced off with the pail. The water was not hot but in that climate it wasn't cold, either. The same system worked with the toilet. In the bedrooms were good chests of drawers and small mirrors, but Priscilla and I discovered that any predinner primping we wanted to do had best be done before dark, as the kerosene lamps did not give quite the effect of the fluorescently lighted mirrors of Hollywood and television studios.

The question of the beds was delicate. In a regular hotel one could complain, but although, just as in any hotel, we were paying for our rooms, Mr. Pandy was also our host, a host in the sense that the Messrs. Hilton and Statler are not. How to say tactfully, as we sat over friendly cocktails—our gin, his vermouth—"Mr. Pandy, honey, your beds are murder"? Yet alas they were. Wood. Wooden slats and the thinnest of cotton mattresses. We assumed it was because of the heat. Feathery stuff would have been intolerable and sponge rubber is cloying too, but what about good thick firm hair mattresses, the world's best; wouldn't they have been all right? Probably, but far too costly and in that part of the world I dare say unknown. The picturesque element was the Dutch wives, those long bolsters that are used in hot countries and that, placed between the legs, are supposed to keep you cool, and the mosquito-netting canopies that let down from round wooden rings fixed in the ceiling.

The one disappointment of Bali was the swimming. With the house located directly on the beach we went galloping into the waves, only to find that we could walk from there to Australia. Any real swimming was out. This is because the island is ringed by coral reefs and between shore and reef it is shallow, the water to the knees or only a little higher. Beyond the reef it is deep, but beyond the reef are sharks, or so they said, and for a curtailed stay it didn't seem worth while proving them liars.

One curious custom we noted was that although the natives bathed naked along the roadside and a few of the women wore no tops most of them strode through the water to the reefs, where they chipped away at the coral, fully clothed in sarongs and long-sleeved kabayas. Since the wind blew continuously they must have been cold in their clinging garments, but we never saw them discard them. They would return to shore bearing on their heads great baskets full of coral that was later ground up to make cement.

Two little boys hung around Jimmy Pandy's, selling long strings of tiny shells they had made into necklaces. Their English was sketchy, but they were sharp merchants and made it clear that they preferred dollars to rupias. It was uphill work, but we made it clear that we intended dealing in coin of the realm. Their realm.

Denpasar is not a beehive of commercial activity, but I should say that whoever has the bicycle concession has a good thing. Shanks' mare, pony carts, and bicycles are the chief means of transportation, with women's bicycles the odds-on favorite. This is because both men and women wear sarongs and that bar on men's bikes is very awkward if you're in a long, tight skirt. It is a get-there-and-carry-it-yourself civilization, and we saw one woman who seemed to be moving house walking down the road with a large kitchen table on her head, big bowls and baskets piled on top of it.

Our purchases in Denpasar were two coin dolls and a picture. The dolls are twenty inches high, made of ancient Chinese coins with holes in the middle and woven together in such a way as to form flat, stylized human figures. Their heads, hands, and feet are molded and gilded, and they wear filigree collars and sashes. They are of no particular value, an interior decorator, I suspect, would consider them junky, but, appropriately hung, against a narrow, flat surface, for example, they can be amusing and decorative.

The picture was typical of Balinese art; pretty, pastel, and a scene of village life: a half-naked maiden fetching water at a little fall, a youth in a straw peasant hat up to no good following her in a flowery, rocky spinney. The day we looked at the picture we saw that the woman who waited on us was pregnant. Balinese women are often slight of frame and the baby protruded like a round melon. A sarong is not the most concealing garment in the world for what American maternity shops refer to coyly as ladies in waiting. When we decided on the purchase and went back the next day to fetch it, the proprietress was again in the shop but the melon had disappeared, the baby had been born.

Although we were traveling everyplace by air and were already loaded to the gunwales, we were able to make these purchases because Priscilla said that she and Leonard would send them to Singapore for us in the company pouches and from there they would be sent on by boat. It was more satisfactory than having them pass through the port of Djakarta, where unfortunately there was a tendency to pilfering.

Speaking of sending things, Traveler's Tip No. 19: Take with you Scotch-Tape, labels, and manilla envelopes. They are hard to come by in the Orient and you will need all three. The big envelopes are invaluable for sending home scarves, postcards, catalogues, small guidebooks, and suchlike.

There is no theater in Bali such as we know in the West, but like the Thais, the Balinese love to dance, and their dancing is very similar to that of Bangkok except that the performance we saw was given by children and out of doors. We went one evening after dinner. The stage was a widening in the road in front of a temple constructed of reddish brick, with the usual stepped façade heavily ornamented with carved stone demons. The audience sat on straight-backed wooden chairs or on the ground, forming a square around the earthen dance floor, and there were several hundred, possibly a thousand, people, three quarters of whom were children. The most prominent guest was the Rajah Ginjar, on whose property the temple stood. He was a portly, aging man attired in a turban and sarong and surrounded by several wives and masses of children, all his own.

The performance, like some of its sophisticated occidental counterparts, was an hour late in starting, but we sensed the happy moment was at hand when a young fellow propped a bamboo ladder against the front of the temple and shinnied up it like a monkey to light candlewicks floating in coconut oil in little stone cups that were part of the carved decoration. The footlights were kerosene lamps shaded by black boxes. The dancers performed to the accompaniment of hide drums and gamelan music. The gamelans were placed on the ground, the musicians sitting cross-legged behind them. The gamelan is something like a xylophone, but not very, and its front is of carved and gilded wood so that it looks like a low piece of furniture.

The program opened with four girls wearing lovely saris of red and blue, green and gold. Their attitudes and posturing were Thai-like, but the dances seemed to have more movement. They were followed by a child, a little girl of eleven, who was presently joined by two more, aged seven and six. They were like exquisite exotic flowers, with their tapering jeweled headdresses, the upper halves of their fragile bodies swathed in golden bandages, their slender legs moving through shimmering green and gold. The suppleness of their hands and arms was extraordinary, and their artful enameled make-up would have had more than one Broadway actress swearing bitterly under her breath should she have tried to duplicate it. The girls, we learned, were the daughters of an Indonesian father and a Dutch mother who sat in front of us.

After them came a fierce small boy who hurled himself passionately into a warrior's dance, a little thunderbolt of a creature with staring, dramatic eyes. There were several more numbers, but we were tired from our late party in Djakarta the night before, our early rising, and the host of new impressions that had crowded in on us during the day. We left before the performance ended and returned to Jimmy Pandy's and the beds so adapted to mortification of the flesh.

The next day we drove to Ubud and on our way into the hills stopped at an open-air market to take some pictures. The produce was pitiable. Three or four eggs would be offered in a little basket, a few pieces of fruit, a little pile of beans tendered on a leaf. The poverty is conscience-disturbing, made bearable only by the climate, a communal way of life, and, one must suppose, habit. Men and women till the rice paddies that belong to the village as a whole, and each one puts a tablespoon a day into a common sack. This is sold and the proceeds distributed evenly among the contributors. They subsist chiefly on rice and fruit, since the fishing is only fair, but, judging from the livestock along the road, we concluded that pork and duck must be reasonably abundant. We were told that the great delicacy is turtle meat. For feasts the entire community sets out to capture a giant turtle, and they are so enormous that one will supply meat for an entire village.

Our goal at Ubud was the museum, where they have some good examples of Balinese art, sculpture and painting. The pictures were the same kind but greatly superior in quality to the one we bought in Denpasar. The exterior of the museum was a piece of art in itself, with a charming lily-filled pond surrounded by bamboo and fern trees and approached by a bridge like that of San Luis Rey, a frail swinging walk spanning a ravine. Priscilla and I were scared, but we agreed to cross provided that our two beaux, both hefty specimens, waited till we reached the other side before stepping foot upon it. We had visions of hurtling into the chasm like the hapless characters in the television production of the Thornton Wilder story.

Ubud has a sizable artists' colony that includes Westerners who have fallen in love with Bali and settled there. One cannot accurately say settled down, because foreigners are not allowed to buy property. They may lease it for a five-year period and must leave and go someplace else, if only for a visit, after two years. This is a ruling the Indonesians inherited from the Dutch, who instigated it to keep out the Chinese who came into Indonesia, worked hard, and bought up the land. Who wants *that* kind of an example set before him?

In the evening on our return from Ubud we went to watch a *ketchak*, a monkey dance. This is a curious spectacle rehearsed with considerable care and performed about once a week for tourists or on occasions when it is especially requested for a private party, and then the performers are paid extra. Leonard had arranged to have it laid on, as the English say, before we left Djakarta.

We drove through the night to a clearing in the jungle and were

given seats on a palm-thatched platform, one guttering candle inten-
sifying the shadows. Presently the drums began and out from behind
the trees the dark people started gathering.

This was a commercial venture frequently undertaken, and Leonard
and Norton were large men, presumably relaxed and anticipating
pleasure, but Priscilla and I glanced at each other and each knew what
the other was thinking. There were only four of us and hundreds and
hundreds of them, and they were preparing to work themselves up into
quite a frenzy, and we were in the middle of a jungle. In the pitch-black
night. And I had read *The Tribe That Lost Its Head*. Of course that
had been Africa, still . . . So all right, do you want adventure or do
you want to spend your whole life in a New York apartment with
steam heat and a freezer?

A tall, heavy iron candelabrum was set in the middle of the clearing
and on it were hung little cups of coconut oil with floating wicks, like
the ones on the temple the night of the children's dance. Presently
these were lighted, and then, leaving space immediately around the
candlestick, about a hundred twenty-five men formed themselves into
four concentric circles, one inside the other. They knelt on the ground,
sitting back on their heels, the lower parts of their bodies draped in
sarongs, their brown torsos gleaming in the flickering light. Swaying
from side to side, they sang, *a cappella*, their voices deep and resonant,
their arms waving and gesturing. They sang and they made strange
guttural chattering sounds, for they were the monkey army of the Rama
legend.

The story was that of Rama, heir to the throne of Ajodhya, who is
exiled from his father's realm and goes into the forest with his wife,
Sita, and his younger brother, Laksamana. One day while Rama is
hunting the deer with the golden horns, Sita, thinking she hears a cry
for help, sends Laksamana to investigate. The cry, however, is a ruse.
Once alone, Sita is kidnaped by the followers of Rawana, king of the
demons, whereupon Rama, with the assistance of an army of monkeys,
attacks Lengkapura (Ceylon), where Rawana lives. Still with me? It
isn't as complicated as the plot of *Die Walküre*, for heaven's sake. Rawana isn't a bad sort of demon and he refrains from violating the lady,
instead asking her hand in marriage, but, as the one-page libretto explained, "she then burst all into tears."

Menelaus, seeking to regain Helen . . . no, no, sorry. Rama, battling
to regain his kidnaped Sita, meets Meganada, Rawana's son, who
shoots his arrow at him. Well, as you may imagine, Rama is fit to be

tied, which is just what happens, because the arrow turns into a serpent and twines itself around Rama like a rope. He beseeches the gods for help, and presently Vishnu's bird Garuda—remember the sculptures in Bangkok and the air line?—is sent to free him.

In the meantime Hanuman—no, we haven't met him before, but he's the king of the monkeys and a good Joe—confers with his monkey generals and mobilizes his troops, and the denouement is a raging battle between the monkeys and the demons and the monkeys win. I *think*.

This tale was told mostly by rhythmic dancing and chanting, but there was a little dialogue, too, brief scenes played in the center of the rings of swaying men. There were Sita and her handmaiden *au naturel* and the demons and the Garuda bird *sous cloche* in fearsome masks. Reversing Shakespearean custom, the leading man's part, that of Rama, was played by a young woman, the daughter of the village elder. The harsh minor chanting, the swaying bodies, the flickering candlelight under the great trees combined to form an eerie spectacle. The performance lasted a little under an hour and stopped abruptly. The men rose to their feet, the circles disintegrated, and the actors wandered back along the jungle paths to their homes. We emerged unscathed.

A less spooky piece of real estate but a memorable one was the monkey forest. It was laced with broad green avenues, and one bought nuts from an old attendant and wandered about feeding the monkeys and taking pictures of the sad-faced babies clinging to their mothers' bellies, the mothers with faces like those of resigned old men. They swung down from the trees and searched each other for fleas and ran after Priscilla and me, clutching at our skirts and holding out their hands for peanuts. While we were there a couple of truckloads of school children drove up, and the youngsters scrambled down to observe the fauna and flora of their native land and to stare at the countless shrines.

There were all kinds of shrines, some merely façades or gateways of brick, the edges and corners demon-encrusted, and there were others that rose in diminishing tiers, each tier roofed with palm thatch. There was one that was very large, a great square shallow well of wood that was also palm-thatched and lined with benches, and that because of its size we took to be an especially holy place and we gazed at it with the respect due the ancient altar of a great people. We learned later it was a pit where cockfighting took place.

We had arrived in Bali Wednesday morning. Early Saturday, 6:30 A.M., General Astley-Bell again rallied his troops for the return flight to Djakarta, and I must say it was good to get home and to lunch on simple, expertly cooked food in the air-conditioned study.

We had only a few hours, however, to enjoy the luxury, for our plane left for Saigon in South Viet Nam at two fifty-five the next morning. We were going to Saigon because we were going to fly from there to Siem Reap, in Cambodia. To get to the great temples of Angkor Wat and Angkor Thom, you don't always have to do this, and indeed it is the undesirable roundabout way. But at the time we were booking our trip the border between Bangkok and Cambodia was closed, a misfortune, as the flight from Bangkok to Siem Reap is only an hour. By the time we had arrived in the Orient, that particular spurt of tension had dissipated and the border had reopened but, wanting to detour via Indonesia, we followed our schedule.

When roused by Ah Chai at two o'clock in the morning we had only ourselves to get to the airport, as Leonard's secretary and the night chauffeur had already coped with the luggage. We bade a fond farewell to our host and hostess, who, though drugged with sleep, had the courtesy to get up to wave us on our way. At the airport I received a nasty shock. We had been told they would want to check the number of my typewriter, so we had sent it along with the other luggage. Since they fitted perfectly I had inserted under the canvas cover the two cardboard-bound notebooks I was using as diaries. No secrecy was intended, merely convenience.

As we were wandering about trying to collect ourselves and our possessions, which had been delivered a couple of hours before, I happened to glance casually at one of the long counters. There, tumbled among bags, coats, and baskets, mauled and shoved about, were my diaries. I leaped upon them as a mother panther upon wounded cubs. They were of no conceivable value to anybody in the world but me, but to me they were my all. I fiercely demanded of the young woman behind the counter what had occurred, how they happened to be there? No malice, it turned out, just carelessness. They had taken the canvas cover off the typewriter the better to check the number and when they'd put it back they'd forgotten the notebooks. She shrugged and smiled amiably. I smiled weakly. No harm had been done, but it was a close shave.

Our plane was an hour and a half late in arriving and we watched with admiration the aplomb with which the members of the Italian Ambassador's household, who had come to see him off, were able to keep up a sprightly conversation in drab surroundings and in the humid, languid atmosphere, while we sat yawning and scratching. It was one of the few times on the trip we were bothered by mosquitoes.

The plane came in at last, a TAI. Many people, we were among them, assume the line has something to do with Thailand, but the letters stand for Transports Aériens Intercontinentaux. It is a subsidiary of Air France and first rate.

Traveler's Tip No. 20: Let each member of the family of writing age have his own pen. Even on a long flight there's never enough time to fill out the countless forms you are handed, and on a short one papers whirl through the cabin like snow. God knows why they want them, since they never look at them. Extra cards with heavy print demand that you declare the amount of money you have, but we never met any official who so much as glanced at them or who asked to see either our currency or our traveler's checks.

CHAPTER SIX

Saigon ✳ Siem Reap

FRENCH INDO-CHINA! The name rang like a gong. The very syllables dripped glamour, it was right up there with Samarkand and far Cathay. Then it had to raise a stink and go and get decolonialized and now what have we got? North and South Vietnam. North and South Dakota. There's romance! There's the tinkle of temple bells and elephants bearing golden howdahs trailing lengths of flaming silk. There's the thin blue smoke of incense rising and porcelain teacups petal thin. What is this passion to do away with all that is colorful and rich, romantic and individualistic in life? One is tempted to snort in outrage like a crusty British colonel.

But we were beginning to learn a tiny bit about the Orient. Europe, I think, differs enormously from America; in civilization and tradition, art and architecture the schism is great, but, allowing for variations of temperament and climate, the difference between one European city and another is not all that sharp: Paris, Rome, Vienna are of one world.

But as the contrast between the United States and Europe is striking, so is that between Europe and Asia. We were to find, however, that in the Asiatic countries we visited the same pattern of civilization and geography prevailed. Rice paddies, tea gardens, water buffalo are as indigenous to the East as are boulevards and cafés to Europe and skyscrapers and superhighways to America. Africa, I suppose, has another and different personality all its own.

Fortunately, where South Vietnam is concerned the country is more beautiful than its name. The part we saw was flat, and flying over it is like flying between two mirrors; the whole land reflects the sky. It is a vast checkerboard of glinting rice fields looped and laced with rivers large and small. A floating area anchored to great clumps of trees, a liquid world where the fluid grace of the women's clothes delights the eye. They wear long loose trousers, usually black or white, surmounted by long tunics. The tunics have the high, stiff little collars of the Chinese *cheong sam,* but are infinitely more graceful than the Chinese dress, for, slit up the sides, almost to the waist, they form two panels that float and flutter as their wearers walk or ride bicycles. The material, frequently diaphanous, is either printed or of lovely colors, mulberry, bronze, and olive.

The money of Saigon is piasters, and there are seventy-two to the dollar. Having been occupied so long by the French, Saigon is like a French provincial town, with broad streets and old trees, French-planted. In contrast to Bangkok and Djakarta it is very clean. People in that part of the world say the reason Bangkok is dirty is that it has never been occupied by Europeans, but Djakarta was occupied by the Dutch for three hundred and fifty years and it is filthy. People in that part of the world say that is because the Dutch have been out of it for ten years and the Indonesians are running things themselves. You can't win.

We arrived in Saigon on Sunday and, everything in town being closed, hired a car and drove out to a lacquer factory where the show-room was open to visitors. The boxes and bowls and cabinets were beautiful, but expensive even there. I cast covetous eyes on a superb Coromandel screen, but as it cost three thousand dollars I quickly retrieved them.

In Saigon we stayed at the Majestic, which was well air-conditioned, and even I, who say so many mean things about the system, was grateful, for the weather was frightfully hot and humid. The floors were tile but apparently seldom washed, and in our bathroom was a bidet with a life of its own. Twenty minutes after the toilet had been flushed and when no one was near it, the bidet would begin to rumble and snort and gurgle. We thought we had hygienic ghosts. Norton said it was because the drains were clogged and it took the water that long to run from one appliance to the other.

The food was indifferent and the breakfast tablecloth was soiled. When I asked the little Vietnamese waiter if we could please have a clean one, he smiled charmingly. *"Mais oui, madame,"* and he whipped out a minute napkin that he placed over one offending spot.

We grumbled a bit about these shortcomings, spoiled darlings of fortune that we were. We little knew what lay ahead.

The trip to Phnom Penh, the capital of Cambodia, was made via

RAC, Royal Air Camboge, where we met up again with our friend Roberto Carriciolo di San Vito, en route, as we were, to Siem Reap and the great monuments of Angkor Wat and Angkor Thom. Also on board were Blanche Thebom, of the Metropolitan, and her accompanist.

Pomp and circumstance had invaded Phnom Penh. The Cambodian Army, fifty strong, was drawn up at attention, the bandmaster stood, his baton at the ready, and heads of departments in their whites were massed at the entrance of the terminal. In front of them jiggled a couple of small girls carrying large bouquets, the excitement and splendor of their mission increasing the urgency of their need to retire.

Were I to see them today, appealing though they were, I should be able to think of them only as "the little creeps with the flowers," a phrase lifted from Mr. Robert Newhart's incomparable monologue about Khrushchev, the definitive version of an Official Arrival at an Airport.

Our official, as it turned out, was Mr. Fred Seaton, the United States Secretary of the Interior, who touched down in a small, unpretentious U. S. Government plane. He was certainly a long way from our interior, but deep in the entrails and, so we must hope, heart of an ally, for his mission was to open the Khmer-American Friendship Highway, cut from Phnom Penh through a hundred thirty-four miles of rice fields and jungle to the Gulf of Siam. It cost us thirty-two million dollars and was a steal, they said, in view of the fact that the French were building and paying for the new seaport. We only picked up the tab for the road.

I wish I *knew* about such things. Are they worth it or are they not? One faction will tell you one thing, one another, and I suppose the only way ever to prove it would be to live a hundred years and see what happens. In the meantime the taxpayer shivers in his barrel.

Anyway, Mr. Seaton was greeted by Mr. Chea Chinkok, Cambodian Minister for Foreign Affairs, and Mr. Phlek Chhat, Minister of Public Works, and the band played *The Star-Spangled Banner* as though it were the "Death March" from *Saul*, and Norton and I were impressed by the correctness and discipline of His Excellency, the Italian Ambassador to Indonesia, who even though he was now out of office and on holiday stood stiffly at attention throughout.

The brass finally departed for town; we got back in our plane and took off for Siem Reap. On the way we tried sorting out our money, for we had a salad of leftover rupias from Indonesia, piasters from Vietnam, and an unexpected windfall of reals, Cambodian currency. While we were still in Bangkok going down in the hotel elevator one

day, a tall, good-looking American spoke to us. "You people going to
Cambodia by any chance?" We said we were. "Here," he said, thrusting into our hands a small verminous wudge of bills, "take these, they're
reals. I'm not going back and God knows they're no use in any other
country," and as we hesitated, "Go ahead, take them, it's a *favor*." We
took them, gingerly—they were really scrofulous—and I'm sure that was
the only time in our lives we'll ever be subsidized by a stranger.

We landed on a tablecloth that is the Siem Reap airport and took a
beat-up taxi to the hotel. Siem Reap was a surprise. We had understood
that the Wats were in the jungle and jungle was what we expected, but
the eight-kilometer drive to the hotel was as open as Kansas. Suddenly
we saw it, le Grand Hôtel d'Ankor, in all its grisly glory. Set in the
middle of nothing, it was a large pile of concrete, bilious yellow on the
outside, *couleur caca*, mission style within.

The floors were tile and had not known a mop for many a weary
day. We were taken up to our room, there was an elevator but it was
capricious, so we walked—and discovered it to be quite large and reasonably dirty. The ceiling fan worked, but the electric lights had been
placed far far from bed and dressing table and their shades were cunningly designed to expose the bulb so that the light hit you right in the
eye. Not that it was any third degree. The wattage of the East is frail.

The bathroom door didn't close, but there was an enormous earthen
jar filled with water in which floated a rusty tin dipper. Despite an
overhead tank it was suggested that we use it to expedite flushing. I
thought we were to use it for bathing purposes as well. Trained at
Jimmy Pandy's, I was getting quite deft at this, but it developed that,
though the shower had only one tap for cold water, the water was
plentiful. It was later that we realized that primitive though conditions
were there was one thing you had to say for those people. They had done
a great deal of painstaking research and come up with a substance far
harder than granite and out of this they made the beds. The lack of
resilience was amazing. If there was ever a diamond big enough to sleep
on, I fancy the sensation would be much the same. The beds smelled a
little too. Of stale sweat. The beds of Jimmy Pandy, so unyielding at
the time, in retrospect seemed like fleecy clouds.

There were mosquito-netting canopies that let down and that, after
you had joined battle with them and killed the mosquitoes who got inside when you did, proved quite effective.

A couple of carafes stood about half filled with water, and the boy
assured us it had been boiled, but we were dubious. Instead of being

depressed, however, the doctor's mood seemed to lift. Here at last was a chance to test the halazone tablets and play with our gadgets! He got out the blue plastic bag that had followed us to Greece and that we had been carrying unopened ever since. He inserted the little tube and spigot, and I held it while he poured water over the crystals. We waited a few minutes, opened the tap, *et voilà!* Pure as a mountain stream. After showers and a couple of highballs, warm but antiseptic, we descended much refreshed to reconnoiter and meet Roberto in the bar.

The bar proper was at the end of a long, dreary room and behind it stood a sad little brown man. We ordered a round of highballs. I craved ice, but the doctor said, "No. Ice is made of water." "I know," I said, "but cold things seem less germ-ridden." "Ice melts," he said. A simple declarative sentence admitting of no argument. At that the bar highballs were superior to our own, as at least the soda had been kept in the icebox and was cold, and the drinks distracted my attention from the little lizards who clung to the neon light tubes and who were called *jikis*.

We saw Blanche Thebom and her accompanist having drinks at a table down the room, and Norton went over to them and doled out a ration of halazone tablets. Not having realized how near they had come to bubonic plague, they were simultaneously alarmed and relieved by his largess. They said that they had hired a pedi-cab and were going to view Angkor Wat by torchlight. Didn't we want to come? We decided against it, as we would have a chance to visit it only once and thought we would see more in the daytime. We were glad later but sorry for them when a torrential downpour split the heavens.

Someone suggested dinner and we left the bar and went out and down the hall to the dining room. It was a big room quite full of people, and I noticed that the floor was shimmering. Like that of the rest of the building, it was of tile, and I thought the shimmer was some kind of mica. We were shown to our table and sat down. A closer view disclosed the fascinating fact that the shimmer of the floor was in reality thousands of ants on the march. An unexpected invasion, but who would be an old sorehead and complain? They were tiny, after all. We hooked our heels over the rungs of our chairs and went to work with the enemy on the table. It was the only place we've ever been where it was more prudent to place coasters on top of the glasses rather than underneath. Kept the bugs out better. We found that the best way to drink was to bring glass and coaster very close to the mouth

then cautiously raise the coaster-lid just a crack, take a hasty sip, snap
it down again, and replace the glass on the table. Those bugs! There
were minute little black fellows that got in your hair and there were
small round ones like mobile lentils. They were exactly the shape, size,
and color of lentils and they swarmed up over the edges of the plates.
They were quick and resourceful and you had to *snatch* the food away
from them. It was hard to say why either they or we wanted it, but
eating is kind of a habit, and even if the food wasn't good there was a
lot of it. Consommé, canned so it seemed safe, safer at least than the
villainous-looking hors d'oeuvres, followed by hash in pastry—that
brave we weren't—then a lone vegetable, then roast duck, salad, which
we skipped, and chocolate pudding. There was of course one saving
grace. French wine was expensive but it was available, and the beer,
which was reasonable, was good.

Over coffee in the bar I expressed my exasperation. "Really," I said to
Norton and Roberto, "this is ridiculous. With soap and water and DDT
and screens in the doors and windows they could be rid of those bugs in
no time." Norton's theory was that the management probably encouraged them. "They're a talking point," he said. "Tourists will never forget the Grand Hôtel d'Ankor. Its fame will spread around the globe."

Roberto shrugged. "Why should they fuss, *les frères Vergoz?*" They
were the proprietors. "There isn't another place for travelers to stay
within two hundred miles. The temples are among the wonders of the
world. People will always come here."

In justice it must be said that the eggs at breakfast the next morning
were fresh and hot. Actually, since we were there, we have heard that
some of the old zing is fading. Today's tourist does not have to be infused with the same stern stuff that activated us. I understand the place
is under new management and is becoming effete, although there is a
school that holds that if it is a certain Royal Personage who has taken
over, and when we were there, there was a rumor that he might, there
may well be an intensification of the old spirit. His adherents defend
him hotly. "*He's* never made good at *anything*," they say. "Not at government, not at women, not at sports . . . why *should* the hotel improve? What is this canard being foisted upon us?"

We did notice, not far away, a quite attractive, small modern establishment that looked as though it might be an inn or guest house, but
it was reserved, we were told, for the prime minister or the king or
somebody.

On our arrival we had had one real disappointment. A few months

before we started the trip I had lectured in Kansas City and at a charming party given by the Irvine Hockadays had been introduced to
Laurence Sickman, director of the William Rockhill Nelson Gallery of
Art, who had written and also given me a letter to Jean Laur, *Con-
servateur des Monuments du Groupe d'Ankor*. I had written Monsieur
Laur from Indonesia and received a card in reply saying he would be
glad to see us when we got to Siem Reap.

Once at the hotel I went directly to the desk to ask if there was any
message or if Monsieur Laur lived close by. The drive from the airport
had shown us that if you were in Siem Reap at all you were close, but
one of the Vergoz brothers told me that Monsieur Laur had left unexpectedly that morning for Phnom Penh and would not be back for
two or three days. It was a blow, but I suppose he had gone to meet
Mr. Seaton.

We were up early in preparation for our pilgrimage to the Wats;
also, as I have indicated, the couches provided by the management
were not conducive to dalliance. Looking out the window, we saw a
little vignette typical of the Orient. The squat is the posture of Asia,
and squatting on the grass in front of the hotel under the lifting mist
were two men eating with chopsticks, their breakfast served them in
bowls by a girl who carried her little restaurant with her. She bore a

yoke on her shoulders, and suspended from long cords at either end were trays with food and a little brazier. It was nice.

A French couple, Roberto decided the husband was a merchant from Lille, Roberto himself, Norton, and I set off at 8 A.M. in a small, rickety bus to view the ruins of Angkor Wat and Angkor Thom, and a fabulous sight they are. *Wat* is "temple," *angkor* means "city," and *thom* means "large." They are all of that. Angkor Thom was built around A.D. 900 and it took five hundred thousand people fifty years to do the job, and Angkor Wat was completed in the twelfth century. They were deserted in the fifteenth century for what reason is not definitely known. Various theories are held, one being that the Khmers, as the Cambodians were then called, were vanquished in war by their enemies, probably the Siamese—although in that event why would the community have been so completely deserted—and another being that the race was decimated by a terrible epidemic. In any event the people vanished, the jungle closed in, and the vast buildings slumbered unknown for four hundred and fifty years until in 1856 a French archaeologist came upon them, surely one of the stunning discoveries of world history. Great trees had grown up, prying apart stones that still were held in position by strangling vines. They say there are no lions in Cambodia. I do not believe it. Surely through the centuries these were the courts the lion and lizard kept.

The French have done with great skill an enormous amount of restoration and reconstruction and the work continues, but the impression one receives is still one of antiquity, remoteness, and brooding solitude. The day we were there the silence was desecrated only by ourselves. I do not want to sound misanthropic, but I can understand those who cherish ruins. They are a record of human ambition and skill and achievement, with the humans themselves mercifully absent, no mean advantage.

We visited Angkor Thom first. The buildings are constructed of huge pieces of gray lichened sandstone brought from quarries forty-five kilometers distant, and the gateways and towers are carved in the form of four gigantic human heads facing the four points of the compass, some with benign Buddha smiles. One clambers up and down terraces and incredibly steep staircases with the narrowest of treads. I could only assume that the Khmers had tiny feet or else that they walked with their feet turned sideways the way they are shown in their sculptures and carvings. There are countless small chambers opening into one another, each of which was a chapel with its own Buddha. The proportion of the rectangular doorways, every one cut from a solid piece of stone, is beautiful. The bas-relief carvings on the walls are irresistible, graphic, and comedic. There are thronging battle scenes with generals on elephants surging into battle, serried tiers of parasols over their heads: the more exalted the rank, the more the parasols. Fierce naval battles are depicted with madly rowing galley slaves and luckless specimens being tossed overboard into the jaws of hospitable crocodiles. There are fish galore and market scenes and cooking scenes with fish and meat *en brochette*, and there are, of course, dancing girls. Exquisite creatures with toes and fingers turned back so far they are practically inside out. There is a corner carving of an elephant with his trunk wrapped around a naked girl. The idea I believe was that he smashed her against a tree until she was dead, a reprimand conceived by the lord of the manor for ladies who had incurred his displeasure.

Although it is known that there were palaces that housed the court, nothing remains of them but a few stones, the traces of their foundations. They must have been built of wood, which rotted away in the climate. Stamina wilts quickly too, and after a couple of hours of exploring in that heat and humidity we began dreaming of a white Christmas and an ice-cold bottle of beer.

There are still a couple of huge square swimming pools that were used by the royal family and the ladies of the court. One might think that we would have been tempted, and offhand it sounds like a good idea, but although they are green and mysterious they are not exactly inviting. What lurks beneath the slime? It was curious to compare the two great monuments we saw on the trip: the pale, sun-drenched Acropolis of Greece, where aridity is the characteristic of the land, and the green dank jungle and the gray humid stones of the Wats. In such an atmosphere I kept glancing around apprehensively for snakes, expecting momentarily to see one coiling down a steep staircase, but whether out of sympathy or veracity the guide assured me that they were very rare. We did see a long string of enormous ants coupled together like trains dragging behind them a helpless captive caterpillar and we heard a tree crash in the forest, reviving the old philosophical discussion about when a tree crashes in the forest and nobody hears it, has it made any sound? I maintain that obviously it has, but I believe that from the electronic or some such esoteric point of view sound is sound only if the pass so to speak, is completed, if the waves are received by an eardrum or its equivalent.

We wandered about, for there are lovely walks through forest glades, and took pictures and gazed upon statues of assorted Buddhas, and finally returned to the hotel for the cold beer and luncheon.

Angkor Wat, with its great cone-shaped towers, which we visited later, is much more open than its sister temple, set on a square island surrounded by a broad, shallow moat, now the village swimming hole, and approached by a tremendously long, broad causeway. Walking along it, for the first time we really suffered from the grueling sun. Like that of the Grand Canyon, the stillness of Angkor Wat is an element in itself, broken only by bird calls. The galleries and chapels are infused by the smell of bats.

We wanted to stay another day in Siem Reap, but the difficulty was the plane service. Not only there but in many other places planes do not fly every day, so the tourist is forced to choose between two alternatives, neither of them satisfactory. He has either too little time or too much.

We missed seeing the magnificent Temple in the Forest because it was some distance away, but had we stayed we would then have had to pass another day and a night before we could get out and back to Saigon and from there on to Hong Kong. Knowing the hotel, this latter prospect did not appeal. Roberto was going the other way, to Bangkok and then on back to Europe, and because of schedules had decided on the more extended tour. He stood on the hotel steps waving good-by as our taxi pulled away, the sweat running down his face, and I'm not sure it wasn't mingled with a tear or two. We had been comrades in arms, however briefly. It is a poignant moment when companions leave and one must man the fort alone. Carriciolo at the Grand d' Ankor! Who shall forget that gallant stand! The Alamo of Southeast Asia!

However much I may have ribbed it, there was one great asset possessed by the Grand that even the stately Waldorf cannot provide. Eastern potentates stop there when they are in New York, but does it supply them with that one little touch of home that can mean so much to a traveler far from native land and dear ones? Does it supply elephants? It does not, but the Grand does, two beautiful authentic living beasts for guests to ride and a high platform from which they may be mounted. I was heartbroken that I had not seen them in time, but they hove into view only when we were on our way to the airport. They'd been grazing down the road a piece and were on their way back, and the driver told us they lived at the hotel.

We returned to Saigon, where we passed a fairly tedious thirty-six hours due to the pixie air schedules, but since the hands of the clock do move, however leadenly, our moment finally came. We took off in an Air France Constellation for Hong Kong, one of the high and shining peaks of our journey.

CHAPTER SEVEN

✴ Hong Kong

The Hong Kong flight was comfortable and pleasant, with an appetizing dinner for diversion. The flying time was three and a half hours, but it was nine forty-five local time when we landed. We were one of the first planes to come in at night, as their airport lighting system had only just been installed, but it is a fine one, and as the plane slips down between the hills the twinkling city is a magnificent sight.

A small cordial delegation was on hand to meet us: Joe Sykes and Rita Xavier, a beautiful young Chinese girl who was working for Northwest Airlines with whom we were coming home, and Noble Smith and his wife from American Express. Again customs were a simple matter of smiles and chalk marks and we were whisked to the Peninsula Hotel. The Peninsula is large, stereotyped, and comfortable and overlooks the waterfront. I have never seen Rio, but surely Hong Kong must rank with it, New York, and San Francisco as one of the great harbors of the world. That first night, when our friends had left us after a nightcap, I was so keyed up over being there I had to take a sleeping pill before I could close an eye.

The next morning the impact and the geography lessons began. Hong Kong was the first city of the Orient we had been in that seemed like a great city rather than a picturesque Asian community. The harbor divides it into two parts. Properly it is named Victoria on the island of Hong Kong, but to call it that would be to draw blank stares. Everybody refers to it as Hong Kong. Kowloon, the other half, is on the tip of a peninsula of the mainland of China. The two parts form a whole referred to as the Colony. The word "China" is taboo; strictly for communists. The harbor between Hong Kong and Kowloon connects rather than separates them and is as much the city as is the land. It takes six or seven minutes to cross on one of the Star ferryboats, so widely publicized in *The World of Suzie Wong*, and there are many of them and they run in endless chain. Ocean-going liners and United States carriers anchor in the harbor—when we were there so was the *Shangri-La*—and the junks, the lovely junks, with sails like great leaves, tobacco brown and violet, inky gray and rust and rose, as typical of the city as are the gondolas of Venice, ride upon it. Junk wood is old and weathered and the figures working the boats are dressed in parchment-colored round straw hats, black trousers, and jackets of deep brilliant blue.

Whole families are born and live and die on the junks, and the river people are suspicious of land people and keep to themselves and their own ways.

There are hotels on the Kowloon side and shops and restaurants. Hong Kong boasts the older business establishments, the banks, and of course shops and restaurants too. The Peak, accurately named since it is the highest hill of an island that is all hills and baby mountains, is the swank residential area where the well-to-do Chinese and most of the British and other foreigners live.

On the far side of Hong Kong is Repulse Bay, a beautiful spot away from the city proper, with a big, comfortable, old-fashioned hotel over-looking the brilliant blue water, green islands, and curving white sand of a lovely bathing beach. It would be a pleasant place to stay during hot weather if one were going to be there for an extended period, but for the average tourist intent on shopping and with limited time at his disposal it is a bit remote.

We lunched there one day with our friends Wally and Julie Kwok, Chinese who had lived in New York and were patients of Norton, and a group of Chinese guests: Mr. Fisher Yu, a banker—Harvard, the house of Morgan, and now his own company; the editor of the Hong Kong *Standard*, Woo Kya-tang; and a man in the textile industry, Ping Yuan-tang, known to everyone as P.Y. The communists, he said, could take Hong Kong any time they wanted to, but leaving it alone is greatly to their advantage. "To begin with," he said, laughing, "there's got to be someplace besides Switzerland that's neutral where the two sides can get together and talk. Furthermore, of course, it gives them a trad-ing area and access to free currencies. With what they sell here and the remittances to families from overseas Chinese they do a brisk business amounting to between two and three hundred million dollars a year."

Most of the Chinese we met who were living in Hong Kong and had established businesses were already refugees from Peking and Shanghai.

Where they will go if the communists do sweep down on the Colony is a poignant question.

Since we, ostensibly, do not trade with Communist China, the United States Government is very firm about having certificates of origin for any goods exported from Hong Kong. This means they are certified as not having come from the mainland, but I don't know where our dear customs department thinks they do come from. Where are Hong Kongese supposed to get commodities and raw materials? They're a little island, gentlemen, they have few resources. Naturally they deal with the communists. Practically all the food is imported from the mainland and there is a store, a sort of bazaar, selling sleazy merchandise, cheap rayon underwear, thin tin pots and kettles, toys and questionable jade and ivory, known as China Products, where all the merchandise is from the communist mainland. Material of this class is not exported. Everything we have is infinitely better.

Hong Kong is an exotic, dramatic, and beautiful spot and, for the visitor whose days are filled with shopping and fittings and sight-seeing time passes quickly. Thanks to those Chinese in Norton's practice who were in Hong Kong for the summer and who entertained us with the greatest hospitality, we met and talked with other Chinese, so we did not feel isolated, as one frequently does in a foreign land. The twelve days we were there flew by, but we wondered occasionally how we would like to live there. A person in business or doing a job necessarily has a different attitude, but if you are used to a great city you miss the theaters, museums, picture galleries, opera—the whole intellectual life of a capital. Good works one *could* engage in. That, yes! With the thousands of refugees pouring into the Colony the need is desperate and the opportunities unnumbered.

When you think of the magnitude of the problem they have to cope with, the government and private agencies are doing incredibly well. They are exerting terrific efforts to abolish the miserable shanty-town shacks made from flattened tin cans, tar paper, and bamboo thatch that crowd the hillsides, and to move the hundreds of thousands of families who have fled the communists into the barrack-like cement blocks of flats that mushroom on Hong Kong and the neighboring islands. The flats are pretty bleak but they are shelter, and some kind of sanitation is possible. Wherever the Chinese poor congregate laundry flutters like tattered banners from their balconies. With the dirt and sweat constant washing is necessary.

We went to visit the Family Planning Association, which is an affiliate of America's Planned Parenthood, where Chinese and English women work together, and we found a very well-equipped clinic that has been given them by the Jockey Club, a swank and eleemosynary organization that contributes to many Hong Kong causes. The clinic doctors and nurses feel they are making some progress in educating the poorest Chinese women in the use of contraceptives, although it's hard to say, "There, that one really understands and is going to follow through." The extreme intimacy of life on the junks—as many as ten and twelve people existing in a stringently confined area—makes their use difficult. On the other hand, it's hard to see why those same conditions don't inhibit the practice that brings the pullulating children, but they don't.

One trouble is that the women who are poor and uneducated get confused. Once away from the clinic they forget the instructions and wear the diaphragms as amulets or give them to the children to play with.

The clinic's small triumphs occur when a woman living in wretched poverty discovers that the contraceptives do work, that it is possible to limit one's family to the number of children who can be cared for and fed and educated and who brings a friend whom she has convinced to the clinic to be instructed. As in the rest of the world the Catholic Church in Hong Kong is rigorously opposed to family planning, but there was one remarkable woman, a nun, who could understand and appreciate its values. She had been trained in medicine and was an expert in tuberculosis. Hundreds of tubercular babies pass through her hands yearly. She knows that, even if she does manage to save them in infancy, with the lives they have to look forward to the chances of their living beyond the age of twenty-five is negligible. She questions the wisdom of unlimited human life. Now that the pill is proving effective in preventing conception, it is to be hoped that its distribution and use will not be too long delayed. The population problem is already desperate, the fate of millions, heartbreaking. In the evenings along the Hong Kong docks we saw families eating a small bowl of rice for their supper and afterward settling down on filthy old newspapers to sleep, fathers, mothers, and litters of pitiably scrawny little kids.

It is heartbreaking, too, for those who live there permanently and are engaged in a daily struggle to help raise the standard of living, but now there are many family planning centers, and inch by painful inch they progress.

We admired these dedicated men and women the more because they had little release from the pressure of their jobs. A change of pace in Hong Kong is virtually impossible. There is no such thing as going away for the weekend. With the possible exception of a brief trip to Macao, which I shall touch on later, there is no place to go. China is a vast land and it is communist and not many outsiders can get in even if they want to.

Beyond Kowloon lie the New Territories. This is a tract of land that was leased to the British by a former Chinese Government. The lease was for a hundred years and expires in 1997, at which time it is supposed to revert to China. Whether or not the communists will hold off that long is a moot question, but Britain recognizes their government and may be able to make a deal. In the meantime the British are going ahead with a cautious ten-year plan, hoping it won't blow up in their faces.

One can drive into the New Territories, as we did, but it's not much of a change, although we were fascinated by a walled village, still, in the twentieth century, curiously medieval. The common grounds where ducks and chickens picked and goats were tethered lay outside. Within the cramped houses adjoined each other, separated by the narrowest of passageways so that only the thinnest slices of sunshine could enter. We had the feeling that the inhabitants could not breathe properly except outside the walls.

There are no charming inns or forest resorts or beaches in the New Territories to provide recreational facilities—by far the best beaches are around Hong Kong—so that after a prolonged stay in the Colony, despite its charm, color, and fluctuating population, I should think one might begin to go a little stir-crazy.

As with insular life anywhere the inhabitants are torn. Should they follow an understandable disinclination to entertain visitors who in all likelihood they will never see again and whose repetitious questions must be answered, whose criticisms should be parried, or should they welcome them with open arms just because they *are* new faces and bring with them the breath and aura of the outside world?

Again, thanks to the Shell and Astley-Bell contacts throughout Southeast Asia, we were handsomely entertained by, among others, the Grossets. He was a colleague of Leonard in the oil business. They had a large comfortable house at the very peak of the Peak, with a superb view of the harbor and of Kowloon. We were invited for dinner and saw the view at sunset and watched the fairy spectacle it became after dark, with the millions of twinkling lights, and we were lucky. Mrs.

Grosset invited us to join them in a picnic the following Sunday, when
we were to take the launch and cruise around Hong Kong, but the
following Sunday it teemed all day and a thick fog shrouded the entire
community. At eleven in the morning she phoned. "The boat part's
called off but we're having the picnic anyway here at the house. Come
along and Jock will meet you at the ferry and drive you up." The picnic
lunch, a curry served at the comfortable dining table, was excellent, but
the magnificent view was blotted out. Among the guests were a Briga-
dier and Mrs. Chestnut and a couple called Smith-Wright. Ah, those
hyphenated names. We felt right in the swim, as we were always introduced as the Norton-Browns.

The Smith-Wrights were old Shanghai hands and were trapped
there when the Japanese came in during the war. He had had a
grueling experience. The English colony had formed a hard-working
amateur theatrical group and were about to put on a performance of
Richard the Third. Smith-Wright was playing Richard. He was in costume and make-up, it was just before curtain time, when a group of
Japanese soldiers arrived and with small ceremony hustled him away
to Bridge House. Since Bridge House was where the torture chambers
were, his own apprehension and the anguish of his wife and friends
may be imagined.

The Japanese grilled him for hours, bedeviling him with constantly
repeated assertions that Shakespeare was anti-Axis. He tried to reassure them, but it was a losing battle. Finally they let him go, having
subjected him to nothing more lethal than their tormenting idiocy.
Later he was held as a political prisoner, but they didn't treat him
badly. Despite what they had undergone at their hands both Smith-
Wright and his wife were pro-Japanese. They love the country and
think them a great people, certainly a remarkably civilized and very
British attitude.

The colonial British I find endlessly fascinating. There are families
who have lived for two or three generations in the colonies; India,
China, Africa, wherever it may be, and very few of them ever dream
of learning the language or of mingling with their foreign peers. The
men are usually better than the women—business has obliged them to
exert themselves at least to the extent of being able to communicate—
but some of the ladies are lulus.

We met one Englishwoman who lived in Shanghai—her husband
was in business there, and she took the train down to Hong Kong quite
frequently—and she said to me with a pleased air, "You know, I take

a lesson once a week to learn to say please and thank you, just simple things like that, and you'd be *surprised* how the Chinese warm to you." I refrained from asking why she didn't take three or four lessons a week and have the populace at her feet. Anyway I knew the answer. She wasn't interested. Were it not for the climate and the fact that they have many more servants than they could afford at home, most British colonials could be living in Little Tooting. Norton and I noticed that when we mentioned our Chinese friends they smiled vaguely and changed the subject, careful not to hurt our feelings by any implication that we were Americans who didn't know better than to mingle.

The Chinese are tolerant of the British, but they think they're bats. As Wally Kwok said to us one day, "I have been in English clubs. They are most boresome."

Wally in an English club I would like to see. He is a small, sturdy Chinese extrovert who loves sports and dancing, and Julie is his beautiful, gentle wife. Norton has considerable staying power himself and he is twice Wally's size, but one afternoon they played three sets of tennis together and then went for a half-hour swim. The doctor arrived home exhausted. His oriental chum took off for an evening of song and dance. Wally refers to his profession as the rag business and is involved in the manufacture of inexpensive underwear.

The Kwoks and three other couples in the textile business gave a big party one night at the Miramar Hotel and asked us to come. We were about eighty people. The Chinese women, many of them glittering with jewels, wore *cheong sams* of soft, glowing brocades. One of the guests was a six-foot-six Dutchman, Mr. de Jong. After even a brief time in Southeast Asia it is hard not to be influenced by the Asians' attitude toward the Dutch, whose reputation is mud, but Mr. de Jong seemed attractive and he was tall. For a tall woman like me—five feet eight— this is important. I found that I was liking him. Tch, tch, tch, sex. Would I have liked a six-foot-six Dutch woman or would I have looked up my nose at her, concentrating on her country's colonial malfeasance? I like to think I judge on personal integrity, and down with guilt by association, but who is ever sure?

A portion of the main floor of the hotel had been screened off, and behind the screen cocktails were served, just like New York. Later we went in to dinner. Not at all like New York. Very Chinese—long, long, long, but good, good, good. Just before satiety the fried rice appeared, and I gave thanks that we had but one course to go. After dinner, dancing. I love dancing, but I was no match for our demon host, Arthur

Murray's star. Wally could conga, and mambo, and samba. The can-can, the Highland fling, and the fandango would present no problems. At these I do not shine under the best of circumstances, and Wally came to my chest, but he would not be denied. "Do not be shy, dear Ilka, I will teach you," and off we went, butting and stumbling, but he gripped me firmly, the zeal of a missionary bringing light to the heathen blazing in his eyes.

The party had been dandy, complete with floor show—a young girl in brief turquoise satin and white fringe, her male partner in yellow and a monkey mask, good old Rama—but it was getting late and I was tired and wanted to go home. I glanced toward Norton. Small solace did I get, he was in his element.

On our arrival in Hong Kong a zany thing had happened. Jane Wang, of whom more later, had thoughtfully had calling cards made up for us, our American names on one side, their Chinese equivalents in Chinese characters on the other. In a little note she translated their meanings. Mine was dull. It meant, in effect, good, kindhearted scout, something worthy like that. The doctor's, God save the mark, trans-lated out to Precious Orchid. His Excellency in Greece, Precious Orchid in Hong Kong—there was no living with the man.

At the moment Precious Orchid was having a ball, and as we were on the Kowloon side only two or three blocks from our hotel, there wasn't even the goad of the last ferry to get him away. The Star ferry stops running at one o'clock, and from there on revelers homeward bound must bargain with the "walla-walla," privately owned taxi launches. This is a tricky procedure for foreigners, but he didn't have to face it. Whoopee!

However, I could hardly stay annoyed at Wally just because he had more energy and was a more accomplished dancer than I. He and Julie turned themselves inside out for us; because of them we enjoyed pleas-ures we would otherwise not have known about.

One of them was the Bird Club. This is an organization of bird lovers, all men, who every week meet in a fifth-floor restaurant for Sun-day breakfast. They arrive early, usually around seven, and stay till about ten and with them they bring their pet birds in cages. They dis-cuss birds, they exchange them, they buy and sell them, and they teach them to sing. This is done by putting a cloth over their cages and letting them hear other birds.

The restaurant itself is large and white-tiled, not picturesque, but the habitués and their pets are. So are the waitresses, who not only wait on table but sell charming tiny porcelain dishes for the birds' cages. There is also the grasshopper man. He comes around with an enormous big round basket, closed at the top, filled with live grasshoppers, and the club members buy a week's rations for their birds. Oh dear, oh dear, animals' inhumanity to animal. The grasshoppers are put to other uses as well. They box. I know it sounds unlikely, but they do. There's a whole arsenal of grasshopper equipment. There are little nets to catch them with, tiny wicker cages in which they are kept, and the Chinese make small clay arenas like bowls with rough inside edges on which the grasshoppers' feet can get a grip. In this arena they place a pair of male insects and then they take marsh grass and strip it down to the feathery inside bits, and with this they tickle the grasshoppers' private parts. It makes them angry. Understandably. Aroused and outraged, they have at each other, stridulating and flaying away furiously with forefeet and antennae, and the Chinese crowd around cheering them on and betting heavily. The grasshopper who first cries uncle loses the bout.

While we were at the Bird Club there were a couple of violent showers, but the sky cleared as we left, and we went to visit the municipal market. It was in a great big concrete building with separate floors for meat, fish, poultry, and vegetables. The vegetable stalls were the prettiest, the green and white and purple plants freshly sprinkled and glowing. At the meat stalls hung several benign cows' heads skinned, slabs of beef and tattered scarlet shreds of unknown cuts fluttering like rags. But the extraordinary thing was that in the whole immense market, although there were no screens, we didn't see a single fly or mosquito. We concluded that their sanitation department was highly effective. The poultry and fish certainly were fresh, as they were still alive in tanks and crates.

I have come upon a note in my diary that I pass along for what interest it may have. "Chinese kill poultry with a deft twist of their necks. Have equally quick way of removing snake's bladder: make tiny sharp incision, send snake on its way good as new. Use bladder juice as aphrodisiac." Cocktails, anyone?

From the municipal market we made our way through the crowded colorful streets to the Thieves' Market. The streets of Hong Kong are one's dream of China come true. Many of them are steep and staired, and the colorful perpendicular signs in splashy Chinese characters, which, for all the foreigner knows, may be saying "Joe's Eats" or "Going out of Business," are wonderfully decorative.

There are, as a matter of fact, lots of Joe's Eats; food stalls under awnings, their counters, loaded with strange shiny comestibles, flanked by long benches. The Chinese, however, do not sit on them, they sit on little low stools placed along them at intervals and rest their feet on the benches, thus attaining the ubiquitous squatting posture.

Bowlegged men in white shirts worn outside their short black pants trot through the street bearing yokes with swinging baskets and little kids half naked, but some of them, thank God roly-poly, lie kicking on the sidewalks. In Thailand and Indonesia babies were carried in slings and worn on the hipbone. In Hong Kong the slings are worn on the back à la papoose. Their little heads bobble over the top of the sling, and one is strongly tempted to walk behind the mother with a supporting hand under the baby's neck. We saw a few, but only a few, pigtails —they are on the wane—and we watched a tall, thin nun with long black garments go by carrying a black umbrella over her shaven head. She was quite beautiful in a lean masculine way. Wally Kwok said there were many Chinese Lesbians but few homosexuals. A good many rich upper-class Chinese families want to have their children educated in Europe, but hesitate about sending them to English public schools because of the prevalence—or so they have heard—of homosexuality. Continuing our promenade that day, I was reminded of Drue Parsons in Paris and her concern about the toilet paper. Scot Tissue girdles the globe. In the crowded streets were several shops festooned and garlanded with the product. American toothpaste is in good supply too.

The old and the new in Hong Kong are still contemporary, with automobiles and street cars jostling rickshaws. The rickshaws are the old-fashioned kind, with men running between the shafts. The foreigner, I think, is of two minds about them. The pedi-cabs are acceptable because the chauffeur rides too, but is it ignominious for one human being to pull another along by hand and foot? The line of demarcation is subtle, and since they were there and rickshaw men made their living out of customers, I occasionally took one. Norton never would. With him it was a matter of principle, but the distance from the Star ferry dock to the Peninsula Hotel is only three or four blocks, and he also said I was a sissy not to walk it. Sometimes I did, but sometimes I was tired and would pick up a rickshaw at the pier. The ride is a bit jouncy but fairly rapid; they can do about seven miles an hour on flat ground. When it rains they put up the rickshaw's green hood and attach a tarpaulin in front so the passenger won't get wet. When the carriages are empty it is a quaint sight to see them lined up in a row, the shafts lying on the ground, the bodies tipped forward, all politely bowing. In Hong Kong, as elsewhere throughout Asia, the rickshaw is on the way out, and from the humane point of view that is a good thing. A rickshaw man's life is brief; most of them, probably because of their scant diet and sweating and cooling off so frequently, die of tuberculosis. One evening we saw a poignantly thin man, his chest bones like a washboard showing through his torn shirt, asleep on the pavement between the shafts of his carriage like a tired old horse.

Still en route to the Thieves' Market we passed a stall where they were selling brushes, the kind the Chinese use for writing. I use them to apply lipstick, so I bought a half-dozen for thirty-five cents, the price of one in New York. Wally told the woman what I wanted them for, and she told two or three friends and a few children who were hanging around and they all went off into gales of laughter.

The Thieves' Market—its geographic name is Cat Street—lies at the foot of a flight of steps. Not very long, it is lined solidly on both sides with open shops and it proved my undoing. I couldn't keep away from it. Norton called me the Mother Superior of Cat Street. The wares it dispenses are a marvelous conglomeration of junk and quality. Jades and scrolls and lamps and carvings, coins and jewels, and baskets, everything abounds in Cat Street. Its prices are not high, but the tourist is warned, and by the Chinese, not necessarily other tourists, to beware. This is the home of the haggle and the bargain at which skill I am deplorable.

First crack out of the box I spotted something I craved; a scroll and I am sure a good one. One beige horse at a dull red hitching post against a tobacco brown background. Price seven dollars. "No, no," cried Wally, "don't get it. This is only the first stall, there are masses of them. You're sure to see something you like better. You must see everything. Come back another time with Julie and let her bargain for you."

"But I want it," I said. "I want it *now*."

"Nonsense, there are others far better."

"Wally's right," from Norton. "Seven dollars is probably more than it's worth. Let's look around."

Like a triple-starred jackass I listened to them. Had it been exorbitantly priced that would have been one thing, but seven dollars I could afford. I went back the next day with Julie. I rushed her to the shop. "It's gone," I wailed. "Yesterday it was hanging right here, right outside."

"He's just put it away," she said. "I'll ask him." She inquired of the proprietor. He remembered me well. "Yes indeed," he told Julie, "but about half an hour after your friend left another American lady came by and bought the scroll." I took an intense dislike to my unknown compatriot. She obviously had had all her marbles, which Mrs. N. S. Brown as obviously had not.

In the end I bought another scroll from that man and two more from a shop farther down the street. They were nice but they weren't my love. The authorship of one of them is rather curious. It depicts the classic eight horses and a lake and was done on silk by an eighteenth-century artist, an Italian who went to live at the Chinese court and learned to paint in the Chinese manner.

We also bought four charming opium lamps made of flowered porcelain and brass with fat little glass chimneys. One evening, at home in the country when we were giving a buffet dinner party, I wanted to use them on the card tables. "I will fill them with the proper oil," said the doctor, "trust me, they will work like charms." I trusted him. The result was clouds of smoke, a heavy, oily stench, and no flame. It was midsummer, but fortunately I had available some Swedish Christmas candles that served very well, burning with a clear, pure northern light. Not to run down the little lamps, they *do* work when properly fueled.

Besides the Kwoks we had another Chinese friend who rendered us great service as a Buyer's Guide. This was Jane Wang (pronounced Wong), whom I have already mentioned in connection with Precious Orchid's calling cards. Jane works for Sears Roebuck. I believe she is considerably older, but she looks all of twenty-four, speaks perfect English, has an ingenuous air and a great deal of intelligence under her shining black hair. Because of her job she knew all the best merchants of Hong Kong, and she and her boss, John Waddell, shepherded us about with friendly and unflagging zeal. Jane even chose a hairdresser for me, Yvette, a Chinese woman who hailed from Australia and spoke excellent British English. I risked a permanent and it was reasonably good. Also the price was right; nine U.S. dollars. I discovered, however, that just because many oriental women are small-boned and delicate-looking it is illusory to assume they will be skillful manicurists. I had a little charmer with the instincts of a butcher, but as she poked with an orangewood stick instead of metal my wounds were not lethal.

Between our acquaintances, our own discoveries, and recommendations from friends who had passed that way before we visited a good many shops and tailors. Everyone has his favorites, and I do not doubt that we missed a few pearls, but as it may be helpful to any reader who plans a visit to Hong Kong I will list some of those we found to be the most satisfactory.

For a man's tailor Norton says to be sure to recommend George Chen, in the Peninsula Court just back of the Peninsula Hotel. The good doc was very pleased with his suits and made-to-order shirts. The shirts were five dollars apiece and the suits averaged less than sixty. It is not true, however, that you go to a Chinese tailor at 9 A.M. and he delivers a perfect suit that evening at 5 P.M. without any fittings. The Chinese tailors, like any others, are human. They need time, and the more fittings you have the better the suit fits. Plan to stay long enough in Hong Kong to assure yourself of workmanlike jobs.

Ying Tai at 88 Nathan Road, Kowloon, made up two dresses from the Thai silk I had bought in Bangkok—$34.50 for the two. They also made me a *cheong sam* of soft green brocaded satin that fitted beautifully. When I got it home I had a moment of misgiving. It had seemed perfect in the Orient, would it seem like a costume in the U.S.A.? The answer is no. Everybody liked it and I wore it so much—it is good whether the men are dressing or not—that I sent it back to Ying Tai, they copied it exactly, this time in a turquoise blue brocade, and I wear the new one with pleasure. They sent the old one back, too. For rainy evenings. Even in Hong Kong, however, the prices are creeping up. The first one cost $16.50, the second $19.

For suits or regular dresses I cannot too highly recommend Zou Nan at 5 Pratt Avenue, Kowloon. Their fit is superb and their British woolens and cashmeres are top quality. A gray herringbone cashmere suit cost me $95. At home they cost anywhere from $250 up.

Our experience was that Chinese *couturiers* are not great designers, they do better with something to copy, but it doesn't have to be an actual dress. At Zou Man's I leafed through a pile of American and European fashion magazines and found a Nina Ricci model that I fancied; a dress with a pleated skirt and a jacket. They made it, I still wear it, and people say to me, "W*here* did you get that good-looking outfit?" It cost $80.

For shoes, Benny's—Mr. K. Ben Wong, 15 Cameron Road, Kowloon, around the corner from Ying Tai. Julie Kwok suggested others as well, but we had already gone to Benny's and we both liked him so well we stayed with him. Handmade shoes run around $10 and $12 a pair. Lizard somewhat higher, about $21. The shoes are not only good-looking, they are marvelously comfortable.

We were told that there was a woman at the Repulse Bay Hotel who had lovely clothes, and I was in the shop briefly one afternoon but did not have an opportunity to order anything, so I cannot speak from first-hand experience.

While discussing shopping it may be germane to observe that we found that the merchants hated credit cards. They would, in a pinch, accept them, but they resented the commission they were obliged to pay the issuing companies and infinitely preferred either cash or personal checks on American banks.

Indeed their willingness to accept the latter we thought rather surprising and concluded that by and large the American tourist must be honest. Also, of course, one's passport number goes on the check, so the merchant does have a means of tracing any dispenser of rubber goods.

Lane Crawford, on the Victoria side, is the big good department store that renders many services including the setting of jewelry. Charlotte Horstmann in the Old Printing House, 6 Duddell Street, also on Victoria, is an interesting woman, half Chinese and half German, who has lived most of her life in the Orient and who sells clothes and beautiful antiques and art objects. Her good things are not cheap, but her taste and knowledge are great. There are also a great many linen shops with beautifully embroidered table settings, blouses, and handkerchiefs, and shops with finest jade.

For basket lovers—and we are a formidable group, nonlovers little wot how large—there is Kowloon Rattan Company, 4 Honkow Road, in back of the Peninsula Hotel, where they sell irresistible baskets and furniture, toys, ornaments, and bags. The doctor groaned and took me by the elbow, hustling me along every time we passed it on our way to and from the hotel.

The Peninsula, by the way, is something of an institution, with very high ceilings and very long corridors. The downstairs lobby is enormous and every afternoon is crowded with tea and cocktail drinkers sitting under the revolving fans. Inevitably those residents who are there for any length of time get to know each other, and the refreshment hour is a babble of note-taking and comparative shopping for the best restaurants and the best bargains.

Many of the restaurants are excellent. Maxim's in Hong Kong, the Marco Polo in Kowloon, and Gaddi's in the Peninsula Hotel. The first time we went into Gaddi's was at noon and the place was nearly empty. They did their big business, they said, at dinner. I certainly hope so, as the food was notable, and if they didn't do better than that it was going gravely to impair my firm conviction that the best will always attract trade.

The restaurants I have mentioned for the most part serve European food, but one evening we went with a group of friends to a Chinese place, the Golden City. The food was good but the décor was memorable! It seethed with dragons and pagodas and colored lights. I think it was what the proprietors thought foreigners thought Chinese restaurants were like.

Our friend Robbie, Harold Robinson, an Englishman who had lived for years in the Orient, introduced us to the P.G., the Parisian Grill, in Hong Kong. It is always crowded and the fare is fine. At our first luncheon I ordered a curry, but subtle Dr. Brown ordered fish, a delicious native catch called garoupa, a species of rock cod. He has a really uncanny intuition about what's going to be best on the menu. He loves fish and time after time comes up with a succulent and unusual dish.

It was Robbie who drove us to the New Territories and took us to the Jockey Club. I am sure that at times it is very gay, but Sunday afternoon at half-past three is not one of them. However, even at that hour he clapped his hands, called for a boy, and tea was served. On another day he also introduced us to the Shek O Country Club. The club is on a bluff with a superb view over Repulse Bay and is very, very British, complete with Union Jack, a golf course, a big airy veranda, and a fine swimming pool.

After a midmorning gin and tonic we went on to a luncheon party given by Bill Stanton, an American in the gold business who had lived in Hong Kong for thirty-six years. Two of his servants had been with him for thirty-five. I can think of no higher reference.

His small house is magnificently located above a little cove and a bathing beach. The beach is public but charming, and we were told that most of the property in that locality is leased from the Shek O Club the way it is here at home at Tuxedo and Piping Rock and others. There were two Stanton dogs, a beguiling pointer pup and a disagreeable chow named Jimmy.

Another pleasant meal was one at Aberdeen when we were the guests of Chinese friends, Tsuyee and Eileen Pei. Aberdeen is a fishing village on Hong Kong teeming with life, the harbor packed with sampans. We reached it in a launch belonging to an American couple named Hughes. Mr. Hughes is the head of a large insurance firm, and during the Korean War he had been a correspondent in that country. He and his wife picked us up at the dock and we chugged through the harbor on our way to open water. The picturesque harbor of Hong Kong turned out to be like the English channel. *Rough.* As I slowly turned apple green our skipper assured us cheerily that it was always this way. "So much shipping, you see, and the water slapping hard against the sea wall. Be all right shortly." Fortunately the good man spoke true. Once clear of the harbor we could settle down to enjoying the coast line of the green mountainous island and the evening sky.

At Aberdeen we went to a floating restaurant, the Sea Palace, a brilliantly painted houseboat reached by sampan. They specialize in fish, and one knows that the fish is fresh, since they are swimming about in tanks anchored to the boat. You pick out the beauty you wish to consume, a bowlegged old man with a wrinkled parchment face scoops him up in a net, he is done in and grilled on a brazier over charcoal. He is The Best. The Pei party was quite large and we dined at two tables on the upper deck. Norton and I had been there once before with the Kwoks, but that was at teatime, so this was our first encounter with the commendable cuisine.

When we came back on the sampan after dinner, Norton sculled. A wiry little girl who had taken us over—she was the daughter of the woman who owned the boat and couldn't have been more than ten or eleven—showed him how. I was sitting in a wicker chair in the stern and happened to glance down. There, in the narrow space between the chair and the hull, asleep like a kitten or a puppy in a dirty nest of rags and newspapers, lay a tiny baby. The chances are that she will grow up, live, and die on that sampan or its replica.

I have mentioned John Waddell, of Sears Roebuck, and how helpful he and Jane Wang were on our shopping sprees. It was largely due to him that we went to Macao. He assured us we'd love it, so picturesque, he said, and a big change from Hong Kong. We had mentioned the project to Bill Stanton the day of his Sunday lunch, and he had said at once, "If you do go, let me know. I'll get in touch with my man down there and you can stay in my house." That sounded rather festive, so with our orders all in at the tailors' and a day or two between fittings at our disposal we decided on the trip.

Macao, for those as ignorant as we were, is an ancient Portuguese settlement. Established in 1557, it is on the coast about thirty-five miles southwest of Hong Kong at the mouth of the Canton River and is today the free territory nearest to Communist China. It is necessary to go by boat, as the land between the two settlements is communist-controlled, and we passed two or three of their gunboats patrolling the coastal waters on the lookout for escaping refugees.

Our boat was the *Tai-Loy*, small, clean, and comfortable. Everything about her was highly professional, including "All ashore that's going ashore," and beating the gong, just like on the *Queen Mary*. A worn old record wheezed out *Anchors Aweigh* as we cast off. We had a nice little air-conditioned cabin and the second class had a big, airy dormitory filled with double-decker beds. There were round, smiling Chinese nuns in white habits and coifs, and an old woman who hadn't had time to attend to all the details at home was cutting her toenails on deck. There were few Americans on board, mostly Chinese and Portuguese.

I went to our cabin to stretch out for a while, but didn't stay very long as the trip is only three and a half hours, and a pretty run, passing small green mountainous islands, fishing junks, and the gunboats. One island we saw, I think its name is Lan Tau, is larger than Hong Kong and there was talk of building a big reservoir on it. If that project should go through, they would be able to house thousands more refugees from the mainland.

We had tea, served in tall glasses, with two Englishmen, Mr. Roberts and Chris, the only names we ever learned. I do not know what noisome crimes the latter poor devil may have committed in a previous incarnation, but he was certainly expiating them in this one. He had already been three months in Macao, installing a Diesel electric generating plant and after a brief recess in Hong Kong was on his way back. Roberts, who was going to be there only nine days, was already singing the blues. Norton and I, who were going to be there only overnight, began to shiver.

We were met at the dock by Chang, Bill Stanton's boy, who drove us to the house. It was a big, bare, rather shabby old place situated on the waterfront between a Christian school and a playground. It didn't look very lived in, and we supposed that Mr. Stanton kept it for business reasons, for it was nothing like as attractive as his place at Repulse Bay.

We asked Chang if we might have a drink, and he said we could have either whiskey or gin free and beer if we paid for it. This seemed a little mysterious—shouldn't it have been the other way round?—but we thought to solve the mystery the next morning when we were presented with a bill for breakfast and a taxi. We assumed that Chang picked up a little baksheesh from the overnight guests of the master. He made a profit on the beer, but the hard liquor was from the boss's store, and for this he scrupulously did not charge.

A balcony opened off our sitting room and we sat out there sipping our cold drinks—blessedly there was ice—and I observed with delight that I had made a conquest. Chinese chap of about five in the playground next door kept blowing me kisses. We watched him and his two or three playmates laboriously clambering up the high ladder of their slide and then zooming down the chute, and reflected that life's lessons are learned young: a lot of hard work for a brief moment of pleasure.

We were glad of showers, for Macao was hot and steamy like Hong Kong, and afterward we went next door to the Bell Vista Hotel for a prearranged cocktail with Mr. Roberts. Oh yes, said the round Portuguese lady at the desk, he had a room there, but Mr. Perrera, his boss, had telephoned him and he had gone out. We said we were sorry, but since we were there we decided to have a martini anyway. We sat at the primitive bar and under Norton's tutelage and beady eye the result placed before us was quite savory. We finished it, strolled about a bit, and were just leaving, when Roberts came barreling down the stairs. He'd been in his room all the time waiting for us. We told him what the landlady had told us and he said dryly, "Her communications system broke down. Perrera did telephone me, but she should have kept on listening. She'd have learned I'm not meeting him until later."

Chris joined us and we had another round. As the cocktails were set before us, Roberts looked at mine and said thoughtfully, "The martini. An American invention." "Along with the wheel and the sail," I said. Nothing happened for a few seconds and then he smiled slowly. He was a sweet fellow.

After a bit Norton and I left the two men and went off to dine at the Pusada, an inn that had been highly recommended. We sat out in the garden, which was pretty, and ordered African chicken, which had been highly recommended. "Don't fail to try it," people said. We didn't, which was too bad. The chicken tasted like Uncle Fred's mistake at the barbecue: burned on the outside, raw on the in, with a sauce hot enough to take the roof of your mouth off. The only palatable item on the menu was a bottle of good Portuguese wine.

After dinner a guide whom we had previously engaged picked us up in a car and drove us around town. Macao is on a peninsula and covers an area of about five square miles. We drove up a road and were stopped by a sentry. He was amiable enough, and our driver said that he said it was all right if we wanted to walk the rest of the way, but we declined. A few yards up the road was a barrier gate, and beyond it lay Red China.

We turned back and went to a huge outdoor swimming pool where a big race meet was in progress. As a group of adolescents dove in and started thrashing their way down the lanes to the finish line, the guide hissed in my ear, "Communists." My skin prickled, but, truth to tell, at night, half-naked, and underwater a communist is hard to tell from a member of a 4-H Club. Friend or enemy, the doctor was unimpressed by the performance. He is an old college swimming-team man himself. "Their kick," he said, "is lousy."

From the pool we drove through Happiness Street, a sad little thoroughfare where dwell the daughters of joy. The doors of the houses are painted green, and in the old days one went through the green doors to such bliss as he might find. Today matters are more Americanized and the girls are telephoned to and come to the hotels. Most of the doors stood open to the hot night, and we heard the click of mah-jongg tiles and saw groups of men and women playing under the feeble electric bulbs dangling from the ceiling.

Unseduced by the lures of the flesh, we went on to the Central Hotel, the Casino of Macao where the much-vaunted gambling games of fan-tan and Grands Pequenos are played. Fornication and gambling are supposedly the big attractions of Macao, but the exhibits we saw were skimpy and drab. I guess it was the off-season for sin. The Encyclopædia Britannica refers to the "unrestricted gaiety" of the place that "has attracted many well-to-do Chinese and European residents." Unrestricted gaiety, eh? I have news for the Encyclopædia.

At the Central Hotel the fan-tan game was going on on two levels. We went into a room where there was a long, narrow oval counter. The center of the oval was a well. You leaned over the counter and looked down into a room on the floor below to the fan-tan table, the dealers, and the money. The game is a simple one of pure chance, requiring, I should say, no skill whatsoever and netting dubious profits. This opinion probably betrays my ignorance, but I simply do not believe you can beat the house.

There is a square plaque on the table inscribed with the numbers 1, 2, 3, 4, and you bet whichever number you prefer. You then put your money in a little basket on the oval counter and it is lowered on a string to the room below. The game is played with a big pile of pearl buttons and a small metal cup. The cup is placed over the mound of

buttons and those that remain outside are separated from the main
pile with a bamboo stick, four at a time. When the last set of four has
been scraped away, the remaining number of buttons, 1, 2, 3, or 4,
wins. If you've bet on the right number you're in the chips, if not you
lose. That's it. I know I am devoid of the gambler's instinct, but how
long can you keep that up? I'd as soon pick feathers off my molasses-
covered fingers.

We learned later that you don't *have* to play from upstairs, you can
be right at the table if you want to—the double-decker arrangement is
for taking care of crowds, so they hope, at the weekends. We'd just happened to stroll into that particular room, but that night there was only
a handful of players.

The other game, Grands or Petits Pequenos, is something like roulette without the wheel. It is played with dice and there is a numbered
red and green cloth. You can play individual numbers, split your bet, or
bet on the high or low groups. We watched both games for a while and
played a little, and, having lost three Hong Kong dollars, decided to
call it a day. They must have missed us.

On the way out we were shown one or two small rooms that still
had their opium beds, although there is now very little public opium
smoking. The beds are quite wide and made of teakwood, and the pillows are porcelain. I should think one would *need* a little opium if
planning to get any sleep. Apparently opium is like alcohol, only infinitely more so. Some can handle it, some can't. Jane Wang told us
that in the old days in Shanghai her father always offered an opium
pipe to guests at a dinner party, it was like cocktails or wine.

There is not much to see in Macao, and apparently we missed one
of the few pretty pieces there are. Vincent Sheean had told us that
Marian Anderson had told *him* that there is a charming little baroque
theater, but we didn't find it. We did visit the ruins of an old Portuguese cathedral on a hilltop. It was built in 1602, and the façade is
rococo and decorative, but that is all there is; the body of the church
was burned in the nineteenth century.

We had bumped into Jimmy Sheean, as he is called, one evening
on the ferry. I hadn't seen him in years, "But," I said to Norton, "I'm
going to take a chance, I'm sure it's he." I went up to him and said,
"I beg your pardon, but aren't you Vincent Sheean?" He looked down
—he is a tall man—put his arms around me, and said, "Why, God bless
you, love, how are you?" It was a pleasant reunion, and I introduced
the two men, and we saw him several times during our stay in Hong

Kong. He was there making a television film for Westinghouse to be called *The Hong Kong Story*.

We wandered through the Macao market taking pictures of vegetables and trays of spices and nuts, dried fish and mushrooms in wonderful colors of rusty red and gold and of great heaping bins of rice and watched women washing clothes at the village well where three or four narrow streets come together, forming a little square. A block away from this primitive scene an overhead traffic light blinked green and red, signaling the pedi-cabs on their way. Macao is squalid and filled with pitiable refugees, for while the communists brutally restrain most of those who try to escape them, with equal callousness they boot over the border the maimed, the ill, and the blind. Beggars are rife in the streets and they follow after you, whining and picking at your clothes and keeping up a constant nattering. It is repellent and heartbreaking. We gave money to several of them, which of course brought hordes following at our heels, and we were hard put to it to break away. One woman in particular was persistent as a gadfly. We finally turned on her impatiently, and, muttering and gesturing, she fell behind us, but to this day I feel mean when I think about her. We could have afforded a little more and she could have had a meal. Not, for her sake, the one we had. We went to a place that had been recommended to us by Bill Stanton's houseboy, Chang. We decided that it must be run by his brother, for the food was awful and for what it was, expensive; three U.S. dollars for an inedible little mess.

That same afternoon we took the boat back to Hong Kong, the *Takshing*, bigger and even nicer than the *Tai-Loy* had been, with thoughtful little touches such as fresh hot tea in a thermos in our cabin. As the boat pulled away we watched women porters in blue cotton trousers and jackets helping the men load cargo. They would take one end of a great bamboo pole while a man took the other and hoist aboard the heavily laden baskets. Women also worked on the roads, repairing damage done by landslides caused by the heavy rains.

We had gone to Macao because several friends had spoken of it with enthusiasm, because to them going there at least means taking a trip, getting away from Hong Kong, but if you are doing a good deal of traveling anyway, our feeling is that you can skip the Portuguese colony and still live the rich full life and save time, money, and above all effort.

We found that on a concentrated tour such as we were making it is absolutely essential to arrange occasionally for stopovers of some duration, not only to see something of a country, but also to get your clothes unpacked and settle down a bit. Prolonged living out of suitcases becomes wearisome, and you begin to yearn for closets and a dressing table and a bathroom where you can set out the bottles and jars and know they're going to stay there for a while and not be fitted back into the toilet kit the next morning.

There is another philosophical reflection learned in the school of experience that I would pass on to the reader. It is nothing to feel afraid of or worried about, but there may come a time when a loving couple traveling together begin to grate just a teensy-weensy bit on each other's nerves. As I say, it's nothing serious, it doesn't mean that you're unloved or that either party would so much as glance at a member of the opposite sex, but it does mean that husband and wife are getting a more concentrated dose of each other than is customarily the case.

You know how it is; at home the fellow goes off to his office in the morning and comes back at night. There are the children to romp or argue with or you're dining out or friends are coming in. In short you're diverted. But when traveling, unless by chance you meet with a congenial couple or group, you're TOGETHER, just the two of you. Furthermore you're together when you're tired or your stomach is upset by the rich sauces of the French or all that olive oil the Spaniards use in cooking or by the chancy water and vegetables of the Orient. The husband usually is wondering how things are going at the office or wishing to God he could get in a game of golf instead of moseying through one more blankety-blank museum or cathedral. Or possibly he gets a gander at those bills you're running up in Paris or Hong Kong . . . in short there are any number of reasons why one's nearest and dearest can seem not quite the creature of dreams he or she once was. But be of good cheer. The affection, let us hope, is real, the prickly feelings transitory, and few things unite a couple more closely than adventure participated in and memories shared. And if you take pictures you can relive the happy times through many a winter evening without the inconveniences and delays and fatigue that attended them in actuality. You can bore your friends quite a lot, too. Oh yes, travel is *well* worth it.

One evening we appeared on television as the guests of Major Harvey, a newscaster and Hong Kong TV personality. He picked us up at our hotel and we crossed the harbor in a walla-walla to the broadcasting studios on the opposite shore. The studios were comfortable, modern, and well equipped, although minus a make-up department. This didn't inconvenience me too much as I am the prudent type who never travels without her false eyelashes. I stuck them on in a trice, and in my new pale brocade *cheong sam* hoped to charm my way into countless Chinese hearts. As a rare concession Norton appeared with me. We felt the interview was going swimmingly—how did we like Hong Kong, what did we think of the refugee problem, of the communists, what about American aid, did the food agree with us?—after twelve days we obviously weren't at a loss for a single answer, but we noticed that Chinese cameraman Number One was making peculiar noises and gesturing frantically. He suddenly gave an odd swooping signal that Major Harvey understandably enough took to mean "Cut," so he bade us a cordial good night. We were off the air three minutes too soon. Knowing what the results of such crossed signals would have been at home, we thought that it showed admirable British restraint when the only reaction from the major was a rather hurt, "I say, old boy, that's not quite cricket, what?"

After the broadcast we went next door to the Luk Kwok hotel, the original of the Nam Kok in *Suzie Wong*. Reacting to its fame, it has been cleaned up and respectabilized and is full of chrome and neon and boredom. The bar was dark and noisy with sailors and girls dancing, but no going upstairs—the front desk indeed looked like the Y.M.C.A., and the whole thing had a drab, antiseptic air infinitely depressing. We paid for but did not drink two fearsome dark brown concoctions and went on to dine at Jimmy's Kitchen. Jimmy's name is Landau, and he is the brother of the Landau who runs the immensely successful Parisian Grill, but blood is thinner than money and the competition is keen.

One of our nicest evenings was Sunday supper with the Kwoks. We knew that we were in for a heavy luncheon with other friends and had begged them to have something light and simple. Wally raised his right hand and swore to the Chinese equivalent of a light soufflé: four hot dishes and four cold ones. "And you know Chinese food, dear Ilka, you only eat a little bit of each and that will be all." I hope the angel marked *that* one down in his big black book.

The Dutch Mr. de Jong was at the party, and we had asked if we might bring Jimmy Sheean. We had told him about the Bird Club and the grasshopper boxing matches, and he was eager to get them for his Hong Kong film and to meet Wally.

Course after delicious course was served, ending with a fruit, a sort of lichee nut called dragon's eyes. It was the best meal we had in Hong Kong, and we had some memorable ones. Julie is a real gourmet. Her mother died when she was a child and she was her father's hostess from the age of nine. I asked her how long it took to prepare such fare. She shrugged. "Not very long. The cook was ironing and she asked me how many were coming and when we wanted dinner and I said we would be six and to plan to serve around nine. She finished what she was doing and started about six to prepare the dinner." Some people have talents other people don't have. They also have cooks that others don't.

The Kwok apartment is pleasant and modern, with the great harbor view, and, besides Wally and Julie, is inhabited by a sweet Pekinese, a true little dragon.

Another evening we shared with Jimmy was one at which he was the host. We dined at the Marco Polo with him and another American, who was in the textile business, Martin Cole. That was my lucky day, three beaux, but I should say that throughout the trip there wasn't a restaurant in the Orient to which we went that a woman could not have gone to alone, and two women together could go anyplace. Probably few people go alone from choice, but if a woman has the wherewithal and enjoys travel, lack of an escort is no reason for her to stick in the home-town rut.

The day came inevitably when we had to pull up stakes, have the final fittings, pay the bills, and say good-by to our friends. We had had such a good time in Hong Kong we felt very much at home and were sad at leaving, but on Tuesday morning, August 4, the telephone pealed at six-fifteen. At six-fifteen in Asia it is still pitch black, and we dressed by electricity and went down to breakfast in the lobby. Whether it was exhaustion or woe at leaving the wonderful city I do not know, but I was good and sick and spent most of the breakfast hour in trips to the ladies' room. The little attendant in her black trousers and white jacket was most solicitous, murmuring, "You sick, missy? You take care, I help you." She did, too, bringing me the little tightly rolled towels of the Orient, saturated with hot or cold water and cologne. She finally got me out into the lobby, Norton got me into a cab, and we took off for the airport. Once aboard CAT, Civil Air Transport, I perked up and we had a good flight, two hours and fifteen minutes to Taipei on Taiwan, or Formosa.

We went to Taiwan because it is the center of American Medical Aid to China, and Norton, largely because of his friend Dr. Magnus Gregerson, who has done such fine work there, was interested in seeing the country and meeting some of the men involved in the aid program.

Our hotel was the Grand, the Golden Dragon Annex, with a fluted, painted roof and beams, columns, and railings of bright scarlet. The Chinese love that color, they say it's imperial, but to me it looks kitchen red and I get sick of it.

Our room was nice. On the ground floor it opened onto a little terrace bordered by the driveway. The layout didn't permit much privacy, but the room was air-conditioned, with curtains we could draw at night, and was divided by a permanent screen of canework into two sections, a sitting room and a bedroom. There was a good bath, and an efficient shower that we put through its paces, for they were expecting a typhoon and the weather was hot and steamy. The hotel also boasts a big swimming pool, tennis courts, and ping-pong tables.

At the Peninsula in Hong Kong we had been amused by the paging system. Very small boys in white suits went through the lobby carrying a long stick with a slate at the top on which was written the name of the pagee. At the bottom of the stick was a bicycle bell the boy rang to attract attention. Everyone would look up, and the person who was wanted went to the phone. At the Grand in Taipei they had more or less the same system but the sign was illuminated. One's name was up in lights like a star's.

Our first afternoon we were driven around by Mr. Lu, the young assistant manager of the Bank of China, who was a mine of information. I relay a few of the things we learned from him and elsewhere, because from time to time we in America become very conscious of the island, yet to most of us it is largely an unknown quantity.

Taiwan, originally called Formosa, which is the Portuguese word for "beautiful," is indeed just that. Lush and mountainous, it supports a population of about ten and a half million, produces two and three rice crops a year, lots of bricks, there are kilns all over, and nine hundred thousand tons of sugar, which it mostly exports to Japan. The island is about three hundred miles long by eighty miles wide. They tell you it is the size of the Netherlands, but with all that upping and downing must, I should think, embrace much more territory.

Actually the Taiwanese aren't so madly enthusiastic about the Nationalist Chinese as Americans tend to believe. What they would really like is an independent little domain. Since the time of the Chino-Japanese War in 1894 until V-J Day in 1945 the island was under Japanese domination and feels itself more strongly drawn to Japan than to China.

There are about eight million native Taiwanese, the rest Nationalist Chinese. The older generation speaks mostly Japanese, the young people are being taught Chinese and English. Buddhism is the religion, although Christianity is popular with the younger element.

Within limits farmers can own as much land as they can pay for, and their living standards are considered the highest in Asia, although not, I should imagine, higher than the Japanese. The average wage on the island is twenty dollars a month. Given today's circumstances, though I doubt that many would care to, Americans can buy land in Taiwan provided they don't come from states that don't recognize marriage between whites and Orientals, mostly those of the South.

I do wish we had better sense. It's not that I am particularly concerned over whether we are loved or not—I know quite well we won't be—but who is? Where is the country that loves or is loved by another? Do the French love the Germans? Do the Italians love the French or the Egyptians the Israelis? Are the Chinese and the Russians soul mates? Do Scandinavians have a soft spot in their hearts for Latin Americans? Are Britain and the United States serenading each other in the moonlight?

I do not speak of individuals who may love each other very dearly, but governmental alliances are made by political necessity and commercial advantage, not by affection. As one who does love America, however, I don't like to see us making fools of ourselves, which we certainly do when we take the attitude that Orientals, members of ancient races civilized while we were still in the trees, are not as good as we are.

Mr. Lu, an educated, intelligent Oriental whose legal marriage, were he married to an Aryan, would not be recognized by the sovereign states of Mississippi and Maryland, explained that Taiwan itself is run by a provincial government. The Nationalist, or Chiang Kai-shek, Government theoretically runs only foreign affairs. It is rather as if the mainland of the United States were lost to an enemy and the federal government moved to Hawaii. Inevitably it would take a keen interest in local affairs. So it does in Taiwan. And just as in Taiwan the Hawaiians probably wouldn't be overcome by their good fortune.

Taiwan may be Nationalist China, but it is not Free China. It was and is in a state of semisiege and wartime restrictions prevail. People are not allowed to leave it without special permission and for what the government considers good reasons. When they do go they can only take two hundred dollars with them.

On arrival I had expressed a desire to meet Madame Chiang Kai-shek, as I thought an interview with her might be interesting for my column, and our friends were doing their level best to arrange an appointment. They said, "If only you had let us know sooner there would have been no question, it could have been done, but this is very short notice and her schedule is always crowded." In the end, through no lack of trying, their best efforts failed and I had only myself to blame.

The nearest I got to the lady was a visit to her pet project, the Chinese Women's Anti-Aggression League, which was established in 1950 and has two hundred thousand members. They make underwear for the soldiers, build housing units for their dependents, visit them in hospitals, and run an orphanage for 385 children, twice as many boys as girls. The league headquarters are decorated with pictures done by Madame. Seascapes.

I was taken around the orphanage, the Hua Hsing Children's Home, by Mrs. Sheman Chang. It was very clean and the children ranged in age from four to eighteen. The nursery walls were covered with cutouts of extremely Aryan tots with masses of blond curls and big blue eyes. To the small Chinese they probably all look alike.

The double-decker beds in the dormitories were neatly made and the children's few clothes neatly folded on shelves. They are housed, fed, and educated, but the life seemed meager and pathetic. Although it was holiday time many of them stayed there because they had no other place to go. We went into a classroom—since they had to be there the teachers felt that they were better off occupied and learning something —and the children all rose and bowed. A group of very small girls playing bowed deeply and sang out in Chinese, "Welcome, honorable guest."

Everybody I met handed me his calling card. The calling-card industry must be one of the largest in the Orient. They don't wait for a hat to be lifted from the head, let alone dropped, before thrusting a bit of pasteboard into your hand.

Not wishing to be outdone in courtesy, I handed them mine with the Chinese characters and regretted that Precious Orchid was not with me. He would have impressed them, but I had gone alone to the orphanage because the doctor had been away from a hospital far too long and seized the opportunity offered him by medical friends to see the one in Taipei. From the point of view of one poor patient it was a lucky visit. There was a chap who had a fearful and hideous, burgeoning growth on his face and body. From the photograph Norton showed

me and judging from other pictures I had seen, I diagnosed leprosy.
There was an interesting thing about that diagnosis, too; it was wrong.
The ailment was kala azar. The dreadful lesions are caused by a para-
site, a small protozoan that usually attacks the viscera and only rarely
invades the skin, but where it does one's appearance becomes repulsive.
It was a particularly poignant condition for the man whom Norton
saw, for he was still young, in his early thirties, and had been an
aviator during the war.

Some of the doctors discussed the case with Norton, and he was
able to suggest a drug and treatment they had not known about. New
York medical men are sometimes quite knowledgeable about tropical
diseases. We get all kinds from all over the world streaming through
the port. From time to time after we got home Norton received pictures
of the man, and it was heart-warming to see the enormous improvement he was making. Eventually he will be almost as good as new.

The doctor had Chinese friends and patients in Taipei too, and one
evening we were invited to dine in a private house. It was a small
house furnished in Western style and terribly hot. Each room was air-
conditioned, but the electric current was not strong and only one room
could be cooled at a time. We were only *in* one room at a time, so
theoretically the system should have worked, but the conditioner was
reluctant about building up speed. When we passed from the living
room into the dining room, for instance, the first fifteen minutes were
stifling. A strong overhead light blazed down on the table, and
although the dinner was good it was very long. I folded after the
first thirteen courses. Actually I hadn't had so much to eat as may appear, for I was erratic with chopsticks. Some of the succulent morsels
landed, others went skidding across the table in a flurry of confusion
and apology. Precious Orchid was a star at chopsticks, maneuvering
them with the greatest finesse and delicacy, eating his fill, and watching my fumbling efforts and slow starvation with detachment.

We were six in the party and our hosts' little daughter, a beguiling
child of five, trotted about during the evening. One would think the
incidence of kidnaping throughout the Orient would be high, for the
children are absolutely irresistible. I dare say one factor that keeps them
all in their own back yards is that everyone has so many of his own
that the reaction to a suggestion of kidnaping could only evoke a
squawk: "Oh, God, not another!"

There were naïve and engaging vignettes of daily life. We saw a merchant ride by on a bicycle loaded up behind with bird cages filled with

little birds and in front of him he balanced a cage of monkeys, with one rakish fellow riding the handle bars.

Those who ride bicycles and pedi-cabs are brave, frail adversaries of grim foes who give no quarter, the drivers of cars. All Asia rides on the horn, barreling by at a terrific clip, honking madly as it goes. The tourist must look sharp, for the traffic rules change from country to country. Hong Kong, being a British colony, drives to the left, but Taipei, indeed all of Taiwan, is on the right. The traffic was of interest to us, for we were motoring to Taichung.

Tai by the way means a jutting up, a platform, or plateau. Wan means gulf. For Pei and Chung you're on your own.

We were interested in Taichung, for we were to stop there on our way to Sun Moon Lake, a mountain resort we had heard was very beautiful. We were also told that Kaohsiun was a lovely spot, its Grand Hotel even grander than Taipei's Grand, which is already quite grand. We couldn't manage Kaohsiun, but we were eager to be off to Taichung, as the city of Taipei itself is dreary, with little to offer in the way of shops, restaurants, or amusements, although Grass Mountain is a pleasant woodland park with pretty bridges and little waterfalls and a slight odor due to sulphur springs.

The fine museum of Taiwan is in Taichung, where they have some exquisite jade pieces and incomparable scrolls spirited away from the mainland communists to safekeeping. One may now see reproductions of the Taichung Palace Museum Collection in that superb book published by Skira and distributed in the United States by the World Publishing Company and called *Chinese Painting*, the first of a series, *Painting in Asia*.

Once out of Taipei the country is very beautiful, and with Jim Kelly of Northwest Airlines and a colleague of his, Bill Sun, we bowled along well-paved roads between cork and camphor trees, rice paddies and bananas planted high on the mountainsides. Between the paddies are windbreaks of bamboo just as we use eucalyptus trees in the orange groves of California.

Besides visiting the museum in Taichung we wanted to meet Dr. Howard Levy, who since 1956 had been in charge of the school of languages for United States Foreign Service men. This school, started in 1954, is fulfilling a vital and badly neglected need. Our lack of civil servants and diplomats who can speak anything other than English has embarrassed us long enough. The study periods are six to seven hours a day and the course lasts two years. Teachers get fifty cents an hour, which, in Taiwan economy, is considered fair even if it seems a bit meager compared to the wages of cleaning women in the United States.

We visited the school and met a few students and then went to lunch with the doctor.

Although in Japan we were obviously to see many of them, that luncheon with Dr. Levy was our introduction to a truly Japanese house. On entering we took off our shoes to preserve the *tatami*, the grass mats, and we sat on the floor. These houses are absolutely charming, their subtle and sophisticated architecture today is highly regarded in the United States—the uncluttered look being the big chic—and I can imagine nothing more wildly inappropriate to the climate in which they are used. In the summer months Asia is hot and humid. In the winter it can be very cold. Since the inhabitants know this, one can only conclude that their style of architecture must have been conceived in a vacuum. Since I have never experienced a Taiwanian or Japanese winter I shall not dwell on one other than to say that a house made of paper, bamboo, and thin wood is an inadequate shelter in cold weather. I have been there in July and August, however, and feel qualified to speak.

In a climate where, in summer, if electric fans or air-conditioning are not available, high ceilings and cross-ventilation are essential, the ceilings are low, and there is no draft even if one entire side of the house stands open, which is possible because of the sliding panels that form the walls. The reason no air gets in is that a wall of wooden boards or close-set bamboo screens the house from the road. This ensures privacy and from that standpoint is very pleasant, but the house is set only a few feet behind the wall so that any breeze from that direction is effectively blocked. If there is enough space to permit of a garden on the opposite side, that too is cloistered. The French would be very happy in Japan. Their dreaded currents of air don't exist. The summer sun beats down on these little hotboxes, and to a visitor unacclimatized an hour's visit can be an ordeal. Norton and I were embarrassed by the perspiration rolling down our faces at the lunch table, but there was nothing we could do but mop as unobtrusively as possible. Precious Orchid wilted before my eyes. Dr. Levy seemed in better shape. I imagine he was accustomed to it.

I realize that time and again in this chronicle I have said "the food was delicious," "the food was unforgettable," and I have not told what it was. Poor reporting. The truth is I have forgotten the unforgettable and half the time I didn't know what I was eating anyhow, but for some reason I set down Dr. Levy's menu. Clear soup with thin slices of cucumber, North China pork, noodles, string beans, juicy tomatoes, and local pineapple more delicate even than Hawaiian. We were very grateful.

We left as soon as we decently could, regretting our departure, as Dr. Levy was an intelligent man and a charming host, but we had to breathe. We set out with Bill on the two-hour drive to Sun Moon Lake.

Bill Sun was a Chinese, the district sales manager for Northwest Airlines, but he had at one time been Madame Chiang's secretary. He was tall and thin and, when he spoke of the old days, inclined to tearfulness. He had his moments of jollity, though, and would close his eyes tight behind his glasses, open his mouth very wide, and no sound would emerge. It was his way of laughing.

The road to the lake was wild and beautiful, and high in the mountains we passed an old man straight from an ancient scroll. He wore a round straw hat and a sort of turtle shell of rushes over his back. On the underside were straps through which he slipped his arms to keep it on. It was a raincoat.

The Taiwanese do not use clothespins, as we do. Laundry drying along the roadside was either draped over bamboo poles or poles were run through the sleeves of jackets, the jackets hanging in rows with outstretched, suppliant arms.

Sun Moon Lake, so called because its contours are both crescent-shaped and round, is a big body of water in the heart of the mountains very like our Adirondack lakes. The hotel is first class. It is built on several levels, and its balconied rooms overlook the water. As we stepped out to admire the view a rainbow shimmered through the parting mist. Mist we were growing accustomed to. It was the rainy season, and precipitation, ranging from showers to floods, was the pattern of our days.

The Ever Green Hotel is comfortable, but although it is an ideal place for a rest, there is nothing to do but swim and paddle about in little boats. I would not recommend it for cardiac patients—too many steps and terraces.

We arrived in the early evening and Bill enthusiastically promoted a jaunt on the lake. We set off down the hill to the shore, but returned abruptly, our enthusiasm dampened by a deluge.

Later when it had dried and Norton and I were having a cocktail before dinner on the wide terrace opening off the bar, Bill Sun forced down a beer. He assured us that the Taiwanese were heavy drinkers, but as he himself is virtually a teetotaler we thought possibly their excessive indulgence was only in comparison with his abstinence.

After dinner we sat on our balcony talking quietly in the moonlight, but Bill kept glancing nervously over his shoulder, fearful, he said, of eavesdroppers. Our conversation seemed to us quite innocuous, so we began to wonder if Free China were not, perhaps, something of a little dictatorship. On the other hand, possibly his apprehension was unfounded. Traveler's Tip No. 21: Try to hold on to a sense of values.

The following morning, although the sky was overcast, it wasn't raining, so we hired a launch and went across the lake to a small village we had been told about to see the aborigines dance. My idea of aborigines is either American Indians before they struck oil or something out of Africa with fuzzy hair and a string around its middle. The aborigines of Taiwan were sloppy girls fully dressed, with heavy lipstick and not very good skins.

The main square of the mud village where they lived had been prettied up with stagnant ponds, a few discouraged bushes, and plaster casts of elephants, fish, and deer of a truly inspired ugliness. The local Fifth Avenue was a muddy alley lined with stalls selling poisonous souvenirs; varnished wooden eggcups, stuffed bats, and shell ornaments. Norton was convinced the merchandise had been imported from Newark, New Jersey. "It has the aura of *professional* junk," he said.

The atrocious taste might have been touching could one have felt they were trying, but a crushing air of lethargy and indifference hung heavy as the rain clouds over everything.

A few members of the Chinese Navy were on hand and they wandered around as we did, waiting for the dancing to begin, but time dragged on and nothing happened, so eventually they left. About fifteen minutes later a group of girls wearing weary old cretonne sarongs and shapeless jackets were herded together by the sound of long sticks, like outsized wooden potato mashers being pounded on flat stones. They formed a circle and, taking hands, started a listless shuffling in rhythm to their chanting which sounded like "Hi yin hi ya." The performance seemed to us to lack animation and the professional touch, but we were only three in the audience and it is hard to play with spirit to an empty house. Actresses like Mary Martin little know the trials their colleagues undergo.

At the end of the performance we paid and thanked them and went off to visit a brand-new temple. The building was rather pleasant, of

gray cement, and simple, with a gay tiled Chinese roof, but the Buddha
inside was a horror, a bright pink glazed face and garish gold body.
Since the great era of the Italians and Flemish I do not think one can
judge a people by its ecclesiastical art, which in recent centuries has
sunk to unspeakable lows, but good taste would not seem to be a natural attribute of modern Chinese. At the temple the only charm element was an enchanting little bald, white-robed Chinese nun who
showed us around. There were several Chinese tourists there at the
same time, one with a portable radio playing "It's a Long Way to Tip-
perary." News travels slowly in the Orient.

We left Sun Moon after luncheon and set off for Taichung, from
where we planned to take a CAT plane back to Taipei and a dinner
party at our friends' the Stanley Shens. We reached the airport in good
time and there we sat. For an hour and a half. For a long time we
could find out nothing. It then developed that the plane had been unable to take off from Taiwan due to a storm, Typhoon Ellen, who made
history in the Pacific.

Although at that time we didn't know the magnitude of the trouble,
we were concerned because much of the country had already been dev-
astated by floods that swept over the thousands of acres of rice paddies,
uprooting millions of plants, each one of which is set out by hand, and
destroying the ingeniously engineered little dikes that hold the water on
each terrace or allow it to drip into the level below. A hundred fifty
miles had been flooded, ruining a crop destined to feed millions of
Asians.

Finally after our long wait at seven o'clock a bus was rounded up
and with a roar we set off, racketing down the road like a machine
gun, blazing our way into the railroad station, and swinging aboard the
train just as it pulled out.

The train, the original rattler, was jammed. Greatly to our consterna-
tion Bill Sun started shooing people out of their seats that we might
sit down. They got up and wedged their way through the throng with
great good grace while Norton and I, feeling like the ugliest Americans, admonished him in heaven's name to stop ousting the natives.
"Not at all," he said, "you don't understand. In China when we buy
a ticket it only entitles us to ride on the train. We only get a seat if we
pay extra. I've paid extra for all of us, we *should* sit down, they quite
understand that." This made us feel better and we were glad of the
seats, for it was a two-and-a-half-hour ride worth the price, just under
one U.S. dollar.

Our posture was very good, for the seats are leather-upholstered, but the backs are bolt upright and fixed. No lowering them and lolling about. There are two places to a bench and four people sit facing each other with very little leg room, but as the doctor said with justice, "Don't complain about being crowded, after all very few Chinese are my size." From under the window a small shelf juts out, holding four tall, thick drinking glasses with lids on them. The aisles were packed with standing passengers, but the tea boy with his big kettle burrowed his way through them like an agile mole, with one deft movement removed the glasses from their rack, lifted the covers, poured in the tea, replaced the covers, set them back, and moved on. The tea was hot and freshly made but so full of leaves you had to strain it through your teeth. We all looked like cats who had swallowed green canaries. The second time around it was less good. Standing had made it strong and terribly bitter. Service, however, was continuous. Girls like air-line stewardesses dressed in white blouses and dark blue serge skirts slit up the thigh passed up and down the aisles with the little rolled-up wet towels, and we wiped our hands and faces many times, as there are an inordinate number of tunnels and whether the windows are opened or closed is purely at the whim of the fellow who has the window seat.

As we passed check points along the way, we watched the conductor lean from the train and swing out at a signal with a big ring. The train never slowed and I was certain he would break an arm, but he was expert and it never happened.

The trip passed surprisingly quickly and we arrived in Taipei at 10 P.M., but too late, alas, to make the dinner party. It was a big disappointment, for we liked the Shens and would have liked to see another Taipei house.

All of the Chinese from the mainland whom we met dreamed of someday returning to their homes, most of our friends to Shanghai. If this will ever happen no one knows. Even were communism to fail in this generation, certainly all of them now on Taiwan could not go back, and any returning government would face a formidable task organizing a civil service to govern between six and seven hundred million people.

CHAPTER EIGHT

✳ Japan

THE NEXT DAY we left for Japan on a Northwest Airlines plane, a big, roomy DC-7C. Excellent flight, excellent martinis, fair food. Canned peas and carrots and canned pineapple. It was hard to understand the reason for the latter when the native Taiwan pineapple is so delicious.

We were held for a few minutes over Tokyo due to our friend Typhoon Ellen, but finally touched down on the rainy tarmac and were met by Paul Benscoter, the Tokyo representative of Northwest, by the press, and the faithful American Express.

Again the magic touch worked and we were bowed through customs and driven to our hotel, the Imperial. The Imperial Hotel, designed by Frank Lloyd Wright in 1916–20, is world famous, having withstood earthquakes, war, and an occupying army, and is probably the ugliest structure ever built by man. Dear God, is the Imperial ugly! Dark and squat, it looks like the abode of trolls, with labyrinthine warrens for their dwarf servitors. Any minute I expected to see Mime and Alberich pop from a tunnel.

The Japanese respect the Imperial, however. They are proud of its imperviousness to what our little Japanese guide used to refer to as "erse cakes." The most serious cake of recent times was that of 1923, when many lives and millions of dollars' worth of property were destroyed.

I should think the arcade would be a depressing place in which to pass one's days, but since the hotel is filled with tourists many of Tokyo's best shops, including that of the famous pearl merchant Mikimoto, are located in the gloomy subterranean quarters. During a period of heavy rain—we were there in August, the typhoon season, and it rained almost constantly—the shops are flooded, with the merchandise piled on chairs and tables, while the proprietors, with rolled-up trousers, do their best to sweep away the water and bail themselves out. We began to understand why the Japanese have a large red sun on their flag. It's the only place they ever see it.

I will admit that my early impressions were jaundiced, as for the first and I sincerely hope the last time in my life I was suffering from an acute attack of bursitis in my right shoulder. Lollipop Land would have elicited from me little more than a snarl. Of our first few days I spent several hours a day in bed nursing my arm, trying to catch up on correspondence and dictating to a Japanese secretary who, the hotel assured me, was experienced, understood English, and wrote it perfectly. The letters she brought back for me to sign were piquant, full of surprises and turns of phrase far more original than my own, but at least our friends and business associates knew that we were thinking of them.

Norton got a little desperate because, as I was feeling extremely sorry for myself and wanted everyone to share my misery, every time he came into the room it was to hear a slightly reworded version of "I am suffering the most excruciating pain." "Never in my life have I known anything like this." "Bursitis is the punishment of the damned," occasionally varied by my turning to him and wailing reproachfully, "You're a doctor. Do something." Bursitis, alas, just as he said it was, is a self-limiting disease. When it has run its course it stops, and in the meantime there is very little anyone can do to relieve it. My husband is one of those doctors who know that there are times when the best thing to do is to do nothing. A dubious gift because impatient patients get quite enraged by it, yet it can spare them all kinds of complications and quite often saves their lives.

I knew that but I was the troublemaker. To cosset me, he did buy a hot-water bag and some Butazolidine Alka, which seemed to help a bit, although he himself was more pleased with the devil plasters he unearthed in a Japanese drugstore. Considered them a real find. Like old-fashioned mustard plasters, they set up a counter surface irritant so you forget the more deep-seated pain.

One of the few rays of sunshine penetrating to me during our first days in Tokyo was a letter from Daphne Lyall. She and her husband were taking care of Thor, our Weimaraner. In her letter Daphne said, "I thought you would be interested in knowing that Thor came to church last Sunday. We were sitting in our pew waiting for the service to begin when he strolled up the aisle to the altar. He was quietly asked to leave, which he did with quiet dignity, and we are now waiting to learn whether or not he has decided to become an Episcopalian."

Oddly enough we saw no dogs in Tokyo, but, traveling around the country, we encountered a lot of them. Japanese dogs are, by far, the best off of any in Asia, well fed and petted. We saw one woman picking fleas off her darling while he lay in relaxed boredom, humoring her, several were being carried, and one was riding in a baby carriage.

We were also told about a couple who raised canaries. One clutch or pride or whatever newborn canaries are called consisted of three birds. As a joke the man and his wife made little beds of wood with coverlets and pillows. Two of the birds ignored them but the third was crazy about the idea and went to bed every night with his head on the pillow and peeped and chirped indignantly until he was covered up.

Tokyo is an enormous city, now the world's largest in both area and population, having nine million inhabitants as against New York's eight, but with the exception of some enchanting gardens, not at once visible, physically it has little beauty. Large parts of it were destroyed during the war and have been rebuilt with small regard for a harmonious or homogeneous whole. Since they had the opportunity to start from scratch, it's a pity they did not do so with more foresight and taste, but it must be remembered that their resources were practically nil. Even so one searches hopefully for one's preconceived notion of oriental atmosphere, but streets such as the Ginza, an artery of large stores and neon lights, are more reminiscent of Chicago and West Forty-second Street than of Madame Butterfly.

Once indoors there is a change of heart, and one of our most charming experiences occurred the evening of our arrival. I have mentioned that Paul Benscoter of Northwest Airlines met us and drove us to the hotel. He did better than that. When we had bathed and changed—I wore my *cheong sam* from Hong Kong; Tokyo might not be oriental, but I was—he called for us and took us to dine at the Hanacho, a restaurant specializing in *tempura*. This was it! The restaurant was like a private house, and we were met at the door by two smiling, kneeling little Japanese women in enchantingly pretty kimonos. I wish the phrase "living doll" were not such a cliché, for in Japan, when in native dress, that is indeed what the women and children are. We were asked to remove our shoes—we quickly became accustomed to the ritual—were given scuffs to put on in their place, and were escorted upstairs. At the threshold of the room we shed the scuffs and entered in stockinged feet, me in my Peds.

We sat on the floor on the *tatami*, the clean, fragrant grass matting, and since we were Americans and Mr. Benscoter was an old client, scotch and soda were placed on the low table. The Japanese, who spend a great deal of time on the floor kneeling and sitting back on their heels—to a Westerner an intensely uncomfortable position—have very strong backs and depend on themselves. As a concession to our weaker physiques the Hanacho provided back rests.

For hors d'oeuvres we had strips of not unsavory rubbery fish and another kind, minute fellows on tiny sticks, that had a sweet-sour burned taste. I looked at the doctor, the fish fancier, looking at his plate. He sampled them, smiled politely, and concentrated on his highball.

The treat came later, and what a treat it was! We went into another room and again sat down on the floor, this time around a crescent-shaped table with our feet in a hole, a kind of trench that was, I should say, two or three feet deep. It was explained to us that in wintertime that is where the brazier is placed to keep the pedal extremities from dropping off from frostbite.

Opposite us, in the concave side of the crescent, sat the cook in a dazzling white robe. In front of him was a bowl of hot sesame oil with a brazier under it and a metal shield in front to keep it from spattering. At his left elbow was a big bowl of batter. He would take thick chopsticks, pick up a prawn, a slice of eggplant, or a chunk of crab meat—there were any number of bowls of bite-sized delectables surrounding him—dip it in the batter, pop it into the hot oil, where it sizzled for a moment or two, lift it out, and deposit it on a paper napkin placed in front of each diner, who then picked up the morsel with his own chopsticks and dipped it into an individual sauceboat. The ingredients are soy sauce, mild, freshly grated horse-radish, tender green ginger shoots, salt, and a few drops of lemon juice. One starts eating and a long time later one stops.

You have to like fish, but if you like fish *tempura's* your dish. The doctor, who hasn't lived many years of his life in San Francisco for nothing, was in his element. He got the basic recipe in Tokyo and on returning home worked out certain refinements, and is now *tempura* king of our region. Because he is filled with love for his fellow man and because he subscribes to the theory that, if others enjoy in their own houses a savory feast first sampled in ours, we are in no way diminished, he has allowed me to give his recipe.

>   *Batter:*   1¼ cups wheat cake flour
>   4 tbs. rice flour
>   4 tbs. cornstarch

Mix one egg yolk with ½ cup water. Add flour slowly, mixing from outside to center of bowl. When well mixed add egg white stiffly beaten.

For cooking use sesame-seed oil or two thirds sesame and one third salad oil.

Tempura Sauce: To three parts of stock (homemade or canned consommé) add a few drops of lemon juice, one part soy sauce, and one part white wine. The Japanese use *miriin*, which is a sweet rice wine or *sake*. We normally use Chablis, which serves very well. If possible put in a little dried bonita fillet and *koubu* (seaweed), which may be obtained from Japanese stores. Add a little Ac'cent, grated ginger, and horse-radish. The bottled kind will do, but it is of course much better when freshly grated. Each guest should have his own individual bowl for the sauce.

Foods to use—and they should be set around the cook within easy reach on small plates—are any or all of the following cut into bite-sized pieces: fresh shrimp, peeled and deveined, lobster tails, scallops, crab meat, clams, mussels or small pieces of any delicate white fish, celery, zucchini, eggplant, radish, squash, and squash blossoms.

The last of course are possible only in summertime, but guests swoon over them in rapture. Don't forget the paper napkins on the plates, as they absorb the few leftover drops of hot oil.

When Norton works his magic at home, he puts the oil in an electric casserole with a thermostat that controls the temperature: 360°F.

Four people are the ideal number for tempura, and one should not have more than six, otherwise the hapless chef has to rent another pair of hands and has no time to snap a snack himself.

Usually I think odors are the most potent memory revivers, but the first time we had tempura after we got home it was the sizzling sound of the hot oil that instantly evoked the pale pretty room of the Hanacho and the round, imperturbable chef. When the meal was finished he pressed a button and revolved away from us like a lordly lazy Susan and was hidden from view by a small screen with miniature potted pines in front of it. It was really strikingly different from Schrafft's.

We returned to the front room for dessert: the most succulent, flavorful peaches I have ever eaten. In August grapes, melons, and figs are also at their best. Japanese pears are peculiar. Crisp, cool, and refreshing, with no taste whatsoever.

Another tempura restaurant, possibly even better, is the Tsubaki, but it does not have the charmingly antic quality of Hanacho. No revolving chef.

By way of a change we lunched one day at the *smörgåsbord* buffet in the Viking Room of the Imperial. The food was very good but the spaghetti was a mistake. Via Scandinavia and Tokyo the road is long to Italy.

Another time we were taken by Chinese friends, the Foks, to Suehiro, a well-known sukiyaki restaurant. I have since learned from Oliver Statler's enchanting book *Japanese Inn* that *Suehiro* means "folding fan." It was charming, a good deal bigger than the Hanacho and without its intimacy, but we went upstairs to find the same low tables and bowing, smiling waitresses in kimonos. We were getting so that we kicked off our shoes with the flip of an ankle at the first whiff of *tatami*. There were a good many Americans at Suehiro's, mostly men. It was understandable. I should think the American male would be highly susceptible to the gentle, submissive charm, or so it seems, of young Japanese women.

We ordered cocktails—the American clientele had gotten in a few licks of its own—and shortly a brazier and frying pan were brought to the table, and the sukiyaki of tender beef, spinach, onions, mushrooms, and bean curd, with a stock made of sake and soy sauce, was swiftly cooked. It was ambrosial if somewhat too sweet for our palates.

Sake I cannot go for. They serve it warm and it is sweet and tastes like an inferior Graves; also Japanese green tea was a disappointment. I was once nearly drummed from an American dinner table for saying so by an American green-tea aficionado, and conceivably, if served some of only the most superior quality, my palate might become acclimated, but the first few times around are a let down. I am convinced they make it out of old tatami mats when they are taken up in the spring. The delicious drink of Japan—and this came as a real surprise—is the beer. Japanese beer is grand. Asahi was our favorite brew, and we drank it in quantity. The other great dish in the land of the cherry blossom is beef. Meaning no affront to Texas or Kansas, I have never tasted meat to equal Kobe beef. The Japanese massage the cattle, literally they do, and the resulting tenderness must be sampled to be believed. We tasted it for the first time at the American Embassy. Drue Parsons in Paris had written to her friend Laura MacArthur, the wife of our ambassador, Douglas MacArthur II, who is the nephew of the general, and she had invited us to luncheon at the residence. It was a pleasant party of about eighteen, including Cecil Brown, the CBS correspondent in Tokyo, and his wife, Martha. All the food was good and the beef was lyrical.

The MacArthurs also asked us to their twenty-fifth-anniversary party, which we were obliged regretfully to refuse because on that date, August 26, we would still be out of town on our junior tour of Japan. When he heard we were traveling the ambassador said at once, "You must come and see me on your return. I'll want an hour and a half of your time to talk to you." We were rather flattered. He finds us intelligent and wants our opinion, we thought. Later we did have a talk with His Excellency, not quite along the lines anticipated.

After luncheon we went shopping. The things to buy in Japan are cultured pearls—which start at ten dollars for a reasonably pretty single strand and keep going—kimonos, transistor radios, and camera lenses. Their lenses are extraordinary. The good doctor succumbed to a Nikkor F1-1. Says anything the human eye can see it can see and, to prove his point, he has taken some remarkable colored pictures in theaters without using a flash. He got it in a shop called Matsushima, at 3-Chome, Ginza. They also have excellent binoculars, and we bought for Jimmy and Pete, Norton's two sons, Minolta cameras, which have served them well.

For those interested in modern Japanese art I mention an excellent small gallery, Yoseido at 5-5 Chome, Nishi Ginza, Chuo-Ku. "Ku" is district or zone.

Bargains in the Orient are irresistible, but of course you are paying for the trip and there is a cold, uncomfortable statistic that is prudent to remember. I set it down as Traveler's Tip No. 22: Like building a house, travel *always* costs more than you estimate.

Almost our favorite shop in Tokyo was one of the burrows in the Imperial Arcade, or alimentary canal, as we came to think of it. It was Odawara Shoten. They have all kinds of attractive things to buy— screens and prints and ceramics—but their forte is packaging. You pay for the service, but they will pack anything in the world for you and send it to any part of the world. They do a commendable job stitching unbleached muslin over the box or case and printing the name and address in broad, beautiful black strokes. There's a post office just down the warren where you pay the postage and get a receipt, and Norton and I were constantly ferrying parcels—it was usually moist so "ferrying" is reasonably accurate—and feeling like Mr. Mole in *The Wind in the Willows*. I don't suppose we actually crouched on these missions, but in retrospect I always see us at half-mast burrowing through the tunnel.

One of the chances you take in traveling that give the enterprise a certain spice, like Russian roulette, is the kind of bag you will draw with letters of introduction. Sometimes the people are darlings, and sometimes the friends of our friends seem a rum crew indeed. In the darling category were Keyes and Linda Beech whom we came to know through friends in Taipei, Robert Phillips and his wife. We went one day to the Foreign Correspondents Press Club to meet Keyes and found him an intelligent entertaining man. He is a Pulitzer Prize winner to boot, won it, I believe, for his coverage of the Korean War. From the club we then went on to the Crescent, a pleasant restaurant serving good Western food. Later, on the way to a night club in a taxi, we saw a demonstration, the kind of thing I have read about but never before witnessed except in newsreels. A great crowd was marching with red banners, chanting and shuffling along. Uniformed police lined the route carrying paper lanterns in their hands. Keyes said the demonstration was over the Matsuka-Wa case, a train derailment that had occurred in 1949 involving seventeen defendants. We were in no way concerned and our cab was unmolested, but it is, just the same, a curious feeling to be caught in a current of thousands of sullen, muttering people whose anger, whether inspired or spontaneous, might explode at any minute.

The night club we visited was the Papagayo, presenting an old familiar routine. Girls came out wearing little but fringe, danced a bit, untied their bras, danced a moment or two with naked breasts, and departed. They were a watered-down sissy version of the luxuriantly displayed charms we had seen at the Moulin Rouge in Vienna.

From the Papagayo—Keyes wanted us really to savor the night life of Tokyo—we went to the Albion Club. The Albion is the anteroom of hell. To begin with, it's in the subway. You go down stairs from the street to the first level, part the short cotton streamers that frequently serve as doors in Tokyo, and enter pandemonium. The place was fairly crowded, the clientele was mostly male, there was a shrieking rock-and-roll juke box by way of music, and girls in yellow satin shorts and tops jigging in front of every table. The ceiling was low and the din reverberated endlessly. To spend time in such surroundings while suffering from bursitis would be a hell that Dante never dreamed of. We stayed about five minutes and fled.

A far more tony cabaret to which we went another time was Oscar's. Here the production was quite ambitious, with a group called the Don Yada dancers, a Eurasian mistress of ceremonies, a Hawaiian band, and a Japanese chorus. We were still not converted to night life.

One of our evenings we devoted to culture, a mixed bag. At five o'clock we went to the Takarazuka Revue, the famous all-girl vaude-ville-musical comedy-spectacle show that is a staple of Japanese en-tertainment. Lovers, old men, bellhops, business tycoons, all are played by girls. Sets and costumes are literal, in primary colors, and brightly lighted. The humor is not subtle. The biggest laugh came in a scene where a woman, rattling along at a great pace spits in a man's (another woman's) face so much that he (she) whips out a big handkerchief and holds it between them as a screen. That brought the house down.

There was actually a quite charming interlude, a folk dance called *Hana Taue*, in ten scenes depicting village life, with rice planting, lan-tern festivals, comic rustics, and prayers for rain. It was a riot of color and was followed—they give you your money's worth in the Japanese theater—by a musical comedy in twenty scenes called *Invitation to the Alps*. The plot was pretty intricate, but seemed to have a Romeo-and-Juliet basis in that children of feuding families fell in love with each other, but it was all very modern and the feuding fathers were business competitors who had apparently gone to the Tyrol for a holiday. The costumes were Western, the girlish men very natty with their sack suits and cropped heads, but a bit too broad in the beam to be entirely con-vincing. They were, in a curious way, faintly distasteful.

My favorite bit was two people in a cow. I've often seen the act done with a horse and it never fails to amuse me, but this was the first time I'd seen a people-propelled cow cavorting on an Alpine slope.

We left before the show was over, as we were eager to get to the *kabuki* theater at a certain time. *Kabuki* first got its name in the seven-teenth century, when a handmaiden performed a dance in order to raise money for the shrine at which she was an attendant. She called the dance *kabuki*, and it was the first public entertainment for which an admission fee had ever been charged. The word at that time meant "novelty," and it was only later when it came to be represented by three Chinese characters that it assumed its present meaning. *Ka* is "singing," *bu* "dancing," and *ki* "acting."

The performance had begun at noon and was still going strong when we arrived at half-past seven, to find a highly stylized dance in progress. It was in slow motion, and as we did not understand the significance of the postures and gesturing, we found the action somewhat tedious, but visually it was lovely. There was a bank of musicians stage left garbed in blue and black and playing curious stringed instruments, and three fishermen stage right in ocher and blue. The backdrop was stylized waves, the dancer a fat gentleman of dubious sex wearing layers of magnificent kimonos, gold, pink, black, lilac, and vermilion, which he peeled off slowly in the course of his slow gyrations.

Pace and interest quickened in the second scene, an underwater ballet called *tamatori* that boasted a squid in an imaginative gray and white costume, lobsters, prawns, and a wistful pink octopus.

After a long intermission came the play of the evening, a tale of passion and murder entitled *Kurayami No Ushimatsu*. An English synopsis was provided in the program, so we could follow the action reasonably well, and we found it a unique experience, visually an incomparable production. The action took place in a Japanese house and in an inn, and the restrained line and muted colors, beige and brown and olive green, russet and eggplant and parchment, with here and there a sharp note of coral or vermilion, were breath-taking. An actor called Shoroku played the lead, and he and the entire cast were impressive. I think it is now generally known that in the kabuki theater men play all the parts, including those of women, and that as a rule talent is a family matter; knowledge, experience, and the roles themselves handed down from father to son. The actor's skill in playing women's parts is absolute. Whether homosexuality is involved I do not know, but observation, art, and communicative ability certainly are, and the characters emerge as women, not as travesties of the female sex. The wife and a servant at the inn were marvelously portrayed.

It galls me to admit that we left before it was over, not only because, having touted the beauty and interest of the production, departure makes us sound like hicks, but because we ourselves longed to see the last act and to this day regret that we missed it, but at nine-thirty a power stronger than ourselves drove us from the theater: that of starvation. We had lunched early, we had had no tea, and come nine-thirty we were famished. Had the play kept going we would have too, but we could not last through a twenty-minute intermission before the final stanza. Plucking the hayseed from our hair and trying to deaden the sound of our hobnailed boots on the parquet, we slunk from the theater. We slunk back to the Imperial to dine in the Terrace Café, which has the greatest indoor effect of a starlit sky I have ever seen. It also has good food. Someday we will return to Japan, we will find out when *Kurayami No Ushimatsu* is playing, we will time the performance, and we will catch the last act.

A spectacle that is interesting, if not on a par with the kabuki, is the Imperial Palace Gardens. Thanks to Drue and her lofty connections, an embassy car called for us one morning and we were driven to the palace grounds, two hundred acres moated and walled within the heart of the city.

One need not be as chichi as we were to view them. I believe a pass is necessary, but it is not difficult to obtain and the visit is a pleasant excursion, although the general upkeep of the grounds we found to be rather slipshod. I expect the manicured part is encircled by the great white wall enclosing the palace proper and through which we were not permitted to pass. A beautiful spot in the grounds is a long, wild ravine with thickly treed, sloping sides alive with white herons.

We were met at the gate by a guide who showed us the state carriages, which were nice, but we were a bit blasé, having seen the great carriage museum in Lisbon with far grander equipages. What was interesting was the hall where they perform *gagaku*. *Gagaku* means elegant and authorized music, the term for ancient Japanese compositions, and the concert takes place on a square stage not unlike a prize ring surrounded by a lacquer-red railing. The performance may include dancing and singing as well as instrumental music and is then known as *bugaku* and *kangen*.

A charming department of the palace theater was the wardrobe room, where the rich and colorful costumes worn by the performers hung on ropes so that they looked as though their wearers had flopped over in exhaustion.

It is sad to see the waning of native Japanese dress. When we were there I should say there was perhaps one out of every eight or ten people who wore the kimono and obi, the *geta*, or wooden clogs, and little white cotton socks split to accommodate the big toe. Everyone else wore dresses and sack suits and all color and individuality had been expunged. The trend in gent's footwear is lamentable: pearl-gray, glazed-kid shoes. Saville Row would turn quite faint. Once we saw an unusual group of five or six women in kimonos come laughing and chattering down the street. It was an entrancing sight, a group of butterflies on the wing, and small children with their black bangs and kimonos are edible. A remnant of the old ways still lingers in the Japanese gentlemen in Western suits who ply small paper fans when they are warm.

Norton and I succumbed to kimonos as presents, and I got one for myself and even persuaded him to buy one to wear at home on evenings when we are alone. He looks fine in it, like a shogun, one of the early war lords. We got them at the kimono mart, K. Hayashi, where the prices range between 550 to 6800 yen or $1.59 to $9.10. Superbly embroidered or old kimonos may cost in the thousands.

One night when we dined with the Beeches, Linda was wearing a very pretty one and it became her admirably. That was a cheery evening. Martha Brown, of the sleek, shining braided coronet, picked us up and we drove to the studio to get Cecil, who had just finished broadcasting, and then on out to the Beeches' house, which was remote from the center of town but attractive and with a pretty garden lighted by Japanese lanterns. The party was small and informal, just ourselves and Ambassador and Mrs. MacArthur. The dinner was buffet, including among other delights delicious cold lobster and piping-hot corn on the cob.

Afterward we sat around chatting informally and having a very pleasant time, but Mrs. MacArthur apparently was not feeling well. An abrupt explosion of rage, triggered no one knew quite why, burst from the lady, and shortly afterward she and the ambassador left. The rest of the evening passed agreeably. The Browns drove us back to the hotel, urging us to spend only a day in Nikko, after we told them that we were going there and that the Japan Travel Bureau had booked us for three days, which we had already cut to two.

In Japan their own travel organization takes over from the American Express. They are efficient, but you have to watch them like hawks, for they will blandly book you for three days in places where a morning or afternoon or sometimes even an hour would give you ample time to see all there is to see. This leads not only to unnecessary expense but to boredom and frustration as well. A sure danger signal is when the typewritten itinerary they give you reads, "Guide released on arrival," or "Visit shrine. Guide dismissed. Hotel overnight. Pick up guide next morning." If it says anything of the sort, beware! Flee like the hunted doe, for you are at the nether end of hell. You can bet your bottom dollar that the guide's relieved because there is not so much as a blade of grass that is worthy of inspection. There you are, the captive tourist, without a single solitary thing to do or see until the guide returns to liberate you twenty-four or forty-eight hours later. Your only occupation will be packing and unpacking your bag and forking over too many yen. Aware of this, however, go ahead, for within Japan travel is a must. One may see only London or Paris or Rome or New York and still have had a great experience. This is not true of Tokyo. In Japan the country is more interesting than the capital.

Our own guided tour was conducted by an engaging little creature called Kaori Yokoyama. When we first met, her name seemed to us something of a stumbling block, but she said at once, "Please call me Baby, everybody does." It is easy to understand why. Every adult in the world is bigger than Baby, who stands, I should say, an imposing four feet eight in her stockinged feet. It was quite a sight to see her trotting along, the six-foot-one doc following docilely in her wake.

Our first destination was the Fujia Hotel at Miyanoshita in the Hakone mountain range. We went by train and the train was excellent; modern, clean, and comfortable. The country was beautiful, and infinitely more mountainous than I had realized, checkered with rice paddies and tea gardens, and occasional patches of wheat. On this trip a question that had long haunted me was answered. I always wondered how in a land that is about the size of California and that supports ninety-two million people it would be possible to have any countryside at all. Wouldn't every inch be built up? The answer is that they have and it isn't. There are big unoccupied areas, but every arable inch of land is under cultivation, since only 15 per cent of it can be worked; the rest is too mountainous.

The Fujia Hotel, built originally in 1888 but destroyed a couple of times by fire and rebuilt, is a vast, rambling behemoth of a place not unlike the old summer resort hotels of New England. It doesn't have verandas for rocking rows of dowagers, but somehow, despite the fluted, turned-up Japanese roof and the balconies and, I am sure, at the appropriate season, cherry blossoms, the atmosphere is the same: staid, roomy, comfortable, and *eminently* respectable. The rooms—there are one hundred forty-one—are all named after flowers, Acacia, Pear, Japonica, Plum . . . we were Camellia. Opposite us was Rhododendron. The bee nesting there, an American with a penetrating voice, must have been in residence for some time, for now that she was packing it took her many hours of concentrated effort, with many a shrill cry for help to the floor maids.

The food is Western and only fair, but there's a great deal of it, many courses, so no one need go hungry if he picks at the more savory morsels as they meander by. The service is leisurely.

The place actually has a good deal to offer either for a weekend or a more protracted stay. There is a delightful garden with winding paths and ponds and waterfalls, beautifully shaped and cultivated trees, and a mill wheel and little millhouse. There is an indoor swimming pool as well as an outdoor, and in the latter five gnomes were scrubbing away like mad, clearing up the effects of the typhoon. The hotel also provides tennis courts, a pool table, hot mineral baths, and the eighteen-hole Sengoku golf course, five miles away, which has girl caddies. Miyanoshita is at 2500 feet and there are miles of mountain paths for walking.

I took the steamy sulphur baths, hoping they would help my bursitis, and to some extent they did, especially when I was in them and could move my arm freely. One evening, weary from junketing about and wanting to forget my shoulder, I had taken a pain pill at Norton's suggestion and was writing postcards home, occasionally sipping a glass of Asahi beer. One minute I was a candidate for the Supreme Court Bench, the next I was cross-eyed. Getting seven feet from the chair to the bed took on the aspect of climbing Mount Everest. I did it the same way, too, lifting my knees very high as though pulling my legs out of deep snowdrifts and hitting my chin in the process. The doctor, that character dedicated to alleviating the suffering of mankind, could barely give me a hand he was so doubled up with laughter. I see that I noted in my diary the next day, "Not at my peak." Peak! I was wallowing in the coastal plains. Tip No. 23 (not confined to travelers): Do not mix sedation and drinks of even low alcoholic content.

I rose above my condition the following morning, and we went for a long walk along the winding mountain paths. For almost the first time since we had been in Japan there was a little misty sunshine, and we determined to take advantage of it. Also, the hotel management assured us, we would see Mount Fuji. Fuji is the big spectacle in those parts, and we didn't want to miss our opportunity.

After climbing steadily for forty-five minutes we came to the Fuji view stand. This was a little bench and behind it a primitive painting on a wooden panel, by an untalented Grandma Moses, of the district we were in: fields and rolling hills and lesser mountains rising to the climax of the lordly snow-capped peak. We were grateful for even this facsimile, for it was the only view we got. The feeble sun had retired, it was hot and humid and Fuji was obscured by clouds. The doctor normally is a soft-spoken man, eschewing four-letter words and profanity, but for a while there his comments waxed virulent as he gave his opinion of the symbol of Japan and what it could do hidden away in the dense bank of clouds.

We continued climbing, the way we had come was steep and zigzagging, and we thought to do better if we could get over the ridge and come down the other side. The mountain was thickly covered with trees and undergrowth, but was eerily silent, for in all that verdure we heard no bird sing. After walking for about two hours we had to admit we were lost. It wasn't necessarily serious, as if we kept going down we must eventually come out at some cleared space even if it weren't near the hotel, but the descent was steep and paths split and wound and doubled back on themselves. From time to time we would spot a signpost and make our way to it as quickly as we could to find arrows pointing in three different ways, all printed with Japanese characters. There are few things more frustrating than to know that there, before your eyes, is the key to the puzzle and you can't decipher it. It should scarcely have surprised us to find the directions written in Japanese, but Hakone is after all a tourist center, they are accustomed to English and American visitors, the very ones likely to be roaming the mountain paths, and it did seem that it might have occurred to them to erect an occasional sign in English. The irony of our situation was that that was the one time on the entire trip when my boy scout, who, since we had left Paris, had never stepped outdoors without his compass, didn't have it with him. He had laid it neatly away in the top bureau drawer in our hotel room and was equipped with only two cameras and his binoculars.

We came at last onto lower ground and into a beautiful wooded area bisected by rushing streams and walled by rocks veiled with tumbling waterfalls. The place is called the Thousand Threads Water Falls and is well named. The sun came out and pierced the heavy foliage and the spray shimmered and the waters sparkled in their headlong course. The cool, dank atmosphere was very welcome after the airless mountain.

That evening we went to the village square to watch folk dancing. The local Japanese inns have an engaging custom of providing their guests with kimonos to wear during their stay. Each inn has its own design and people put on the kimonos and go for walks and meet and exchange greetings with groups from neighboring inns. One is, as it were, a member of the team. Four or five inns were represented at the dance, but as the music started so did the rain and the party broke up.

The next day, led by Baby, the mighty mouse, we set off by car for Numazu, where we were to take the train to Kyoto. The Hakone National Park is truly a beautiful area, mountains covered by pine and bamboo, with a large and lovely lake, Ashi, for boating, fishing, and swimming, and there was one moment when the shoulder of Mount Fuji emerged from the mist. Frustrated in his photographic efforts, the doctor was obliged to cheat. He bought a set of commercial colored slides of the mountain in every mood and every season. Snow, cherry blossoms, the golden leaves of autumn. People to whom we show our pictures sometimes get confused, saying, "What time of year did you say you were there?"

The train stopped at Numazu for only two minutes, so with our luggage we had quite a scramble to get aboard. It was a good train, with comfortable parlor-car seats, but so violently air-conditioned that our teeth were chattering. We had to open our bags to get out sweaters, and a group of noisy Belgians who were with us were flailing their arms like Russian coachmen, breathing on their fingers, and calling down the wrath of heaven on the Land of the Rising Sun and all its inhabitants.

I watched a Japanese man eating with chopsticks a box luncheon provided by the train, and marveled at his dexterity, especially when Baby told us that he was eating fried eels. He had a kind of junket, bean curd, I expect it was, and he was able to eat that with chopsticks too, and he drank tea out of the top of a tiny teapot. Baby also ate the box lunch, but there was Western, if stereotyped, food for the foreign passengers.

It would seem foolish to go to Japan and not see Tokyo, but if one were forced to a choice I should say don't miss Kyoto. The capital of Japan for over ten centuries, from 794 to 1868, it has a population of over 1,200,000 and is the seat of or adjacent to all kinds of marvels: shrines and gardens and palaces. There are also excellent Japanese inns. Ours was the Tawaraya. On a side street, behind the usual board fence, at first sight it is not particularly prepossessing, but once you're within it is a pet.

We were greeted by a smiling, bowing personnel, the maids in kimonos, and, automatically now, took off our shoes at the front door. We left them in the entryway, where they were set on shelves, and slipped into the scuffs provided by the management. We shuffled down the clean waxed floor of the narrow corridor and emerged into a small inner court or garden, crossed a railed bridge over a pond, and came to the door of our suite. There we kicked off the scuffs and entered, in stocking feet, a narrow sort of anteroom opening onto a tiny walled garden with bamboo trees, stunted pines, a pebbled path, a stone-lipped well the size of a tankard with a bamboo dipper and a stone lantern. In the room was a modern occidental couch cushioned in foam rubber, a comfortable chair, and a writing table. We also had a television set on which we got vaudeville, capsule musicals, and baseball. One step up and the apartment opened into a quite large square room carpeted with *tatami*. The proportion of this room was lovely and the matting immaculate and shining. In a little alcove hung a scroll with a pale moon, shadowy flowers, and a dark bird. Beside it stood a dark, gleaming vase with two yellow chrysanthemums and a spray of dried grass. In the center was a low table with a few flat cushions around it and two back rests and two armrests so that when sitting on the floor we could lean with one elbow on a rest in picturesque attitudes. The effect was very beautiful; the ancient, restrained, civilized art of Japan in microcosm. The whole thing was in fact so exquisite, so sophisticated and meticulous that we noted with a perverse relish and slight relief the one incongruous note: white muslin antimacassars on the back and armrests. The Japanese are avid for antimacassars, use them on trains, in hotels, restaurants; on any surface that might have contact with any portion of the human anatomy there's an antimacassar.

The walls dividing the two sections of our living quarters and the bath-dressing room were sliding paper panels. The dressing room was a felicitous marriage of East and West. There was a long shelf with a well-lighted mirror in the center and at one end a commodious stall shower. The floor was wooden slats and there was a regular Western shower head and a sunken Japanese wooden bathtub. The idea was to soap and rinse off under the shower, then to step into the tub for contemplation and relaxation in hot clean water. Obviously the management can't stand guard, but, knowing Western ways, it does urge guests not to *sneak* into the tub and get the satiny wood all smeared up. Norton and I, both being shower types, were happy to comply. The toilet was at the opposite end of the dressing room in a closet lined with cedarwood, with a window looking out on its own minute fragment of garden. Native Japanese toilets are usually porcelain-tiled holes in the ground, but those of the Tawaraya are Western. Sliding panels concealed shelves on which the mats that were the beds were folded during the day, and while we had hangers for our clothes there were no bureau drawers. Underwear lay in piles and it behooved us to keep them neat, as their visibility was high.

One's first night on a Japanese bed is quite an experience. Especially was it so for the doc. Each bed was made of three thick cushions placed end to end on the floor, and over these were laid two thin pads, then a sheet. We had quilts to cover us, with sheets sewn onto them, and flat pillows. I was quite comfortable, but my dear one was not a happy man. We had noted before the disparity in his and Japanese sizes. The under-cushions and mats weren't long enough, so his feet dropped over the end onto the floor. If he pulled the quilt up around his shoulders his naked toes pointed, unprotected, to heaven. If he tucked it around his feet, his shoulders were cold, for, although the weather was hot and humid, we were amply air-conditioned. Also the flat pillow slipped out from under his head and lapped on the floor like a Dali watch.

In the morning when Butterfly came in to pick up the beds and fold them away, the doctor re-enacted the night's experience. He had her, I may say, in stitches. She laughed and laughed, revealing a daz-zling array of gold and silver teeth that would have distressed an Ameri-can dentist but delighted a jeweler. His was a telling performance just the same, for the next night there were extra cushions and quilts, and he was comfortable.

One aspect of life in a Japanese inn is a delight. Because of the feel-ing of privacy and the individual attention each guest receives, it's like living in your own home without the responsibility. You merely tell them if you plan to be in for luncheon or dinner, they market to suit your wishes, and when you get back at mealtime in comes your own maid with her brazier and a tray of food, sets the low table, and, squat-ting beside you on the floor, prepares a delicious meal.

Our first evening at the Tawaraya, however, we were not to sample one. Baby did let us have tea and a drink—the gin of Japan does not rank with her beer—but then hurried us out. That night was the Cere-monial Grand Fire Burning on Mount Daimonji. The Feast of the Dead, a thrilling spectacle not to be missed. The mountainsides would flame with torches in the shape of gigantic Chinese characters. From far and wide people were gathering. There was a big fleet of busses, but we must get into the first one because parking space at the foot of the mountains was limited and the first bus there got the best view.

We scuttled along to the depot, which was not far from the inn, and sure enough secured seats in the first of what must have been twenty or twenty-five busses. This was a few minutes past seven. The others were quickly loaded and off we rolled. After an exhilarating ten-minute run we stopped. We were against a sheer cliff of rock on one side and another bus drew abreast of us on the other, so our range of vision was somewhat curtailed. After a bit Baby said she would reconnoiter and returned with the glad tidings that there would be an hour's wait. Why she could not say. The Japanese adults behaved with patience, and the Japanese children clambered around over the seats, knocking us in the head with their dear little feet in their dear little getas.

Still, things were better than prophesied, and after only about forty minutes we started off again and presently, by George, there it was. High on the mountainside we saw a blazing Chinese character, the one that looks like a capital "A" with turned-up toes. There wasn't any parking place, however, we just kept going along the road, and when trees and houses didn't interfere with the distant view we saw it again.

Baby's prognostication of people coming from far and wide proved true. The roads were jammed with traffic and red lights were frequent. It was just like getting back to town from the country on a summer Sunday night at home. After an hour or so of laborious snail-like progress we saw another flaming mountain, this time a boat design. I think it was the boat that bears the dead. We drove on. Brief runs, long inexplicable stops. Fortunately the street life was colorful and entertaining to watch. There were more kimonos than there had been in Tokyo— almost all the children were dressed in them, as were many of the men as well as the women. Although it was late because of the festival the shops were open and lighted, and we counted dozens of bookstores, there were customers in them, too, but of further mountain conflagrations we spied not a spark. The most charming moment of the venture was when crossing a bridge of the river Kamo we watched thousands of little paper boats like lanterns, each bearing a candle, borne down the tide. They light the souls of the dead back to paradise after their three-day visit home.

That was rewarding, but we didn't return to the depot till twenty-past ten and three hours on the none too comfortable seats of the bus were a high price to pay. We were exhausted and famished, but the good restaurants were all closing and turned us from their doors. The best we could find was an appalling juke-box joint where the food was frightful and not improved by warm sake.

Baby was desolate. The poor child had never made the trip before— it comes but once a year and is supposed to be a great festival—and she had assumed it was something touring Americans in her care should definitely see. We consoled her as best we could, assuring her we were seasoned voyagers and that it was all part of traveling. We refrained from adding, "The grisly part," and tramped home, exhausted and hungry, to our mats.

There had been some talk about the possibility of a geisha party, but it left the doctor cold. "To hell with geishas," he said, "play damned parlor games and make like happy." If there is anything he loathes it's parlor games. I said it was my understanding that the services rendered by these charming ladies were not quite in that category. "They are really very accomplished. They play and sing and dance as well."

"As well as what?"

"That's the part I'm vague on."

Gradually we accumulated a little knowledge, much of it from Mr. P. D. Perkins. We had heard of Mr. Perkins from David Jampel, a journalist in Tokyo who suggested that we look him up, for he was a man wise in the ways of the Orient.

We found him living in a Japanese house on the outskirts of Kyoto. Beside the front door was a hideous but traditional statue of a badger —great big fellow. The tradition is that you rub his nose for luck and it was all shiny from the caresses of luck hunters like the boar's nose in Florence. Mr. Perkins was a tall, thin, ashen man, an American, who looked very ill but received us with great courtesy. He was wearing a kimono and spoke to his household in what sounded to our ears like perfect Japanese. He is indeed an oriental scholar and deals in oriental books. Norton was interested in books on Eastern medicine for the library of the Academy of Medicine and Mr. Perkins promised to keep an eye peeled.

We spoke of geisha girls and he said he would take us the next evening to their own theater and that we should meet some. At the mention of geishas there was a good deal of laughter between him and a couple of secretaries, and much palaver, and then they explained that he took lessons from the girls' drum teacher and sometimes played in the theater orchestra. He played the samisen as well. That day he had canceled his lesson because of the heat and an accumulation of work, but he had said it was because of ill health. "That's why I suggest we go to the theater tomorrow," he said. "If I go today and the teacher sees me how can I explain it?" "Easy," I said. "Famous doctor arrives from New York, cure instantaneous." He laughed, but still clung to the morrow. When he saw us to the door he sank to his knees and dropped back on his heels in the most casual fashion, a mark of courtesy, as he bade us farewell.

In doing a little homework on geishas we discovered there were three degrees. The *maiko*, who are very young, wear exquisite kimonos, and flowers in their hair, and who sing, dance, and converse exclusively. Then come the geishas proper. They are a little older, their clothes are rather simple, they sing, dance, converse, *and* engage in other activities. The third degree is the mothers, who are retired from business and keep a kindly, maternal eye on their young charges. They are cozy madam types. *However*, everyone assured us, just because a fellow had a geisha in his house or in a private room at a restaurant or whatever, we were not to think that carnal commerce was automatic. That was definitely not the case. If the lady doesn't care for the gentleman she simply says no and that's that, and regardless of what he's paid there's no court of appeals. On the other hand it would seem that if a rich patron who subsidizes a geisha asks that she entertain a client whose ideas of entertainment are other than singing, dancing, and conversation, then, out of a simple sense of reciprocity, she may oblige.

Their great appeal besides their talent and looks—most of the ones we saw were pretty—is that they keep their mouths shut, not telling one customer's business to another and not indulging in blackmail. Apparently they work union hours and the wages are good. From 6 P.M. to 11 for just entertainment, a host with three or four guests can easily pay between $200 and $250, and if the geishas do agree to stay the night the price is a great deal higher.

When Mr. Perkins came to pick us up to take us to the theater, he was accompanied by a plump, good-humored Japanese woman we had met at his house, and we drove to a building that was part theater, part restaurant. The auditorium was on one side of a very wide corridor, but it was dark and the bottoms were out of the seats. The performances would start in a couple of months. On the other side of the hall was a pantry and bar, and we went outdoors to a wide wooden terrace overlooking the river and the railroad station on the other side.

Two, three, four young men sat at every table, and at every table was a geisha girl. They all wore kimonos of the same design, white with black butterflies, but their obis were different. Only beer was drunk and only decorum prevailed. No lolling and no arms around the girls. According to Mr. Perkins, the girls would not receive any money for their time and the young men would expect nothing further. This was public relations month, when they created good will and drummed up trade for the theater.

After a few minutes a very pretty and gentle young woman, I should say she was in her early thirties, who knew Mr. Perkins—he was an old friend, a pal who played in the orchestra—came and sat at our table. He, and of course his Japanese companion, could talk to her, but we could not. She must have found us crashing bores, but we would never have known it from her attentive courteous manner and the charming smile that displayed her beautiful teeth.

She had had a great sorrow in her life, for she was truly in love with her patron and was heartbroken when he died. She was intelligent and talented, with a repertoire of four hundred traditional Japanese songs each of which runs an hour in length. Mr. Perkins said with a sigh that he was studying hard but so far knew only thirty-seven. There were one hundred fifteen girls in that particular house or unit, of whom fifteen were *maiko*, the young ones who would make their debuts in the theatrical presentations in October. Some of the more gifted girls appeared on television as well.

It would seem that like the kimono the geisha too is a dying custom. As the average Japanese woman becomes better educated the need for geishas will wither. For hundreds of years they were the cultivated women of Japan. They were accomplished in the arts and many of them became highly knowledgeable about the business and professional worlds, for a man would take his business associates to a geisha house in preference to his own home, knowing that the women there would be more companionable and better informed than his wife.

But times are changing, the women of the East are entering politics and business, and the geishas will probably evolve into singers and dancers and actresses who will lose their professional standing and indulge in carnal commerce only out of love, desire, boredom, status advantage, or financial gain.

Since Mr. Perkins was on a stringent diet he declined our invitation to dinner, but offered to drop us off at an authentic Japanese restaurant. It was the oriental equivalent of Hamburger Heaven, though not so sustaining.

We sat at a scrubbed wooden counter and over a low glass partition watched them preparing raw fish for the other customers. The plump Japanese lady had specified nothing raw for us, so we had little squares of rice accompanied by tidbits we couldn't decipher, then a piece of very good roast pork, then a long wait. Norton, who's a shrimp fiend, drew a little picture of a butterfly shrimp, which just at that moment arrived. He showed his picture to the waiter, who rocked with laughter and passed it up and down the counter. Everybody looked at it, looked at us, and doubled up with joy. We were happy to have supplied so

much gaiety, but, considering the simplicity of the meal and the surroundings, thought the five-dollar tab a little high.

Kyoto is a great sight-seeing center, and among other pilgrimages
Mr. Perkins urged us to make one to Kiyomizu Temple. Composed of
various pavilions, it stands on a high hill commanding a splendid view
over the city. Unfortunately the most insistent objects are the gas tanks,
although there was one group of roofs tiled, peaked, their eaves turned
up like brownies' toes, that had a traditional Old World charm. Also
we were blessed by the day, which while a little hazy was at least sunny
and rain free.

Kiyomizu was founded originally in 805 but today's buildings date
from about 1633, and the central shrine is a four-tiered pagoda representing the four elements, although the Japanese often use five tiers, for
they count the wind an element as well as air, earth, fire, and water.
Near it hangs a round bronze gong with a heavy rope hanging in front
of it. You whack with the rope to make it boom. When Buddhists
pray they simply clasp their hands because the statue of their God is
there, but Shintoists, like Moslems, do not portray God as a human
figure; they therefore clap their hands to attract his attention. In one
of the Kiyomizu shrines are row upon mounting row of Buddha-like
dolls dressed in bright little capes and caps, the clothes of dead children
given by their mothers.

When visiting the temple we stopped off to browse in the shops of
Tea Pot Lane, a street of steep steps, so called because the shops all
specialize in china. We watched a young chap bent over a whirling
potter's wheel, skillfully manipulating the wet clay into pots and
vases. While not so spectacular as the work of the glass blowers of
Venice he was incredibly dexterous, and it was fascinating to see the
rounded shapes forming between his thin hands as the wheel spun.

The day's disappointment came as we crossed the Katsura River.
We had hoped to see the women washing the newly woven textiles and
stretching the lengths along the grassy banks. There is apparently a
mineral in the water that sets the color, and it is a gay sight to see the
brilliant fabrics drying in the sun. Unfortunately the river had been so
muddied by the typhoon that any washing was impossible. The same
thing held true of the cormorant-fishing. We wanted to watch the men
releasing the birds, which dive-bomb the fish but can swallow them
just so far because of a ring around their throats. They return to the
boats and spit them out and the fishermen take them to market. I
should think continual frustration would give the poor birds ulcers—not

to mention the shock to the fish—but cormorants are strong, so they must be fed something, possibly a tithe of what they produce. We didn't see this exhibition of skill and cunning, due again to the waters' being so roiled. It is better to go to Japan in August than not to go at all, but if you have an alternative month, take it. For one thing the gardens will show to better advantage, and Japanese gardens are among the loveliest in the world. We are used to blazing color, and they too, in the spring, have iris and azalea and cherry, and chrysanthemum in the fall, but basically, I should say, Japanese gardens are planned with emphasis on subtlety, if that is not a contradiction in terms. The shape and texture and variety of trees and bushes, the placement of stones, the contour of a lake are factors more important than the massed color of flower beds. And of course they are more enduring, they last the year round.

When possible the Japanese prefer to lay out a garden at the foot of a mountain so that it forms the background; they call it "borrowing the mountain," and it is an intrinsic part of the design. They say of their gardens that they are like the human body; the rocks are the bones, the water blood, and moss and grass the skin.

Many of the ponds and lakes have thick, round steppingstones set in them, and there are also the famous "dry landscapes," areas of sand or gravel raked in geometric patterns bounded by meticulously pruned bushes punctuated, perhaps, by one deliberately placed rock or a path of flat stones. To the untutored eye they seem a little vacant, one must grow accustomed to them, but their appeal, though subtle, is persuasive, and I can well imagine that if one lived in Japan for any length of time they would become immensely satisfying, and exuberant gardens burgeoning with bloom would seem as overstuffed as a Victorian parlor. Like the houses they enhance, the appeal of the gardens is one of simplicity, elimination, and purity of line.

Our first Japanese green and water garden was that of Heian Shrine, with its vermilion columns and large, graveled courtyard, and our first dry one that of Ginkakuji, or the "Silver Pavilion." It is a small, two-story, L-shaped structure and it was the intention of the shogun who built it to cover the whole thing with silver foil so that it would reflect the moonlight. I don't know why this praiseworthy project never developed. Maybe he didn't have the money or maybe he got liquidated by a rival.

The garden is of raked sand, and there are strange mounds of white sand whose meaning is obscure. I was interested to read (at a later date) an article by Christopher Tunnard, professor of city planning at Yale University, who says of them, "[They] are something of a puzzle, even to the initiates of Zen. They have a hard crust and may conceivably have been there since 1479 when the garden was laid out. Were they platforms for moon viewing? Were they piles of sand kept in readiness for covering the paths where royalty came to see the Silver Pavilion? Were they elaborate devices for reflecting moonlight? Were they imitations of snow? Each explanation is plausible but their main interest today is that they are unique in the world of gardening and probably irreplaceable."

From the Silver Pavilion we went on to the gold one, Kinkakuji. Built originally in the fourteenth century, it was destroyed by fire in 1950 so that the present structure is modern but an exact reproduction of the old. Silhouetted against Mount Igasa, it is an airy, square, three-storied pagoda rising from a lake filled with water lilies. Anchored on slender pilings, it seems to float above the water and its own glimmering reflection. The lower wall is white, the upper two covered with gold leaf. It is very pretty but serves no purpose other than an aesthetic one. No religious services are observed there and no tea ceremonies are held, but it is a gratifying source of revenue and tourists, mostly Japanese, flock to see it.

The great gem of Kyoto is Nijo Castle. It was begun by the Shogun Tokugawa Ieyasu in 1603 and is a masterpiece of Japanese architecture. A broad corridor, or veranda, encircles a complex of enormous inner rooms, their walls and sliding panels of gold leaf painted with dark green pines and fantastic tigers and birds. The transoms are teakwood, solid blocks carved on one side with peacocks and peahens and on the other with peonies. Hammered and intricately traced brass plates on beams and uprights, decorative in themselves, conceal nails and joints underneath them. The public rooms are of strong and startling design, while the private apartments allotted to wives and concubines are softer and more intimate in feeling.

Sliding paper and wood screens along the corridor open onto a magnificent garden of water and rock arrangements. It is the oldest castle garden in Japan, was designed by Kano Tanyu, a famous artist, and dates from about 1626.

The corridor is floored with highly polished boards. They looked very handsome but squeaked as we walked along, like the new French shoes of my Paris school days. Norton and I, as visitors from a foreign land, didn't like to criticize, but we did murmur under our breath, "It's lasted but it's jerry-built." Baby informed us otherwise. "It squeak on purpose. Is called nightingale floor but does not sound like," and she laughed merrily. The idea behind the squeak was ingenious enough. The boards were deliberately laid to protest under the tread of anyone approaching, and the sound would alert the shogun and his entourage so that no enemy could creep up unobserved to plunge a snickersnee into an un-protected back. This was particularly important for those in the fourth room of a Japanese house. This number, for centuries, has signified death. Today hotels, for practical reasons, are beginning to override the supersitition, but hospitals never put a patient in Room No. 4, just as in many of our office and apartment buildings there is no thirteenth floor. I've never understood who's fooling whom in this nonsense gam-bit, but I realize that it's widespread and popular.

After our day's sight-seeing we dined cozily in our hotel room on an excellent tempura prepared by our kneeling maid as we sat at our low table. The Japanese have a proverb about crawling around the room all day, and it has the same connotation as our "Woman's work is never done." I don't know why they fancy the floor so passionately. Maybe because they are a comparatively short race with short legs and it's easier for them to sink to their knees than it is for us, but anyway much of their furniture is built proportionately and their door handles are set low in their frames to facilitate access.

Some of their habits are catching though. For one who wasn't going to have any part of Japanese shenanigans, geishas and kimonos and such, the doctor, I noticed, seemed quite content to relax in his robe, a white one with charcoal blocks and a tobacco-colored sash, reading and taking an occasional pull on the Asahi. The long kimono sleeves he found very handy for his pipe and tobacco pouch. He never got to the point of venturing out of doors in it, which I regretted, as I would have liked to have a picture of him looming out of the mist that was our faithful companion on all but a few days of our stay, silhouetted against the ordered pines and rocks of a Japanese garden.

One of the most famous and beautiful of the gardens is Katsura. To visit it, one must apply for tickets through the Imperial Household Agency, and it is better to do so in advance, as there are only two tours a day, at eleven and one-thirty, and only thirty people are allowed in at a time, a wise ruling but one that caused us a spot of difficulty. When we came along, tickets in hand, twenty-nine had already been admitted to the gatehouse. We were two and that made thirty-one; however, as we had on matching wedding rings and Baby vouched for

our characters they agreed to make an exception this once, and we were passed as a unit into the magic precincts.

The Katsura Garden surrounds what is referred to as the Detached Palace. The architecture is similar to that of Nijo, but smaller and more intimate. The landscaping, done by Enshu Kobori around 1630, is very lovely with ponds and little islands, rivulets and miniature promontories and stone lanterns. There are four teahouses for the four seasons, with benches outside, sheltered by roofs of bamboo thatch, where one is supposed to sit and relax until he has achieved a contemplative mood for the tea ceremony.

We were in Japan for three weeks and never attended one. Thinking back on our negligence, I don't understand it, but possibly they were never going on when we were around or maybe we never got relaxed enough.

Despite the bad day, not raining but overcast, hot, and humid, we enjoyed Katsura. It is truly a delight. The thing that today evokes it most vividly for me is not a mossy bank or the scent of pine trees, but the smell of citronella. This is due to Baby, who was obsessed with the notion that her native land abounded in mosquitoes, and drenched herself for protection. We never suffered so much as one sting, but we suffered fairly intensively from the overpowering aroma of our little guide. She even put it on when we were going inside to visit the Ori-Dono Textile Gallery. This is an entrancing shop in a house built around a beautiful garden dating from the same period as the Katsura Garden and designed by the same man. There were some exquisite brocades and embroidered organdies and silks. I refrained from purchase, having reached my limit in Bangkok and Hong Kong, and the saleswoman said wistfully, "Oh, you've already been there." Had I known about Ori-Dono I would have held back a little, for it is a treasure house. I do not understand the Paris *couturiers'* not having bought fabrics from them, but the saleswoman had never heard of Dior, Balenciaga, et Compagnie.

We watched a man weaving a narrow strip of brocade meant for an evening bag. It was intricate and beautiful and required skill and endless patience. Under strands of silk drawn taut on a loom is a thin piece of paper on which is sketched the design to be followed. He weaves through the warp with a bobbin of colored silk and then draws the strand down into place with his fingernails that are kept especially long for the task. An experienced man can weave about two inches a day. Despite the satisfaction he must derive from his handiwork it is a constricted life, and blindness must be an occupational affliction, so that, humanely speaking, I suppose one must hope that the profession is on the wane, but, humanely speaking, one may be forgiven for regretting the demise of a lovely art.

I passed up the silk, but purchases we did make in Kyoto were scrolls, prints, and decorative trays. It is also the place to buy wood-block prints. We saw some old ones that were enchanting in color and design and I would recommend the Uchida Woodblock Printing Company in Marutamachi Street, Kawaramachinishi.

So far, with the exception of the weather, our Japanese interlude had been purring along like a plump-bellied kitten, but perfection, alas, is transitory and infrequent. We awoke one morning to find our maid, she of the dazzling smile, kneeling before our mats, her forehead touching the floor, imparting the information that "guide Yokoyama sick." Norton and I looked at each other and our hearts sank. As we spoke no word of Japanese, what would we do without our staff, short to be sure, but staunch as oak? "Maybe we're misunderstanding her," I said, "maybe she thinks the English word sick means something else."

"She sure as hell doesn't think it means well and happy," said the doctor, and he was right. As far as the maid was concerned, Dr. Brown San had proved himself Marcel Marceau with his pantomime about the inadequacy of his bed. It was a form of communication between them, and she was now clasping her brow, cushioning her cheek on her hand, rubbing her stomach, and groaning. Baby was sick, all right, and the message was coming through clear as a bell.

"You're the boy with the mask and drums," I said, "want to go see her?"

"Not I," said my loved one. "I don't know the procedure around here and I don't want her thinking that just because we won the war I assume Japanese doctors are no good."

"But maybe she hasn't seen one."

"Look, she's a very intelligent little cooky. I don't doubt for a minute that a doctor's been to see her. She knows enough to tell them to send for one."

"But likely he's a quack."

"Why should you think that? Go up and have a look at her."

"Me! I'm not a doctor."

"You're a woman, as I have reason to know. Go upstairs and see what this gaggle of hens is up to."

"To hear is to obey, Doctor San." I went. There, on her mat, and it truly was a mat, not gussied up with cushions for the foreign trade, lay prostrate Baby. The poor little soul was obviously wretched and told me that the night before she had fallen down and now could not stand without feeling giddy and nauseated. Yes, she said in response to my question, a doctor had been to see her. Had he taken her temperature? No. Quack, I snorted inwardly. Armed with Norton's props, I took it. He was considerately traveling with a flat thermometer with red mercury so I was able to read it. Normal. This was deflating. Maybe the Japanese doctor was a reasonably astute diagnostician? Sometimes medical men can sense these things. I remembered Norton, the most thorough of men, telling me that when a new patient walks into his office, between the threshold and the chair in front of his desk he can usually assess, to some extent, what the trouble is likely to be. Maybe allee samee Japan?

Baby had already been in touch with the Tokyo office and another guide was on his way. She assured me that we were not to worry, she had many friends in Kyoto, would be well looked after, and would join us, she hoped, tomorrow. If not in a few days.

Norton went up to say good-by to her and returned with the opinion that, while the illness was genuine, he suspected that her misery was largely psychosomatic. "Our first night here," he said, "the fiasco bus tour upset her terribly. She felt it was all her fault or that at any rate we would think so and blame her. She's been in a tizzy ever since and what with running around and the heat and maybe something she ate . . . anyway, don't fret. She'll live."

She did and we later joined forces, and how we appreciated her! The guide sent from Tokyo by the Japan Travel Bureau to take her place was an elderly gent, a tedious, platitudinous, name-dropping old bore we couldn't stand.

Our first goal under his guidance, however, was something of a show stopper: Sanjusangendo, the Hall of Thirty-three Ken, so called because of the thirty-three spaces between the pillars of a long, narrow pavilion erected in 1266, which means it has achieved an age extraordinary in a country where the wooden structures are frequently destroyed by fire and earthquakes, though we were to come to a still-older one. The temple was erected to Kannon, goddess of mercy. She is an enormous Buddha figure of gold-painted wood seated on a lotus blossom and her outstanding characteristic is her one thousand hands. The primary pair, with arms attached to the shoulders in the conventional way, is joined in prayer. Then from behind her back, forming an enormous sort of round fan, sprout the remaining, so we were told, we didn't count, nine hundred ninety-eight.

This is a curious enough conceit, but the viewer is bowled over by the gigantic phalanx of one thousand and one standing figures, each, save for its upright position, a replica of the great mother—a statue of gilded, carved wood with a spiked halo, two hands clasped in front, and, to be sure, a more modest number of hands and arms, only four-teen in all, flaring from its shoulder blades. The figures stand in rising ranks ten deep and one hundred long, with an extra one for good measure. Kannon cures mental diseases, and since the emperor who ordered the thronging company was off his rocker the affinity is under-standable.

Despite the opulence such unbridled repetition seems a little absurd, yet there is in it something curiously pathetic too. Possibly the emperor had lucid moments when he realized his mind was deranged. One god-dess could not cure him, but maybe he had not tried hard enough. If he ordered ten, one hundred, one thousand goddesses to be carved, together they would be strong enough to rescue him. I should like to have known more about him, a wistful, desperate man.

Ranged about the shrine are twenty-eight other carved statues, sup-posedly the followers of mercy, but they are all of a furious and menac-ing aspect.

Our next stop en route to Nara was the Todai-ji Temple, dating, in its present tense—there were earlier manifestations—from 1708. It is the largest wooden structure in the world—for those who relish statis-tics 160 feet high, 187 long, and 166 wide—and houses Daibutsu, the largest bronze statue in the world. If you count the thick, cushiony lotus blossom on which he is seated, and you might as well, he is 71 feet 6 inches high and weights 500 metric tons.

There's a square hole in the bottom of one of the wooden columns supporting the temple, and through it a whole string of little boys were wriggling one after the other. The attraction of the hole is that it is the size of one of Buddha's nostrils. Personally I doubted it, as the nose is only one foot six inches long and the hole looked to me bigger than a nostril could be. Norton says I'm a cynic. I'm not a cynic, I'm a skeptic.

Nara, some twenty-six miles south of Kyoto, was the capital of Japan even before Kyoto and is noteworthy today for its lovely wooded park and Kasuga Shrine. The park abounds in awful little souvenir shops, but tame deer come up to you to be fed and that part is delightful, but I was miserable because in a small, low enclosure was a little kitten who was being tormented by a monkey on a chain. It wasn't that the monkey was so big or cruel but he'd grab hold of the kitten in a relentless search for fleas and pull his fur, and the poor little thing was crying and couldn't escape, while the Japanese stood around laughing. I complained a good deal about that, and when we came back from feeding the deer I was happy to see that both kitten and monkey had been removed and, I could only hope, separated. The owners, seeing us return, had doubtless muttered, "Here comes that nutty American dame. Let's scram."

The Shinto shrine of Kasuga is a beauty. It is painted a bright vermilion that somehow—perhaps it had weathered more—was more appealing than the kitchen red of the Golden Dragon in Taipei and is surrounded by three thousand lanterns presented by the faithful. About half the lanterns swing from the eaves of the various buildings, the other half are stone, their carved and curious shapes, some quite lovely, clustered along the temple paths.

There is a graceful five-tiered pagoda near the hotel, its reflection piercing the lake, and the night we were there a festival was in progress and gay lanterns were strung along the shore.

The hotel itself from the outside is picturesque with its lilting, fluted, peaked roof and smooth façade, and one is eager to get to it. Inside, shock value. Pure Ulysses S. Grant *cum* Theodore Roosevelt: walls stretched with cut velvet, brown fretted woodwork, fat plush armchairs and sofas and a snowstorm of white crocheted antimacassars. In its own way it's kind of wonderful.

The ceilings are high and the electric fans efficient. We had a large suite, grander than we had anticipated or reserved, but they said it was what was available. The living room and bedroom were separated by a fancy wooden grille, and the bathroom was American except that the plumbing didn't work. We sent for the room boy and demonstrated our problem. He grinned happily. "All hotel like that. Water stay. No plessure."

The Japanese and Chinese interchange of R and L takes getting used to. Just as you think to pounce on the use of one letter, the other pops out in an unexpected place. You cross from Hong Kong to Kowloon on the Star felly, but a girl named Helen is called Heren. Man, a creature of instinct, is partry good and partry bad. The arried victoly of the rast war seems to cause more admilation than lesentment, and there is no plessure in the plessure tank. But what can you do? That's rife.

The hotel dining room maintained the architectural tradition and was cavernous and ornate, but the food was respectable. Dismay set in later on. The so fragile, the so pretty paper lanterns we had noticed along the lake shore portended no good. There was indeed a festival going on, a sort of water frolic, seemingly innocent until we retired and its full impact broke upon our ears. The voices of those calling the boats into position for every race were amplified through a loudspeaker until we thought we'd go crazy. Great bellowing squawks reverberated across the water, beat their way up the hillside and into our bedroom windows.

A call downstairs to the desk elicited the information that the crackling commands of the games master would surely stop at ten o'clock. It was then ten minutes to ten, so we shut up. At ten minutes to eleven it was still going on. I called down again. This time *my* roar was enough to blanket that from the lake, and seconds later silence fell on Nippon.

Before quitting Nara the next morning we tried to telephone Baby back in Kyoto. The distance was only about twenty-six miles, but the service was that of Monaco at the time of the wedding. We waited over an hour and then gave up.

Fortunately we had been released from our dreary old boy bore and a nice little woman named Kay guided us onward to the Horyu-ji Temple. Just as the Todai-ji is supposedly the largest wooden structure in the world, so is Horyu-ji the oldest, dating from 607.

The temple encompasses in all some forty structures, of which the octagonal Hall of Dreams, with its seamed roof of convex, lead-colored tiles, is probably the most picturesque. It houses an exquisitely graceful statue, a Korean wood carving, another version of Kannon, the goddess of mercy. She is lovely, tall, and very slender, with ribbonlike draperies dropping from her arms and curling about her feet. There was also a bronze statue of the goddess to whom one prays to turn bad dreams to good. What an enviable gift.

We enjoyed Nara and its environs and all that we saw there was rewarding, but it is wiser to make one's headquarters in Kyoto and radiate from there rather than go to the extra expense and fatigue of packing and unpacking for the sake of a night at the Nara Hotel, piquant though the furnishings be. All the temples and shrines I have mentioned—Sanjusangendo, Todai-ji with the colossal Daibutsu Buddha, the Kasuga Shrine, the park of Nara, even Horyu-ji Temple, only a few miles farther along the road to Osaka—can be visited in a day. It would be a full one to be sure, but with a reasonably early start, bright eyes, and a receptive mind it would be possible to savor the beauty and bizarre charm of all these monuments and still not be the comical American tourist of legend who rushes through the galleries of Europe and Asia, his nose in the guidebook. Or, if interested in pushing on from Kyoto, bid the native inn good-by and head for Osaka, taking in the sights en route. Obviously, if going the other way, reverse the itinerary.

Bidding the inn good-by, incidentally, is a nostalgic experience full of the old *sayonara* charm. The whole staff comes to the door to wish you Godspeed and they do not do it with outstretched palms. They seem genuinely sorry that you are leaving and urge you to a speedy return. We spent only three nights at the Tawaraya, but we left with a tug of the heartstrings.

Osaka is very different from Kyoto, different from Tokyo, too, but it's a good city: big, lusty, industrial—the Barcelona and Chicago of Japan. There's lots of night life, big cabarets, restaurants, and stores. Also it has one of the most famous puppet theaters in the world, but, in August, it was unfortunately closed.

Osaka is ugly because it's industrial and gives rise to melancholy reflections on how unfortunate it is that industry, which enables so many to have a so much more comfortable life, obliges them to live that life in surroundings totally devoid of charm, surroundings that can only cause them to say, "How can I most quickly get away from this place where I am earning all this money?"

One of the virtues of a big city, however, is apt to be the food. In the grill of the Grand Hotel we ate one of the best lunches we had had in all Asia.

Leaving the lobby afterward, we were sidetracked by a rustling of flowers, a twittering of birds. A group of geishas, they were very young, I think they must have been *maiko*, came hurrying in giggling and chatting. Not only were they in beautiful kimonos and obis, their faces and the backs of their necks were whitewashed, and they wore their hair in the high, formal lacquered manner. We gathered they had come to entertain a convention of Japanese businessmen. We watched them for a few minutes and then left the hotel, the doctor on notably reluctant feet.

We were going to Kobe because we were on our way to Hiroshima via a cruise on the Inland Sea, but Kobe as a city is drab and dreary and the road between Osaka and it one of unrelieved ugliness, a long, unbroken industrial belt the entire way.

We found our surroundings so depressing that they caused us to

cancel our plan of going to Hiroshima. We had wanted to see it because of its historic value, but it has been rebuilt and we were told
that it is one more industrial city without any features of specific interest to the traveler. Another Kobe didn't seem worth the long trip
required to get there. Our one regret was missing Miyajima, a small
offshore island that is supposedly very beautiful, one of the scenic trio
of Japan, the other two being Amanohashidate, not far from Kyoto,
and Matsushima, near Sendai.

We went to the Japan Travel Bureau to arrange for a rerouting of
our itinerary, skipping Hiroshima, and then, having little to do, wandered about the city looking for a sustaining bottle. A man at the
Travel Agency had said, so we thought, "Go to the so-called department store." I considered him a sophisticate languishing in the prov-
inces far from Tokyo. "Oh, Brother! The kind of merchandise *they*
have," I imagined him saying, had he been more familiar with the
American idiom. What he had actually said was, "Go to the Sogo Department Store." That was its name. Unfortunately it was closed. We
wandered through a long shopping arcade and came upon a Japanese
product called Hermes Gin. We were tempted but refrained, and ten
minutes' further search brought us smack up against a bottle of Gordon's. We concluded that we lived right and snapped it up.

Traveler's Tip No. 24: Carry one or two small bottles or flasks with
you. Plastic ones are the lightest, but sometimes they affect the taste
of liquor, especially scotch, yet you will need some container in which
to pour the residue from a large bottle when it is too much to leave
behind and not enough to make toting the parent bottle worth while.

In the evening we got in touch with a Dr. Monkichi Namba, a
friend of our pal Paul Fejos in Austria. The doctor was the president
of Kobe University for Women, eighteen hundred students, and although he had already dined he came to our hotel and guided us to a
very good restaurant where we ate a toothsome Kobe steak, one that
had been most lovingly massaged, while he himself downed a repulsive-
looking orangeade dear to the Japanese stomach. He knew the United
States and spoke with enthusiasm of the university he had attended for
a year, "Hairbairt." It took us a minute or two to work that around to
Harvard, but it created a bond because Peter, Norton's younger son,
was there, so we had a rooting interest.

"Back to the mats!" cried the doctor when on waking the next morning he consulted our itinerary and discovered we would be spending

the night at another Japanese inn, this one in Takamatsu, on the island of Shikoku.

With no regret at all we bade farewell to dreary Kobe and boarded the boat, the *Otowa Maru* (*maru* means "steamship"), for our trip through the Inland Sea. The boat, though small, was not uncomfortable. It was not very clean, either—that is to say, the decks and public rooms weren't—but we had a pleasant cabin with fresh tatami on the floor and mats on which to relax. I napped and read Mitchner's *Return to Paradise*, which I had missed when it first appeared, but Norton spent most of the day on deck. He loves the sea, even after sixteen months in the Pacific during the war he hasn't had enough of it, and the weather, for a glorious change, was bright and sunny. The deck space was cramped, however, and I should say that on that ship, even though the voyage was only a few hours, a cabin was imperative for comfort, but we learned that the line was building a new vessel to be ready in 1960 that would make the Osaka-Hiroshima run in about twelve hours. It should be a pleasant trip.

There were a few French passengers on board and a horde of Italians, the Italian Press Club on an Asiatic junket. We stopped briefly at a pretty island, Shodo-shima, and then went on to the port of Takamatsu, where we put up at the Tokiwa Honkan Hotel. It is a native inn, but after the unpretentious, genuine little Tawaraya the public rooms had a certain chop-suey grandeur that we found suspect. In the heart of Japan it seemed about as Japanese as the butterfly shrimps of a Howard Johnson restaurant.

The approach to our rooms was over vermilion bridges arching above small ponds in which darted large goldfish. The hotel boasts nineteen rooms in all, three Western, sixteen Japanese. We were first-floor-Japanese types; tatami matting, low lacquered table, back and armrests, antimacassars. Less convenient than the Tawaraya, it had no desk and no writing table. We looked out on a lanai or tiny, narrow garden; a little lane, really, with slim bamboo trees growing against the wooden wall, a narrow flowing stream, and small steppingstones.

We dropped our bags and set off by car to the *raison d'être* of the Takamatsu stopover, the Yashima plateau, a thousand-foot eminence that one ascends by cable car. It is very steep and I am afraid of cable cars—I have Newton and his basic law ever in mind—but there are times when fear is preferable to exercise. Holding our breath, or at any rate me holding mine, we ground up the face of the cliff, to be greeted at the top by cheerful, grinning bearers of bamboo palanquins equipped with scarlet cushions. They were charmingly picturesque, but, having reclined all day on the boat, I gathered myself into one only long enough for Norton to take a picture and tip the men for posing at the end of their poles while I sat enthroned. We then set off on foot, following the winding path that ended abruptly as the promontory dropped to the sea. The view out over the water was magnificent. At the foot of our towering cliff stretched the salt flats and the harbor, from which rose another mountainous island. The sun setting in a bank of clouds was reflected on the water as on a gleaming sheet of steel. The film in Norton's camera was running low and in the failing light he didn't want to take too many pictures for fear of wasting it. He posed me against the awe-inspiring backdrop of sea, sky, and mountain, clicked once or twice, and remarked briskly, "Well, let's not waste any more film." My tactful love.

Back at the cable-car station was a television set. The reception on the mountaintop was exceptionally good, and while waiting for the car to arrive at the pinnacle of its long ascent we watched a program. Japanese actors in native costume were performing a tense drama. A beautiful maiden was beseeching a mean-looking guy to grant her request —probably to lift the mortgage. When he remained adamant she went into a room and drew the sliding, transparent-paper panel behind her. Silhouetted against the light, she was an easy target. The mean-looking guy outside drew his gun, leveled, and ventilated her. The dastard! She dropped like a partridge. It was terrific. Eastern-Western.

On returning to our hotel for dinner we learned that the splendors of the be-chromed and lacquered dining room were to be denied us. The large Italian Press Club had descended upon the hotel and its facilities were overtaxed. "If you do not mind, sir, madam, will please dine private rooms? That way no waiting." We did not mind.

We bathed, donned our kimonos, and at precisely seven forty-five, as we had requested, dinner was brought in by two maids, one in kimono, one in Western dress with glasses and a phalanx of false teeth. The service was excellent but the food lamentable. We didn't have the heart to complain, however, as the poor little things seemed to be run ragged by the influx of Italians, who, somewhat to our surprise, also descended upon us.

As we sat cross-legged on the floor eating from our low table, about a dozen of them, in kimonos, passed our window. It was a large sheet of glass, floor to ceiling, and we were sitting close to it, so it was almost as though they were in the room.

They were exploring the little passagelike garden and were obviously as surprised to see us as we were to see them. A couple of them waved in rather self-conscious fashion and the long single file passed from view. Norton and I went on eating. Moments later they were back. The tiny garden ended just beyond the wall of our room in a dead end. There was nothing for them to do but return the way they had come. This, however, they found embarrassingly intimate so they filed back Indian fashion, stepping high on each stone in the little stream, facing the board wall rather than look into the room in the vain hope that if they didn't see us we wouldn't be able to see them. They were rather large Italians and their Japanese kimonos flapped around their calves, and Norton and I got to choking over our tempura, and the little maids, while clucking in distress over this invasion of our privacy, began rolling about helplessly on the tatami, convulsed between their concern and hysterical laughter.

It wasn't only Italians who were trooping in. The tourist trade is flourishing in Japan. So much so that the Tokiwa Honkan Hotel was building an annex to accommodate the overflow of guests, although, besides the superb view from the plateau and a pretty park, the city has little to offer the transient visitor.

The park contains a charming, irregular lake with a deeply indented shore line and lovely trees. There is also a zoo of mangy aspect.

Our luncheon in the hotel dining room the next day was extremely good, a great improvement over dinner the night before, for the Italian Press Club had departed and we were the only people there, and the cook's attention was focused upon us exclusively. On the way to the boat that was to take us back to Osaka, Norton said, "Want to bet? We may be the only people on board." He surprised me. "But surely," I murmured, "the natives, don't they travel?" They do. They came surging up the gangplank in battalions, and when we pulled alongside the pier at Shodo-shima, what looked to be about a thousand Japanese kids streamed aboard. They were all carrying weighty knapsacks, wearing shirts and arm bands emblazoned with "Camp Yoshima" and "Y.M.C.A.," and sporting vaguely sombrero-like straw hats. Paper streamers appeared from nowhere, and we were tethered to the shore by countless colored ribbons, vermilion and crimson, green and blue and yellow.

It was like the old days of the great transatlantic sailings, when a trip to Europe was a voyage and not a meal in the sky, when there were delirious farewell parties where champagne flowed and departing passengers were bombarded with telegrams, baskets of fruit, forests of flowers, and heavy libraries of light reading matter and more than one well-wisher had to be smuggled off with the pilot.

One tragedy marred our departure. One sombrero overboard. Shrieks of woe from the bereft cowboy. I went down to our cabin to catch up on my diary, but I could hear the children singing on deck. When we arrived at Kobe most of them debarked. Masses of parents were waiting on the pier, pointing out their own children, laughing, jumping up and down in delight at seeing them, but when they actually met the mothers and fathers merely patted them on the shoulder or shook hands. Apparently Japanese do not kiss very much in any event and not at all in public.

Back at the Grand Hotel in Osaka we found Baby waiting for us, looking a little pale but feeling ever so much better. We said good-by to Kay, who had been an able, nice little soul but without the appeal of General Mouse.

That night we dined, admirably, in the grill and the next morning flew back to Tokyo in an hour and forty-five minutes, via Japan Air Lines.

In the afternoon we went to see our second all-girl show, Kokusai Gekijo. Those whose birthdays, like mine, coincide with the War of 1812—may remember New York's Hippodrome and the big thrill when ravishing damsels on horseback descended a flight of shallow steps and kept on going, horse and girl, right down into a big pool of water until even the tops of their heads disappeared. *That* was living! Where is the thrill today that can equal it? I'll tell you. At the Kokusai Gekijo. That finale would have Billy Rose gasping. The scene is one wild glitter and roar of leaping, splashing fountains and a pounding waterfall, plunging and foaming across the entire width of an enormous stage. The audience yells. Zowie! There isn't any question, though, that the customers need something this spectacular to take their minds off the entertainment that has preceded it. Les Girls are not good. Scarcely a pretty face in the lot, and those legs! "Remind me of potatoes," said the doctor. There was a long line of precision dancers composed of rugged individualists, and a lot of recorded singing on a blaring sound track. As at the Takarazuka Revue the leading men were girls, the star a big, robust Lesbian with lacquered haircut like a man's and thick hips.

The star turn was a song and dance act performed by eight girls, "The exotic peaches cream of the Kokusai lovelies take to pirating to

capture your heart." They had cute pirate costumes, too; the briefest
of skirts cut in points, high-heeled boots coming to the knees, and pi-
ratical hats turned up in front with skull and crossbones.

The spectacular aquatic finale was preceded by an enjoyable scene
of pure delirium that took place in an Italianate square with the entire
cast in wildly garbled costumes of every period and nation belting out
"Funiculi, Funicula."

It was too bad there was such an air of absurdity about the proceedings, because they work unremittingly and spend a packet producing
four shows a year and giving three performances a day seven days a
week. A performance runs about an hour and a half without intermission.

Returning from the theater to the hotel, we once again underwent
Ordeal Japanese Taxicab. Having experienced Paris, Rome, and our incomparable Albert in Lisbon, Norton and I thought we were pretty
seasoned. We had got a bit complacent, the hair-raising taxicabs of the
world we had had; there was little anybody could tell us about *those*.
How true it is that pride goeth before a fall. We spoke loudly, we were
puffed up, we flaunted our hairbreadth escapes, and we got our come-
uppance. All our experience had been B.T., Before Tokyo, and we were
babes in the woods. Talking it over after our first jet propulsions from
the launching pad, Norton and I concluded that our original impression was wrong. The drivers weren't escapees from the city lunatic
asylum as we had assumed, they were the leftover kamikaze pilots of
the war, those who had taken the oath to hurl their planes and themselves straight into the American carriers, ending all in one vast *Göt-
terdämmerung* explosion. The scheme had fouled when they ran out
of fuel or something, but their spirit was unimpaired, and they were
now driving cabs in their capital city and would soon achieve eternal
life among their honorable ancestors.

Their arrow flight, splitting two cars ahead of them with an eighteenth of an inch to spare on either side, the headlong lunges at brick
walls executed with ecstatic abandon, the way two cabs going in opposite directions at eighty-five miles an hour magnetized each other so
there was only a breath before crashing head-on—all this so unnerved
me that I sank to the floor of the taxi and crouched there, eyes tight
shut, whimpering with fear.

The Japanese drivers' behavior in motion is all the more unexpected
because when stationary they seem amiable enough chaps who devote
a good deal of time to housekeeping. Every driver has at least one

feather duster, the more meticulous have two, and they are forever
flicking away specks of soot and polishing the hacks till they shine.
We decided it must be that they wanted to make a good impression on
honorable ancestor, who, given their determination, might be only a
fare away.

The taxi tariff by the way starts at sixty, eighty, or a hundred yen,
depending on the size car you get. A guidebook put out by the Travel
Bureau, called "Your Travel Companion in Japan," states with admirable candor, "For tourists who prefer careful driving . . . hire car service is recommended."

Mostly, however, the Japanese are skillful craftsmen and artisans—
come right down to it, I don't suppose it's *skill* the drivers lack, merely
a sense of self-preservation—and everything they do with their hands
they do well, including hairdressing.

In Tokyo I went to a salon called Arden, Arden Yamanaka in the
Nikkatsu Arcade. Elizabeth would probably not be pleased, but they
were pretty good. Trim, shampoo, rinse, set, manicure, yen 1250, or
about $3.50.

When I had finished I was some time getting away, as the proprietress of the salon, kimono-clad, and a gentleman—I gathered a business
acquaintance—were taking leave of each other in the doorway. In
Japan in polite society this is not done quickly. None of that "So long,
be seeing you" stuff. It is a matter of an exchange of compliments and
much bowing. The gentleman would bow deeply and the lady would
bow in return. Since obviously he couldn't allow a woman to outrank
him in courtesy the man would then bow again whereupon the lady,
recognizing the lordly male, would, in her turn, bow even deeper. This
went on for a good three minutes. I don't know what finally stopped
them; I imagine the clockwork ran down.

That night Norton and I were dining at a highly recommended
restaurant, Happo-En, at Shiro-Gane-Machi, Minato-Ku. Japanese addresses kill me. They kill the Japanese, too, who realize that they go
on and on and who think they're ridiculous. Japanese, while doubtless
filled with poetry, seems to be an involuted, somewhat long-winded
tongue. When the stewardess in the plane on our flight back from
Osaka had talked for quite a while, I asked Kay what she had said.
"Nothing," replied our guide with the gesture of one struggling with
a nonsensical burden, "absolutely nothing. What she mean in effect
is 'fasten seat belts.'"

In any event Happo-En was set in one of the two beautiful gardens we saw in Tokyo; the other one was also a restaurant. There used to be many great gardens in the city, but much of the beauty that had endured for years, sometimes for centuries, that had taken many lifetimes of love and care and knowledge to bring to fruition, had been ravaged by the war.

At Happo-En there are dwarf trees of silver fir varying from two hundred to five hundred years in age. There are great pines and thirty stone lanterns, one known to be eight hundred years old. There is a thousand-year-old pagoda and one of thirteen stones, or tiers, and herons and teal return to the ponds season after season and kites nest in the tallest trees. The restaurant itself was once a private house, the only really big house we saw in Tokyo. There are doubtless many, but we, alas, did not know their owners. The rooms, their beauty derived from proportion and a sense of space, had a quality of light and airiness enhanced by their sliding walls, which, pushed back, framed the green trees and sloping lawns. It was, we decided, an ideal place for a party and we wished we had more Tokyo friends and were staying a little longer so we might organize a gala.

As we dined we were surrounded by pretty bowing kimonos quick to anticipate our wants, but the food, a sort of barbecue dish, after exotic hors d'oeuvres of celery, tomato, and Kraft cheese, was only fair and cold to boot. Before that party we would certainly have to have a conference with the chef.

As far as Norton was concerned the flavor of the food wasn't helped any by his state of health. The poor chap had a cold and was feeling like the devil. It seemed to have started via sinus and hay fever possibly contracted while sleeping on the mats on the tatami. It is, after all, vegetable matter and some people are susceptible.

So wretched did he feel in fact that the next day he decided he would not go to Nikko, but urged me to go anyway, with Baby, as we had planned. It was a sorry loss for Nikko Castle is one of the splendors of Japan. It is situated in Nikko National Park, a vast area encompassing 206,665 acres of mountains, woodland, lakes and waterfalls about two hours from Tokyo by train. It is a pretty route past rice fields starred with white herons and up into the mountains.

Baby and I took an early train, 8:40 A.M., and had comfortable reclining seats. I prized a slip of paper that, referring to a guidebook of Nikko, urged us to "Please order it to the waitress in this romance car." It seemed the least we could do.

At Nikko an avenue of ancient cedars leads to the great central temple of Toshogu. The trees were planted at the time the shrine was built by the same shogun who inhabited Nijo Castle in Kyoto. I suppose he had his shortcomings, but he was certainly a man of taste who also kept his eye on the kitty. His warriors were expected to contribute heavily to the new temple—politics then were no different from politics today—but one fellow simply couldn't ante up, he had no money. However, feeling it the better part of prudence to do his bit, over twenty-four years he planted forty thousand cryptomeria trees along twenty-five miles of highway. Today more than three hundred years later, seventeen thousand of them still stand.

Toshogu reminded me of Bangkok. The silhouette is very different and there are no broken bits of china and mirror, but, like Bangkok, architecturally speaking, something is going on every minute. It is an ecstatic triumph of Japanese rococo and baroque. The temple complex is composed of twenty-three buildings in a twenty-two-acre enclosure planted with huge, dense cryptomeria trees, and the predominating colors are the gray of the tiled roofs, the white and vermilion of the columns, and the gold of the ornamentation. The entire effect is thick, glowing, and indescribably rich. The Yomei-mon, the principal portal, is known either as the Twilight Gate, because you stand, lost in admiration of it, till sunset, or, in the same vein, the Gate Where One Waits All Day, the delay to be ascribed not to a lethargic ticket taker but rather to the beauty of the edifice, which is so intricately carved with such wealth of detail and proliferation of flora and fauna that it takes all day to assimilate it. White curly gargoyles peer from under the tilting, fluted eaves, which are supported by chunky golden leaves as many-layered as a strudel but thick instead of paper thin. Golden wind bells pendent from the corners swing in the breeze, and the whole affair is an exuberant yet disciplined eruption of deeply indented carving, sculpture and fretwork.

Branching out on either side of the Yomei-mon are galleries or corridors of breath-taking splendor. They are about 665 feet long, the solid wall of the building on one side, round columns on the other opening onto a courtyard, the whole—wall, floor, ceiling, columns—painted with cinnabar, or dragon's blood, a rich vermilion lacquer. At the top of the wall, adjoining the ceiling, is a deeply carved and gilded border.

One approaches the entrance gate by a long, wide alley and broad, shallow steps arched by the torii gate that is the tallest stone Shinto shrine in Japan, embellished by stone lanterns and a vermilion and gray, five-storied pagoda. The gate itself is guarded by hideous red

Vasiliv

demons—the one on the right has his mouth open, the left one's mouth is closed. The open mouth signifies the Word, as in Christianity: "In the beginning was the Word, and the Word was with God." The closed mouth is the end, Silence. Considering the profound and serene philosophy they symbolize, I do not know why they carve the demons with such ferocious and furious expressions. They are really quite alarming.

The Sacred Stable, off to one side, is a lovely little building with a gold-bedizened and tiled pitched roof, its smooth façade of satiny gray wood ornamented with gold-studded crossbars and a carved, painted frieze involving water-lily pads, leaves, peonies, and the famous monkey trio See No Evil, Hear No Evil, Speak No Evil. The monkeys have round white faces, white waistcoats, and warm brown fur, and there is a good deal more to the legend than just that one group. There is a whole philosophic cycle of monkey and, *ergo*, human life.

There are eight frames in all, and as they have considerable charm I enumerate them. The first one shows a mother monkey, her baby beside her, shielding her eyes with her paw as she looks into the future of her child. Then comes the famous three of See, Hear, and Speak No Evil, ending with the admonition "and grow gently." Number Three, a solitary monkey, "When alone look around carefully for the way one wishes to follow." Number Four, a pair of the boys are peering upward from under carved branches—"The higher one seeks the more he wants; know when to stop wanting beyond one's needs." In the fifth frame a highly perched monkey is looking out over two rather stooped and downcast characters, and we are exhorted to be kind and considerate to those less fortunate than ourselves. Number Six, a married couple. She, I take it that it is she, is swinging blithely from a branch —she has doubtless just been on a shopping spree—while her morose mate sits cross-legged with a "This is a hell of a note" expression on his face. The motto there is, "A mate helps one enjoy life but he must remember that life is not always honey." Number Seven shows waves and the couple more engrossed in each other, and we learn that turbulent life can be sailed through peacefully when man and wife cooperate. With the eighth panel we have come full circle. A pregnant mother monkey contemplates the future, symbolizing, so we are told, God's love, paternal love, and child's compassion. It is only the last that is puzzling, a compassionate child being hard to find.

Over the lintel of one of the buildings is a delicious carving of a cat asleep among peony blossoms, and the legend has it that the sculptor

Hindari Jingoro was so skillful that in a fit of jealousy one of his rivals cut off his right hand, but that didn't phase Jingoro, who simply went ahead and carved the elegant puss with his left hand and was still better than his rivals.

The Inner Shrine, or Offering Hall, is a vast apartment floored with long strips of tatami and has a carved and painted ceiling of incredible richness divided into squares by strips of dark teakwood studded with carved gold crosspieces at the intersections. Against the walls hang long, thick tassels. The upper part of the tassel is yellow, the center red, and the lower part black. Yellow is the past, a clear color because we see the past clearly, red is the burning turbulent present, and black is the dark enshrouded future.

On the floor a great sheet is spread to catch yen dropped by visitors, and behind a long, low table two or three monks wearing curious black Punch-like caps on their heads sat back on their heels selling books and pamphlets about the temple.

The day Baby and I were there the place was thronged, mostly by school children, boys and girls all wearing white middy blouses and shirts and black pleated serge skirts or pants. There was a delegation from a Japanese inn wearing their team kimonos, and we saw a tiny little old woman in kimono and clogs being carried piggyback down the steps by her son.

After luncheon we drove to Kegon Falls, of which the Japanese are rightly proud. Arrived there, you descend in a huge, crowded elevator, make your way along a moist, slippery passageway cut out of solid rock, and emerge onto a big platform from which the view of the falls is spectacular; a roaring, gushing cataract plunging downward into boiling rapids, crashing and foaming over the rocks. The drop is three hundred thirty feet and, for any who attempt it, mortal. Baby told me it was a popular suicide spot. "Many peoper jump for ruv," she assured me soberly. Aras, in what heart has ruv not prayed havoc?

There are other fine sights in Nikko Park, including a magnificent highway with fifty hairpin turns that snakes its way up into the mountains, and there is Lake Chuzenji, from which the falls descend, lying more than four thousand feet above sea level.

As we had a little time before the Tokyo train was due to leave, Baby took me to an antique shop set in a lovely garden reminiscent of the one in Kyoto where we had gone to see the silk.

I bought a sake set with a charming design, *millefleurs* in gray, green, and gold. We use the bottle as a single rose vase and the little cups as salt cellars. There was also a four- or five-ply gold screen with white and soft rose pink chrysanthemums after which I lusted, but we had been a long time from home, I feared for the exchequer, and I refrained. Now, of course, every time I think of it and of what a bargain it was I could kick myself. I am aware that a bargain for which one has no specific use is probably not a bargain, but that's not the way a collector's mind works.

We returned to Tokyo in time for dinner, which as Norton was still in bed, we ate in our room, and afterward bade a sentimental farewell to Baby. We were staying on a few days more but not planning to leave the city and would no longer need her services.

The doctor perked up the next day in time for an amusing luncheon at the Correspondents Club with Keyes Beech, Robert Trumbull of the New York *Times* and Alexander Campbell, bureau chief of Time-Life, a man with the world's most engaging Scottish burr.

Two days before we were to leave an incredible thing happened. The sun came out! The weather was hot and brilliant and the breeze was cool. We took a new lease on life and, one of our letters of introduction having turned up a gentleman named Mr. Yoshitaka Horiuchi, we accepted his invitation to dine in a garden on a balmy evening. He said he would pick us up at the hotel at five-thirty. This seemed a rather odd hour, but we accepted it as Japanese. At five he phoned to say he was downstairs in the lobby. Norton and I looked at each other, question marks stabbing the air, and scrambled into our clothes and went down to meet him. The lobby was not very crowded and we didn't see anyone to fit our imagined image of him, so we had him paged, whereupon he instantly materialized from the depths of an apparently empty easy chair. He proved to be a merry fellow with a high-sounding job, president of the Japan International Public Relations Institute, and he had had a solid schooling in his profession via eight years in Hollywood.

He drove us to a restaurant called Chinzan-So, set in seventeen acres of garden right in the city, and he had very wisely suggested the early hour so we would have an opportunity to wander around the grounds by daylight. Paths wind through the gently rolling land among pine and bamboo trees and over a stone bridge spanning waters stocked with carp, some of which are *said* to be three hundred years old. Seems they have pedigrees, just like horses and dogs.

Also in the garden is an eleven-hundred-year-old pagoda that was brought from Hiroshima in 1934. As darkness comes on they floodlight it and it seems to float under the stars. On May 26, 1945, the American

Air Force bombed Chinzan-So—which means the Villa Camellia, as originally thousands of the flowers used to grow there—and the villas and most of the ancient trees in the garden were destroyed. By a fluke the pagoda and a shrine escaped damage. The present owner, Eiichi Ogawa, through a Herculean effort over a six-year period worked to restore the premises, putting up the present buildings and planting more than eight thousand trees.

Throughout all of the part of Japan we saw there was one attitude we found striking. They might say of a city, Takamatzu, Tokyo, "This section was virtually destroyed during the war," but they said it as a matter-of-fact statement—no bitterness, no hatred, no self-pity. One may ask with some reason why, given Pearl Harbor, should they behave any differently? But that is not usually the way human nature works. Resentment and the desire for revenge more frequently prevail, but after the war the Japanese had, and, I believe, most of them still have, a genuine admiration and respect for America. They want to do things in their own way perhaps, but vengeance plays small part in their feelings toward us. Or in ours toward them. It is not easy to forget Corregidor and the Bataan death march and the other horrors of war, but most Americans we have met who have traveled or lived in Japan and have come to know the Japanese people respect them and have grown fond of them.

At Chinzan-So we dined outdoors on the broad terrace of one of the pavilions. The speciality of the house is a Genghis Khan, or Mongolian, meal. Shrouded in enormous bibs, the kind we use for shore dinners, guests sit at square tables that have a charcoal pit sunk into the center. Each table has its own waitress-cook, who deftly lays the meat and vegetables on the grill with chopsticks. There are morsels of beef, pork, and chicken, green peppers, onions, mushrooms, and fresh bamboo shoots. The food, eminently satisfying, has nevertheless a delicate green springtime flavor. The garden, glowing with soft lights under the stars, was very beautiful, and with the small, flickering fires quite romantic, the only drawback being that the grills get pretty hot so that one tends most unromantically to sweat in front and feel chilled behind.

We returned early to the hotel, as the next morning we were to be at the embassy at nine for our hour-and-a-half meeting with Ambassador MacArthur. Our idea, that possibly he wanted to hear our impressions of Japan, turned out to be erroneous. He wanted to tell us his impressions, which, we had to admit, made more sense. He'd been there a long time and knew a great deal more than we did. He is an intelligent man and while in that post was certainly a dedicated one, working hard to maintain peaceful, prosperous relations between Japan and the United States.

Two of the most charming Japanese we met were Ise and Fumuhiko Togo. We had a letter to them from our mutual friends in New York, Jane Grant and Bill Harris, and they had called, inviting us to dinner.

Traveler's Tip No. 25: When coping with letters of introduction make a double list. On one side the names of the people to whom you are sending the letter with a covering one of your own, on the other the names of the friends at home who know them and who gave you the letter. This is especially necessary when you're not accustomed to foreign telephones and have difficulty in understanding what's being said anyway, and when the names are wildly different from sounds you've been accustomed to all your life. As Norton and I discovered to our discomfiture, if you neglect to follow this golden rule, you'll forget whose friends are whose and will be telling Mme. Gouchigami that dear Jane sends her warmest love, when dear Jane never heard of her, and she will quite naturally think you're bats. And Mme. Togo, who *does* know Jane, will be surprised to learn that never a day goes by without that sweet Harold, of whose existence until this moment she was ignorant, remembering the happy time they had together at Kyoto.

The above course of wisdom I neglected to follow. Therefore, when Mme. Togo arrived, as she had sounded charming over the telephone, and I had accepted her invitation with pleasure, Norton and I spent the first half hour in tentative little sorties trying discreetly to find out whom of our friends in New York she and her husband knew. When it turned out to be Jane and Bill, our relief, I like to think, was not too apparent and we sailed smoothly on through the suddenly charted social sea.

Mr. and Mrs. Togo took us to the Akai Hane, Red Feather, restaurant. We were eight for dinner, including a man from the Foreign Office, as was Mr. Togo, his wife, and the sister of one of them, a ravishingly pretty movie star, and her husband, an architect. Like a dolt I slipped up on the movie star's name, but in her white kimono and blue obi she was a delightful sight, and the dear doctor, who sat next to her, simply couldn't believe his eyes when we got back to the hotel and he saw how late it was. It was amazing, he said, how the evening had flown.

We didn't get there for some time, however, as the dinner was long, leisurely, and succulent. As we had on our first evening at the Hanacho, we sat around a low table—this one was oblong instead of crescent-shaped—with our feet in the trough where in winter a brazier would be lit.

The meal opened with a drink that looked like spinach juice—it was green tea—and we were feeling a mite melancholy when presently the hors d'oeuvres arrived, accompanied by sake and beer, and our spirits perked up. The beer we had enjoyed from the start and by now we were even getting acclimated to sake.

The hors d'oeuvres were unusual and a nice change from that bromidic old olive wrapped in bacon. They were toasted bees and un-expectedly good; as crispy, crunchy, and nutritious as Corn Flakes. One course was little squabs. They looked so pathetic lying on the plate their tiny claws curled up, I almost wept, but swallowed them and my tears, reflecting that at least they no longer suffered. After them came delicious fried chicken, and after that charcoal braziers, the *habachi*, were brought to the table and a sort of junior barbecue ensued. We began to bog down, but after a while along came noodles and soup and tender, rolled-up ginger root, the equivalent of the penultimate rice course in Hong Kong, and then fruit and tea.

Our hosts and their friends were intelligent and gay, speaking perfect English, while we of course could not utter one word of their language, and we greatly enjoyed ourselves. We sat around chatting after the meal, but gradually a rather heavy silence began to fall. Then one or another of the party would take a deep breath, spring upon a topic, and spark things up again.

Norton and I were getting sleepy, and as the next day was our last we had a good deal of packing and organizing to do, but it seemed rude to make a move to leave before the host and hostess did. In a private house the guests' departure after dinner is a simple matter; in a restaurant it rather seems as though the one doing the entertaining should give the first signal. We learned later that the custom is re-versed in Japan—the host waits upon the guest. At last, despairing, I suppose, of our manners, one of the men glanced at his watch, ob-served that he had a heavy day at the office, and the party broke up. With the exception of the last few minutes, however, it had been a de-

lightful evening, and I can only hope Mrs. Togo did not hold our ignorance against us.

Apparently the bad weather spell had been broken. We did our last-
minute shopping on a brilliantly sunny day and after some rather intricate formalities but no real difficulty took off from the Tokyo airport
at twenty minutes past seven on Saturday evening.

Despite our bad luck with the weather we had found Japan a fascinating country, but if one goes there purely as a tourist and plans to
visit other countries within a limited period of time, I should say that
to stay three weeks, as we did, is not necessary. I am aware that such a
comment sounds fatuous. Japan is an ancient land marvelously rich in
art and tradition, humanly intricate and rewarding, politically challenging, and it is of course ridiculous for anyone to assume that after
so brief a stay he *knows* it. That is not what I mean. I do mean, however, that within ten days or two weeks, given health and interest,
one may see many of the country's great treasures, experience and take
delight in many of her customs, and establish, one hopes, a beach head
of friendship with the individuals one meets.

Northwest Airlines calls its great eastbound flight—Tokyo, Anchorage, New York—the Imperial Polar Flight. It is also the Add-a-Day-to-
Life-Flight, which while interesting is not necessarily desirable. We
left Tokyo Saturday evening. We flew all night across the Pacific and
landed the next morning in Anchorage and what morning was it?
Right, Class! Saturday. That international date line is a scamp. The
doctor, having crossed and recrossed it times without number during
the war, was completely *au courant* with it, but despite his tutoring
on the subject, which has gone on at intervals throughout our married
life—he's devoted to the thing—I don't really grasp it and it makes me
peevish.

Something else made me peevish too. In our compartment was a
young American couple, Army, I imagine, homeward bound with three
small children. The father was a stripling and the mother looked a ripe
eighteen. The little girl and little boy were well-behaved moppets and
sweet. They kept trilling to each other like birds in Japanese. The
third one was a baby in arms, and throughout the twenty-five hours
of the trip that infant never stopped crying once. He can grow up, get
to be ninety-five, smoke twenty packages of cigarettes a day, and he
will *never* die of lung cancer. His are made of leather. We know.

The personnel of the Northwest plane were of course American, and
the first homey touch after a three-months absence amused us. When

I asked the stewardess if I might have tea with my breakfast instead of coffee, she replied with a wink, "You sure can." We had left the lands of courtesy and entered that of familiarity.

The weather at Anchorage was sunny, the air cool and refreshing. A nice customs man let me go through with my handbag, which, if you're not going to clear customs, they sometimes won't do. You might be smuggling diamonds to a chum. As we had a layover of two and a half hours we went snooping about for souvenirs, but the only things that tempted us, engaging little animals carved from bone that for fifty cents or a dollar would have been fun to have, started at $2.50 and ranged up to $45. We thought perhaps it was just a tourist trap at the airport, but a very nice woman, a Mrs. Snowden, who had been vacationing in Alaska and joined the plane, said the whole country is frightfully expensive. Maybe now that it's a state things will be different.

The trip itself is now very different. By jet only about fourteen hours, compared to our twenty-five.

We touched down at Idlewild at eight-thirty Sunday morning, our lovely adventure at an end. The New York weather was as hot and humid as Tokyo had been, but our apartment was shining clean and we would spend the day in utter relaxation. On the morrow would come the bills, bank balance, and reality.

Traveler's Tip No. 26: When you get home you'll be tired and excited at being there. Try hard to leave twenty-four hours for readjustment, forty-eight are preferable. There is the family to see, mail to be got through, friends to be telephoned to, and dinner invitations issued so that one and all may hear about your *glorious* experience. Also, as soon as your pictures have been developed, you'll want to share *those* with your dear ones. We have noticed that sometimes our closest friends have steered clear of us for a month or so. Could they be giving our enthusiasm over our art work time to cool off?

CHAPTER NINE

* The British Isles

January 1960

"Sweetie, there's one thing I want you to promise me. It's a resolution we simply have to make." The doctor said this as we were sitting down to dinner one evening.

"Of course, darling. Anything. What is it?"

"We will do *no* traveling this year. There's an awful lot I want to do around the house and garden next summer and besides, we can't afford to go anyplace. We've got to recoup and I've got to stick on the job."

"All right, darling, I don't mind. We had our wonderful trip last summer, that'll do me for a long time."

"It must. It's unheard of for a doctor to take three months off, and I only did it because it just happened we could swing it, and lots of my patients are away in the summer anyway, but it was a once-in-a-lifetime thing, you've got to realize that."

"Yes, darling. I realize it."

"Then it's a promise? We stay home?"

"That we do."

June 1960

"Norton, you look kind of peaked. You feel all right?"

"Oh sure, I'm just stale, that's all. Same old grind; office, hospital, apartment, house. Same thing week in and week out. I wish *I* could get a change the way you do."

"Me? A change? I don't even have the office and hospital for variety. Just the country and the apartment."

"That isn't so. You're *always* going off someplace glamorous. Where were you just the other day when you spoke at that club women's luncheon?"

"Columbus, Ohio."

"There you are! And where is it you're going to play summer stock in July?"

"Vineland, Ontario. I understand the place is a motel in the middle of nothing. Right on the highway with a theater attached."

"Oh. Still, you probably can get into Buffalo."

"That will be lovely but I've been to Buffalo."

"You can see Niagara Falls."

"I've seen them."

"Mmm. I wonder . . . nah, that's foolish."

"What's foolish?"

"Well, I was just thinking . . . with jets and all. We haven't been in England since 1951."

"ANGEL!"

"Listen, even if we could afford it it can't be for any length of time."

"Of course not. No more than a month but even when we just stay home you do take a *month* off in the summer. You *have* to. A doctor's got to have some rest and relaxation. What good would you be to your patients snapping their heads off? Shall I call Mr. Guthrie?"

"Well, don't set anything definite, but maybe you and he could work out a little tour through Ireland and Scotland or something. Find out what it might come to."

Late July: A Desk in the Fifth Avenue Office of the American Express Company.

MR. GUTHRIE: "Here you are, Mrs. Brown. Here are the tickets and the itinerary. London, then over to Dublin, where you pick up the car for the tour around Ireland. From Belfast you fly to Glasgow, pick up another car for motoring through Scotland, then back to London and home. Just under six weeks. I hope you and the doctor have a very pleasant trip."

MRS. BROWN: "Thank you so much, Mr. Guthrie. Uh, I haven't mentioned it to the doctor yet, but to be that near and not go to Paris . . . well, I mean, it does seem . . ."

MR. GUTHRIE: "I quite see your point. Just call our London office, they'll get plane reservations for you any time."

That's how it happens. Have a talk with your husband, apply the tip of the fountain pen to the surface of the check, hand it to sainted Mr. Guthrie, and in no time at all you've got a fat wallet full of vouchers and tickets and instructions.

In comparison with our round-the-world trip of the previous year the preparations were the soul of simplicity, requiring little time or discussion. We did send off one big suitcase air freight, as it was $1.27 a pound, opposed to $1.96 if it accompanied us, and at that it cost $60. These, unfortunately, are the extras one tends to overlook in budgeting a journey.

In view of the fact that it was a flight of only six and a half hours, when Norton and I learned the difference in price, $828 worth, for a round trip for two between New York and London, we decided to go economy class. That is a sum of money worth saving, but there's no doubt you'll save more happily if you're young and/or small. The young are hardy and a little physical discomfort is good for them, keeps them from getting uppity, and the small fit without great inconvenience into a confined space, but the doctor and I are high ones and Economy doesn't give you much *Lebensraum*, at least not on a Comet 4.

Since we were flying east the sun rose at about midnight our time, and just as we were hoping for London the captain announced over the intercom that we would be making an unscheduled stop at Shannon, as due to head winds we had to refuel. This we didn't mind too much, the smell of Shannon is always delicious, and it gave us a chance to stretch and get a breakfast of fresh eggs and Irish bacon. Irish cooking arouses in me emotions not incompatible with homicide, but to their eggs and bacon one can usually accord unstinting praise.

Shannon has greatly changed in recent years. It used to be one of the bustling airports of Europe, but the jets do not stop there unless, as in our case, they must refuel. It is now relatively quiet, but we were grateful for our brief interlude and appreciated our breakfast, for by the time we arrived in London the six-and-a-half-hour flight had stretched to nine and we had made a firm resolve that we would ever afterward cross the Atlantic by daylight. The impression that one saves time going at night is erroneous. As I have said, one is too tired the next day to be of much use.

Our hotel was our beloved Connaught in Carlos Place where we had a room on the top floor known as the Penthouse. It overlooked the roofs and chimney pots of London and had a cozy, kind of *On m'appelle Mimi* atmosphere.

Even in the dear Connaught, however, the number of showers is limited. Our bath had none, nor were we to find any in a month of motoring around Great Britain. Make up your mind, they just don't have them.

There's something else they don't have and that's washcloths. We assumed that we spoke the language, but when we asked for a couple they looked at us blankly. Certain English words I grasp quite easily, they even have logic behind them: flat for apartment, lift for elevator, lay-by for emergency parking. I also like dual carriage-way for two-lane traffic, but I am stopped by the British phrase for washrag: face flannel, for God's sake. We had to go to a chemist's and buy our own, indulging in pantomime to make our need clear.

This little matter attended to, our first morning was spent in Establishing Our Contacts, telephoning to several old friends and making engagements, and the early afternoon was passed in napping. The only fly in the ointment was the discovery that dear old London was being torn apart quite as ruthlessly as little old New York, and the gnomes with the riveting machines were hard at work under our windows and six stories did not deaden the sound of their conscientious endeavors.

Refreshed by a rest and tea, in the soft light of early evening we walked up Carlos Place and into Grosvenor Square. It seemed wonderful to be in London again and strange to realize that it was our first visit in nine years. When we were there before Pete had been with us, a schoolboy. Now he was twenty-two, through college, and doing his military service in the Navy. London too had changed. Even in 1951, six years after the war, austerity still ruled. Now, if one were to judge by the flow of traffic, the economy was booming; Mayfair was awash with Rolls-Royces, Bentleys, and Jaguars. We walked around Grosvenor Square and gazed upon the new American Embassy. I am prone to modern architecture but cannot say I am swept away by that particular building; however, the controversial eagle perched atop it we thought harmonious and well proportioned. The brisk skirmishes about him between the English and the Americans had gone on shortly before our arrival, the English declaring that he was overbearing, haughty, and above all *large*—he would dominate Grosvenor Square—the Americans maintaining he was merely the national bird, gentle as a dove, and, if anything, on the small side, a Rhode Island of a fowl, not a Texan. Though a little sensitive to our national trait of exuberance and braggadocio, Norton and I felt that in this instance our countrymen were right. The eagle seemed to us a handsome creature that adorned the embassy with distinction and without arrogance.

We continued our walk through Brook Street, Hill Street, and a few mews and returned to the hotel and a cocktail before dinner. In a land that has ever done right by bottled spirits it came as a shock to discover that British cocktails are *very* small and costly. The heart-rending cries of our countrymen echoed around the bar, "A double martini, please," "A double whiskey and soda." At first it sounded rather coarse and alcoholic, but after we had been served our maiden thimbleful we too automatically called for doubles.

One of the most notable changes we found in England from the last time we were there was the food. There are any number of first-rate, charming restaurants not only in London but all around the country-side. The inns are a delight and the fare excellent.

The London restaurants we enjoyed most were the Mirabelle in Curzon Street, the Guinea in Bruton Place off Berkeley Square, and the Caprice in Arlington Street. Also a few doors down from the Connaught in Mount Street we happened, undirected, upon the Marquis, which, while perhaps not the hautest of cuisine, is still eminently satisfactory, and we noted with pleasure that in most British restaurants the natives were drinking wine with their meals with the relish and connoisseurship of their abandoned French neighbors across the channel.

The Mirabelle is a pretty restaurant. You go downstairs to a sort of patio surrounded by columns and covered by a glass roof that rolls back to admit air and sunshine, when there is any. We had a few sunny hours in England and lots and lots of clouds and rain.

The Caprice is attractive too, and the Guinea is a pet. It is small and so popular that the crowd at luncheon often overflows into the street. You see chaps with their beer and wineglasses in hand standing on the sidewalk munching a roll sandwich or balancing their plates on the window sill. It too has a small patio and a couple of little rooms where you sit on banquettes against the wall. To get to them, you pass through the kitchen, selecting what you'll have en route. The menu is limited and delicious. You may start with artichoke, asparagus, or smoked salmon and you go on to steak, chops, or kidneys, salad, fruit, and cheese. As a man given to broiling steak on the terrace, the doctor was charmed by the grill. "It's so intelligent," he said. The smart thing it did was to have its narrow round bars running at a slant rather than horizontally above the coals so that the fat slipped down into a trough fastened to the bottom, thus ensuring that the meat itself didn't catch fire from the hot fat. Luncheon for two at the Guinea, wine included, runs between eight and ten dollars.

Theatergoing in London is as pleasant as restaurant dining, and the ticket holder is actually made to feel welcome, not given the reception those impostors who stand in line at the box offices of Broadway eager to spend their money are subjected to. Of the several plays we saw we considered Robert Bolt's A Man For All Seasons, starring Paul Schofield as Thomas More, to be by far the best. The title was taken from a passage composed for Tudor schoolboys to put into Latin: "More is a man of an angel's wit and singular learning; I know not his fellow. For where is the man of that gentleness, lowliness and affability? And as time requireth a man of marvelous mirth and pastimes; and sometimes of as sad a gravity: a man for all seasons."

Another nice thing about the English theater besides the possibility of getting tickets at human prices is the seven-thirty curtain time, which still prevails so that one can have supper afterward—we found Prunier and l'Ecu de France and the Ivy to be excellent after-theater restaurants—and get to bed at a reasonable hour.

The really disappointing show in London, to our way of thinking, was the old classic, Madame Tussaud's waxworks. One trouble is that in viewing what they've done to Marilyn Monroe, Bob Hope, and their own queen, whose persons and pictures are ubiquitous, suspicion over the resemblance of the historical wax effigies to their prototypes is keen.

The other letdown is the Chamber of Horrors. If I'm going in for horror I want to have the living gizzard scared out of me, but very few of the depicted fiends are engaged in fiend's work, and it's disconcerting to discover that when not involved in their unspeakable crimes, when, just lolling around in the dock, fiends are very hard to differentiate from good guys.

An exhibit we found more stimulating was the Picasso Exhibition at the Tate Gallery. We were lucky because although the exhibition had been open for a month the pictures from the Hermitage had only just arrived and been installed. There were ten that the Soviet Government had finally agreed to lend, including the tender, emaciated Old Jew seated on the ground, his arm around a little boy, and Acrobats, a muscular figure seated in the foreground, a slight young boy balancing on a big ball in the middle distance.

The famous Las Meninas series inspired by Velázquez was on view, as were the gay and adorable pigeons in a window in Nice. Some

Picassos give me a pain and some certainly rank with the great art of the world, and everyone, I think, must agree that the man is a titan. The doctor was willing to go along with this viewpoint, with reservations, for he could not curb his exasperation induced by the master's playing fast and loose with human anatomy. I don't care for that dame on the beach with mechanical claws and a triangular lizard face where her head should be, either, nor would I care to own, except for financial reasons, *Les Demoiselles d'Avignon*, but I don't mind *looking* at them.

We spent a pleasant week in London renewing old friendships, seeing, among others the Frank Hoares, with whom we had had so much fun on our cruise of the Greek islands. For once the Hands Across the Sea policy worked without disillusionment. Among the gray stones of London they were as sprightly and amusing as they had been against the wine-dark Aegean. We could only hope that they on their side were not disappointed.

Every time I go to London I realize anew how much I like Englishmen. We had an especially good time lunching with John Foster, a member of Parliament and a brilliant man in the fine tradition of English individualists.

The rumor that the English never introduce their guests to each other is, by the way, a canard. We were ten for luncheon and we were all introduced to everybody by everybody else and by several names. Norton was called Mr. Brown and Mr. Chase—the latter didn't go down too well—and I ended up as Mrs. Chase.

The luncheon was stimulating because many Englishmen, it seems to me, are full of intellectual vigor and, if one is lucky in one's contacts, colorful and entertaining eccentricities. The conforming mold, too prevalent in America, has not closed over them.

Although this is obviously a generality, I do not feel that Englishwomen match their men in color and personality. *My* friends naturally are brilliant and delightful creatures, but I think that what Mrs. Oliver Wendell Holmes said (approximately) of Washington women may be said of many English females. Corresponding with a friend, she wrote, "I have met many interesting men here and the women whom they married when they were young."

On the afternoon that we left London for Dublin, driving out to the airport, we were struck afresh by the truly offensive ugliness of low-cost English architecture and the incredible beauty of the tiny plots blazing with flowers in front of every house. The houses are built with a lumpy stucco that looks like peanut brittle combined with tile and brick and wood trim often painted poison green or lavender, but the flowers are breath-taking. Gardening is the people's art.

The flight to Dublin, though late in starting, was smooth and took an hour and twenty minutes. There were clouds in the sky when we arrived, but clean blue stretches, too, and our driver on the way in from the airport said they'd just had a violent thunder shower but were hoping that the worst was over. This was August 9. The month of July, he said, had been unusually rainy. The month of August was unusually rainy too. I believe they all are.

We put up at the Shelbourne because it, along with the Gresham and the Russell, have old and established reputations, and Elizabeth Bowen wrote a book about it. But should we visit Dublin again we would go to the Royal Hibernian. Food's a lot better. We were comfortable enough, however, and a fortuitous encounter the first evening led to a couple of very pleasant interludes.

Norton and I were sipping our drinks in the bar when an attractive-looking woman came in and sat down on the banquette at the table next to us. She was obviously waiting for friends and looked very smart in a black and white checked silk suit. Over her arm she carried a lovely soft tomato-colored woolen stole. I coveted it. "I think I'll ask her where she got it," I murmured to Norton out of the corner of my mouth.

"But you don't know her." Honestly, men are hidebound.

"What of it? It won't do any harm."

I leaned over. "Please don't think me rude," I said, "but I admire your scarf so much. I wonder if you'd mind telling me where you got it?"

"Not at all," she said pleasantly. "It comes from my shop. I have a shop around the corner, Anna Livia in Dawson Street."

On the bench beside me I heard a low moan. "Oh, God, a shop."

The lady's name was Kay Petersen, and the friends she was waiting for were the Digby Mortons. He is the British designer. We met them when they came in and renewed a tenuous acquaintanceship that went back many years to a time when my mother was living in England and working on British Vogue.

The next morning dawned radiant—many of them did, we were to find, but that didn't mean the whole *day* would be clear, not by a long chalk—and we set off down Grafton Street, the swank shopping thor-

oughfare, to the American Express to cash a traveler's check and find
out about the car we were going to rent for our Irish tour. En route
we stopped to buy a sweater for David Lyall. David and Daphne, those
holy people, were again boarding Thor for us as they had when we
went around the world, and the salesman suggested we try a spot of
local color. "Davey Byrnes in Duke Street," he said. "Gaelic coffee, I
think you'll like it." Like it was the year's understatement. It's a magic
brew and here's how they do it. Into a glass, preferably a fair-sized gob-
let, pour a generous jigger of Irish whiskey. Then a little sugar, brown
barley crystals are best although white granulated will do. Fill the
glass nearly to the top with strong black coffee and *then*, and here's
the tricky part, add cream. Irish cream is very thick, like Devonshire or
crème d'Isigny, and floats. The way the Irish apply it is to take a spoon,
bottom side up and hold it over the glass and over this, with another
spoon, they spread the cream so that it slips into the glass and rests on
the surface of the coffee like the collar on a glass of stout. The cold
thick cream, the hot strong coffee, the stimulus of the whiskey . . .
what a drink!

Here at home it's hard to get proper cream. The normal product simply sinks down into the coffee and the whole effect is lost. The helpful
thing to do is whip it.

Refreshed by Mr. Byrnes's speciality, we continued on our way
to the American Express, where there was a nice young chap in
charge, Mr. Joyce, who suggested that we go along Westmoreland
Street and have a look at O'Connell. We crossed over the Liffey, reflecting the colorful quais and floating an occasional swan, and wandered along a wide street for a while. We weakened at the thought of
trying to review Ireland's turbulent history, including the Trouble of
the Twenties, but we did ask who was the Mr. O'Connell who had
such a fine broad street named after him and discovered he was Daniel
O'Connell who in 1829 secured the passage of an act whereby privileges
of citizenship were reinstated for Catholics, who had been barred from
them for centuries, and later he had been elected lord mayor of Dublin.

With Anna Livia in mind we started retracing our steps, passing on
the way Trinity College on College Green. We went into the great
quadrangle and were admiring the beautiful eighteenth-century buildings and the lovely hand-blown glass windowpanes with a sheen on
them like silk, when we saw the little sign with the arrow: "Book of
Kells." "Hey," I said to the doctor, "this is it, this is where it lives.
Let's go." We went up a flight of stairs into the university library, or

Long Room, as it is called. It is one of the beautiful rooms of the world, a superbly proportioned long, high, narrow apartment with an arched ceiling. On either side are deep embrasures each ending in a window set with panes of hand-blown glass and lined from floor to ceiling with magnificent calfbound volumes. The width between each embrasure is only the width of the stacks themselves, and abutting them are pedestals with marble busts of the world's great literary figures. They gaze with marble eyes upon the glass-enclosed housing of the Book, the gospels illuminated, done on vellum by monks of County Meath probably in the eighth century. It is one of the oldest books in the world. Nearby, in a large double frame, are reproductions of the most colorful pages; although the pages of the book itself are turned from day to day, it is naturally impossible to see them all at once. We gazed with admiration and dropped a coin in the slot available to those who want to contribute to the maintenance of the incomparable library.

Trinity is interesting among other reasons because, although the buildings that compose it today are of the eighteenth century, the college itself was founded in 1591, a strictly Protestant proposition intended to further the Reformation in Ireland.

From the Book of Kells to Anna Livia was but a few blocks, several centuries, and a different mental outlook. We hurdled the gap and I ordered some clothes, including two or three bawneen sweaters. These are the chunky hand-knit oatmeal-colored sweaters that Irishwomen knit in their cottages and sell to Dublin and London merchants. That is to say, theoretically they do, but like many artists these ladies are temperamental. They may be having babies or attending wakes or bringing in the harvest or cutting peat, and these activities are far more vital than sweaters for city slickers, so the deliveries are chancy. The shops are good about sending things on to you, but under the circumstances it's more prudent to order merchandise already in stock. It is also cheaper to pay in pounds than in dollars, pleased though the merchants are to accept the latter. In the better shops articles are priced in guineas rather than pounds, a guinea being a shilling more, but they translate a guinea as $3.00 instead of $2.94, which it is. Two or three guineas perhaps make little difference, but as they mount, so do those extra six cents. It is better for the American traveler to pay in the coin of their realm rather than his own.

As we were about to leave Mrs. Petersen said, "Why don't you join the Digby Mortons and me for lunch? If you go on over to the Buttery in the Royal Hibernian, just down the street, I'll be along in a few minutes."

Delighted to accept this pleasant invitation, we went to the hotel but could not at first glance find the Buttery. (It's downstairs.) We sat in the lounge for a few minutes, thinking we would spot the Mortons or Mrs. Petersen as they came in but spotted instead Margaret Webster and Pamela Frankau, the novelist.

"Peggy," I cried, "what on earth are you doing here?"

"Directing Noël's play of course, what else? Pamela's lending moral support."

Noël Coward's new play, *Waiting in the Wings*, was trying out in Dublin preparatory to its London opening. "Coming to see it?" Peggy asked. Norton and I glanced at each other. "Well, uh, the fact is we've only got this one evening and we have tickets for the Abbey." Having learned our bitter lesson about the opera in Vienna it seemed idiotic to go to Dublin and not see the Abbey Players, so we had ordered seats in advance.

"You won't like them," Peggy said, "they've gone off terribly."

"Oh come, the Abbey?"

"All right. You'll see." I did a little mental tongue-clicking. Really, theater people, these petty jealousies. Even darling Peggy. Margaret Webster's a grand woman. I have never worked with her in the theater, but there was a time when we both served on the Council of Actors Equity and a more levelheaded, intelligent, courageous person I have yet to see. Those Council meetings used to get pretty heated—I suspect they still do—and self-control, fairness, and clear vision are no more common to actors than they are to politicians, but Margaret had them in abundance. She had something else, too, that for all their stage training most of the male thespians lacked. She had a sense of timing. She would get to her feet, say what she had to say, and sit down. Once the boys were on, it was mighty hard to get them off.

We finally did spot the Mortons, and after lunch I went with Kay Petersen to the opening of a big art show, held in the National College in Kildare Street. It differed from any other exhibition I had ever seen because many of the artists were priests who were on hand for the gala event, keeping a sharp eye on the way their entries were hung.

That evening, when Norton and I went to the Abbey, we found to our disappointment that they were out of their own theater, which was being renovated, and were playing in the somewhat ramshackle old

Queens. The production was *The Country Boy*, by John Murphy.
Yoo hoo, Lady Gregory. Yoo hoo, Mr. Yeats, Mr. Synge and Mr.
O'Ca-a-a-sey!

We didn't think much of the play, but the acting was truly distress-
ing. Where was the skill that made the Abbey renowned around the
world? I had thought ill of dear Peggy Webster, who spoke no more
than simple truth. Such truth in fact that in the first intermission I said
to Norton, "How about it? Shall we go have a whack at Noël's play?"
My husband has staying power and was taking a collector's interest in
the shenanigans transpiring on stage and rather wanted to stick it out,
and I would have been staunch too had we been going to be in Dublin
another evening, but we were starting our tour in the morning and if
we were to see the Coward play at all this was our only chance. Theater
tickets in Dublin are even cheaper than in England; twenty-five shillings a pair ($3.50), so we felt we had already got our money's worth

and would not be too wildly extravagant if we took in two shows in one evening.

We hurried away, arriving at the Olympia just as the curtain was going up on the second act. I should not say that *Waiting in the Wings* was one of the master's best, but it was warmhearted with funny and touching moments, and the cast, although a little unsteady—it was, after all, only their third performance and they were coping with changes—included such wily players as Sybil Thorndike, Marie Lohr, and Margot Boyd. They were a big relief from the Abbeyites.

We had asked Margaret Webster and Pamela Frankau to lunch with us next day at Jammets, old-fashioned but one of the best restaurants in Dublin, and afterward, having bought an umbrella, as necessary in Ireland as in Bergen, Norway, which is the wettest place I have ever been in my life, we bade them an affectionate farewell and set out in our rented Austin. I am loath to run down a product manufactured by men who, I do not doubt, are kind to their old mothers and cherish their wives and kiddies, but the Austin is a gem of discomfort. It is cramped, it jolts and jars, and every curve is an affair of clenched teeth and dogged determination to hold it on four wheels on the turn. It *is* economical. Five gallons of gas, all it holds, will virtually see you over Europe.

We enjoyed Dublin immensely; the people, the winding Liffey, the beautiful Queen Anne and Georgian buildings, St. Stephen's Green, the park at the top of Grafton Street . . . there had been only one chilling note: a small truck, on its side the legend "Swastika Laundry" and the hated symbol. During the war the Irish acted to what they doubtless thought was their advantage. It is shocking to see the point of view prolonged to this day.

The drive to Wexford, about three hours and a half, including a stop-over for a wretched tea at Gorey, was very beautiful. Indeed we were to find that Ireland, the part we saw at least, the south and west coasts, is one of the beautiful countries of the world; rolling, green, and seemingly fertile, although it can't be as fertile as it looks or they would have vegetables other than the eternal potato. Their little round red tomatoes are delicious too, but there, apparently, they stop. The food is of an incredible monotony and its preparation, with the exception of top restaurants such as Jammets and the Royal Hibernian and a few other rarities, is a disaster.

Almost all the roads we traveled were excellent, although sometimes it was hard to see the fields because of the walls and high hedges. The hedges, however, are entrancing. Fuchsia—millions of tiny crimson bells ringing silent melodies against the dark, bright leaves.

Usually the roads have no more than two lanes, but they are well graded and well surfaced and two lanes are all they need, since, even if they lacked colleens and smiling eyes, Ireland is indeed heaven in one respect: There is no traffic. New York taxi drivers should be sent there to spend a month bowling over the smooth open roads by way of therapy and to restore their sanity. Also it is instant country. The cities don't sprawl forever into slums and suburbs and developments that, in turn, merge with the next city so that green secluded places are non-existent. In Ireland you go through a town, even a big one, you round a bend in the road and there they are, the fields and the moors again.

I expect that this adorable condition exists because of the poverty and lack of industry, but I'd be for the whole world chipping in to subsidize Ireland forever, if she would control her birth rate so that with the money given her her people could have decent lives and education, and provided she promised *never* to become industrialized. There should be at least one unspoiled spot on earth where the people of other races would be allowed to go for holidays, to escape the crowding industrial horrors of their own native lands.

The Talbot Hotel at Wexford is the good place to stop, although one needs to be quite athletic. We walked for miles up and down steps and along winding corridors to get to the new wing, where we were to be accommodated. The appointments were all very modern and there was a formidable panel of switches and buttons, like the instrument panel of a jet, that was the lighting system. The bath, too, was imposing, and, joy of joys, there was a shower, but our rapture over this, was premature. Neither it nor the telephone worked. They were like handsome props in an expensive stage set, installed but not functional. That part, we understood, would come later, workmen were still all over the building. I assume that by now one can shower and telephone around the world in jig time.

A club at Ballynahinch, on the west coast, famous for its fishing, was our destination, so we were staying only overnight at towns on the way. The next afternoon we set out for Cork, stopping for tea in Dungarvan at a sinister hostelry called the Devonshire Arms. The coziness and color of the English country inns were notably lacking. It was bare and dreary, with the railway hotel atmosphere of a provincial town.

About a quarter of a mile out of town the Austin sneezed, coughed, and came to a dead stop. The doctor, usually highly knowledgeable in these matters, was stymied, even with the thought of having to return and spend the night at the lethal Devonshire Arms spurring him to superhuman efforts. After a time a friendly chap came along, peered under the hood for a while, and then said he would phone for a mechanic from the garage down the road. He went into his house, and five small, ragged boys sprang up from nowhere and stared at the engine in silence. We prayed that they might be precocious engineers, but nothing happened. After a while the mechanic arrived. With the most nonchalant air in the world he unscrewed a gadget, blew into it, spit on it, screwed it back, and the Austin began to purr. We went on to Cork.

Cork is the third-largest city in Ireland with a population of about eighty thousand, but you have to know it to love it. As two who spent only a night there at the Imperial Hotel, our advice would be to scurry through town and get to the next stop as quickly as possible. Cork is like Ravenna, but no mosaics. Our dinner at the hotel was the nadir in Irish food. Too late, alas, we learned from perusing Mr. Ashley Courtney that we would have done better at the Oyster Tavern.

This Mr. Courtney is quite a fellow, and anyone touring the British Isles cannot do better than to buy his book *Let's Halt Awhile*, a mine of valuable information about the hotels, inns, and restaurants of Great Britain and Ireland. We found, almost without exception, that everything he said about a place was true. Our faith was momentarily shaken when one hotel manager told us they had to pay to be included in the book—his establishment was in so it wasn't a question of sour grapes— "but," he added, "pay or not, if your place falls off you're yanked out. You quickly learn to read between the lines. You can tell when the food is nothing special." I should say it was only on the food that Mr. Courtney did occasionally go overboard, but the poor chap must sample so much that is awful that he gets a little delirious when it becomes palatable.

Wishing to drown the taste of the appalling dinner we'd had at the Imperial, we strolled the streets of Cork looking for a pub. We popped our heads into one that was obviously not what we wanted, but a nice-looking man was just coming out so I asked him where we might find Irish Coffee. " 'Tis Gaelic coffee you're wanting, is it? I can show you a good spot," and he led us down the street. I never mind picking up strange men when Norton is right behind me. He is large, with an authoritative air. Besides, I am now at an age when, if a man makes a tactful approach shot, I am rather pleased, although not yet, I hope, grateful. Reactions of the male young are likely to be filial rather than lecherous, and I obviously never have any trouble with men in my own age brackets, since they are all interested in girls in their teens.

The pub to which Mr. O'Keefe, our pickup, guided us was of somewhat mangy aspect, but the Gaelic coffee was reasonably good, though not of the caliber of Davey Byrnes. In the course of our conversation we learned that he was a laborer and he was deeply concerned with unemployment insurance and the parsimoniousness of same.

It is easy to understand why the Irish leave their country, beautiful as it is, to seek jobs elsewhere. They want work that will pay. At home even when they're employed they can't hope to make more than seven to nine pounds, or between nineteen to twenty-five dollars, a week. Judging from his conversation, however, we suspected that our pal was something less than a dynamic go-getter. Apparently he'd had three or four opportunities to get to America, but, like those Chekov girls who never made Moscow, his goal was still to be achieved.

Wanting to shake the dust of Cork—although it's hard to speak of dust in Ireland, with the amount of rain they have—we left the city early the next day and headed for Blarney, six miles away. Today there is nothing left of the castle but the tower, or keep. Still, it's an impressive ruin, dating from 1446, although even that early date is late, for the first castle, of wood, was erected in the same spot in the tenth century. It was replaced by a second, of stone, which in turn made way for today's Revered Remains.

In her informative little booklet about the castle Mary Penelope Hillyard tells us that "the MacCarthy who reigned in Munster during Queen Elizabeth's time was able to talk the nose off his head and the word blarney meaning in conversation fair words in soft speech dates back to that time.

"In his dealings with the Queen while professing to be her loyal Baron of Blarney, MacCarthy never fullfilled any promise or condition he had made. Procrastination followed dalliance, delay and subterfuge followed device and evasion until eventually, in disgust, the Queen cried out: 'Blarney, Blarney, what he says he does not mean. It is the usual blarney.' "

From the top of the tower the lush, rolling fields and woodlands of Muskerry are a green-gold dream, but one must close one's eyes to a modern development lying in the folds of the nearby hills for an unblemished effect. The development is a try but, we felt, an abortive one. The ice-cream colors, pink and pistachio, turquoise and yellow, in which the houses are painted are fine under the Mediterranean sun, but under the rain-washed skies of Ireland, the gray stones, the muted hues of the villages, and the opaque, whitewashed huts of tradition are more becoming.

Blarney's renowned stone is at the very top of the tower and, having wound our way up the precipitous, spiraling staircase and emerged on the terrace, we decided to take its magic powers on faith and refrain from kissing. To get at it, you have to lie flat on your back on a dubious old blanket spread on the stones, and then wriggle your way outward and with head and shoulders dropping off the parapet crane upward in order to apply your lips to the fabled hunk of masonry.

The architecture of the keep is curious. The topmost battlements project several feet beyond the walls themselves, making an effective sort of slot through which to pour boiling tar and oil on any foolhardy aggressors storming the keep below. As the famous block of limestone was set in the outer battlement, in the old days it was quite possible for the kissing tourist, if his legs were not securely held, to drop one hundred twenty feet to certain death. It sometimes happened, too. To-day any untimely demise has been obviated by two iron bars secured in the rock walls on either side of the stone, forming an effective barrier between the acrobatic tourist and mother earth.

Poking about in the ancient ruin—exploring the tiny stone rooms, peering through the narrow slits through which the archers shot their arrows, looking into the black and fearsome dungeons—is to realize anew what a hard, brutal, dirty life our ancestors lived. They were a tough tribe who, if they did survive the arrows and the boiling oil, spent their days incarcerated behind walls five feet thick and through which no ray of sun could penetrate. On sunny days when they could escape the keep for a few hours they must have been delirious with joy. The grounds are lovely. A purling brown river, the Martin, gurgles over a stony bottom, and along a winding, wooded path one comes to the Rock Close, one of the quiet places of the earth. The Close is an outdoor cathedral of ancient trees and even more ancient stones. Although there is no proof, it is thought that it may be of druidic origin and that the rock garden constructed there in the latter part of the eighteenth century, by the owner of the castle, might to some extent have been inspired by the ancient formations.

In any event, it is today a marvelously still and peaceful place in which to invite one's soul. Until of course the charabanc arrives with the other tourists. We were very lucky, for we were there entirely by ourselves.

We had learned, via Mr. Courtney, of Ballilecky House at Bantry and were sighting it for lunch. A remodeled and enlarged old farmhouse, it is charmingly situated at the head of Bantry Bay, separated from the water by a garden and croquet course and while waiting for luncheon we watched an English family hard at play: a mother, her two young daughters and son, and the menace. The menace was a fair-haired party aged eight months who crawled about the lawn gleefully misplacing balls and frustrating any devastating sends the players may have had in mind.

The food at Ballilecky was the best we had had since the Royal Hibernian. Excellent eggs in aspic with tarragon and mayonnaise, a good lamb stew, delicious, fresh little carrots, and a salad. The coffee was instant and weak. If one were going to stop there for a few days, and there are pleasant rooms for guests, not to mention fishing, boating, and golf, a little talk with Mr. and Mrs. Graves the owners—Madame and the chef are French—would, I am sure set that straight.

Back home, some months later, having got thus far in this chronicle, I said to the doctor, "Now we're at Ballilecky. That nice little inn at the head of Bantry Bay, remember?"

"Do I not! And the good lunch."

"I've mentioned it."

"I hope you've told about the bartender, too?"

"Well, no. Matter of fact I haven't. As it is, I'm afraid the reader's going to get the impression we drank our way around the world. I didn't think I'd say anything about the Ballilecky bar."

"*That*," said the doctor, the garlic clove with which he was massaging the steak poised in mid-air—he was preparing Sunday lunch in the country—"is grossly unfair. He was a very *good* bartender. I don't see how you can't make *some* comment about him."

Comment: The bartender at Ballilecky House was young—nineteen or twenty—slight, and blond and created a peerless martini. Minute, to be sure, just as they are in England, but excellent. The doctor, as persnickety about this special brew as any other self-confident American, took a first skeptical sip and his expression changed. He looked with respect at the stripling who had manufactured it, and obviously concluding that age be damned, art is art—look at Mozart, look at Keats—raised his glass in serious salute.

As we drove into the afternoon the country beyond Ballilecky changed, becoming wilder and rockier, the moors were the moors of Scotland. We rode out a few quick, violent showers and rolled most of the time under a high blue vault in which tumbled clouds of pearl and inky black. One aspect of Irish highways is immensely pleasing, a great boost to the ego. The trains wait for cars and pedestrians instead of the other way around. In Ireland when you come to a grade crossing the bars are not down across the roads when a train is expected; they are set at right angles to the tracks so that automobiles and pedestrians continue on their way and the iron horse jolly well reins up and waits for a clear interval. When this occurs the gates are raised and it proceeds.

As I have said, the traffic is not heavy. Eight to ten cars a day is bumper to bumper, but there are caravans and donkeys and goats, herds of sheep, and an occasional cow that meanders by, that do cause some reduction of speed—no hardship, since every prospect is lovelier than the last and one has a chance to absorb it leisurely.

All the way from Dublin to Killarney we were traveling the coast road and were surprised to see how sweeping are the Irish tides. At full ebb the mud flats extend far out and the channels are very narrow. Although the countryside is enchanting, the tides do not make for a pretty coast line and must create a serious navigating problem, and we did not see many boats.

Coming into Killarney, the road winds through the uplands, with the purple mountains in the distance, and one comes to an irresistible stopping place, a roadside shop called Ladies View, where they sell the bawneen sweaters and Donegal stoles and Irish linen. It is a tourist convenience, but not a trap, for the merchandise is authentic and a little cheaper than the same things in city stores. The selection is quite wide and we found the proprietors completely trustworthy. We ordered a few sweaters and scarves and had them sent directly home as presents so as to avoid the nuisance of carrying them, and everything arrived in due course and in good condition, and as they were each valued at less than ten dollars the recipients didn't have to pay any duty.

Approaching from the south, as we did, one comes down upon Killarney from the heights and has a sweeping view of the lakes stretching away below. On the level the road is narrow and winding, with a high wall on one side, and we drove slowly, for there was a whole caravan of high, Irish jaunting carts loaded with children. It must have been some kind of an outing, and they were having a high old time. I would have liked to go on a cart myself.

The Great Southern Hotel is big and reasonably commercial but

pleasant and comfortable, and there was a welcoming open fire crackling in the lounge. The food was par for the course, but the bedrooms
were modern and comfortable, with private bath, a convenience not
necessarily automatic in the British Isles.

We had been told of one very beautiful drive, which we did not take
because we were doing so much motoring, but I think we were wrong.
I think the traveler should definitely "do" the Ring of Kerry, the hun-
dred-mile drive around the irregular peninsula jutting into the Atlantic. Spend a day doing it and at least half a day sight-seeing in Killarney
itself. "If we had it to do over again," that's one thing we would do.

Before leaving on Sunday morning we walked in the park bordering Lake Killarney and admired the hydrangeas and dahlias, which in
August were in high beauty all over Ireland. About eleven-thirty we
drove into Adare. That was it! The village of legend, with adorable
little cottages, thatched roofs, and lyrical flower gardens. We stopped
to take pictures and noticed that we were right in front of a delightful-
looking inn, the Dunraven Arms. "Let's go in and have coffee," I said.
It lived up to its façade. Pretty, cozy sitting rooms, comfortable, overstuffed furniture with chintz covers, open fires, flowers, magazines,
beautifully manicured lawns, flower and vegetable gardens. "Ashley
Courtney should learn about *this*," we said. "Takes the pioneering
Americans to discover delectable places every time." Then we looked
in the book. Of course. Mr. Courtney knew it well, had been going
there a mere ten years. "The wide tree-lined village street, thatched roof
cottages and generally well-groomed appearance reflect great credit on
the previous and present Earls of Dunraven who, as ground landlords,
have done so much for the betterment of the village and the social
conditions of the inhabitants . . . we doubt whether there is another
Irish hotel where the profits have been so steadily ploughed back."

Breakfast was over, the coffee had all been consumed, and it was too
early to lunch, so I settled for tea. The doctor allowed as how he could
go for a beer, but it was Sunday and the bar would not be open for
transients before twelve-thirty. Having seen the vegetable garden, I was
all for exploring the village and waiting around till lunchtime, but this
was one of the occasions when my dear one was adamant and masculine
on the subject of our schedule. He had estimated Limerick for luncheon, and that, by God, had to be it. "We must make Ballynahinch before dark," he said doggedly. "The road may be mountainous." I
pointed out that in this latitude it didn't get dark till nine o'clock, but

Limerick loomed and off we went. The punishment was inherent in the act.

I do not know whether the doggerel rhymes of the same name originated in the town of Limerick, but the more bawdy ones may well have. The inhabitants would have to have some diversion from their surroundings or go mad.

Limerick on Sunday is like a graveyard that's closed. The effect was numbing. But this was before our Sabbath orgy in the twin cities of Belfast and Glasgow. That glittering debauch lay ahead.

The Brazen Head, a restaurant that had been tentatively recommended, although not by Courtney—*nothing* in Limerick was recommended by him—was closed. The Savoy restaurant, which we thought we might try, was closed. The Savoy, incidentally, was in a movie house that was closed. "But," said the doorman, "we have a grillette, very nice, come and see." The Grillette was a low-grade coffee shop in a cave. We then made tracks for the Cruises Royal Hotel, arriving just before a busload of tourists, which meant we at least got a table. When we first walked into the dining room, I thought it was reserved for women only, there were so many of them. Closer inspection, however, revealed a few men and several priests. I should think Irishwomen would look upon priests with mixed emotions. It is noble to dedicate oneself to God, but in a land where women greatly outnumber men, to do so on a celibate basis seems rather unkind.

The mayhem that had been committed on the food in the Cruises Royal kitchen was indescribable, and we fled the premises with the last swallow, pushing on to Galway, a somnolent-on-Sunday but still-picturesque old town well known to the Spaniards, who traded there through many centuries and this despite the fact that the Anglo-Norman colony who settled it were a close-knit crew wanting no part of outsiders. Certainly not of the native Irish. In 1518 there was a law providing "that neither O nor Mac shall strutte ne swagger thro' the streets of Galway." They probably intruded to some extent, however, for at one time over one of the gates was the inscription, "From the fury of the O'Flahertys good Lord deliver us."

The road from Galway to Ballynahinch seemed long, but it wound over the moors and uplands, and men had been cutting in the bogs, for great piles of block-shaped peat were stacked along the way. Also the sun was out in glory, and the only obstacles we encountered were black-faced sheep and a few donkeys with their babies lying in the roads. They slowed the wheels of progress a little, as I had to get out and hug

them—the babies' fur is deliciously soft—and take their pictures. Norton muttered about this, but he was co-operative about stopping the
car and collaborating on light-meter readings and distances.

Curious about his concern with darkness and the mountains, I asked
him what he had been worried about. He started to laugh. "I was
wrong, I admit. I think it must have been because of my California
days. When we drove into the mountains on camping trips when we
were boys, it was important to reach our destination before dark because the good roads narrowed to trails and the trails finally disappeared altogether. If you didn't know where you were, you were in a
bad way. Also," he added, "I sensed donkey-petting coming on. You've
been raving about them ever since we've been in Ireland."

We arrived at the gates of Ballynahinch still in broad daylight, at
ten minutes past five. The drive winding up to the castle is banked with
hydrangea and rhododendron and the place is not a castle in the sense
of crenelated towers and battlements, but rather an enormous country
house that was once owned by an Indian maharajah who used it as a
fishing lodge. It is made of cement stuck with pebbles, brownish in
color, and is set on a height terraced down to the river. The river is
lovely, swift-running, and clear, brown or blue depending on the light.

Before the maharajah came along, it was the ancestral home of the
O'Flahertys, perhaps those feared by the inhabitants of Galway? In
the seventeenth century it was acquired by the Martin family, whose
most famous member was Humanity Dick who founded the Royal
Society for the Prevention of Cruelty to Animals.

While the Ballynahinch Castle Hotel is sometimes referred to as a
club, one does not have to pay dues or be elected in order to go there.
It caters chiefly to people recommended by friends or by members of
the syndicate that controls it. The Gilbert Smiths, who are friends of
ours, are interested in it, and it was they who told us about it.

It's homelike, comfortable, not exactly shabby, perhaps, but certainly not "smart." And the rates are reasonable. Including four meals,
if you count tea, which is excellent, they are three pounds eleven shillings and sixpence a day, or about ten dollars, and eighteen pounds, or
$50.40, a week per person. The non-tea food is indifferent, but they
have a cellar and the management is kind and courteous. I suppose
the servant shortage is a universal problem and good cooks hard to
find, but our disillusionment with the food didn't spring from the fact
that we were spoiled Americans. One of the English guests comment-

ing on the meat served the previous evening at dinner remarked grimly, "That roast beef certainly took the biscuit."

We were, however, comfortable in a large room with good beds, windows to the floor, ugly furniture, and a delightful view; the river, fir trees, rolling moors, and one stark nub of mountain. I suspect the fire-fighting apparatus is primitive, so we were not allowed a fire in our grate, but we had a hazard worse than a carefully watched open flame would have been.

Our bathroom, having been at one time, I imagine, a regular room, was *large*, with wall-to-wall carpeting and lined with jerry-built closets of thin wood painted mustard yellow and filled with masses of old newspapers. Not folded in neat stacks, just stuffed in loosely and so dry they crackled. When, baffled, we inquired their purpose, we were told that they were used to wrap blankets, but all the blankets were now on the beds so the papers were just left there. It struck us as less than meticulous housekeeping, but as we had enough room for our clothes in the wardrobe and bureau drawers we rose above it.

The ventilation of the bathroom was odd too. A square of ceiling had been cut away and a high shaft rose above the tub. It was topped by a skylight, but windows from bathrooms on the floor above us had been let into the sides so that if anybody chose to lean out of them he could have looked down upon us in the bath. Actually, since the windows were frosted and hinged at the bottoms and opened in, it would have taken something of a gymnast, but all during our stay we couldn't quite get over the feeling that a peeping Tom with time on his hands might negotiate them.

Fishing being the purpose of our Ballynahinch stopover, Norton reserved a boat, engaged a gillie, and every day of the three full days we were there set out conscientiously to court the wily trout, but not once did the trout succumb. The weather, for Ireland, was unusually fine, only two or three showers a day. The rest of the time the sun shone, the waters were comparatively low, and the salmon and trout were laughing their heads off at the tourists so expensively equipped with rod, reel, and flies. I was indignant for Norton's sake, for he's an experienced fisherman and the gillie, a nice little chap who wore a dark blue serge store suit whether in the boat or along the river's edge, supposedly knew his stuff, but neither scale nor fin did they snaffle. All the poor doctor got for his pains was a miserable dose of hay fever.

Despite the chancy quality of the fishing, and I expect your true fisherman takes chance in his stride, I would recommend Ballynahinch if

only for the incredible beauty of the adjacent countryside of Conne-
mara. We drove one morning to the little village of Clifden going the
long way through Roundstone. It is eighteen miles of woodland, nest-
ling villages bounded by the fuchsia hedges, crimson and dark, glossy
green, rolling moors covered with great splashes of golden gorse, purple
heather, and blue lupin, and scored with white sandy beaches and bays
of sapphire blue. To inhale the freshness and fragrance of the air is to
be reborn.

Clifden is a village of two broad streets, a population of nine hundred
five, and Millars, a shop where one may buy more stoles and bawneen
sweaters, which I did, and my husband said, "Bedad, you're on a
sweater toot." "Bedad," I said, "I am." I haven't regretted one of them.

The road in Clifden has a high crown, and Norton parked the Austin
at right angles to the curb, its nose pointing downward. This must
have done something to the gasoline, and the ignition wouldn't work,
but two co-operative fellows came along and the three men lifted the
car up and shook it and set it squarely down, whereupon it pricked
up its ears and started off.

Another day we decided to drive to Ashford Castle at Cong in
County Mayo for lunch, about thirty-two miles distant. Ashford Castle's reputation is extensive, and indeed our Mr. Courtney refers to it
as "Ireland's most spectacular fantasy."

Situated on Lough Corrib, with a fine sweeping view of the island-
studded waters, it was originally owned by the Guinness family and is
now run by the Noel Huggards, well known in Irish hotel circles. The
Huggards have really gone to town. Their domain of three hundred
acres is beautifully tended, and they can offer swimming, shooting,
boating, yachting, riding, croquet, golf, and tennis. They also embrace
dancing, billiards, and a weekly movie. There is a shop for woolens
and woven ware, but the prices are a good bit higher than those of
Dublin and much higher than Clifden and Ladies View.

The exterior of the building satisfies any romantic cravings for
castles, being very castley indeed, with turrets and towers and crene-
lations and a drawbridge, but it is all modern restoration and copy. The
interior is unsettling: curly iron standing lamps with shades of red velvet and parchment engraved with eighteenth-century gallants and pan-
niered ladies, patterned carpets, and patterned cretonne slip covers and
heavy oak tables. It is also immaculately clean, but we preferred the
unpretentious, shabby charm of Ballynahinch despite the fact that its
staff and cooking are not first rate. The Ashford Castle staff looked very

spruce, but their cooking is not first rate either. That's the trick about Irish food. Even when that of one place is a great deal better than that of another, it's still no good. With Irish cuisine you start in a deep hole and pull up to level ground. Getting off the ground is another stage altogether.

On the menu it says that Mr. Huggard considers it his privilege to overlook the planning of the food. Having eaten a luncheon, one is tempted to the thought that, while his privilege, it is perhaps not his province.

The chicken broth was thin and completely tasteless—what *is* this antipathy the Irish have to seasoning?—and the roast goose was tough and without flavor. We were served two kinds of potatoes, which seemed unnecessary, and a frightening vegetable known as broad beans. They are huge lima-shaped pieces of leather and bear about as much relation to fresh baby limas as cattle corn does to sweet corn. Drinks and coffee were good. We did not stay beyond lunch, but I imagine the bedrooms would be comfortable, and if one were planning an extended visit in the neighborhood there is certainly more diversion at Ashford than at Ballynahinch.

Back in our more humble surroundings Norton plotted our itinerary for the next couple of days, and I wrote to the people in Scotland to whom Malcolm Douglas Hamilton had sent letters telling of our arrival there. Malcolm, who lives in New York, is the brother of the Duke of Hamilton, and he had alerted assorted chums when he heard of our trip. "Be sure to let them know your dates," he said, "they're expecting to hear from you."

Feeling it entirely possible that the news of our arrival might be greeted by a riot of apathy, I did my best to make the letters sparkle, and although I am by no means sure that I succeeded, our reception proved what we had long known to be the case: Scots, far from being dour, are among the hospitable peoples of the earth. Thanks to Malcolm's forethought and Natalie's wifely admonitions—"Darling, if you're going to write those letters for Norton and Ilka, get *to* them"— we had some very pleasant times.

Delightful as her husband's connections would prove, however, Scotland still lay ahead. We still had Irish driving and sight-seeing to do and after Ballynahinch, with a brief Irish-coffee break at the Pontoon Bridge Hotel at Foxford—reputed to have some of the best fishing in Ireland, but by now the doc was a bitter skeptic—we pushed on to Sligo for lunch. It was sleazy Sligo for fair and the Great Southern a dreary commercial hotel, the only bright spot a merry luncheon party of priests and nuns, the men of the cloth drinking beer right along with the laity. We had originally been scheduled to stop at the Great Southern, but, thanks to Mr. Courtney, we improved our lot considerably, we went to Ardnamona Estate on Lough Eske in County Donegal.

The prospectus he had received, said Mr. Courtney, was headed "The Most Beautiful Place on Earth" and, he continued, "incredible as it may sound we thought so too." It was, we gathered, a Georgian country house bathed in sunshine and furnished in perfect taste. There was also five hundred acres of beauty. That was for us.

We were following the map faithfully and when after a time it seemed as though we must surely be there or hard upon it, we stopped to ask the way. "Indeed yes, it was but half a mile," we were assured. We pushed on, Norton with eyes glued to the road, me vacillating between speedometer and signposts. When we had covered nearly four miles we saw a modest shingle, "Ardnamona Estate." We thought that possibly Irish miles were longer than ours or that the man had not really known where the place was, but we found out no. It was just the Irish way. It is unjust to accuse them of tampering with the truth, however, or of maliciously confounding the ignorant foreigner. It is because of their kind hearts; they want to encourage you. Four miles at the end of the day seems long.

While Ardnamona did not perhaps quite live up to its own or Mr. Courtney's description, it had a good deal to offer, including fabulous banks of rhododendrons and azalea bushes that in spring must be quite breath-taking. It's an undistinguished but pleasant country house, its limited accommodations, six double bedrooms, two single, and small, cozy public rooms making it the more homelike.

An unkempt flower bed and hayfield in which grew some enormous beautiful trees sloped away from the curving terrace to the shores of Lough Eske, whose opposite shore rose gently in a patchwork of farms and fields to the moors beyond, a gentle rural scene.

On the second floor was the personal library of the late owner, Sir Arthur Wallace, with masses of leatherbound copies of *Blackwood's Magazine*, published in Edinburgh. The earliest volume I found was dated 1830, the most recent 1904.

We had asked for a room with bath and we got it. Our bedroom was large with a high ceiling, a big wardrobe, and a bay window. Between the wardrobe and the window was a tub. Even though it was our own, taking a bath in all that open space seemed quite public.

Our window overlooked a lawn where a little goat was tethered. He was a sweet creature, but my heart ached for him because he was lonely. A very small rock jutted up out of the grass and he would stand upon it bleating in a sort of pathetic triumph. He was a mountain goat.

There were two other couples staying there besides ourselves: the Lancelot Jeffersons from Belfast; he was a solicitor and his wife, Janet, a psychiatrist interested in retarded children; and the Rodney Drakes from Warwickshire. Their two children—like so many young English were charming to look at—had delightful manners and were somewhat immature for their ages. They had the hardihood of blue druids. On a gray and gusty morning I asked them where they were going and they said, "Oh, we're off to fetch our bathing dresses and have a swim." I had barely been able to bring myself to the large tub.

The Jeffersons had a son too, Ian, about sixteen with red hair and a skin like pink and white flowers. It embarrassed him to death. Elvis Presley was his dream. He was faintly impressed when he heard I had worked in *Ocean's 11*, a picture of Frank Sinatra's; he tolerated Sinatra —graciously implying that snow on the thatch didn't necessarily mean there wasn't fire in the hearth—but Elvis obviously would have been far better. He was passionately curious about everything American. Our roads, "Very straight, I imagine—how wide? How fast can you go?"; our apartments, "How are they, your apartments? Are they all right?" When I told him ours had eight rooms, he was overcome. "Here when we say a flat we mean a poky little place of two rooms." He was dear.

The first evening before dinner we heard of the Ardnamona mystery. Just who was running the inn was a moot question. The manager had recently and mysteriously vanished—no foul play was implied; still it was very odd—and the owner was far away, no one knew where. The place seemed to be run by the cook and Miss Williamson, who had been senior maid and was now housekeeper, with two young girls to assist her. They were a bit older than the children of Bourdzi had been, but they were performing the same tasks.

The bar arrangements were relaxed and the tariff was right. As I recall, a shilling or one and six a drink: between fourteen and twenty-one cents. There was an array of bottles, and a pad with a pencil attached to it by a string. You mixed your own and wrote down on the pad how many you'd had, and they were added to your bill. It was the honor system par excellence. I think I may claim that the Drakes and ourselves were scrupulous and the Jeffersons had no temptation. They were teetotalers.

The food at Ardnamona was above the native average. Fish was fresh and well cooked, and there were actually salads; not tossed, of course, but still a few lettuce leaves with a couple of thin slices of tomato, radish, and cucumber. We gobbled them down, feeling that we had warded off scurvy for another day. I think that is the difference between French and British salads. In France one eats them because they are delicious, in Britain because they are good for one.

We spent a couple of remarkably pleasant days, although Norton had a thin time with the fish there too. He rowed over the lake for several hours, but all he caught were two infinitesimal fingerling trout, which he threw back.

When they learned that we were leaving for Belfast the same day they were, the Jeffersons kindly asked us to dine with them at home that night.

We left Ardnamona about eleven in the morning, and after driving for half an hour and seeming to get nowhere, we asked an Abbey Theatre character sitting on a fence, Barry Fitzgerald to the life, if we were on the road to Londonderry. His patois was a bit thick, but the salient fact emerged right enough. We were headed in the opposite direction, a good twenty miles out of the way. Since I was custodian of the map I appreciated my husband's restraint, but he and I both wish he would give up having confidence in me when it comes to map-reading. I *think* I'm right, it looks as though I *couldn't* fail, and then, in some mystic way, it turns out that the map is upside down.

We learned one curious thing about Londonderry. It's the "London-derry Air" and it's written that way on the map, but guidebooks, sign-posts, and people never call it anything but Derry. The stretch of country between Ardnamona and Derry is entrancing, green and fer-tile, and beautiful. We lunched at the North Counties Hotel (dark and brown and gruesome) and saw a man eating pork and mashed potatoes and boiled potatoes and broad beans and baked beans. That surely could not have been good for his complexion.

As we had agreed, Lancelot—I always wanted to call him Gobbo— Jefferson picked us up at our Belfast hotel, the Grand Central, around seven-thirty, and on the way to their house drove us by the House of Parliament. It stands on a rise in Stormont Park and is approached by a long, wide, sweeping avenue. The building is enormous. It would be enormous in a large country, and we thought it a bit top-heavy for six counties but tactfully refrained from saying so.

We had a pleasant evening with the Jeffersons, but, knowing they would have a great deal to do getting home from their holiday, we left early and returned to our gloomy Grand, where we went to bed and read.

Traveler's Tip No. 27: There are bound to be slack moments, sometimes depressing ones, so never fail to have a few books handy, including a hair-raising murder or two; they will tide you over the bad spots.

Belfast and Glasgow on a rainy Sunday are a brace of spots requiring the combined efforts of Edgar Allen Poe and Agatha Christie, and don't think we didn't wish for them. Churchgoers perhaps would find occupation for an hour, but once service is over they too would be in the lurch. The plane for Scotland didn't leave until two, so we lurched till luncheon, which was unexpectedly excellent. Perfect smoked salmon and a well-grilled *entrecôte*. The coffee was all right too. Our spirits began to perk up.

The flight to Glasgow took forty minutes, and it was just as gray and bleak there as it had been in Belfast, but we had Brooksie to look forward to—Brooksie, Christina Brooks, who had been my friend and secretary for nine years and in whose company I had passed some of the most contented hours of my life.

Brooksie had left me in 1954, and after a period spent with relatives in the Middle West had returned home to Scotland and was now living with three sisters, Peg, Flora, and Jean, in Kirn, a small village not far from Glasgow across the Firth of Clyde. She was coming up to see her dear "Doc" and me. We appreciated her visit all the more, for we knew that she was badly handicapped by a broken hip, but she arrived indomitable, convoyed by Peg, her left leg in a brace, leaning on two sticks, but her spirit and her bright black eyes undimmed.

She brought us presents—she is the present-givingest woman I know —and we opened them and had a fine gabby reunion. She didn't look a bit changed from the last time I had seen her in New York three years before when she had come for a visit, and I was pleased to see that her interest in the royal family was still keen. As she is Scottish, there is no kowtowing in her attitude, she simply likes to keep a sharp eye on their doings, and very little escapes her. "Margaret," she will observe, "wore a brown and white tweed when she went to Balmoral," and she will flash a glance from her bright black bird's eye as if to say, "What about that? Pretty significant if you ask me."

We had hoped to dine at the Gay Gordon, which we understood was a good restaurant that had been amusingly decorated by the Mr. Hicks who married Pamela Mountbatten—Brooksie had taken a keen interest in Princess Ann's bridesmaid's dress—but it was closed on Sunday. It's a wonder to me that the Scots don't close the kirks on Sunday, so we stayed in the hotel, where we had a reasonably good meal and a warming bottle of wine.

Before setting off the next morning I phoned Inverary Castle—we had a letter to Ian Campbell, the Duke of Argyll—to ask if His Grace was at home. We were told that he was away and wouldn't be back for a few days, but we decided it would be interesting to see the house anyway, so, taking a somewhat choked-up farewell of Brooksie—it is sad not to know if, or where, we shall ever meet again—we started off in our rented Ford along the banks of Loch Lomond. The Ford was a big improvement over the Austin, and we felt as though we were in a car instead of on a bucking bronco.

The banks of Loch Lomond are bonnie-ish but thick with trippers and caravan sites, flattened tin cans and waxed-paper bread wrappings, and kids with long bare legs and packs on their backs who tramp the roads between youth hostels.

I felt a bit wistful about Loch Lomond. I had been in Scotland in 1938 and in my memory it was more attractive. It was certainly less frequented.

We lunched at Inverary at the Argyll Arms, and then paid our two and six to go through the castle. Two or three big parties are usually circulating through the great houses at the same time, and I should think the dukes of Britain must make quite a good thing of it, although with taxes and maintenance they probably only break even.

The most striking feature of Inverary is the high central hall, with its collection of guns and swords arranged in big, decorative medallions on the walls and fanning over the doorway. There is also a room, with lovely William Morris wallpaper, the bedroom of Princess Louise, Victoria's daughter, and her husband, Lord Lorne. There are ancestral portraits galore, among them a Gainsborough and a Winterhalter. The present duke, in kilts and ruffles, is represented by a colored photograph. Good-looking chap, too. Sorry to have missed him.

From Inverary we drove through a blinding, flaggelating storm to Fort William in the Highlands. Once escaped from Glasgow, we didn't mind the weather. Scotland has always seemed to me a romantic land, and although sun is nice, rolling clouds and thunder and storms are no more than to be expected in the land of Macbeth and wild border raids and skirling pipes and kilts and haggis.

At the Alexandra Hotel we found a message from Mr. Joseph Hobbs, to whom Malcolm Douglas Hamilton had written, that they were expecting us for the night.

Delighted, we drove three miles beyond the town to Inverlochy Castle, set in thousands and thousands of Hobbs acres. The squire also controls twelve and a half miles of river and a large lake, owns a salmon cannery, a distillery, and raises cattle; an enterprising man who hailed originally from Canada.

Our host and hostess were at the door to welcome us as we drove up. "We were expecting you for tea," they cried. "Whatever detained you?" We hadn't known we'd been expected and we'd been delayed by the storm, which was now over, but we expressed our pleasure at being with them at last.

Inverlochy, built in 1861, beautifully situated on a lake filled with water lilies at the base of Ben Nevis, has only fifty-two rooms, but it's home to the Hobbses. One might think that coziness would be difficult in a setting of such magnitude, but with the magic knack of the British they have achieved it. Our room was large and flowery and very pretty, opening into an even larger one, which, we were told, was Norton's dressing room. He looked alarmed and when we were left alone said to me, "My God, I don't really have to dress in there, do I?"

"No," I said, "you dress here with me and then we'll go in and scatter your things around so Effie won't be shocked." Effie was the maid, a sweetheart with a black mustache.

Our co-guests at dinner were General Harding, in his late seventies, Admiral Hose, eighty-five, and our host, who announced that he was seventy. Norton and I began to feel quite skittish. Mrs. Hobbs is her husband's second wife and many years younger than he. Admiral Hose wore a hearing aid, but other than that seemed to have all his faculties, although Norton said he felt a bit inept when the old boy began fielding him questions on the activities of the Canadian Navy in World War I.

Leaving the castle the next morning, we drove north, skirting long, narrow Loch Ness to hilly Inverness for lunch. Mrs. Hobbs, who having business in town, had left ahead of us, had said she did it in one hour and ten minutes, but the lady is either not very time-conscious or is heaven's child. Norton, when pressed, is a dedicated driver, but to drive to Inverness from Inverlochy in an hour and ten minutes and arrive in one piece would require, quite simply, a miracle. Uncertain as to whether it had taken place and genuinely concerned for Madam's safety when we recognized her white Jaguar parked in the street, Norton scribbled a note that he tucked under the windshield: "You are a bad girl. God."

A little later, lunching at the hotel, we spotted her a couple of tables away deep in conversation with two eminently respectable females. We waved and she responded abstractedly. We were worried. Had we unwittingly flunked the guest test? Was she only too relieved to see the last of us? We hoped not and later learned the reason for her absorption in her two companions. The clubhouse for young people she had built and equipped had burned down during the night, and they were discussing ways and means for replacing it.

We drove on and stopped overnight, quite unnecessarily, at a ratty hotel in Nethy Bridge because dear Malcolm had stalked the stag or something with the proprietor when they were both striplings and felt we should go there. We felt we should not, but our irk faded once we had made our getaway early the next morning, for the scenery became spectacular; mile after mile of wild rolling moors, dark purple mountains, and waterfalls.

Along the way we stopped at Blair Castle the seat of the Dukes of Atholl, parts of which date from the thirteenth century. It is rather like a more primitive Azay-le-Rideau and contains some beautiful furniture and charming "conversation piece" family portraits.

Our target was Gleneagles, where, once arrived, we spent some time murmuring over clasped hands, "Ralph, dear Ralph, forgive us." This was because our friend Ralph Reed, a Power in the American Express had kept saying, "Go there, stay there," but we insisted we wanted to do more motoring around Scotland, not be stuck in one place. Will one never learn in this world? Will the voice of experience forever count for nothing? Yes, it won't, would seem to be the answer. Intelligent, right Ralph. Obstinate, wrong Norton and Ilka.

At first glance we curled a little around the edges, for we prefer the human scale, and Gleneagles, while undeniably magnificent, is a colossus, a Buckingham Palace of a hotel, a Buckingham Palace *cum* Versailles, but once acquainted we fell in love with it. It was our sweet, our intimate, our little Ardnamona in the Ochils. It's a great spot.

It may come as a surprise that we should have been so charmed, considering that its *raison d'être* is golf and neither Norton nor I plays a stroke. All we could do about the vast sweeps of greensward, three superb courses, Kings, Queens, and the nine-hole Wee, was to admire them and think of Ike. We could, however, appreciate the comfort, service, and above all the food offered by the establishment.

We lunched in the Restaurant du Soleil, which we later learned was not the regular dining room but corresponded to the Ritz restaurants on ocean liners, but we continued to patronize it because one of the delightful things about Britain is that even the de luxe restaurants are reasonable by our standards.

A formal dinner at Gleneagles, beginning with hors d'oeuvres, melon, or whatever, continuing through soup, fish, including superlative smoked salmon, entrée, which at that season included grouse, dessert, and cheese, came to thirty shillings, or $4.20. Coffee, served only in the lounge, was extra, as of course was wine, but good French wine is still less expensive there than in the States. I admit they make it up, to some extent, on the cocktails. A double martini, but a single one by our standards, was $1.40.

A tour of inspection of the hotel revealed a squash court, swimming pool, movie and hairdresser indoors, four tennis courts, croquet, and gardens out. Fishing trips are easily arranged. Budget allowing, the most agreeable way to see the central part of Scotland would be to establish headquarters at Gleneagles and explore the country from there. The tariff ranges in the neighborhood of twenty dollars a day for two, including breakfast. Everything else is European plan.

In the evening we repaired to the lounge for coffee and to the strains of an orchestra of determined ump-pah-pah beat had a gentle fling. There were some sweet and long-suffering parents dancing with their offspring, and we were touched by one kid who must have been thirteen or fourteen, on the plump side, wearing a tartan skirt and sweater, shirt and mannish tie. She came into the lounge with her father and mother just as the orchestra struck up, and began a little twitching, eager dance of her own on the place where she stood. She was obviously longing to be asked for a whirl.

Thanks to our own ineptitude we were at Gleneagles only one night, yet we left it with a pang. We left in rain and a thick fog that lifted as we drove along and we came to Stirling Castle on a wild, gray, windy morning, the very climate in which to see it.

It stands on a great rock above a sweeping plain, and although the castle loomed through the mists of history in the twelfth century, what one sees today dates only from the fifteenth. It was the scene of bitter battles and bloody murders and the birthplace of Scottish kings. There Mary Stuart was crowned as a child and there she returned, the widowed Dowager Queen of France at the age of eighteen. And there on a December night in 1566 the torches blazed striking fire from the gold font presented to her godson by Queen Elizabeth, and ambassadors from foreign lands danced to the music celebrating the baptism of Mary's son, James VI of Scotland.

Today the castle is a barracks, and the roses in the small quiet cultivated plots within the gray walls bloom as peacefully as in a cottage garden.

While we were there several platoons were drilling, and I said that all that arm swinging and foot stamping and sharp turning seemed to me a silly business, to which the doctor replied tartly that it was no more silly than the ballet—he doesn't like the ballet—and I said that at least the ballet didn't lead to bloodshed and slaughter, which army life has a very good chance of doing. It was one of our few spats.

We arrived in Edinburgh in time for lunch and registered at the Caledonian Hotel. After quite a hiatus we were happy to find a welcoming little mountain of mail, which we read, glancing from time to time out of our window at Scotland's other great rock, Edinburgh Castle.

We had planned our stay in Edinburgh to coincide, in part, with the festival, which opens the third week in August and runs through the first week of September. Our first evening we went to hear Verdi's *Falstaff*, sung by the Glyndebourne Company. We were especially glad to hear the singers, as we had not been able to get tickets when in England for one of their performances on home grounds, the lovely estate to which one travels by train or car in full evening dress in the afternoon to enjoy the opera and eat a picnic supper on the grass.

We dressed in Edinburgh too, and found to our satisfaction that several other couples had done the same, but not the majority, and it was not necessary. In a way I'm sorry. One always used to be able to count on a touch of swank in Great Britain, and it is pleasant, makes the evening seem more gala. Besides, it's hard for a woman to endure fittings and hopefully to spend money on pretty gowns only to watch the season wane as the poor things, the gimp gradually draining out of them, hang unused and forlorn in the closet.

The Glyndebourne Company was a salad of Italian, Mexican, Swiss, English, Spanish, and Geraint Evans, a Welshman, as Falstaff. He was magnificent, with a deep-rolling velvet voice, sound acting ability, and a marvelously comic make-up. We enjoyed the performance immensely and returned to the hotel for supper in the Pompadour Room.

The second evening was the Royal Ballet Company. There was a funny, gay, charming one, separate sketches called *Ballabile*, with choreography by Roland Petit, and Dame Margot Fonteyn and Michael Somes danced *La Péri*, in which the ballerina is discovered, a sleeping fairy, lying on her side with a lotus blossom balanced on her hip. Robbed of it by a Persian prince, she is so upset she wakes right up and in a series of exquisite fluid movements with unparalleled grace eventually retrieves it. The suspense is not excessive or the plot electrifying, but how that Dame can dance! The third ballet, *The Prince of the Pagodas*, we found a mighty dull business and left before the end.

The third evening was the most fun, for our dear friend Judith Anderson, now, and so rightly, Dame Judith, was in Edinburgh playing in *The Sea Gull* with the Old Vic Company. Her performance was brilliant, and she appeared, in her red wig and elegant costumes, much taller than she is.

Afterward we went around to her dressing room, for, as there were no seats available for the review that was to be presented following the performance of *The Sea Gull*, she had arranged to have us sit in the wings. "It's the best I can do, pets. Even Isaac Stern is standing tonight." The review, *Beyond the Fringe*, was the hit of the festival. Written and acted by four young Englishmen who took to the stage only sporadically, going on with their professions of medicine and law the rest of the time, it was hilariously funny.

Dressed in slacks and sweaters, equipped with a kitchen table, four wooden chairs, a piano, and microphones, they convulsed their capacity audiences night after night. Their nearest counterparts in America are probably Mort Sahl, Bob Newhart, and Nichols and May.

Seated, as Norton and I were, in the wings, we were worried that we might get in their way or make them nervous, but they whirled about and threaded between us with the greatest good humor, whispering, "Pull your chairs nearer," and then whisking out on the stage, never missing a beat or a cue.

When the performance was over, Judy came back to the hotel with us for supper, and we were joined by the Tony Brittons—he was playing Trigorin in *The Sea Gull*—and their beautiful Afghan, Cleo.

They had just returned from the late performance of *The Tattoo*, which we had seen the night before after the ballet. Despite the high art overflowing every nook and cranny of Edinburgh, the climax, for most people, was *The Tattoo*, an exhibition of drill, dancing, and the military music of massed bands given every evening on the esplanade of the castle. All the great names were represented: The Lorne Scots and The Scots Guard, the Seaforth and the Argyll and the Sutherland and the Queen's own Cameron Highlanders and the Royal Air Force Regiment. More than two hundred fifty men took part and, as the fanfare sounded, the floodlit company came marching out from under the great stone archway, some in leopard aprons, scarlet tunics glowing, kilts swinging, bagpipes skirling—it was a breath-catching moment. A group of men from the Greek Royal Guard, evzones, with their flaring white ballet skirts and pompons on their shoes, had joined the Scottish regiments, and also a brigade of Gurkhas, the sturdy little mountain troops who fought with the British in India and whose uniform is a white shirt and full white Bermuda shorts.

To spirited music they marched and countermarched and drilled and presented colors and nearly at the end the courtyard went dark and the lights swept onto a group of trumpeters on the old walls who played "The Sunset Call." There was silence for a moment and then, high above on the ramparts, a spot picked up a lone piper looming in the drifting mist as the piercingly sweet strains of "The Last Post" floated out on the rainy air. Two thousand spectators wept.

The Edinburgh Festival is a fine achievement worthy of the beautiful city that organizes it. Princes Street and the castle are the city's heart. Today it is the history of the castle rather than the building itself that moves one. There is an inspiring view from the high rock out over the Firth of Forth, but most of it is, by European standards, comparatively modern. Only the tiny Chapel of St. Margaret, with its tremendously thick walls, was constructed before the fifteenth century. It is interesting to see the small paneled room where Mary Queen of Scots gave birth to James, and to make the sad pilgrimage through the National War Memorial erected after World War I.

At the other end of the Royal Mile, or down the street a piece, stands Holyrood house, much more Renaissance in feeling than other Scottish castles. The most interesting apartment to see, as I remembered from my last visit, is the little room in which Rizzio, supping with the queen, was murdered. When our tourist party was shunted away from its closed door by the guide, I asked why. He shrugged. "Too many of you, it's too little, getting everybody in and out—take too long." He was not entirely without a point, but it is ironic that that is what so many people go to see but can't see because there are so many people.

Something else that we enjoyed in Scotland besides the festival, scenery, and old castles was their splendid newspaper *The Scotsman*. It made us feel a little more *au courant* with the actualities. The London *Times* is a venerable institution, and American japes about it doubtless belittle the japer rather than the paper, but getting any information out of it requires a microscope and the patience of a cat at a mousehole.

On a rainy Sunday we drove from Edinburgh out to Barrow Farm to lunch with Malcolm's daughter and son-in-law, the Gavin Youngers. Young Mr. Younger is Younger's ale, one of Britain's finer brews, and we sensed that the countryside through which we were traveling must be lovely, though it was difficult to discern through mist and rain. They live in a pleasant farmhouse set in the midst of fields and sheep, and they have three darling towheaded little boys. There was one, aged three, in a sweater and kilts whom I longed to sweep down upon and spirit away.

After luncheon we drove to Lennoxlove to meet Malcolm's brother, the Duke of Hamilton, who had considerately come in from North Berwick, where he and his family were staying, to show us around the castle.

Although parts of the house itself are very old, it has been owned by the present duke only since 1947. It is an authentic Stately Home with a banqueting hall, a dungeon, superb furniture, and a treasure in Crown Derby and Dresden and pictures by Canaletto, Guardi, Boucher, Raeburn, Lely, Augustus John and sculptures by Jacob Epstein.

The death mask of Mary Queen of Scots is there—she must have had a lovely face—and the duke took a silver box from its case and showed it to us: the casket of the famous Casket Letters. The box had been given to Mary by the Dauphin of France when they were married in 1558.

As the duke and his son, the second of five, Alastair, Malcolm's son, and Norton and I were making the tour, two women who had paid their admission fee joined us. They had no reason to think the boys and ourselves weren't sight-seers too, which of course Norton and I were, and His Grace was very courteous to them, pointing out the pieces of greatest interest and discoursing on the assorted treasures. When the tour was over one of the women whispered to her friend,

"Now *he's* the kind of guide I like. Takes as much interest in the place as if he owned it."

Leaving the satisfied ladies, we drove to the farm, which is a working affair, has electrically milked cows and a great many pigs. The ducal porkers seemed in fine condition, and in one pen was a litter of tiny new ones lying under an infrared lamp. They were surrounded by wooden bars so the sow couldn't roll on them. There were also greenhouses where carnations were grown for market.

We left Edinburgh the next morning and, southward bound, passed through Jedburgh and visited the small stone house set on a lawn smooth and green as a billiard table, and bordered with crimson and yellow flowers, where Mary of Scotland stayed for a month, part of the time very ill, having caught her death of cold riding forty miles in a day to see Bothwell. Mary was really an exasperating woman. Beautiful, glamorous, learned, meeting her death with courage and dignity, but incredibly inept in her conduct vis-à-vis Elizabeth. And those men! Darnley and Bothwell—now really.

Poor Bothwell, though. Even he didn't merit his unspeakable end. By chance Norton came upon an account of his last years in W. T. Blake's book, *Travels of a White Elephant*. Having got in bad with the Scots, he fled to Denmark, where he was betrayed by a former mistress whom he had bigamously married before meeting Mary. The Danes, thinking him a valuable hostage, imprisoned him in a dungeon where he was brutally treated—his left eye was gouged out and where he was kept *with one arm fastened to the wall by a chain for eleven years*, when he died a raving maniac. One can only hope he lost his reason in the earliest days of his imprisonment.

In the Jedburgh house is a bad painting of Mary's execution. She is surrounded by her three attendant Marys, Seton, Beton, and Carmichel with the ghost of the fourth, Mary Hamilton, who strangled her own baby, and inspired the ballad, hovering in the background.

While we were looking at it a Scotsman rushed into the room, his face pale with agitation, "Have you na seen my purse?" he asked. "Have none of you seen it?" There were only four of us and we assured him we had not. "It was here in my sporran and now it's gone, it had everything in it. Keys and license and money. Eleven pounds, not so much perhaps but still . . ." The poor fellow was distraught. "But it *is* much," we said, "we're so very sorry. Can we help you look?"

"No, no, I'll retrace my steps. I had a lemonade, maybe there . . ." He turned and ran out of the room. Later on as we were leaving we saw him standing on the bridge, his head in his hands. "You didn't find it?" "No." He was so despondent we could only hope he wasn't plotting to drown himself, but it is true that few things are as upsetting as losing a purse.

From the house we went to see Jedburgh Abbey. It is Norman architecture a graceful pile with beautiful archways and a cloister, the fretted ruins a lovely tracery against the sky.

We crossed Carter Pass, the border between Scotland and England, about noon. It's a favorite place for picnics, and several families were scattered about on the moor with baskets and thermos jugs. We ourselves lunched at the Percy Arms at Otterburn, an attractive inn with a pleasant dining room and mediocre food.

The afternoon drive was long and tedious, but the White Hart Hotel at Lincoln is a cheerful, old-fashioned establishment with some very good antiques in the public rooms. There is an ancient elevator and long, meandering, rabbit-warren corridors. After our bags had been put in our room, Norton continued down the hall. "Where are you going?" I asked. "This place strikes me as an ideal firetrap," he said. "I just want to see if there's another staircase down here." There was. There were in fact several exits, so we relaxed.

Lincoln is, of course, the site of the great cathedral, and the bells create a deafening cacophony that does stop at ten forty-five but starts up again in the morning at seven. I do wish ancient churches all over the world with established reputations didn't feel they had to work so hard to keep in the public consciousness. They must be terrified of being forgotten, but as most of them are bulky and many of them are of renowned beauty, that is unlikely. Let the visitors sleep at night, O noble monuments. We'll be in to see you in the morning.

Lincoln is enormous and impressive, more beige than gray in color, and, to me, without the quality of Notre Dame, but it is exceedingly old. The early towers were erected in 1093, and the building as it stands today was completed in 1235. There is also an interesting old house in Lincoln called the Jews house, which we unfortunately missed.

We were more alert in Stamford.

Passing through that charming and ancient village, we saw a sign with an arrow that said Burghley House. Somewhere in the dim recesses of memory a bell clanged. What I am pleased to call my mental processes ground laboriously into gear. I was back in the schoolroom. Burghley. Queen Elizabeth. Her prime minister or something, no? A lifelong and trusted adviser. "Hey," I said to the doc, "Burghley's house, that might be interesting." We drove on past a high stone wall enclosing the estate and came, in time, to imposing gates and another Burghley House sign, the arrow this time pointing back in the direction from which we had come. I made a last stab, "Looks good, doesn't it? Very big and beautiful, I imagine." That did it. The pearl to whom I am married pulled over to the side of the road, turned, and drove back to where I had first seen the sign. As any woman knows, this was an act of heroism and self-sacrifice ranking with the fortitude of the volunteers for outer space. More so! The astronauts are journeying into the unknown, a challenging prospect infinitely preferable to retracing territory already covered, especially when it is throwing the ETA (estimated time of arrival) out of gear.

Once back at the sign, we made a right turn and drove down a lane that skirted a couple of miles more of high wall. Six feet of earth may do for eternity but for the short haul let us *breathe*. We were impressed by the acreage even before viewing the house, which, without hyperbole, may be termed a palace. The first Lord Burghley was not, as I had thought, Elizabeth's prime minister—maybe the office as such did not exist at that time—but her secretary of state and high treasurer. His descendants were created first earls and later marquises of Exeter and still live there.

Burghley built the house in three stages, first using the remains of a monastery and later enlarging and completing it in 1589 as it stands today.

A notable exterior feature is the unusually tall, slender chimneys, dozens of them, and always in groups of two and three, surmounted by sculpture and carved chimney pots. The grounds and stables were laid out by a landscape architect called Capability Brown, who certainly lived up to his name.

We fell by chance upon Connoisseurs' Day, which means they jack up the price of admission from two and six to five shillings, but it was an extravagance we were happy to indulge, for we were the only ones in our party and were shown around by a nice woman guide. Fresh from the Duke of Hamilton and Lennoxlove, we eyed her warily. Was she perhaps the marchioness? We didn't think so and in the course of the tour were informed that the family was in Rome for the Olympic Games.

The first room we saw was almost the most fascinating, an enormous kitchen dating from the abbey days in the twelfth century. The walls were covered with gleaming copper pots and pans that made our mouths water, and the spit was still in the huge fireplace, as well as a curious fanlike contraption that controlled the speed at which it turned that controlled the temperature at which the meat roasted. Norton understood it.

Throughout the house there were elegant gleaming steel and silver grates in the fireplaces, and when I asked our guide who kept them in such superb condition she said, "My husband." I asked if he had a magic formula—I could scarcely wait to get back to our brass andirons and the Revere ware—but she said, "Only the Churchillian one. 'Blood, sweat, toil and tears.'" I don't know what there is about life; despite Easy-Off and Mr. Clean one always seems to come back to that.

The chapel in which Queen Elizabeth worshiped is still used for morning prayers and is dominated by a Veronese altarpiece. This house too is a repository of masterpieces of art, including a Rembrandt, his mother as an old woman, and a portrait of Mary Tudor so strikingly like Princess Margaret one looks twice. There is also a fine painting of the aging Elizabeth I have never seen reproduced, and a fascinating picture called *Rent Day*. There is controversy as to whether it was done by Breughel—it has all his human, earthy quality—or by an artist of whom I had never heard, Quentin Massys, who lived from 1466 to 1530. It shows villagers arriving in an office with eggs and pigs and other produce to pay their rent and taxes. The men behind the counter have the unmistakable "Come on, bub, get it up" expression of our own dear inspectors of internal revenue.

The house boasts intricate and exquisite wood carvings by Grinling Gibbons, garlands and overmantels of flowers, fruit and birds. His signature was a pea pod, closed when he had executed the entire work himself, open when his pupils had contributed to it.

Probably the most spectacular work in the castle is the *trompe-l'oeil* painting of Antonio Verrio, whose perspective and shading were such that gods and goddesses, horses and cherubim tumble from the walls and ceilings right into the room. The enormous salon known as The Heaven Room is considered the finest painted apartment in England. The Italian artist lived in the house for twelve years, received wine and sausages, horses and a carriage, and was paid three and sixpence per square yard of painting. This seems somewhat parsimonious in view of his gargantuan achievement, but as he must have painted his way through several miles of walls and ceilings he probably made a reasonably good thing of it.

It is enormously interesting to visit these vast houses, but it is strange to think of living in them. Room after room after room serving no specific purpose. I suppose they were built for prestige, to accommodate art collections and for the occasional reception of monarchs—also we must remember they rose in the good old days of Have Someone Else Do It for You.

At Stamford we lunched at the George. The hotel is old and picturesque and the food is good, and in the afternoon we traveled along M1, the big expressway into London, arriving back at the Connaught around six. English traffic is as bad as our own.

I think I have stated elsewhere that my husband is an antimovie man, but one night I pinned him. *Ocean's 11* was playing at Warners in Leicester Square, and I wanted to go. He couldn't very well get out of that one, but when we got near the theater and saw the long queue waiting outside, my heart sank. I knew he wouldn't go for that and I was right. "My God," he said, "we don't have to stand in *line* to see you, do we, sweetie?"

"Hold everything," I said, "I'll see what I can do." I went into the lobby and asked for the manager. When he came I explained the circumstances. "Why of course, Miss Chase," he said, "you and your husband must come right in. I can manage two seats in the mezzanine." We were about to thank him effusively, when he said briskly, "That'll be one pound, just pay the young lady in the box office." My dear one gave me a slightly sour glance.

Ocean's 11 was a big success whenever it played, but, even being in it, I didn't have the foggiest notion of what was going on in the first half of it. To me it was as confused as all get-out.

One of the reasons we had been eager to get back to England was to see the Tallents, one of the couples with whom we had been so compatible on our Aegean cruise. They lived in Cheltenham, and we had arranged over the telephone that we would meet at a certain place on the road and follow them to the inn where they were putting us up and where we were going to lunch.

We thought we had left London in time, but the traffic was bad, as usual, and when it became apparent that we would be late we stopped in the village of North Leach to telephone. Norton wanted to

424 THE CARTHAGINIAN ROSE

buy some tobacco; also, as so much of his life is spent on the phone with patients and nurses, other doctors and drugstores, he avoids the beast whenever possible. I had the duty. I went into a roadside booth and there I stayed for quite a time. What's that about a riddle inside an enigma wrapped in a mystery? Take a shot at an English public telephone. I had the number, but there are letters and buttons and codes to be dealt with, and no matter what I pushed or turned or how many coins of what denominations I deposited, nothing happened. I was beginning to get desperate. There was a little sign that said, "In case of emergency dial 999." I dialed. "This is an emergency," I said to the answering voice, "I'm an American and I can't find my way around your telephone system. Please tell me what to do." The operator laughed, but she was very nice and gave me minute instructions I tried faithfully to follow. *Still* nothing happened. Feeling like an idiot, I went into the pub across the road and asked the proprietor if he would dial the number for me on his phone. He got it right away. It was humiliating.

We eventually met Philip and Loma at the spot where they said we would be, and had a happy reunion luncheon with them and two of their children, Angela and Dick, at the Greenway Hotel in Shurdington. It is a delightful inn, originally, like many of them, a private house, and the luncheon was sumptuous.

The plot was an afternoon of gentle sight-seeing and Stratford-on-Avon in the evening. En route to Warwick Castle, our immediate goal, we stopped at one of the most enchanting villages in England, Lower Slaughter. It, Upper Slaughter, Lower Swell, and Burton-on-the-Water are a lovely garland flung across the Cotswolds. Philip told us that the rather unfortunate name of Slaughter stemmed from the fact that the famous Cloth of Gold was in truth a Cloth of Wool and Mutton, England's wealth, and it was here that the sheep were brought to be slaughtered after the shearing.

The fifteenth- and sixteenth-century houses are of stone, roofed with beautiful, irregular hand-split stone shingles covered with moss. A stream wanders through the village and a herd of cows was grazing beside it. A true *Brigadoon* spot.

By the time we had absorbed its charm and Norton had got his pictures, we were late getting to Warwick, but Philip gallantly crossed a necessary palm with silver and the guide took us through. The moat today is no more than a depression in the lawn, but it circles a noble pile of late medieval architecture. The origin of the castle was a huge mound of earth, a military rampart erected in 916, interesting because it was the work of a woman, girl called Ethelfleda, the daughter of Alfred the Great. Whether she was a better cook than her father, history doesn't say. Her lieutenants in charge of the mound were the Earls of Warwick. Apparently they started building not too long afterward, for the earliest part of the castle was already standing at the time of the Battle of Hastings. Today it is roughly L-shaped, the entrance gate flanked by two high crenelated turrets. The domestic apartments form a long, narrow wing rising from the river Avon, ending in Caesar's Tower. There is another, tall twelve-sided tower called Guys built in the fourteenth century. The whole exterior of Warwick is intensely romantic, an altogether storybook affair.

The interior of its great hall, fairly named since it measures sixty-two by forty-five feet and is forty feet high, is modern, but contains a fine collection of armor and the enchanting portrait of Queen Elizabeth I at the time of her coronation at the age of twenty-five; a faery creature with her pale face and round dark eyes, her slender hands holding the orb and scepter. Those who have read Elizabeth Jenkins' fascinating study, *Elizabeth the Great*, may remember a photograph of this portrait on the jacket. Holbein's Henry the VIII hangs at Warwick, and a beautiful portrait of Queen Joanna IV by Raphael. There is also a Rubens, a rather institutional one, of St. Ignatius Loyola.

Exhausted from culture, we fell upon tea but had to hurry through it, as the curtain was at seven-thirty and we didn't want to be late. The Shakespeare Theatre at Stratford-on-Avon I found frankly disappointing. It is of raw brick, both material and architecture reminding me of nothing so much as a biscuit factory. The inside is spacious and comfortable but also lacks charm. We had hoped for the *Merchant of Venice*, but the bill was *A Winter's Tale*, one of the master's more preposterous plots. It was well played, however, and directed with imagination and freshness by Peter Brook.

We left the theater in teeming rain, but the Tallents drove us to another delightful inn for supper, the Saxon Mill. There is a square of thick glass in the floor through which one may watch the water racing. The food again was very good, and afterward we drove back to the Greenway Hotel for the night. Fond as we are of each other, in the pitch darkness and through the pouring rain it seemed to us, and, I do not doubt, to the Tallents, one of the longest drives in the world.

We parted from them the next day and on Sunday, with other friends, Christopher and Marya Mannes Clarkson drove into Sussex.

Marya I have known a long time. She is a lady of compassionate heart and an acid pen and is the drama and television critic of *The Reporter*. She also wrote a book of verse, *Subverse*, and published a book of reasonably scathing essays, *More in Anger*, with which she won kudos galore.

Christopher is an Englishman, fantastically knowledgeable about the byways and back roads of his native land, and this despite the fact that he no longer spends very much time there, as he and Marya live in New York.

In the course of the day we passed the house where he had been born, although his family had not lived there for many years, and stopped to take pictures. Christopher stood with his hand on the gate, and Marya and I rather liked the exchange that ensued.

NORTON (peering through his lens): "Take off your hat, for God's sake."

CHRISTOPHER: "But I don't live here any more."

We thought it showed a nice sense of decorum.

We lunched at Midhurst at the Spread Eagle, one of the oldest inns in England and one of the best, and afterward drove to the Sussex Downs and got out of the car and walked over the open fields—the Downs are really uplands—and gazed out over the English Channel, rolling below us. Cows were grazing nearby and it was a peaceful rural scene. On the way back to London we drove past Parham Park, another lovely great house, but Marya and Christopher had a dinner engagement in town, so we saw it only from the outside. We got a catalogue, though, and, on our next trip to England, Parham prepare! Among the joys of England are the beautiful and historic spots where the ghosts dwell, easily reached in a day's outing from London.

As we were on our own in the evening, there were two or three restaurants from which Norton and I thought to take our pick, but they were all packed. It was only by the intercession of Mr. Gustave himself, the manager of the Connaught, that we could get into our own hotel dining room. Traveler's Tip No. 28: In London always book a table in advance for Sunday night. Not many restaurants are open, and those that are are crowded.

When shortly after we had first arrived in London I said brightly to the doctor, "You know, darling, it occurs to me that it would be foolish to be this near and not to go to Paris for a few days—I mean, downright wasteful, don't you agree?" he had replied, "I hope it hasn't occurred to you that it wouldn't occur to me that it wouldn't occur to you to go—I mean, I'm braced." There are times when men's intuition is every bit as good as women's.

We had four luscious Paris days, including a visit Drue Parsons and I made to Balenciaga's to view the collection. Other designers are currently perhaps more in the news, but to me he is a master. I must say, however, the chi-chi attendant upon a visit to the *haute couture* seems ridiculous. One does not say, for example, "Heigh-ho, today I think I'll go see what Cristobal is up to." Far from it! One must play one's cards right, one must negotiate, and go through Channels. It's like being presented at court. Our sponsor, Drue's and mine, was Mr. Widmer of the American Express, and he warned us that we must take our passports, even Drue, who lives in Paris.

"But I used to know Balenciaga," I protested, "he was devoted to Mother. 'Dearest Mrs. Chase of *Vogue*,' he would always say."

"Take your passports," said Mr. Widmer.

"But this is September. The openings have been over long since. It isn't as though we were spies from Seventh Avenue."

"Take them," said Mr. Widmer.

So we did and they checked them, too. The collection was, for the most part, lovely. The suits were simple and elegant and eminently wearable and a few of the evening gowns fabulously beautiful and the prices fabulously high. I spend very little time bewailing my lot, I know I have been fantastically lucky in life, and I'm grateful, but sometimes, just *sometimes*, I wish I were richer than Croesus or a Texas oil millionaire.

I did have with me, however, a suit I rather fancied and in which I had a certain success. Walking one day along the quai of the Ile Saint Louis on my way back to Drue's apartment, I passed two little boys sitting on the wall. They held their chattering for a beat as I passed by. "*Que Madame est belle,*" one of them murmured, and went right on with his gossip.

I was amused that so young a *boulevardier* should be perspicacious enough to appreciate the good feeling a woman has when she is wearing something she likes.

Our last day in Europe dawned a pure and cloudless blue, marvelous flying weather, and just eight hours after take-off we were home. We dropped our luggage at the apartment and after a quick dinner in town drove out to the country and to May, who was waiting for us. It was

good to see our small domain, although we discovered once again how true it is that into each life some rain must fall. Our part-time gardener, in an excess of tidying zeal in the vegetable garden, had pulled up all the herbs, *including* the so-hard-to-establish tarragon. When Norton saw my face he said, "Dear, let *me* talk to him, I think it will be wiser."

There was another slight *contretemps*, too. When we had gone away I had said to our local jewel who sometimes came in to help and who, in our absence, would be dropping by a couple of times a week to see that all was well, that I thought it might be a good idea to pull out the electric clocks. "No use their going all the time we're away and we'll plug them back in when we get home." Acting apparently on the theory that if one pill is good for you the bottle is better, she pulled out not only the electric clocks but every other plug in the house, including that of the well-stocked freezer in the cellar.

It seems that after a few days, the aroma having spread down the driveway and across the lawns, the cops arrived, no doubt having in mind Faulkner's "A Rose for Emily," which tale, as the reader may recall, features a defunct, uninterred, once-loved one who, in the natural course of disintegration, has become a little high.

Seeking to remedy this, the jewel reinserted the plug and refroze the retching mess so that it was a solid slab in the bottom of the chest. Norton's was the pestilential task of hosing it down with hot water and cleaning it out. Ah well, who does not have his ups and downs?

On our first Monday home came a fearful hurricane. Norton had left for town Sunday night, and May and I drove in on instruments. Back in the apartment we unpacked; my secretary, who while we were away had done such a faithful job of letter writing and checkbook watching, now and again uttering a sharp warning chirp, coped with the brief case. I put away my passport. The trip was over.

As I said in the beginning of this book, travel has its drawbacks, its disillusionments, and its irritations, and one of its great advantages is to make one appreciate one's home and one's own country afresh, but if anyone says to me, "You want to take another trip?" I can only answer, "When do we start?" adding, "But hold off a brief moment, let me savor the pleasure of anticipation." How lovely it is to have something to look forward to and in this world rather than the next, of which, despite the dogged assurance of the clergy and hope eternal, we have no proof.

๒